PRAISE FOR GOTTIGUARD

As Kate's hunt for her father's killer progresses, so too does the book's funny bone. Leder has always had a gift for balancing suspense with humor that serve his characters and the story well, but the jokes in *Gottiguard* land fast enough to send even the most somber readers into an uncontrollable fit. Many come in the form of puns that Leder slips into prose while others are long bits of rising hilarity. If laughter is the best medicine, then *Gottiguard* will cure plenty of ailments. Meanwhile, the suspense surrounding Kate's pursuit of the killer proves unputdownable on its own terms. Leder loads the plot with twists that make Kate earn every clue and lead. But amidst all the criminal hijinks, Kate's relationships with friends and love interests alike are genuinely sweet which, in an age of caustic humor, is supremely refreshing. If this is indeed the "final" Kate McCall crime caper, as Leder suggests, Kate goes out with a bang in what may be the best of the McCall books. But let's hope Kate will always be solving her "last" case.

— BEST THRILLERS

PRAISE FOR GOTTIGUARD

Relentless in its pace, with brilliant banter that's a staple of Rich Leder's writing, and a twisting plot that keeps one turning the pages to the last chapter, *Gottiguard* is a stellar final entry in the Kate McCall series. Surprising bursts of action, character revelation, and laugh-out-loud humor make for an uproarious final punchline to the series and and elevate Leder's crime fiction over others in the genre.

— SELF-PUBLISHING REVIEW

I've thoroughly enjoyed this series from start to finish. Mr. Leder has an uncanny ability to create interesting characters that you love, hate and everything in-between. In addition, his ability to paint the scene and take the reader on a fun, curious and sometimes frightening journey makes this series a great read. My only disappointment is knowing this is the last Kate McCall book.

— THE ISLAND WANDERER REVIEW

PRAISE FOR GOTTIGUARD

Once again, Rich Leder brings his Hollywood talent to a Kate McCall page-burner. The familiar offbeat humor is still LOL funny, the hardboiled tone permeates, and the supporting cast adds spice and flair. McCall is for mystery fans who want a fresh, lively, and different whodunnit. If Gottiguard is Kate's last performance, she's going out on a high note.

— READERS' FAVORITE

A wild and crazy romp that will leave you breathless from both laughter and excitement. Had to run pretty fast to keep up with this one. I loved it!

— SWEET MYSTERY BOOKS

GOTTIGUARD

THE FOURTH AND FINAL KATE MCCALL CRIME CAPER

RICH LEDER

LAUGH
RIOT
PRESS

1

———

CINEMATIC INSANITY

I STASHED RICK GOTTI IN MY APARTMENT AND REJOINED THE CAST and crew for the first day of principal photography of the martial-arts masterpiece, the karate classic, the jujitsu gem in the making: *Kung Fu Fu*. It was slated to be a tour de force, an all-out, action-packed magnum opus. What it had was drugs and dealers and dopers and cops and crime and murder and mad scientists and a runaway bomb on an unknown city bus and furious kung fu fighting every few minutes.

What it didn't have was dialogue.

No dialogue whatsoever.

Not one scripted word for any of the characters appearing in the film. Every line said out loud so the audience could hear it, process it, and use it to follow a plotline or a character arc would be improvised. LaTanya had written a treatment that presented a general sweep of the action intended for each scene, but what would actually happen was left to the cast.

For highly trained, talented, and experienced actors, ad-libbing *all* the dialogue in an independent feature film would be a monumental challenge. But the *Kung Fu Fu* cast (me excepted, she said with some modest amount of modesty) was not composed of actors. The *Kung Fu Fu* cast was populated by the irregular residents of the Upper East Side brownstone I lived in and managed—the House of Emotional Tics. So, yes, we were filming scenes out of order with no idea what was said in the scenes before or would be said in the scenes to come. And, yes, cinematic insanity.

Fu Chen, my enigmatic Chinese-assassin maintenance man, had been cast as the star, Detective Fu Steinberg. I played the role of Fu's sidekick and costar, Detective Cassie Barnett. LaTanya, the writer-director-producer and self-anointed future recipient of the heretofore nonexistent Academy Award for Karate (which she predicted Hollywood would invent just for her) had cast herself as NYPD Captain Rashida Jewel. We were all renegade cops. Warren was the renegade mad scientist who'd hidden a bomb on one of the five thousand city buses, and Al and Charlie were renegade drug dealers. Everyone was chasing someone while running away from someone else for reasons that had not been addressed in the treatment, reasons we had to make up on the fly. The story was chaos wrapped in confusion rolled in bedlam but felt tight as a tick compared to the reality of the shoot itself, which was anarchy in a bowl of pandemonium topped with turmoil.

We were shooting in the morning—starting with the second-to-last scene in the movie—because we all had jobs to get back to in the afternoon. It was the climactic scene where Fu, LaTanya, and I take down Charlie and Al—who've been chemically enhanced by a mysterious martial-arts drug invented by Warren's mad scientist character. Outrageous kung fu kicks and outlandish ad-lib dialogue filled the set—which was the hallway on the third floor of the brownstone because the location fee was zero and because no one with a badge would wander by and ask to see our permits. Spoiler alert: we had no permits.

Warren was today's director of photography and camera crew. He had no film experience of any kind. So there was that.

Charlie had brought his badass brass knuckles to our improv kung fu fight and accidentally clipped Fu in the face. This pissed Fu off—never a good idea—and he whacked Charlie with a real-life roundhouse kung fu kick in the chest that sent the three-time ex-con-turned-city-tow-truck-driver careening halfway down the hallway.

"Fu you, Fu," Charlie said, rubbing his chest.

"Fu you too," Fu said, rubbing his jaw.

Then Charlie pulled a knife, and we stopped improvising to make peace between them. That's how much of the morning went.

You might imagine that even under theatrical conditions such as these, being the off-off-off-off-Broadway professional actress I was, I would have been able to focus on the improvisational jujitsu at hand. But somewhere around midmorning, my concentration became less concentrated because the first day of *Kung Fu Fu* happened to fall on Halloween.

My thoughts drifted back to when I was an eight-year-old champion trick-or-treater growing up in Queens. I knew I'd been a champion trick-or-treater because Jimmy, my father, had held my hand, walked me from house to house, and said, *"Katie, I've seen Halloweens come and I've seen Halloweens go, and you are a champion trick-or-treater in anybody's book."*

And because it was Halloween and I was thinking of Jimmy, my thoughts wandered again to the end of this past July, when he'd been found murdered in an insurance-company elevator, eyes shot out of his head. At the reading of his will (in Mel Shavelson's office), I'd inherited his private investigations business and become the McCall of McCall & Company.

And once my mind landed *there*, it meandered through the three cases I'd already solved—workman's compensation, stolen identity, and embezzlement—that were decidedly mine.

And also ambled through the three murders I'd simultaneously investigated that were decidedly *not* mine. Murders that were categorically the domain of NYPD Homicide. Murders where the victims' eyes had been shot out of their heads in the same way my father's eyes had been shot out of his head. Meaning *after* they'd been murdered. Meaning it was the killer's signature—*payment due on delivery.*

I'd worked those murders, pissing off the police (surprise!), because it was the only way I could track the killer, and I'd promised Jimmy up in heaven somewhere that I would catch the creep who'd killed him.

I'd come close on several occasions. Close enough to almost have my eyes shot out one time, my brains blown out another, and to punch the killer in the jaw yet another. Close enough for him to text me clues to his next victims—*personally text me clues!* Close enough for him to give me a pet name: Little Engine. As in *The Little Engine That Could.* Or in his opinion, *Couldn't.* Meaning I couldn't keep up with his ultra-uber-brilliance. Meaning I couldn't stop him from murdering his next target even with the clues. Meaning I was nothing but an entertaining sidebar, a compelling puppet he was playing with to keep him amused while he murdered high-powered people for money and stayed ten steps ahead of the police in the process.

Whoever he was, he had an ego the size of St. Patrick's Cathedral, which is to say you could see it from space. I was the PI in the middle, his bridge to Detective Lew Logan and Logan's recently formed NYPD task force. *Recently formed* because after half a dozen professional hits, the city had decided in earnest it was time to stop this top-tier corporate assassin from shooting people's eyes out all across the boroughs.

So I lost focus on the first day of shooting *Kung Fu Fu,* and then the first day was in the can, and it was time for lunch, so I went into my apartment and started the ball rolling on my fourth case: being Rick Gotti's bodyguard.

2

———————

NOW HE WAS KNOWN FOR MURDER

His professional name was Rick Gotti. But his real name was Richard Gottfried. So no relation to the famed, late New York mob boss. Just the normal NYPD presumed-guilt-by-name association.

Mel Shavelson, my father's disheveled lawyer, who I'd unhappily inherited along with Jimmy's PI business-in-a-box, had sent Rick to me first thing this morning. Rick was a celebrity for some of the right reasons—sitcom star from ages fifteen to eighteen, and cult-status stand-up comedian until he turned thirty-three. Then he'd vanished from public life into a succession of rehab, recovery, and halfway houses. Meaning he was also a celebrity for the wrong reasons—drug and alcohol misuse and abuse leading to exceptionally bad behavior on and off the set for years and years and years.

Now he was known for murder.

In the midst of making a career comeback after fifteen years of hiding from the crushing cogs of the entertainment machine, he'd become famous anew for killing fellow comedian Kenny Cochran after Cochran had blatantly stolen his material. This is what the police said.

Rick said otherwise.

Rick said Cochran had stolen his act, and he, Rick, had walked into the backstage dressing room at The Joke Joint, a popular New York comedy club, to confront Cochran face-to-face, and had seen some big guy holding a plastic bag over Cochran's head. Cochran was already dead. The big guy had been taking an extra few seconds just to make damn sure of it. Rick hadn't seen the big guy's face, but Cochran's *real* killer thought he had.

Indeed, Cochran's real killer thought Rick had gotten a good long look at him while he'd been busy killing Cochran. So he'd chased Rick into the dark, empty club, saying something like, *"You saw me, so you die too."* But the big guy never nailed him because Joke Joint security had grabbed Rick first, and the big guy had vanished without a trace. Which meant security had never seen Cochran's real killer either.

And now the real killer thought he needed to kill Rick quick, before Rick could find out who he was, *actually* was— maybe by picking him out of a lineup; maybe by looking at a mug shot; maybe by describing him to a police sketch artist. Which is why the bodyguard—me—needed to keep Rick alive for the next six weeks so he could prove his innocence at the pretrial in December.

Rick Gotti was three years older than me, so forty-eight give or take a few months, and about two inches taller, so five-nine. He had hip celebrity hair, copper-colored and curly, flecked with gray, a little long, a little wild, a little rebellious. He was thin and wiry. Recognized for the smartass smile he'd flashed on his hit TV show *The Jungle.* Celebrated for his wise-guy delivery of the show's iconic tagline, "Welcome to the jungle!" Infamous for the bad-boy reputation fans had come to know from his time in the tabloids. And now notorious for a murder rap everyone knew from the police reports.

He was sitting on my sofa watching *Animal Planet.* Faded

blue jeans with a white dress shirt untucked, sleeves rolled up. Expensive watch. No wedding ring.

Before you jump to conclusions, noticing the absence of a wedding ring was in no way related to even the slightest hint of a romantic thought on my part. Ever since Tom Mullin, my son Matthew's biological father, had flown all the way west (and turned all the way gay) after impregnating me at age sixteen, I'd been unlucky in love. I'd never let it ruin my life, which I liked just fine—single mother and musical-theater actor working every odd job under the New York City sun—but I'd always dreamed of being in a committed relationship, like Jimmy and my mother, Christine, who'd died of cancer when I was ten. That I'd never been able to make a monogamous relationship work for more than an unimpressive number of months was as much my doing as it was the doings of the men I had chosen along the way. Which is to say I was bad at choosing men.

The late great Kate McCall was not at all great (or even good) at choosing men to be romantically involved with and was equally bad at being involved with them once she'd made her not-at-all-good choice would be a true-that sentence in my obituary.

Honestly, it had been as true these past three months as it had ever been. Indeed, after the men I'd been tenderly entangled with since the end of July, a romantic relationship was the last thing on my mind. The Harriman Affair had nearly destroyed me. The end of the romantic road with the rock star-real estate-decathlon stud—fifteen years younger than me *and* Matthew's friend from law school—had left me despondent, dispirited, dejected, and depressed. And Blue had broken my heart into pieces I still couldn't put back together. Starry-eyed interlude? No, thank you. It was going to be business and nothing but business with Rick Gotti. All bodyguard, all the time.

I stepped into my apartment and shut the door behind me. "What animal?"

"Peregrine falcon," he said. "Fastest bird in the world. Two hundred forty miles per hour when it stoops."

"Stoops?"

"Deep dives from high altitude. That's how it hunts."

"I'm about to deep dive into my kitchen for a BLT. Want one? It's on me."

"There's no such thing as a free lunch," he said, turning off the TV and following me through my railroad flat. "How was the shoot?"

All the apartments in the House of Emotional Tics were railroad flats, meaning the living room, situated at the front of the brownstone, looked out onto East 83rd Street and led into the first bedroom, which led into the second bedroom, which led into the dining room, which led into the kitchen at the back of the brownstone, overlooking the crabgrass garden and grubby shrubs. All the rooms were in a row, like pearls on a necklace or, as the name implies, like the railroad cars of a train.

"Weird doesn't begin to describe it," I said. "Out of body? Out of mind? Out of control? Out of bounds? All of the above? We shot the next-to-last scene of the movie, when we catch the renegade drug dealers, kung fu fight them into submission, and haul them off to jail. But there's no written dialogue."

"None?" he said.

"It's all ad-lib. Every word made up on the spot."

"So how did what you said in the whole movie you didn't shoot yet lead up to what you said in this scene?"

"No way to know. We didn't say it yet."

"And you don't know what you'll say until you—whoa, what's going on in here?"

He'd stopped in my second bedroom, which I'd turned into my walk-in-walk-through closet.

"These are the costumes, accessories, and accoutrement of all the roles I've played for the past twenty-five years or so," I said. "Wigs, glasses, purses, scarves, gloves, bags, shoes, jewelry, and clothes from all the local late-night cable commercials, failed TV pilots, forgotten indie features, and way-off-Broadway plays and musicals that make up my life's work. Plus, my real clothes are in here too."

"Hallowed space on Halloween," he said. "Like a sacred Indian burial ground."

Floor-to-ceiling shelves lined the walls, with racks and hooks and hangers and dressers in between. A vintage armoire, an antique vanity, a full-length mirror, plenty of lighting.

"Except nothing's dead and buried in here," I said, digging deep into the closet. "Including you. So put this on and don't take it off until after your pretrial. You can take it off in the shower, obviously."

I tossed him the concealable bulletproof vest Jimmy had made me wear on an especially dangerous surveillance case involving a manic husband with a gun who'd threatened to kill his wife for cheating on him.

He tossed it back to me. "The camera adds ten pounds as it is, McCall. This thing adds another twenty. It's going to look like I ate my way through recovery."

I tossed it back to him. "You're wearing it."

He tossed it back to me. "No, I'm not."

I decided to fight the bulletproof battle later, put the vest back in my closet, and kept moving. He followed me through my dining room and into my kitchen. The one full bathroom in the apartment was off the kitchen. A large plate-glass window was set on the back wall so you could look out into the yard. It was the mirror image of the window on the front wall of the living room. Because I was on the first floor, both windows had bars over them, like a jail cell. But the building was rent-controlled, and I got a manager's discount on top of that, so I didn't see the bars.

Rick watched me make BLTs for both of us. The bacon was

from the fabulous Florence Prime Meat Market on Jones Street, where they custom-cut slices from an enormous slab. The bread was fresh from the East Side Orwashers, a bakery to which bread-lovers pilgrimaged and genuflected. The lettuce and tomatoes had come from the Korean market around the corner on First Avenue, where it seemed like they grew fresh produce on a country farm somehow hidden in the alley beside the building.

Before you start thinking I was overly overboard with food, you should know I was a lifelong New Yorker. Food was my cultural DNA. When I had money, I spent it on food. When I didn't have money, I spent it on food.

As the bacon sizzled, I grabbed two bottles of Sam Adams from the fridge.

He gestured thanks but no thanks. "Sober for six years."

"Congratulations," I said, meaning it. "I'll drink yours."

I was Jimmy McCall's daughter so I enjoyed a drink as much as the next guy but only when I should, never when I shouldn't. My father had taught me the difference.

"Congratulations," he said, meaning it. "Two for you."

I assembled the BLTs—they were works of art, if I said so myself—and we sat at my small kitchen table.

"So keeping me alive until the pretrial," Rick said between bites. "What are you thinking?"

"I'm thinking you live here for six weeks. Camp out on my couch. No one knows you're in my house. You're safe here. I feed you. I buy you every magazine on the stand. You watch *Animal Planet* until you have a degree in zoology, and you stream Netflix like nobody's business. Binge *The Jungle* for old-time's sake."

He was in heaven, either loving the BLT or my plan for keeping him alive.

"Not happening," he said.

It was the BLT. Not the plan.

"The point of me hiring you to be my bodyguard is for you to keep me alive while I prove I didn't do it, not for you to keep me alive in your living room. Although, when you think about it, the living room is a perfect place to keep someone alive."

It was a funny line because of him. *He* was funny. His delivery was a big part of what made the joke funny. Probably funnier than the joke itself. He had a unique, smart-mouth style that was engaging despite its smart-mouthness. You knew it, and he knew it with you. He was in on the joke with his audience. Laughing along with them—in this case, me. It was part of the fun, part of the funny, that Rick Gotti thought it was funny too. Plus, the joke came with that Rick Gotti sitcom smile at the end, like punctuation, like permission to laugh your head off. I could practically hear his signature line in my head: *Welcome to the jungle!*

"That's funny," I said. "But the answer's still no."

Now I get it, I thought. *It's not that he wants me to keep him alive for the next six weeks so he can prove he's innocent at his pretrial. It's that he wants me to keep him alive for the next six weeks because he's planning to prove he's innocent before he ever gets to his pretrial. He's planning to catch the real killer, and he can't do that if he's dead. He's not going to sit on my sofa like a good boy and watch TV until December. He's going to play private investigator and solve Cochran's murder on his own. What a stupid freaking thing to do. Who does he think he is, me?*

I could tell he wasn't happy with my take. He'd lived his entire raucous and rampaging life disregarding advice, disobeying rules, defying social norms. But he didn't say anything, which surprised me. Shooting his mouth off had put him in hot water a thousand times. He couldn't help himself. It was his nature. His reputation. He was famous for it. So he'd either mellowed over the years or was saving something worse than shooting his mouth off for later.

We ate our sandwiches in silence. He drank bottled water,

and I drank two beers, and then he walked to the back window, looked through the bars, and said, "Your costar is doing tai chi with a parrot on his head."

I put the dishes in the sink and joined him at the window. It was true. But after all I'd learned about Fu, he'd have to do something more than tai chi with Jerusalem Joe perched on his head to shock me.

"He's a Chinese-mob assassin banished to the brownstone for reasons no one wants to know," I said. "Tai chi with a parrot on his head is just one of a long list of things that make him the most unusual maintenance man in New York. Also on that list, his father abandoned him at a Shaolin Temple when he was seven. He has no mother."

"Everyone has a mother," Rick said.

"Not Fu. His shifu taught him ten different martial-arts disciplines. Fu earned the highest possible belt in all of them, the highest possible belt being *Master of Don't Fuck with Me or I'll Snap Your Neck with My Bare Hands*. Which he can do without breaking a sweat, trust me. I've seen him crush concrete with his fingers. But he can also bake like Betty Crocker. Tea cakes are his specialty. And he listens to Italian opera at decibels that make AC/DC sound like a soft breeze. He loves birds. Except pigeons, which he kills indiscriminately with poisons and shovels and slingshots. He knows how to work a boom mic because he made bird movies in China. He's as graceful as a Bolshoi ballerina, as fast as a Funny Car, as agile as an antelope, and as brutal as a bulldozer. Plus, he was a trick horse rider in a Chinese circus before the mob made him an assassin. And, oh yeah, he's saved my life four or five times. One time is in dispute."

"Saved your life?"

"Four or five times while helping me find my father's killer. I mean, clearly, he's helping me if he's saved my life, which he has, four or five times. Don't tell anyone about Fu and my father's case. Especially Logan."

"Logan?"

"Homicide detective working Jimmy's murder from his side of the street. Don't tell him about Fu. Not sure Fu has a green card or a bingo card or any card."

I moved back to the sink and washed the dishes. Rick watched Fu and Joe a little longer, then leaned against the counter beside me.

"So you know where I'm coming from, wanting to catch the guy who killed Kenny Cochran," he said.

I did. Of course I did.

"I can't let you do it," I said. "I'm responsible for your life now."

He took a breath and let it out slow. "I'm still going need stuff from my house. Clothes and toiletries. My laptop."

"We'll go tomorrow," I said. "First place the real killer will look for you is your house. And he'll look tonight now that you're out. That's my guess. We'll let it settle. Make him think you left the city for someplace safe."

He nodded and went back to the window. After a minute, he said, "He just flipped me off. Fu. Without breaking his routine. Double birds. Like it was part of his tai chi."

"Welcome to the jungle," I said.

OPPOSITE SIDES OF THE SERENGETI

I FINISHED UP IN THE KITCHEN, THINKING HOW NICE IT WOULD BE if all I had to worry about was doing tai chi with a parrot on my head. *If all I had to worry about was doing tai chi with a parrot on my head, that would be a vacation in paradise. If I was on vacation in paradise, I would do tai chi with a parrot on my head and hardly worry about anything at all. The only thing on my mind would be vacationing in paradise doing tai chi with a parrot on my head, worried about nothing.* Instead, I had Jimmy's murder on my mind and Rick Gotti's life in my hands, neither of which was a vacation in paradise. Meaning both were another daunting day in the pressure cooker.

My doorbell rang as I put the period on that thought: *pressure cooker.* Probably one of the tenants delivering an unannounced complaint. Or maybe LaTanya with tomorrow's call sheet. Or Fu with bad news about Al's toilet. As resident manager of the House of Emotional Tics, I was, among other things, the designated complaint catcher. The grapevine for grievances.

Rick was in the living room. I yelled for him not to answer, that I would get it, but patience was not part of Rick Gotti's profile, and as I arrived in the living room, he was opening the door.

It wasn't a tenant, but it was a complaint...personified in the form of Homicide Detective Lew Logan.

"Who the fuck are you?" Logan said to Rick.

His jacket was open and his badge and gun were dead giveaways. And Rick, whose run-ins with the police had been tabloid fodder for years, was on his heels just like that, especially with the whole Kenny Cochran case hanging over his head.

But it wasn't the badge and the gun that had him off balance—though no one, especially someone like Rick Gotti, wanted to see those particular items when they opened the door. It was Logan's tone of voice, which was gruff enough to melt glass from the far side of Central Park.

"I'm Rick Gotti," Rick said.

"Stand-up comedian arrested for killing a stand-up comedian. They should give you a medal, then burn you at the stake. You paid his bail?" Logan said to me as I came to the door.

"I'm his bodyguard. What are you doing here, Logan? How did you get in the building?"

"There is what appears to be a zombie washing three identical early-model Corollas in front of your brownstone, and by early model I mean made by the Japanese in Japan during the attack on Pearl Harbor. I asked the zombie if he lived in this building, and he answered that, in fact, he did. I then asked if he knew whether you were home. At which time he told me to, quote, buzz the fucking buzzer like every other fucking delivery boy on East 83rd Street, end quote. I showed him my badge and my gun and told him I'd noticed exactly none of the vehicles he was washing had a current registration sticker and so were clearly not registered and likely not insured. I explained that if he opened the door and spared me the ignominy of buzzing the fucking buzzer like every other fucking delivery boy on East

83rd Street, I would, A, not shove the entire Department of Transportation up his zombie ass and, B, not shoot him in his zombie face. That, McCall, is how I got in. I'm here because I have questions only you can answer. Now, are you going to offer me a cup of coffee, or am I going to kill this stand-up comedian like he killed that stand-up comedian to get him out of my fucking way?"

Lew Logan had even less patience than Rick Gotti. Which is to say no patience at all. Negative patience.

"No," I said.

"No?" Logan said.

"I'll meet you on the steps outside. Two minutes."

There was no reason to subject Rick to more Logan than he'd already encountered. Plus, Rick would find his smartass footing shortly and give it back to Logan as good as Logan was dishing it out, and I didn't want to be in the middle of that unhappy exchange. So Logan left for the front steps, and I told Rick to watch *Animal Planet*, and then I got my shit together and followed Logan outside.

He was sitting on the top step. It was as pretty a Halloween day as I could remember. The end of October can go either way in New York. Cold and gray like winter or bright and fabulous like fall. Today felt like the last breath of spring. That's why Al was washing Warren's fleet.

Warren had purchased three dirt-cheap, totally stripped-down Corollas and was running a black-market rental-car company for people who didn't want any record of renting a car. People who didn't want to answer any questions about who they were or why they needed a rental car or where they were taking it. Off-the-grid people. People who paid cash. Drug dealers and bank robbers and other folks from the shadows. And me. I rented from Warren whenever I needed an under-the-radar ride. *"Part of a PI's life is hiding in the shadows, Katie,"* Jimmy once said to me while we were hiding in the shadows.

I sat next to Logan, and we watched Al clean the cars. Al was Warren's night manager because, well, Al was up.

"Is he a real zombie?" Logan said.

It was a fair question. Al Cutter was thirty-four. He'd lived in apartment 5A since before I'd arrived at the House of Emotional Tics, two and a half years ago. He was tall and zombie thin with stringy, dirty-blond zombie hair that fell below his stooped zombie shoulders. His ears and nose seemed larger than normal because his perpetually bloodshot zombie eyes were set so impossibly deep in his face. His skin was zombie white. Fingers long and bony. The vibe he put out in waves when walking down the street was disagreeable and unpleasant. He was not a nice man. Mothers would keep their kids close when Al walked by because, for all intents and purposes, he was as much a zombie as anyone dead or alive.

"Jury's out," I said. "But he's a real insomniac. Sleeps less than an hour a night for the last sixteen years on account of when he was a freshman at Fordham, his roommate, a premed douchebag named Elliot Morgan, woke Al up in the middle of the night—his name's Al, by the way—shoved the barrel of a loaded .357 Magnum in Al's mouth, and called his biology professor to negotiate an F up to an A in exchange for not blowing Al's brains across the dorm room. The professor's wife called the police on the other line. The standoff lasted ten hours, all of it with the gun in Al's mouth. He never slept after that night. Elliot, now a douchebag bond trader, got off with a slap on the wrist. But every month, Al hacks into ConEd's portal and fucks with Elliot's bill. So for the rest of time, Elliot has to fight ConEd about how much money he owes them."

Logan was unimpressed. "Nobody got murdered, so it doesn't matter if he sleeps or not or why he does or doesn't. What matters is if he's a real zombie, you have to shoot him in the head with your gun while I'm here. It's the only way to kill them."

"Why my gun? And why do I have to shoot him while you're here?"

"It turns up as evidence in half my homicides, and I can never prove it was the murder weapon. If I'm here when you shoot him with your gun, I can arrest you again and put you in prison for your own safety."

From my father's McCall & Company business-in-a-box I'd also inherited his ashes in a German beer stein (now on a shelf in my living room), a bottle of Wild Turkey (which we'd drunk at his wake in the brownstone backyard), a sealed manila envelope with my name written on the front, his most recent case files (open and closed), his satellite cell phone, a miniature digital camera, a very small photo printer, a six-inch restorer's pry bar, an old-fashioned brass nameplate that read *McCall & Company, Private Investigations* (that Fu had affixed to my apartment door without my permission), and his automatic .45 Colt pistol.

Logan wasn't wrong. I'd been forcibly separated from the Colt at several different murder scenes related to Jimmy's case, which was part of the reason he'd arrested me four different times since the end of July. But, like Logan said, it had never been proven I'd shot anybody, so each time I'd slid off Logan's legal hook—and weaseled my way off his shit list too. Though that never lasted long. I was usually back on it before I left the room. Since I'd committed to being a PI and told Logan I wouldn't stop looking for Jimmy's killer, I was back on the list for good.

"You're a morbid man, Logan."

"Everybody says so."

He was fifty-eight. Five-ten and in good shape for his age or any age. He'd been a homicide detective, hunting down the most murderous murderers in the city for more than thirty years. Cranky and crusty rolling out of bed. He detested private investigators as much as he disliked off-Broadway actors.

Meaning two strikes against me before I ever got to the plate. Meaning Logan didn't like me as far as he could spit. He'd said those very words to my very face on multiple occasions—each time he'd arrested me, for instance.

In return, I didn't like him either. Which was as it should be according to Jimmy, who'd taught me on more than one occasion that, *"PIs and cops are not friends, Katie. They're lions and zebras unless and until they need each other, at which time they pretend to be pals at arm's length. But the minute that need is over and done, they're back on opposite sides of the Serengeti."*

But there was something other than the Serengeti between Logan and me. We had a couple connections that couldn't be denied.

Connection one was that Logan had reminded me of my father a dozen times since I'd been illicitly investigating Jimmy's murder. My refusal to stop my investigation, even after Logan had ordered me to, even after I'd promised him I was *all done investigating any damn thing in New York*, exasperated and infuriated the detective to no end. I couldn't say I blamed him. I could be as frustrating and irritating and annoying as my father, who'd been known by the law-enforcement side of the city as a titan of frustration, irritation, and annoyance. (In his defense, at the same time, Jimmy had been beloved by his clients for his honesty, morality, and decency.) Anyway, I was his daughter, for Pete's sake. I'd inherited his DNA. Which meant my father had often—meaning every day of my life— expressed the same feelings of anger, incredulity, and dismay toward me that Logan felt.

From my unplanned pregnancy at age sixteen, to my unconventional acting career that barely paid (didn't pay) my bills, to my endless string of dead-end jobs, including my brief stint as a strip-club dancer (to help pay said unpaid bills), and on and on and on, Jimmy would say in myriad ways, *"Jesus Christ, Kate. Does your brain not work at all?"* But he'd been there when I needed him, heard me out when I had something to say, trusted me when he didn't trust me, believed me when he didn't believe me, and had my back when there'd been no one else back there.

Logan had done the same, though he'd also said on many occasions, *Are you out of your mind, McCall? It's simply not possible for a person to be this stupid.* But in our turbulent time together, the detective had also shown me the hint of a begrudging smile of respect, and even, dare I say, something that passed for not entirely disliking me. Somewhere under his bad-tempered, ill-humored, surly crust, it was possible Logan could accept me as someone he didn't dislike, as long as no one was watching and he'd had a few beers.

Connection two was what Logan had come to chat about.

"Have you heard from him?" Logan said.

"Not since the subway," I said.

He was talking about Jimmy's killer. The professional corporate assassin who shot people's eyes out for six or seven figures.

"Nothing from the task force?" I said.

"Nothing," he said. "Son of a bitch is invisible."

"No, he's not. You know who he is. He told me you did."

It was true. The killer had told me he knew Logan well and for a long time. Well enough and long enough to have engineered this whole stinking shit pile so that Logan would be the detective of record, so it would be Logan's case, Logan's task force, Logan's headache, Logan's ulcer. And because I'd stuck my nose in Jimmy's murder and the murders that had come after, the killer had made me the middleman between him and Logan.

"I've spent enough time in Rockefeller Center, they should give me a fucking office," Logan said. "I've watched hours of security footage from every camera and every angle going back more than a month. We've questioned everyone who works in the building and everyone they know and everyone *they* know. Thousands of people. Nothing. Not one suspicious fucking thing. We went back to Superior Press. Back to Monument Insurance. All the way fucking back. Still nothing."

Rockefeller Center was the location of the killer's most recent professional hits—a law firm where one of the partners had no longer wanted to have any of the other partners as partners. Superior Press was the murder scene before that. Monument Insurance was where they'd found my father dead in the elevator. I'd worked my unwanted way into all those cases.

"He's not done," Logan said. "He wanted a task force to torture me, and now he has one. He's going to reach out again. Test you. Test me. The minute he does, McCall, you are going to dial me directly and put me between you and him. Do you understand what I'm saying today?"

"Put you between me and him," I said.

"He wants to kill me, McCall. Whoever the fuck he is and whatever the fuck he imagines I've done to him, that is his endgame. If he has to kill you to kill me, then he will, and I will not accept your death as part and parcel of this particular case. You are a rank amateur who cannot defend herself against this sick and violent egomaniac motherfucker. You will call me when he texts you, and you will leave him to me. You will not engage him beyond that. I will send your son a record of this conversation so there can be no mistaking my position. You are done. Is there a way for me to be any clearer about this than I have been regarding you and me and the killer?"

Yes, he'd hit a dead end with his task force, and the frustration had eaten him alive because he couldn't uncover a clue and because the killer was one of the gazillion people he knew or had known during the course of his thirty-plus-year career...and he didn't know which one it was. And, yes, he'd hoped I'd heard from the killer so there would be another place for the task force to find footing, but he was worried about me too. I could feel it beneath his short-tempered tone.

"I realize this is the original lie from which all your ensuing falsehoods flow, but one more time for humor's sake, repeat after me," Logan said. "I, Kate McCall, promise Detective Lew Logan, cross my heart and swear to the God of Far-Flung Bullshit Broadway Musicals, that I am done investigating any damn thing in New York."

"Can't do it, Logan. You know I can't. That sick and violent egomaniac motherfucker killed my father. But I promise to call you as soon as he texts me."

Logan nodded. He'd known before he started this was how it would shake out. "You're not going to shoot that fucking zombie in the head for me?"

"No can do," I said. "He pays rent."

4

TODAY WAS NOT A GOOD DAY FOR CLARITY

IT WAS EARLY TUESDAY MORNING, THE FIRST DAY OF NOVEMBER, and the Gods of Weather had snatched the last gasp of spring that was yesterday and replaced it with the first blast of winter —gray-on-gray and twenty degrees colder—as if they'd looked at each other and said, *"That's enough fall for these fucking people. Let's get to the nasty shit, shall we?"* It wasn't supposed to rain but try telling that to the nimbus clouds that were spitting on New York out of spite.

Rick was asleep on my sofa. I shook his shoulder because I'd scheduled a workout with Raul. And if I was going, he was going. I had the feeling he wasn't happy about this arrangement. It was more than a feeling, actually.

"I'm not happy about this arrangement," Rick said, coming out of a good dream. "Sucks enough I'm sleeping on your sofa. I'm definitely not getting up early to go to the gym for you. I don't get up early to go to the gym for myself."

"The irrefutable fact of being someone's bodyguard is that their body must be with you at all moments if you're going to guard it," I said. "So get up and get going. When I'm late, Raul tortures me like the Dark Ages."

We grabbed a cab and headed downtown and west to Raul's Boxing, a Hell's Kitchen landmark in the form of a sweaty, grimy, no-frills, old-school, hard-knocks, second-floor gym that hadn't changed since Raul opened the place more than fifty years ago. Same spit buckets. Same corner stools. Same names carved into the walls. Same lockers. Same sweltering heat. Same sweat-soaked smell. Same everything. Including Raul. He was in his eighties but was tough as shoe leather.

"You're a boxer?" Rick said in the cab.

"Since I was thirteen," I said. "My mother died of cancer when I was ten, and my sister left for college in Cleveland three years later. After that, it was just Jimmy and me. He was still working a lot, and I was on my own, so he decided it was time for me to learn how to hit like a man. He told me I'd love the sweet science if it didn't kill me first."

"Do you?"

"Four days a week for thirty-two years—thirty-three next month—so, yeah, I don't hate it."

I introduced Rick to Raul, who found him a chair where he could watch me suffer, and then I went to work. On any given day, a session with Raul could include some combination of five or ten rounds of speed bag, followed by five or ten rounds of shadow work, followed by five or ten rounds hitting the pads in the ring, followed by five or ten rounds pounding the heavy bag, followed by five or ten rounds skipping rope, followed by five or ten rounds of push-ups and pull-ups and crunches. Each set was three minutes of intense drilling per round, one minute of rest; three minutes of lungs burning like bonfires, one minute of rest; three minutes of heart exploding like warheads, one minute of rest; three minutes of muscles screaming like sirens, one minute of rest.

Raul decided how many rounds per set and what drills in what order you were going to growl-grunt-groan through. A workout lasted two terrible hours. If he was in a good mood, it was two hours of suffering and torment. If he was in a fair mood, it was two hours of agony and anguish. If he was in a bad mood, you barely lived through it.

Raul was unhappy about Rick with me. No guests was the house rule. I explained I was bodyguarding the guy, so he let Rick stay, but since he wasn't happy, I barely lived through it.

I showered and changed and arranged an Uber for the ride to Rick's house in Brooklyn, where he'd pack a suitcase and grab his laptop and whatever else he needed to pass the six weeks he was going to live with me. I told him we'd be in and out of his place like the wind, like we were never there, so that anyone who did come looking for him would think he'd bailed on Brooklyn until his pretrial. He nodded, and we were quiet as the Uber headed across town and south to the Williamsburg Bridge.

"You didn't spar," he said after a while. "You said you hit like a man. I wanted to see you punch somebody."

"I don't train with people who punch back," I said. "I'm an actor. Can't risk messing up my face. Last thing I need is for some casting director to say I look more like Rocky Balboa than Sandra Bullock."

"You *do* look like Sandra Bullock. From *Crash* and *The Blind Side*."

"People tell me all the time."

"I mean, you're not her spitting image, but you've got her vibe for sure."

"I'm not as pretty as she is. Believe me, I know. And I'm not as accomplished or composed or rich either. And I'm *probably* not as talented...see what I did there?"

"I do, yes."

"But she plays a bodyguard in the movies, and I do it in real life. So I've got that going for me. Plus, I hit like a man, and I bet she doesn't."

"You could take her? That's what you're saying?"

"She's going down."

"So if Sandra Bullock comes to kill me, you'll knock her out and save my life?"

"It's my job to KO Sandra Bullock, if that's what you're asking."

We both laughed at the idea of me decking Sandra Bullock to save Rick's life, having a swell time, and I thought, *Hey, whoa, back it up, Kate. You're having a little too much fun with your client. You're not here to be his friend. You're here to be his bodyguard.* And the laughing gradually dissipated, and we were quiet again.

Two hours of grinding through the meat mill at Raul's usually cleared my mind on days when my mind needed clearing. But today was not a good day for clarity.

Today, I was thinking about Logan looking for answers I didn't have. Today, I was thinking I might never hear from Jimmy's killer again and find myself back at square one, a square upon which they had inscribed my name, considering how much time I'd spent there. Today, I was thinking about being Rick's bodyguard, admitting to myself that I had no idea how to be a bodyguard, that I was in over my head, that I should tell the Uber driver to pull over, give Rick his money back, and tell him to find some other bodyguard who knew what the hell she was doing because I sure as shit didn't. So no, even a torture session with Raul had not cleared my mind today.

We went over the Williamsburg Bridge, found our way to Fifth Avenue, took that to Driggs and then to Broadway (passing the legendary Peter Luger, New York's most storied steak house since 1887), then made a left on Union and a right on Scholes.

"That's my place on the left," Rick said. "The firehouse."

"Go around the block," I said to the driver.

Then I turned to Rick. "Let's not tell anyone we're here."

$$5$$

THREE FIFTY A DAY IS NOT ENOUGH
MONEY TO BE A BODYGUARD

Brooklyn was the coolest borough. All you had to do to confirm that fact was ask anyone who lived there. Stop any Brooklynite on the street and there was a chance they might not ever even go into Manhattan, that's how cool they thought Brooklyn was. *"Manhattan? You mean the overrated town for tourists on the wrong side of our bridge?"* they might tell you. That being said, Brooklyn kind of *was* the coolest borough. And Williamsburg was probably its hippest and hipster-est neighborhood.

Located directly across the East River from the Lower East Side of Manhattan, Williamsburg was the first stop into Brooklyn on the L train. Ridiculously rich in culture, it felt as if every ethnicity in New York decided all at once to stake their claim in the same neighborhood. High-end galleries next to bodegas next to nightclubs next to mega-million-dollar apartments next to factories next to fancy five-star restaurants next to cool-cat coffee shops next to indie art studios next to long-time local eateries next to Italian Social Clubs next to Hasidic houses of worship next to and next to and next to and next to. Barry Manilow had Williamsburg roots. So did Mel Brooks. So did Peter Criss and Gene Simmons from KISS. And Peter Dinklage. And the guy who created Tumblr. And Bugsy Siegel, the gangster who made Vegas Vegas.

No matter the borough, for many New Yorkers, music was the ultimate indicator of cool, and Williamsburg's club scene had long been the ultimate incubator for innovative indie bands—punk, rock, fusion, funk, soul, worldbeat, and Latin jazz. Sometimes it felt like they were all playing at the same time. Same thing with art and food and fashion. It was all simultaneously turned up to ten and happening in wild-eyed harmony in this one rad neighborhood. A hipster indie culture clash like no other—vibrant and stylish and walkable.

So we walked.

Starting around the corner on the opposite side of Scholes Street from Rick's place, we walked like we were passing through, like we had no special business on this block of Scholes. Which, like lots of Williamsburg streets, was a mix of four- and five-story residential buildings in need of renovation, worn-out churches requiring repair and renewal, trendy retail shops, casual cafes, fabulous factory conversions, and slummy artist garrets.

I nonchalantly scanned both sides of the street. No idling cars with questionable characters behind the wheel. No losers loitering in the shadows or doorways. Just people going about their Brooklyn business, same as me and Rick.

At the light, we crossed the street and headed back to Rick's, a three-story converted firehouse with a rustic and beautiful brick façade. A second-floor window was nearly as massive as the street-level, roll-up, metal garage door—wide enough and tall enough for fire engines to race off to the rescue back in the day. Built into the door made for pumpers and hook-and-ladders was a small door for people. Rick unlocked it, we hurried inside, and he shut and locked it behind us.

I turned around and my first thought was, *Holy shit, this*

place is tons of freaking awesome. My second thought was, *Holy shit, Rick Gotti has tons of freaking money.*

The ground floor, where fire trucks once parked, had been completely transformed into the most incredible carpentry shop you can imagine. Every possible piece of high-end, state-of-the-art woodworking gear was on the floor, most of it on self-contained rolling tables: lathes and planers and routers and sanders; shapers and miters and jointers and saws of all sizes. Mortise machine. Mobile clamp rack. Floor-mounted drill press as tall as Shaquille O'Neal. A lathe straight out of Bob Vila's private stash of super-cool lathes. A hundred hand tools on long workbenches that stretched to the far end of the room. Custom cabinets to store stains and paints and polys in style. Large labeled lumber racks ran the length of the space: oak, maple, mahogany, cherry, pine, ash, birch, cedar. Plenty of power. Superior lighting. High-tech dust collection system. State-of-the-art air compressor. Wall-mounted flat-screen television with super surround sound. Multiple shop vacs. Office area with a massive monitor.

And there was custom-built furniture. Tables and dressers and chairs and cabinets galore. All in different stages of construction. All beautiful beyond words. It was like being in the middle of the best episode of HGTV I'd ever seen.

"What the heck, Rick?" I said.

"I picked it up in therapy maybe a dozen years ago," he said. "It gets in your blood. The raw wood in your hands, the finished piece in your head. It's kind of a hobby I can't quit. I'm an addict, don't forget. Sawdust in my veins and all that."

I wanted to ask him about the gear, what each machine did. I wanted to ask him about the furniture he was building. Did he sell it? Keep it? Give it away as gifts to, I don't know, his personal bodyguard, for instance? But the questions would have to wait. We had to move fast and leave no footprints, no evidence to say Rick had stopped by.

A long staircase against the left wall led up to the second floor. It had to be a twenty-foot ceiling, so when I say long staircase, I mean thirty steps' worth. Maybe more.

"The actual stairway to heaven," I said.

"Love Zeppelin," he said.

I went first because of the two of us, I was the bodyguard.

"How long have you owned this place?"

"Bought it twenty years ago," Rick said. "Total wreck. Boarded up. Empty for decades before that. I didn't do anything with it until after my second round of rehab maybe ten years ago. Then it was a three-year reno. I did the shop first, then the second floor, then the third. Came out okay."

We arrived at the second floor, and my jaw dropped. It was a stunning, midcentury modern, twenty-five-hundred-square-foot loft-like space pulled from the pages of *Architectural Digest*. Pale maple floors, soft-white walls, sixteen-foot ceilings, gorgeously lit, professionally designed, tastefully furnished, Asian rugs to die for, original paintings and photographs and prints and pottery and glasswork that looked like they'd been made for the room. Everything stylish. Everything elegant. Plush for days.

"Came out *okay*?" I said, blown away by the effortless sophistication.

"Probably better than that," he said.

The staircase opened near the kitchen, which was white on white with professional-grade stainless-steel appliances. The enormous island held a huge premium sink and six leather barstools. To prepare dinner in this space would be Food Network nirvana. Meals cooked in this kitchen would just flipping taste better.

Beyond the kitchen, moving toward the front of the firehouse and the giant window that looked down onto Scholes Street, was the most beautiful, bench-built dining-room table I'd ever seen. Made from exotic-looking hardwood, it sat twelve for dinner. The chairs were hand-built to match. You could feed folks a feast at this extraordinary table or put it in a furniture museum. Flip a coin.

"You built that?" I said.

"And the chairs, yes. In the shop."

"Wow, Rick."

"Thanks, McCall."

Past the table was an enormous living-room space, large enough for three full-size luxurious sofas, several handsome chairs, coffee tables, end tables, lamps, and other living-room accessories that faced a custom-constructed wall unit fashioned from, again, some kind of spectacular wood surrounding a wall-mounted flat screen that would have worked in an art-house movie theater, a sound system that Led Zeppelin themselves would have been proud to play in their studio, and shelf after shelf after shelf of albums. Vinyl. Old school. Thousands of records.

Light slipped through a sheer drape over the front window, and I thought this might be the most serenely styled loft in a converted historic firehouse anywhere ever.

"There's a full bath and a gym behind the kitchen," he said.

"Bedrooms are on the third floor?"

"Two of them. With two full baths. And a laundry room. And about a thousand feet of outdoor deck space. It's nice up there."

"No doubt," I said, moving to the wall of albums. "How's the sound?"

"Pick a record."

Since I had Zeppelin on my mind, I pulled *Led Zeppelin IV* from the shelf. "Just one minute because we really have to go," I said, pushing pause for sixty seconds of vinyl on Rick's killer system.

He smiled, put the record on the turntable, cranked the volume, and "Rock and Roll" filled the room like the band was playing live in the loft. Rick wasn't kidding. The system shook the building.

I closed my eyes, let the band blow me back, and someone behind me put a clear plastic bag over my head and pulled it tight around my neck.

I was stunned and staggered and almost immediately out of breath. I instinctively reached for the hands of whoever was suffocating me and glanced to my right.

Another assailant was suffocating Rick at the same time.

In the next sixty seconds, we were both going to die.

The guy smothering the life out of Rick was well over six feet and had to weigh two hundred fifty pounds at least. Much bigger than Rick. And much stronger. Rick had no shot with the guy. Rick was a goner.

The big guy was wearing a bear mask, of all things.

My guy was about my size. And he was struggling to contain me. Maybe the bear had told the smaller guy to take the woman, that she'd be a piece of cake. But of all the things I am, a fucking piece of cake is not one of them.

Twisting and turning and fighting for air, I stomped on my guy's ankle as hard as I could and bent it sideways. He groaned with pain and released his grip. I spun around and kneed him in the nuts dead on.

He was wearing a pig mask, of all things.

He grabbed his groin, and I lifted a small, heavy African sculpture off the coffee table and smashed it into his face. The pig went down, semi-conscious, bleeding through his mask like, well, a stuck pig. Busted nose for sure.

Forget the pig. Rick was on his knees. The bear was a relentless killer. He would murder Rick and then come for me.

I pulled the bag off my head and dove for my purse—I'd dropped it when the plastic went over my face. Rick fell onto his stomach, maybe already dead. I opened the purse, pulled

Jimmy's Colt, pointed it at the bear, and fired a shot. Led Zeppelin was playing so loud, you could hardly hear it.

I was unsteady as shit from almost being murdered myself, still catching my breath. Plus I'm a terrible shot because I don't like guns, so I'd missed the damn bear, even though he was the size of, well, a bear and was only ten feet from me.

But the gunshot made the bear rethink his situation. He let go of Rick and ran for the stairs. I pulled the trigger again—and missed again—then hurried to Rick and ripped the bag off his head. He gulped air. So not dead.

The pig moaned and moved. I took three steps to him and clocked him on the back of the head with the Colt. He went down like a bag of books.

"Watch the pig," I said to Rick, and ran after the bear.

By the time I got down the stairs, the bear was gone. I went through the small door in the big door and looked up and down Scholes Street. Nothing. No bear anywhere. I locked the door and went back up the stairs, where Rick was recovering on the sofa. He was in shock, but he was alive. I sat across from him.

"You didn't believe me," he said. "When you took the case yesterday."

"I didn't *not* believe you."

It was true. Lying had never been part of Rick's profile. He'd always been brutally honest—in his life and in his act. It's what had put him in hot water so many times. So I hadn't thought he was lying. I just hadn't believed him either.

"Today you're all in," he said.

"All in."

"So you'll help me prove I'm innocent?"

"No. More dangerous than ever. Now you stay in my house until Christmas."

He shook his head. I couldn't tell if he was refusing to

follow orders, expressing disbelief that I wasn't going to let him investigate Cochran's murder, or both.

"We need a cord and duct tape," I said. "We'll take the pig with us for leverage, make Cochran's killer think long and hard before he tries again."

Led Zeppelin pounded through the loft. The double-murder attempt replayed on an endless loop in my mind. It had happened so fast and been so violent, it was hard to process. Finally, Rick walked to the sound system and turned off the music.

"Three fifty a day is not enough money to be a bodyguard," I said.

"Not enough, no doubt," he said. "How about three sixty? You can use the extra ten bucks to take target practice."

Still a comedian. We both laughed. I caught a flash of smar-tass in his eyes and thought, *Thank God I didn't lose him.*

He started across the room. "I'll get a cord and duct tape."

I took my phone out of my purse and looked down at the pig. "I'll call a cab."

6

NO SELF-RESPECTING ACTOR TURNS DOWN THE CINEMATIC CYCLOPS

WE TIED THE PIG'S HANDS BEHIND HIS BACK WITH THE CORD, duct-taped his mouth shut, blindfolded him with a piece of cloth Rick had left lying around the shop, and walked him downstairs to wait for the cab I'd called. The left side of the pig's face was black and blue and purple. His smashed nose had finally stopped bleeding, and he was covered with his own dried blood. I'd never seen him before, and neither had Rick. He looked like nobody special. A schlubby dirtbag, miserable and hurting. I didn't feel the slightest bit bad for him. He'd tried to suffocate me with a plastic bag. *"Fuck him two times to Sunday,"* Jimmy would have said. I'd never known what he'd meant by that until today.

My phone rang, I nodded to Rick, he rolled up the garage door, and LaTanya pulled her yellow Volvo taxi into the building. Rick rolled the big door down behind her.

"What the fuck you do this time, McCall?" LaTanya said, climbing out of the Volvo and looking at our pathetic prisoner.

"He tried to kill me," I said. "The one who went for Rick got away, so we're taking this one hostage, in case they want to talk about it."

"Same motherfucker killed the comedian in the club?" LaTanya said to Rick.

"Pretty sure," Rick said. "But I didn't see his face in the club, and today he was wearing a bear mask."

"Blindfold boy was wearing this," I said, holding up the pig mask for LaTanya to see. "So we call him the pig."

"This little piggy all fucked up," LaTanya said.

"Fucked up and then some," I said.

The pig's shoulders sagged. Even he had to admit it.

LaTanya walked past the pig and me and Rick, took in the carpentry wonderland where fire trucks had once parked, and said, "*New Yankee Workshop* and shit. You some kind of Harrison-Ford-furniture-making-comedian-actor-asshole like *Star Wars* Jesus?"

"She has a way with words," Rick said to me.

"She has a way with everything," I said.

It was true. LaTanya Bellamy had her own way with everything. She lived in 3B and was four years older than me. She owned the yellow Volvo with her twin brother, Anthony, who everyone called Mountain on account of his being six eight and three hundred fifty pounds of pure, well, mountain. LaTanya drove the cab all day. Mountain drove it all night.

She was a few inches taller than me and heftier too. A big-breasted, thick-thighed, strong-armed force of nature. Sharp brown eyes, beautiful brown skin, wide nose, dazzling smile, gorgeous dreads, loud voice that broadcast her unadulterated opinions to everyone within earshot and beyond. She had no patience for idiot behavior. A walking-talking-live-from-New-York-in-living-color-radio-shock-jock all day, every day. A cat-five hurricane of a woman. My best friend in the House of Emotional Tics. Maybe my best friend in the world.

"Including movies," Rick said.

"You got that right," LaTanya said, cruising by the jigsaw.

"And I just now had an idea made of solid gold going guarantee my Academy Award for Karate."

"There's no such thing," I said.

"There will be when I add Rick Gotti to the cast of *Kung Fu Fu*," LaTanya said.

"Me?" Rick said. "I'm your idea made of solid gold? I like the sound of that, and I don't know what the hell it means."

"No way, LaTanya," I said. "Someone's trying to kill him. He has to stay inside my house for the next six weeks."

"Means my movie's got almost every damn thing it needs to be a box-office beauty," LaTanya said to Rick. "Got a mad scientist making a martial-arts chemical cocktail ain't nobody ever seen before; got a zombie drug dealer; got a bomb on a bus; got Fu making moves like Jumpin' Jackie Chan; got every damn thing but one."

"The suspense is killing me," Rick said.

"Romance," LaTanya said. "Poor little Cassie Barnett is all alone in the corner of the movie. All by herself. A poor little peanut."

"No, she's not," I said. "She's kicking butt and taking names."

"What the peanut needs," LaTanya said, ignoring me, "is a romantic rendezvous with a reporter on the run."

"She does not need that," I said, thinking, *on the run, of course. Can't be a regular reporter; has to be a renegade reporter.* "No way she needs that."

"I'm the reporter on the run?" Rick said.

"Damn straight," LaTanya said. "You covering the bomb on the bus and fall in love with Detective Peanut."

"He absolutely does not do that," I said. "And stop calling me peanut."

"All his scenes can be shot in your house," LaTanya said to me. "No break in your bodyguard business. Somebody call me a cinematic cyclops right the fuck now."

"You're a cinematic cyclops," Rick said. "Whatever that is. I don't even care what it is."

"Oh my God," I said. I wanted to say more, but that was all I had.

"Why is the reporter on the run?" Rick said.

"IRS wants a piece of his ass for back taxes," LaTanya said without blinking.

"Oh my God," I said again because nothing else would come out of my mouth.

"So you in?" LaTanya said to Rick.

"No self-respecting actor turns down the cinematic cyclops," Rick said.

LaTanya laughed. It was still one of the most beautiful sounds I'd ever heard.

"Oh my God," I said for the third time, and swore in my head I would not say it again.

Then LaTanya and Rick shook on it, and she went upstairs to see if she could find a free location to use in the film. Rick and I loaded the pig into the Volvo.

"She's way outside the box," Rick said.

"Since the minute we met," I said.

"When was that?"

"We moved into the building the same day two and a half years ago. Jimmy was helping me; her twin brother, Mountain, was helping her; and pretty soon we were all helping each other and drinking beers and having a blast and being brand-new best friends, especially Jimmy and LaTanya. Me and LaTanya too, but she and Jimmy were head-over-heels best buds. It was a great day until somebody stole the Volvo while we were carrying boxes into the brownstone. It wasn't so great after that."

"This Volvo?" Rick said.

We put the pig on the floor in the back seat and hog-tied his feet to his hands. I leaned down and said in his ear, "Are you familiar with the movie *Diner*? It's a classic. Set in Baltimore. I'm paraphrasing here, but if you move a muscle, I'll hit you so hard in the head with my gun that I'll kill your whole family. Do you understand?"

The pig nodded and groaned through the duct tape.

"Yes, this Volvo," I said. "Jimmy said we'd find the cab and catch the guy and bring him back so Mountain could say hello in person. Mountain is the same size as the entire right side of the New York Jets offensive line."

"And you did. Impressive."

"Took a week. I had a snitch who pointed me in the right direction. Jimmy roughed the guy up and threw him in the back seat—not unlike the pig, actually—and we drove the Volvo back to the brownstone. The guy pissed himself when Mountain stood up to say hey. LaTanya and I have been tight ever since."

We leaned against the cab. Thinking about that story, about Jimmy driving the Volvo back to the House of Emotional Tics, about him gesturing down at the bloody shitball on the floor of the back seat and telling me..."*Katie, some people go begging for a good punch in the nose, and it's your job to give them what they want.*"...thinking about that made me remember he was dead now.

"Jimmy's murder hit her hard too," I said. "So she helps me with that case, finding the fucker who murdered him. I'm going to get that guy and fry him."

"So Fu *and* LaTanya help you?"

"And Charlie and Al and Warren. Like *Mission Impossible*."

"You're Tom Cruise? Or maybe Peter Graves?"

"Graves. But only in my dreams and even then not as smooth as he was. But yes, they're my team. That's why you can't tell Logan. I have a PI license—Jimmy made me get one twenty years ago—and even with that in my pocket, Logan's arrested me multiple times. They're just normal Manhattan maniacs. None of them have a PI license. Some are barely legal, some are definitely illegal, the rest already have criminal records. Charlie's a three-time ex-con released early to collect delinquent cars for the city. Fu's a mob assassin. Al's light years off the legal grid. Warren runs an unregistered rental-car company. LaTanya, well, she's LaTanya. And Mountain's been in prison too. I don't want Logan to know anything about them. They're my friends. Something like friends. I don't know. Anyway, I have to keep them in the shadows, away from Logan."

He nodded. "Why'd your father make you get a PI license?"

LaTanya came down the stairs and started through the shop toward the Volvo at the front end of the building. She called out as she came toward us. "Nice crib. You made some scratch, Rick Gotti. Don't deny it."

"Four years on TV, LaTanya," Rick said. "Lucky I didn't blow it all when I was wild. Same business manager for thirty years. I call him every day to say thank you."

"Tell him to manage me and my movie next time you talk to him," LaTanya said.

"Matthew, my son, was born on my seventeenth birthday," I said, answering Rick's question about Jimmy and my license. "When he was six, I got a night job dancing in a strip club. Single mom, shitty day gig, struggling actor, amateur boxer. I had to do something to pay the bills, and I could dance. I mean, I don't look like it now, but I had moves. But Jimmy found out after my second night and separated me from the club—separated the club owner from his nose too—and made me get my license so I could help him with surveillance and other PI particulars when I needed money, which I often did and still do."

"You could dance in a strip club tonight if you wanted to."

"Thanks. Full-time actor. Full-time PI. Currently bodyguard."

"I mean, you *do* look like it now is what I'm saying. It's a compliment, McCall."

Is that Rick Gotti complimenting me or is that Rick Gotti hitting on me? I thought.

He'd been a notorious slutbag when he was wild (his words), before he'd disappeared into fifteen years of rehab and recovery. But a leopard doesn't change his spots, does he? Before I could react, LaTanya arrived at the Volvo.

"Where we taking the pig?" she said.

We got in the car. Rick rode shotgun. I sat in the back.

"Theater," I said. "I have dress rehearsal. Show opens Friday."

Rick hit the button on the app on his phone, and the garage door rolled up. LaTanya pulled the Volvo out onto Scholes Street, and Rick locked and alarmed the firehouse behind us as we drove away.

"What show?" Rick said, turning sideways to face me.

"*Psychedelic Sunday*," I said. "Light-years-off-Broadway musical theater."

"What's it about?"

"Venus, Adonis, and a Columbia art professor on LSD meet in the Met on a sunny Sunday afternoon in 1968."

"And what happens?"

"Singing, dancing, couple orgies. The usual."

7

SOUNDS LIKE A CASE FOR THE SCHMIDT AND PARKER PLAYERS

"IT WAS A BRA FACTORY IN THE 1940S," I SAID, POINTING THROUGH the windshield at the three-story industrial building on the next block. We were at a red light on the Lower East Side of Manhattan. The pig was at my feet. "Built by Irish and Italian immigrants. Dennis Parker and Posey Schmidt bought it ten years ago with a windfall inheritance, quit their jobs as New York City public-school music and theater arts teachers, and founded the Schmidt and Parker Players. They're the godfather and godmother of way-off-Broadway musicals. Or maybe the eccentric aunt and uncle. Or the wacky next-door neighbors. They rent out the ground floor, live on the second floor, and opened the D-Cup Theater on the third floor."

"D-Cup," Rick said. "Portent of orgies to come."

"Word got out that there would be two of them, and the show sold out the eight-week run to subscribers in presale," I said. "No seats for the general public. Sex sells tickets, someone said, and Dennis said sex doesn't sell tickets, it sells guilt-free self-gratification. Posey said *Psychedelic Sunday* is a masturbatory musical for the ages. Or at least for New York. That's the tagline for the show, I kid you not."

They were husband and wife, cofounders of their own theater troupe—of which I was a card-carrying member—and co-creative directors of the D-Cup. All their shows were original productions. Dennis was the venerated, underground, alt-universe writer/director and choreographer. Posey was the adored, cult-queen, mad-mad-world composer, orchestrator, and keyboardist for the D-Cup Band of Bohemians. Their season was four preposterously fantastical shows a year. Eight weeks of performance, followed by four weeks of rehearsal, followed by eight weeks of performance, followed by four weeks of rehearsal...write-rehearse-perform-repeat all year long with four weeks off during the summer. I'd been with them five full seasons and had been the star or costar of a dozen of the craziest musicals ever mounted.

Did I wish my career had taken a different trajectory, a rocket right to Broadway instead of to a former bra factory on the Lower East Side? Of course I did. I wasn't nuts.

What I was, though, was a committed actor and singer and dancer in my soul since I'd played Kim MacAfee in our seventh-grade production of *Bye Bye Birdie*. After that show, I was done. The path of my life had been decided at age twelve (much to Jimmy's dismay). I knew who I was and who I would be. So acting, singing, and dancing in a cool-beans, loft-like New York theater in front of a live and enthusiastic New York crowd—who subscribed to see D-Cup musical insanity for its pure and passionate energy, its live rock-and-roll scores, its high-powered cast of crazies, and, yes, its indecipherable story-lines that were as much fun as they were incomprehensible—fulfilled me in a way that made me matter to myself. Like a pin in a map of the universe...*Kate is here*. I loved it like Lucy. I needed it like air. I was never more me than when the curtain opened and the lights came up and the band began to play.

LaTanya backed the Volvo into the loading dock, and Rick and I put our prisoner pig on the industrial elevator with the sliding cage doors that had been here since the building opened in the '40s. The elevator bell rang—which it did at all hours, even during shows—as we reached the third floor. The elevator simply added another crazy layer to the general insanity of a D-Cup musical, meaning the audience had come to accept the bell as part of the madness. Somehow, we all had.

I slid the cage door open, and we escorted the blindfolded pig into the loft.

Rick looked around, caught my eye, and said, "Wow, McCall. Awesome theater."

"Playhouse paradise," I said.

It was a full-size, former factory floor. Longer than it was wide but plenty wide enough for twenty-four chairs from side to side. Aisles divided the space into three sections of eight seats per row; ten rows front to back; two hundred forty total seats. Small enough to be intimate when necessary but big enough for raucous, rowdy, loud, and bawdy musicals, which was our bearing, bent, badge, and brand. Fourteen-foot ceilings. Ten-foot windows. Brick walls with faded murals of women's torsos wearing bras the size of safari tents. Exposed industrial heating and air ducts. Commercial lighting—Dennis and Posey had re-wired the original fixtures so the place had a rock-and-roll vibe from a bygone era. Two rows of steel support beams that obscured certain sight lines of less fortunate audience members.

The elevator opened along the south wall into the middle of the room. To the left, at the back of the theater, was a full bar with stools and bistro tables and two bathrooms. To the right, at the front, was the elevated proscenium stage, meaning it had wings on both sides and an apron in front of the curtain. Yes, it had an honest-to-God red velvet curtain. Professional stage lighting and a concert sound system made Posey's Band of Bohemians look and sound like *Procol Harum Live: In Concert with the Edmonton Symphony Orchestra.* Yes, there was often dancing in the aisles during the shows.

Behind the stage was one of my favorite places on Earth—the dressing room. Also offices and storage for set construction, props, wardrobe, boxes of paraphernalia from past performances, and one room whose purpose I'd never known.

"There's a room behind the stage," I said to Rick. "Door's always locked. I'm hoping it's a freezer."

"Because you want to keep the pig on ice?" Rick said.

"That's the punchline, yes."

"You've got comedic skills, McCall."

"Coming from a comedian, that almost means something."

"Don't mention it. What's with the cab?"

The stage was set for dress rehearsal (scheduled later this afternoon). An old-school Checker cab had been cut in half from front to back so the audience could see inside.

"Act one, scene one," I said. "Professor Johnny Jedry is on her way to the Metropolitan Museum of Art to rekindle her lost passion for art and love and life. On the ride down Fifth Avenue, she drops a tab of LSD, offered by the well-meaning cabbie who she's never met in her life. Also, she's never taken drugs or done anything impulsive. But still, she drops the acid. So if you're thinking, *Uh-oh, this musical could get all kinds of crazy*, then you win a prize because the LSD inspires her psychedelic trip through the Met, where Venus and Adonis pop out of the priceless Peter Paul Rubens painting, and they all get romantically and sexually entangled in a Sunday-afternoon threesome that leads to not one but two orgies and a duel to the death between Jedry and Adonis. The rest of the story makes less sense than that. *The singing and dancing are off the hook, and the energy is through the roof, but from where I'm sitting, indecipherable only scratches the surface,* some reviewer will write. *From where I'm sitting, it sounds like another unintelligible, incoherent, and impenetrable D-Cup disaster.*"

"Sounds like far-out fun."

"Sounds like another grand and glorious hot-mess success."

Dennis called out from the stage. "Kate, you're early."

"And you've brought company," Posey said.

They were tweaking the taxi set.

"Including a man whose hands are bound behind his back," Dennis said.

"And who's blindfolded and duct-taped to boot," Posey said.

Though neither one was large, as a pair they were larger than life. Dennis Parker was five-three in his stocking feet, thin and limber like a Broadway dancer. He was sixty-two years old and dressed, looked, sounded, and moved exactly like the legendary Joel Grey, who remained a true-blue musical theater hero. Dennis was a brilliant, avant-garde choreographer and counter-culture writer-director. He was the spirit and wisdom and passion of the Schmidt and Parker Players. Its kooky conscience.

His wife for decades, Posey Schmidt was the heart and soul of the D-Cup, its maniac musical muse. If there'd been a five-foot-tall Liza Minelli balloon inflated to a perfect sphere with fire-engine-red frizzy hair, red lipstick, red fingernails, red everything, that would be Posey. She was a brilliant composer-orchestrator-pianist-performer. Her rock anthems were Queen-like in their breadth and drama, Meat Loaf-like in their urgency. Her ballads were beautiful. It was pure joy to sing and dance her songs. She was fifty-five, but rocked like she was thirty years younger.

The one little, bitty, minor, trivial issue I had with them as writer-director-composer of the plays we presented to our fanatic subscribers was that they didn't share an affinity for story logic, character continuity, plot-point reality, backstory clarity, or any aspect of theatrical narrative rhyme or reason that would bring some sense of, well, sense to the blazing fun.

I'd gotten used to it because blazing fun turned out to be a big damn deal to a lot of people.

We walked toward the stage. Dennis and Posey stepped out onto the apron. Rick and I sat the pig in a third-row aisle seat. The guy couldn't see, couldn't speak, could only breathe through his nose, and his wrists had to be numb. He'd had some kind of allergy flareup—dust or duct tape or something in the D-Cup air—and was working extra hard to get oxygen into his lungs. I wanted to say, *That's what you call karma. Bad juju on you-you.* But all I said was, "Stay." He wasn't going anywhere.

We moved away from the pig and joined Dennis and Posey on the stage.

"Dennis Parker and Posey Schmidt, this is my client, Rick Gotti," I said. "Rick, meet my friends Dennis and Posey."

They nodded and smiled at each other.

"And that is the pig who tried to kill me at Rick's house in Brooklyn earlier today," I said. "The pig's associate, the bear, tried to kill Rick while the pig was attempting to kill me. They wore animal masks, which is how and why we named them the pig and the bear. We escaped, clearly, and have taken the pig prisoner."

"Wait a minute," Dennis said. "Rick Gotti from *The Jungle*?"

"Welcome-to-the-jungle Rick Gotti?" Posey said.

"Rick Gotti making a comeback?" Dennis said.

"Rick Gotti arrested for murder and out on bail?" Posey said.

"That Rick Gotti?" Dennis said.

"The very same," Rick said.

"It's a pleasure, Rick. Welcome to the D-Cup," Dennis said.

"Thank you. Really great space," Rick said.

"Off-Broadway musical nirvana on steroids," Posey said.

"Looking forward to rehearsal today for sure," Rick said.

"You're staying?" Dennis said.

"Captive audience," Rick said. "I mean not like the pig."

We all laughed. Rick had a way of making you laugh at things that shouldn't be funny. It wasn't a skill he'd picked up on the side of the road of his life. It was a talent he'd been born with. Maybe he'd fine-tuned it over time with practice, but it didn't seem like something he could have learned. It seemed like a gift he'd been given.

"You've still got it, Rick," Dennis said when the laughter faded.

"Been a while," Rick said, "so, yeah, good to know."

"Changing subjects," Posey said, turning to me. "You clearly used the word *client* when introducing us."

"'This is my *client*,'" Dennis said.

"And the pig was part of the pair that tried to snuff you out," Posey said.

"One under wraps, one on the loose," Dennis said, gesturing toward the pig in the third row and out into the world somewhere.

"So we can safely assume Rick represents your new case," Posey said.

"And that you've come to stash the pig and enlist our help to catch the one that got away," Dennis said.

"The bear," Posey said.

They'd been together for so long they often shared sentences.

"Yes, I've come to stash the pig," I said. "But it's not that kind of case. Not really a case at all. I'm his bodyguard. I'm not investigating anything."

"Which is, I must admit," Rick said, "a bone of contention between us."

"Do tell," Posey said.

"No, don't tell," I said. "There's no bone of contention. No bone."

"I'm sensing a bone," Dennis said. "Are you sensing a bone, Posey?"

"Femur," Posey said.

"Fibula," Dennis said.

"Tibia," Posey said.

"Humerus," Dennis said.

"Big bone," Posey said.

I rolled my eyes. There was nothing I could do to stop this conversation from unfolding.

"I didn't kill Kenny Cochran," Rick said. "McCall knows that's true. The bear killed Cochran, and I got framed. Wrong place at the wrong time. I want to use these six weeks before my pretrial hearing to prove my innocence."

"And?" Posey said, looking at me.

"And he hired me to be his bodyguard," I said. "To get him to his pretrial hearing alive. Not to investigate the murder of Ken Cochran."

"From an objective standpoint," Dennis said.

"Unbiased, detached, and impartial," Posey said.

"It sounds like a case for the Schmidt and Parker Players," Dennis said.

Rick looked to me for an explanation. Unfortunately, there was no one I could look to.

"They help me with my *other* cases," I said to Rick. "And this is *not* one of those other cases. This is me bodyguarding you. This is you staying in my house, watching *Animal Planet* for six weeks until Christmas."

"A true test of human endurance," Posey said.

"Crossing the Pacific in a rowboat," Dennis said.

"The Sahara on a bicycle," Posey said.

"The South Pole on a skateboard," Dennis said.

"You can stop now," I said. "May I please stash the pig in the locked backstage room that I hope is a freezer?"

"So you can say the pig is on ice?" Posey said.

"Does everybody know the punchline before I say it?" I said. "Yes. May I?"

"For how long?" Dennis said.

"Long enough to make the bear think twice about going after Rick again," I said.

"We'll keep the pig in the pokey," Posey said. "It's the least we can do."

"Thank you," I said. "Now, if it's all the same to everyone involved, I'd like to stop talking about bones of contention and murder investigations and obvious punchlines and change into my *Psychedelic Sunday* costume, which, I might warn Rick, is a skintight, flesh-toned, one-piece leotard that mercilessly shows every curve on my forty-five-year-old body and makes me look like a naked dance-club stripper instead of Venus popping out of a painting in somebody's acid trip; although, what's the difference? Any comments before I exit stage right?"

"You could definitely be a dance-club stripper," Rick said, busting my chops. "I'd pay to see that action. I bet plenty of people would."

And just like that, as if their synced-up radar had caught the same imperceptible idea at precisely the same time, Dennis and Posey lost their creative shit on the D-Cup stage.

"And *you* could be the MC in that same club," Posey said to Rick.

"Tossing out jokes and wisdom while introducing the next act," Dennis said.

"Which is Kate singing and dancing and stripping for lonely souls," Posey said.

"It's a love story for the ages," Dennis said.

"An epic musical," Posey said.

"I'm seeing it," Dennis said.

"I'm hearing it," Posey said.

"Must be our sex phase," Dennis said.

"Yes, our sex phase. All artists have one," Posey said. "This is ours."

"What do you say, Kate? Will you star in our next musical as a singing-and-dancing stripper in a juke joint on the edge of town?" Dennis said.

In spite of everything, it's my professional policy never to turn down a leading role in a musical, no matter how inane.

"I will," I said.

"How about you, Rick?" Posey said. "Care to trip the light fantastic with the Schmidt and Parker Players?"

Rick looked at me and smiled. "I never miss a sex phase."

8

THESE ARE THE GIGS OF A LIFETIME

RICK AND I CAUGHT A CAB UP FIRST AVENUE, GOT OUT AT 83RD Street. I'd been careful to look for the bear and anyone following us out of the theater, or following the cab, or following us down 83rd. But no one did. No bear. No anyone. We were in the clear. I imagined the bear was in his den, licking his wounds, wondering what the hell had happened to the pig. All he had to do was ask me. I would have told him. *The pig's on ice.*

The cabbie did all the talking during the ride uptown. He thought he recognized Rick from somewhere—maybe junior high—and of course it came out that he was Rick Gotti from *The Jungle,* and the cabbie wouldn't shut up after that.

So it wasn't until we were walking west on 83rd Street toward the House of Emotional Tics that Rick said, "So how did you think it went?"

"I think it's hard enough to run through an entire show—full tech, full cast—for the very first time when Rick Gotti is *not* in the theater watching you perform," I said. "But when the musical in question is something of a shit show to begin with *and* you add him to the mix *and* you let it leak he's going to star in the next D-Cup production with these same Schmidt and Parker Players, then you're talking about losing your shit during the shit show, which is more or less what happened."

"You more or less lost your shit during the shit show because of me? What, too excited? Trying to impress me? Mind racing? Heart pounding? I both apologize and take it as a compliment."

"The collective *you*, meaning not me, meaning the Schmidt and Parker Players as a troupe. Meaning personally, I'm a professional. I was Venus up there, singing and dancing in someone else's acid trip, but I was also your bodyguard."

"*That's* why you kept looking at me. I knew there was a reason."

He laughed it off, and I laughed it off too. But the vibe had been placed on the table. He was hitting on me, and I knew he was hitting on me, and he knew I knew.

I unlocked the front door of the brownstone and we crossed the lobby to my apartment.

"I didn't think it was a shit show, by the way," Rick said. "I'm not saying the story makes sense because it doesn't make any sense at all. I'm saying the music is great, the dancing is killer, the cast is a blast, and I found myself having a ton of fun even though I didn't understand what the hell was happening or why."

"Par for the D-Cup course."

"The orgies are out of control. Must-see TV. The second one, in the American Wing, with George Washington? Holy shit. That's the stuff of legend."

The first orgy, the big barn burner at the end of act one, took place in the Greek Gallery to a rocking anthem called "Lusty Ladies of Greece" in which the statuary came to life and got it on wearing togas while singing and dancing like the Parthenon was on fire. The second orgy included America's first president, the signers of the Declaration of Independence, and the women of the colonies, who leaped out of Early American paintings and made the first orgy seem like free beer at a ballgame.

"It was fun, I'll give you that," I said. "Otherwise, for a first dress rehearsal, I'll say no earthquakes, tornados, hurricanes, floods, or fires. Not the end of the world, in other words."

We went into my apartment, and Rick's phone rang. He answered it. I stuck around to see who it was.

"Robbie, hey, what's happening?" Rick said. Then he covered the phone with his hand and looked at me. "Robbie Sloane, my agent."

I nodded, went to the kitchen, and started dinner: stir-fried rice with tofu and tons of veggies. Lots of cleaning and chopping but fast and easy to cook when the prep part is done. Not to mention the added benefit of being delicious.

While I worked, I thought about Rick signing autographs for the more starstruck Schmidt and Parker Players. I thought of me squelching the idea of us joining the rest of the cast at the cheap Mexican joint around the corner for nachos and tostadas and quesadillas and Tecate in cans. I thought about Rick hitting on me—not his homerun swing, I felt sure. Sort of his single-up-the-middle swing.

From the baseball analogies, it was a short, clean hop to my father. He'd loved baseball and had been an all-star pitcher in his day. Jimmy had taken me to Yankee games as often as he could get away—from work when I was young; from my mother's cancer when I was little older; then from work again after she'd died. We always sat in the upper deck behind home plate. Jimmy had said it was the best place to score a ballgame. He'd said that was where he'd learned to do it, so that was where I'd learn to do it too. I'd worshipped my father and paid close attention, and soon I could chart like a bench coach. I still remembered the night he'd passed his scorecard to me. My lap. My pencil. I was twelve. At the end of the fourth inning, he'd leaned over, looked at my card, and said, *"That's as good a card as I've ever seen, Katie. Better than most big-leaguers."*

My heart soared that night in the upper deck—*better than most big-leaguers!*—and remembering it now, my heart soared in the kitchen. Which made me sad because Jimmy was gone forever. And so I cried while chopping veggies for stir-fried rice. My father had been dead three months, so I was past sobbing on the sofa for hours at a time—snot pouring from my nose, shoulders heaving so hard they ached, blind with pain and grief—but little things could and did still set me off. You don't realize how much you're going to miss your father until he's gone and there's a hole in your heart that will never be filled. I don't think about the hole all the time, but when I do, like remembering Yankee games while making dinner, the sadness flows through me all over again and the tears fall.

I reached a point in my prep that I could take a break, so I dried my eyes and walked to the living room. Rick was clicking off the call with his agent. He was excited and then some.

"What was that about?" I said.

"Work," he said.

"Job offer?"

"*Two* job offers. It's happening, McCall."

"Your comeback?"

"I didn't think it would happen this fast, but it is."

He sat on the sofa but stood right up again, too amped to sit. I leaned against the doorway that led to my bedroom.

"What jobs?" I said, thinking, *Two jobs or even one job does not sound like a good idea when someone is trying to kill you.*

"Job one is too good to be true," Rick said. "Ruby Gold, *the* Ruby Gold, is casting me in her new sitcom. 'Are you kidding me?' I said to Robbie. 'Because you can't kid me with things like Ruby Gold casting me in her new sitcom.' He wasn't kidding. Ruby Gold is casting me in her new sitcom."

"Wow," I said. I meant it too. Lucille Ball. Carol Burnett.

Mary Tyler Moore. Bea Arthur. Betty White. Jean Stapleton. Estelle Getty. Doris Roberts. Cloris Leachman. Ruby Gold. That was the list she was on. Her name in the same sentence as those names. Incredible career spanning all media. Still working after all these years.

"Big wow," Rick said.

"And job two?" I said.

"Victor Vreeland wants me to host this year's Comedy Camp Cornucopia."

"Wow again."

Victor Vreeland was a New York comedy-club legend. His iconic Upper West Side establishment, Victor Vreeland's Comedy Camp, had been the crossroads of fame, fortune, and funny for forty years. From the renowned to the notorious, four decades of comedians had played the Comedy Camp stage. New Yorkers who needed to drink strong drinks and laugh their asses off had perennially packed the place since it had opened back in the "Golden Age of Jokes and Jubilation," as Victor himself had named the days of his humble beginnings. HBO and Showtime and plenty of other networks had all filmed comedy specials here. Dozens of feature films and TV shows had used Victor Vreeland's Comedy Camp as an atmospheric comedy-club backdrop because Victor himself had invented "comedy-club atmosphere" forty years earlier. As Victor had said in his biography, *"Comedy Camp has enough atmosphere to surround a planet."* Which was a funny thing for him to say because Victor Vreeland was the size of a planet. His ego was even bigger than that. He was one of those particular people that could only exist on the island of Manhattan. There was no Victor Vreeland wandering the streets of Boise, say, or Little Rock. He was a New York original.

As part of owning and operating one of the most financially successful comedy clubs in the country, Victor hosted two nationally known events a year: the Cabaret and the Cornucopia.

Victor Vreeland's Comedy Camp Cabaret was a fundraiser he had founded and produced for twenty-four years in a row to raise money for hundreds of New York nonprofit organizations. Over the decades, he'd raised and gifted just south of three hundred million dollars to these fortunate folks. Tickets to the black-tie affair, which included a half dozen world-famous comedians, a celebrity host, unlimited Dom Perignon, and all kinds of caviar were thirty-five thousand dollars *each*. It was a three-hundred-fifty-seat club. The event had sold out every time, every year. The math was impressive.

Victor Vreeland's Comedy Camp Cornucopia was Victor's very own Thanksgiving celebration. The hottest ticket in town because you couldn't buy a ticket. Invite-only for top-tier entertainment executives, managers, agents, producers, and promoters; world-famous athletes, actors, comedians, and musicians; bigwig bankers, brokers, accountants, and attorneys; friends, family, and other fine folks. An evening of comedy and gluttony. A professionally catered soup-to-nuts Thanksgiving spread emceed by a secret celebrity host with the most for three hundred fifty who's who of the who's who in New York and beyond. The pics from the Cornucopia were always front fold in the gossip rags and entertainment pages. Red-carpet entrance. Paparazzi at the door. Jokes and booze and turkey and fixings and wheelings and dealings in Victor's club. Hardly anyone turned down an invite because no one could put on the Thanksgiving Ritz like Victor Vreeland.

And it was all free of charge, meaning if you were invited, you were Victor's guest, meaning Victor had been footing the bill for this feast every year for close to twenty years. Despite that, he'd made more from the dinner than he'd spent because he used these invite-only tickets to thank folks for favors already granted and to solicit new favors for the future.

"What are the dates?" I said.

"Ruby Gold shoots her pilot tomorrow," Rick said.

"Tomorrow?"

"Victor's Cornucopia is Sunday the thirteenth."

"Of this month?"

"It's a Thanksgiving thing."

"You do know someone's trying to kill you?"

"I realize that."

"I mean right now, as in earlier today, someone was trying to kill you. They'll try tomorrow and less than two weeks from today too."

"I get it, McCall."

"What do you get, Rick? That there's no way you can take these gigs?"

"Your point. I get your point."

"So you agree it's too dangerous for you to be exposed like that?"

"Whether I agree or disagree, these are the gigs of a lifetime."

"The bear almost killed you, us, *inside your own house*. To kill you in a comedy club or on a soundstage somewhere will be a piece of cake. And next time he'll come locked and loaded. No plastic bag."

"I understand what you're saying."

"That you hired me to be your bodyguard, that I'm respon-sible for your life, that's what you understand? That if you get murdered, that's on me? You understand that?"

"I understand right up to that, yes."

"And beyond that?"

"Beyond that is dark and stormy."

He was unhappier than I was, and I was really unhappy. It was suicide. Not just public, *publicized* public. On a soundstage with minimal security? In a dark club with three hundred other people? No freaking way.

"I'm sorry. I can't protect you uncovered like that. You have to tell your agent thanks but no thanks."

He sat down again, and this time he stayed down. Deflated. Conflicted. Angry at the world and at himself and at me. He knew I was right.

"I'll call him tomorrow," he said.

"Better safe than dead," I said.

9

AS FLABBERGASTED AND CLUSTERFUCKED AS I COULD BE

CENTRAL PARK IS THE MOST VISITED URBAN PARK IN THE country, welcoming more than forty million visitors each year, many of whom, like me, I imagine, come to clear their heads. At eight hundred forty-three acres, it's only the fifth largest park in New York, though it's larger than Vatican City, another excellent place for head-clearing, so I've been told. JKO Reservoir, Central Park's blue-water bird refuge—named for Jacqueline Kennedy Onassis—was my go-to run when I couldn't think things through over my morning cup of coffee.

The reservoir takes up most of the area between 96th and 86th, from north to south, and between Fifth Avenue and Central Park West, from east to west—fifteen percent of the total park. There's a one-and-a-half-mile jogging track circling the JKO, so from the House of Emotional Tics to the park, twice around the track, and back to the brownstone was about a five-mile run that usually dissipated my brain fog.

Some mornings are foggier than others, and Wednesday was murkier than most. I woke up earlier than I wanted to, couldn't figuratively see my hand in front of my face, and knew I needed a reservoir run before breakfast.

I quietly opened the door between my bedroom and the living room, tiptoed past Rick still asleep on the sofa, stretched outside in front of the building, and took off for the park.

It was a brisk November morning, a bit of blue in the sky, sun peeking through white cloud cover, the kind of crisp, early autumn day that promised good things were possible and put people in an upbeat mood. Except for me, apparently.

Rick had battled through years of rehab and recovery, had graduated clean and sober, was on the cusp of the comeback he'd come back for, and I'd pulled the plug. Ruby Gold and Victor Vreeland? Those were a couple of major marquee names to turn down the same day. But the bear had made it unwise to be out and about, so safe and sound in my apartment was the smart bodyguard move. It was the right idea at the wrong time for Rick. But Jimmy would have done the same thing. So, yes, it sucked to have made that plug-pulling call, but that's not what had flipped me upside down.

There was no doubt Rick had hit on me. Okay, maybe *hit on me* is a tad too strong a description of what had happened between us. Maybe he'd just been flirting with me. And maybe I'd just been flirting back. Maybe it had just been a trifling, toying tease between two single adults. The problem was we weren't simply two single adults. We were client and bodyguard, bodyguard and client. It was strictly a professional relationship with Rick's life on the line. So, yes, it was sloppy and slapdash and clumsy and crude to be flirting with a client, even though the client had started it in the first place, but that's not what had turned me inside out.

Rick Gotti wasn't typical of the type of man I flirted at, was attracted to, and got involved with. Using my recent relationships as not-so-subtle signposts along my rocky romantic road, Detective Harriman had played the part of the moody macho movie star; Peter Simms had been cast as the rock-and-roll Olympic decathlete; and Blue had stolen the show as the gorgeous professional baseball player I couldn't keep my hands off of. Rick Gotti did not fit the tall-dark-big-strong-handsome-hunk pattern of my admittedly also-ran romances. He'd been everyone's idea of a small-funny-wiry wiseass kid and had grown up to be everyone's idea of a small-funny-wiry wiseass man. So, yes, someone outside my mold had flirted in my direction, and I'd flirted back when I should have kept my professional distance, but even that wasn't what had spun me around.

What had me hot and bothered was that part of me was hot and bothered. Yes, that was it. I'd flirted back because I'd felt an unconscious flicker of attraction. For Rick Gotti. I liked a guy nobody liked. I liked an unlikeable guy. But was he still unlikeable? He'd made me laugh, hadn't he? Sense of humor was a big plus in a man's plus column, wasn't it? He'd been polite and considerate. Two more big plusses. He'd enjoyed my cooking and said so, he'd let me drink my beer *and* his beer without judgment, and he'd slept on my sofa without too much complaining. Plus, plus, and plus. As far as physical chemistry was concerned, he was cuter than I thought he'd be. And that Rick Gotti smartass smile was a freaking babe magnet for sure. There'd been no shortage of beautiful women in Rick's crazy life.

Still, as I crossed Second Avenue, finished my run, and did my cooldown walk to the House of Emotional Tics, I couldn't help but think, *Come on, Kate, snap the hell out of it.*

But that whole Rick Gotti train of thought was run off the rails because as I approached the brownstone, a cab pulled up in front of the building, the back door opened, and my son Matthew climbed out.

He was on the phone, which didn't surprise me. He was a Manhattan assistant district attorney, a rising star in the DA's office, and his cell phone was surgically attached to his hand in the same way his Bluetooth earbud was permanently implanted in his ear. He was my only child. I want to say I raised him alone, but the truth is Jimmy raised us both for the first ten years.

Matthew McCall was smart as a whip, rational, reasonable, and sensible. So the opposite of me. He did not like the fact that at forty-five I was *still* an aspiring actor in way-off-Broadway musicals. He argued, as if in court, that I should put my dreams on some distant back burner and procure a real job with a front-burner future. Private investigating was not the job he envisioned for me, so he debated that life choice too. He did this out of his love for me. I let him do it out of my love for him. We did not see eye to eye on how I actually lived or should live my life, but our bond was unbreakable. A handsome, sensible, successful son and his unreasonable, illogical, headstrong mother.

Matthew and me.

"What a great surprise," I said, walking toward him.

He leaned into the car and told the cabbie to wait two minutes.

I kissed his cheek. He was dressed for court. Conservative suit and tie. Lace-up Oxfords. Leather briefcase. He was excited about something big. Something he couldn't tell me on the phone. Something he had to tell me face-to-face. Seeing him this happy, knowing his heart was filled with so much joy, made my soul sing.

"I can't stay," he said. "I just got called to court. But I had to tell you in person."

And just like that, by the tone of his voice, I knew what it was.

"What?" I said anyway.

"Nina's pregnant. She's due the middle of May," he said. "We're getting married."

"Oh my God," I said, hoping *my* tone dripped with excitement instead of dread.

We were not friends, Loathsome Nina and me. She was a

pompous windbag NYU associate professor of film appreciation, the self-anointed arbiter of good taste in movies and all media. She was beautiful, I gave her that, but she was insufferable, so inside my head, she deserved an adjective at all times—and always got one.

To be fair, she couldn't stand me either. I was everything she stood against in terms of artistic sophistication and chosen lifestyle. The one and only thing we had in common was Matthew. We both loved him, and he loved both of us, so we'd negotiated a mostly unspoken truce whenever we shared the same air. It was catty and snarky, certainly, but it never turned into a barroom brawl.

"I know," Matthew said, smiling with exhilaration. "Just like that, here comes the rest of my life. Crazy how that happens, Mom. I'm over the moon."

Excitement, I thought. *Thank you, baby Jesus, for hiding the dread.*

"You can't stay ten minutes to celebrate with a cup of coffee?" I said.

"I wish I could, but I have to go. Sorry, Mom. We're getting married at the courthouse on the fourteenth. It's a Monday. The judge we want to marry us is on a European river cruise. Gets back Sunday. Put it in your calendar. Monday the fourteenth. We'll do a real ceremony and reception next year when we both have time. Love you, Mom. Have to go. You're going to be a mother-in-law in less than two weeks and a grandma this spring. Holy shit."

He kissed my cheek, jumped back in the cab and was headed toward Second Avenue before I could say, *"Holy shit is right."* November fourteenth? Was he kidding me? My little boy getting married in how many days? Twelve? I wasn't ready for him to be married yet. Especially to Reprehensible Nina. Especially in twelve days. And I definitely wasn't ready to be a grandma this spring. Holy shit times two.

But the feeling disappeared as fast as it first appeared, replaced by true-blue parental excitement for Matthew and, yes, for Abhorrent Nina, who would be the mother of my grandchild in May. I had the urge to tell someone right away, couldn't hold it in for even a single minute. I went into the lobby and looked for Fu or LaTanya or Charlie or Warren or even Al, but no one was around. So I opened the door to my apartment, ready to gush it all out to Rick.

And Rick was gone.

He wasn't in the kitchen or the bathroom. If he had been, his suitcase, his laptop, his *stuff* would still be here in the living room.

And none of it was.

"Rick." I called out so he could hear me in the kitchen, even though I knew calling out wouldn't help because he wasn't in the kitchen. "Rick…"

I raced through the house—bedroom, closet, dining room, kitchen—even though I knew racing through my house wouldn't help because he wasn't in the kitchen. I grabbed my cell, dialed, and got his voicemail.

"Rick, it's Kate. It's Wednesday morning. I don't know if you remember me. I'm your bodyguard. You hired me on Monday to get you to your December pretrial alive. At this exact moment, you are not safely hidden in my house. At this exact moment, in fact, I have no fucking idea where you are. As you might imagine, it is impossible for me to be your bodyguard if I have no fucking idea where you are. If you do not call me in the next five minutes, I will track you down and kill you myself. Goddamn it, Rick. Are you kidding me?"

I clicked off the call and stood there fuming. Now, the thing about fuming is that it's an impediment to thinking. You can't think when your brain is filling with fumes. So I took a breath and poured myself a glass of orange juice. As I drained the glass, my phone rang. I was so fully fumigated by then that I didn't even see who was calling me. I didn't have to. It was Rick. Had to be.

"So you remember who I am?" I said.

"How could I forget you, Little Engine?"

Jesus Christ.

Not Rick.

I knew the killer's voice almost as well as I knew my own. I stopped moving. Stopped breathing. My heart stopped beating. Was the kitchen spinning or was that my imagination?

"I was going to ask if *you* remembered *me*, but I don't hear you breathing, so I assume you do," the killer said.

I wanted to say something but couldn't get my jaw to move. And my mouth was suddenly bone dry.

"I would like us to play a game," the killer said.

"What kind of game?"

"A numbers game."

I knew what he was really saying. *"I would like to give you a numeric clue to my next murder and see if you and Detective Logan are smart enough to figure it out."*

"I'll play," I said.

"Excellent," he said. "The number is twelve. There are twelve men named Ronnie Russo in the New York phone book. You have twelve hours to figure out which one of them is my next professional appointment. Rest assured, Little Engine, one of them will die in twelve hours. The number of consequence in this game is twelve."

He clicked off. I checked my watch. It was only nine thirty Wednesday morning, and I was already as flabbergasted and clusterfucked as I could be.

I called Logan and told his voicemail I had news. Then I sat at the kitchen table and waited for the room to stop spinning.

10

ROBERT THE BRUCE

I left Logan three more voicemails before noon, which was the start time for the second day of shooting *Kung Fu Fu*. Considering the implosions, collapses, and cave-ins happening in my head, I thought my messages had been somewhat composed—although it was possible I'd babbled and even shouted the last one. Logan would let me know if I was losing my shit, I was sure.

I was babbling and shouting and losing my shit—let's just assume I was—because Rick Gotti was gone; because my son was getting married to and having a baby with Repellent Nina; and because Jimmy's killer had moved from texting me clues to cluing me in with actual phone calls.

And the clue he'd called in? The number twelve? What the hell kind of clue was that? It was true—there were twelve men named Ronnie Russo in the phone book. I'd looked it up. So would Logan have to locate and lockdown each Ronnie Russo before nine thirty tonight? No way it could be that simple. The killer was too shrewd, too vain to allow for such an easy answer. So did the number twelve mean something more? Not just twelve names in the phonebook and twelve hours until one of them was dead? Did the number also hold the key to which Ronnie Russo would be found with his eyes blown out of his face? Of course it did.

But what key? I couldn't think it through alone. I needed help. Logan still hadn't called me back. I needed another source. And the only other source at my immediate disposal was the cast and crew of *Kung Fu Fu*, which today was me, Fu, Al, and LaTanya.

We were shooting in the backyard, under the elm tree in the far corner. It was the scene where renegade detectives Steinberg (Fu) and Barnett (me) confront the renegade zombie drug dealer (Al) for the first time to see if they can get him to turn the tables on the renegade mad scientist, who's hidden a bomb on some unknown city bus. LaTanya was doing double duty as director and camera operator. We only had an hour to get the scene because LaTanya had to work, Al was in the middle of an eBay blockbuster, Fu was repainting the laundry room, and I had to find Rick and talk to Logan.

I was telling Fu and Al that Jimmy's killer had called me and I needed their help figuring out the clue when LaTanya crossed the yard with her camera.

"No time for small talk so change the channel on the chitchat. We got one hour, we got good weather, we got to shoot this shit on the run," LaTanya said, getting herself set. "So let's see Steinberg and Barnett flip the zombie and get the skinny on the scientist. All systems go. Camera rolling. Take one means ain't going to be no take two. And...action."

Since every word was improvised, I thought, *Why not keep the conversation going?*

"Listen up, zombie," I said to Al. "Like I was just saying, the 'mad scientist' called me on the phone, gave me the name of his next victim, told me when the hit was going down, and gave me a clue to keep it interesting. So if you cooperate, like a good little zombie drug dealer, maybe we can get this thing figured out, save the poor bastard, and nail the mad scientist in the act."

LaTanya circled us like she was on a dolly track. "Don't forget the bus."

"You can't talk, LaTanya," I said. "You're not in the scene."

"Poor bastard on bus," Fu said, winking at me.

I'd never seen Fu wink before, so I was thrown off balance. But he'd had the presence of mind to wink when he wasn't in the shot, so LaTanya wouldn't know that I knew Fu knew where I was going with this. But did Al know?

"I don't appreciate being called a zombie to my face," Al said, half in character.

"What name appreciate?" Fu said to Al.

LaTanya had only given real names to my character, her character, and Fu's character. In her outline, Al's character was called *zombie drug dealer*.

"Robert the Bruce," Al said.

"Cut," LaTanya said, lowering her camera. "Robert the Bruce? What the fuck zombie drug dealer name is that? Who the fuck is Robert the Bruce?"

"Scottish outlaw became king of Scotland," Al said. "My character's a New York outlaw going to be king of New York."

Since there was no budget, we'd worn our own clothes for the shoot. Fu and I were dressed like we thought a couple of New York City renegade detectives might dress, meaning the clothes hanging in our closets. Al had donned a vintage white tuxedo with a white tie, a white top hat and tails, and white shoes. His deep-set, red-red bloodshot eyes seemed to explode against the blinding bright white of his suit and the pale, pasty color of his skin. He looked more like a zombie than usual, which was saying something. Except now he was a debonair and dapper zombie. A ballroom-dancing zombie. A Fred Astaire zombie. On the one hand, it was an unlikely ensemble to be hanging in Al's closet. On the other hand, it wasn't even a little unlikely. Any damn thing could have been hanging in Al's closet.

"Fine, fine, Robert the Bruce," LaTanya said, getting her camera set again. "Picking up where we at, and...action."

"Cooperation ain't free, Barnett. How much cooperation are we talking about, if we're talking about what I think we're talking about?" Al said.

There was nothing more important to Al than money, than the deal and his end of it.

"We're definitely talking about what you think we're talking about," I said now that we were on the same page. "Two hundred."

"Robert the Bruce don't get up in the morning for less than four," Al said.

"Robert the Bruce already up," Fu said, busting Robert the Bruce's balls with Al's insomnia. A brilliant moment of improvisation. Finding truth in fiction.

"Or Detective Steinberg could break Robert the Bruce's neck," I said. "We're going to flip you one way or the other."

I nodded at Fu, who grabbed Al by the lapels of his white tux.

"Go for it, Fu," LaTanya said.

"You can't talk, LaTanya," I said. "You're not in the scene."

"Did I say four? I meant three. Three is good," Al said.

Fu wrapped a massive hand around Al's neck. Like me, Al had seen Fu crush concrete with his fingers.

"Or two," Al said. "I'll take two."

I moved to Al, opened his tux jacket, slid his wallet out of the interior breast pocket, and removed two one-hundred-dollar bills. Al always carried five of them. *"Five hundred in cold cash in case a deal in a dark shadow develops near the corner of York and 96th Street,"* he'd once told me. I slid his wallet back in his tux pocket.

"Two it is," I said, handing him his own money.

"Renegade cop on the case," LaTanya said.

"You can't talk, LaTanya," I said. "You're not in the scene."

"The poor bastard on the bus, what's his name?" Al said, putting his money back in his wallet and straightening his tux.

"Ronnie Russo," I said.

"If know name, why need Robert the Bruce?" Fu said to me.

"Because there are twelve poor bastards named Ronnie Russo in the New York phone book, but only one of them is the poor bastard on the bus, and we have to figure out which one is the right one in the next twelve hours. Make that nine hours," I said. "And Robert's rig can crunch the numbers."

"Big zombie computer," Fu said.

"Big zombie computer," I said.

"Big Robert the Bruce computer," Al said.

Al's digital rig was illegal in ten states. He'd hand-built it from parts he'd unearthed in devious deals on the dark web, which is where all zombies go when they need computer components that are illegal in ten states. Maybe I'm overstating it. Or maybe I'm understating it. Maybe it was twenty states. Either way, manifold mismatched monitors flashed row after row of code like the *Nebuchadnezzar's* notorious screens in *The Matrix* while strange-looking printers spewed government secrets, corporate confidences, and stock market mysteries. The massive digital alien organism fed into two six-foot-tall mainframes that had to have been stolen from the Pentagon or NASA or maybe even Amazon. Al's mechanized cyber-monster was terrifying. But his deviant mastery of the machinery was more frightening still. He was an underworld wizard surfing where no man had surfed before.

"Big enough to crunch numbers in a hurry," I said. "The real Ronnie Russo dies nine thirty tonight. So the clock's ticking."

"Every Academy Award for Karate got a ticking clock," LaTanya said.

"You can't talk, LaTanya," I said. "You're not in the scene. And there's no such thing."

"There will be once that clock starts ticking," LaTanya said.

"Twelve is clue," Fu said.

"Yes, something about that number," I said.

"Twelve-string guitar," Al said.

"*Twelve Angry Men*," I said.

"Twelve labors of Hercules," Al said.

"Twelve days of Christmas," I said.

"If I can find out which Ronnie Russo is connected to the number twelve in a deeper way than twelve-in-the-phone-book and twelve-hours-to-die, then you can save his ass and nail the mad scientist all at the same time? That's what you're buying for two hundred?"

"That's what it cost to flip Robert the Bruce," I said.

Al nodded, turned, and headed back across the yard toward the brownstone. "You flipped me with my own money."

"What did you expect?" I would pay him the two hundred later, but making Robert the Bruce sweat was all part of the fun.

"I'm Robert the Bruce. I expected more."

"You flip on the mad scientist, you not Robert the Bruce, you Robert the Rat," LaTanya said.

"You can't talk, LaTanya," I said. "You're not in the scene."

"I'll fix it in post," LaTanya said, referencing that mystical land where cinematic miscues are mended.

Al spun around like Fred Astaire himself, nimble and graceful, did some fanciful ballroom moves that would have made Fred proud, and gave us all the finger, flipping the flip on us. I'd had no idea he could dance like that. At twelve thirty

Wednesday afternoon in the House of Emotional Tics' grubby backyard, Al Cutter might have been the best zombie dancer in the city. There were other dancing zombies in Manhattan—no New Yorker would argue that—but perhaps none with Al's 1940s flair.

LaTanya got it all on film. "Cut," she said. "That's a wrap."

11

I WAS ABSOFUCKINGLUTELY NOT GOING TO BE A GOOD GIRL

"My sister's granddaughter, my five-year-old grandniece, came for an uninvited visit and decided to play hide-and-seek with my fucking phone without my personal permission," Logan said. "It was on silent and took four hours to find. That's why I'm calling you back so late."

It was one fifteen. I was on my way to Kenny Cochran's house in Long Beach. I'd rented the White Whale, one of Warren's Corollas—yes, each car in the fleet had a name. Warren was otherwise occupied, so General Manager Al Cutter was general managing the Toyotas. As I paid him for the White Whale, I gave him the two bills we'd agreed on for his Ronnie Russo research. He wasn't unhappy about that.

"Where did she hide it?" I said.

"Big bag of dog food," Logan said.

"No wonder it took four hours."

"Had to finally feed the dog. That's the only reason I'm calling you now."

I told him about my chat with the killer, about Ronnie Russo, about the number twelve.

"Twelve Ronnie Russos and twelve hours to figure out which one?" Logan said.

"Eight hours," I said.

"Might only take eight seconds."

"How do you mean?"

"Ronnie Russo is a Staten Island mob boss with his fat fucking fingers in every pathetic pile of crooked shit in the city. Protection, Russo. Stolen goods, Russo. Drugs, Russo. Money laundering, Russo. Gambling, Russo. Prostitution, Russo. Weapons, Russo. All of it funneled through supposedly legitimate enterprises that are nothing but fronts for fucktards. Which is why his illegitimate ass is still on the street in the first place. They call him Ronnie Raccoon on account of his eyes."

"He has enemies who'd pay to have him dead?"

"Truckloads."

"It makes sense but—"

"But would your boyfriend make it that fucking easy?"

"He's not my boyfriend, Logan. He's your boyfriend."

"The correct answer is no, he would not make it that fucking easy."

"Unless he was playing with your head."

"Unless he was playing with my head."

"So you have to go through the motions either way."

"Do you have any idea how hard it is to turn a task force on a dime?"

"I'm guessing hard."

"Like sending the Seventh Fleet back to Yokosuka when they're halfway to Hawaii."

"The only thing I understand in that sentence is Hawaii, and I wish I was there right now."

"You and me both, McCall. But not together. Don't even think about coming with me."

After that, he told me to keep my nose out of it, not to go

anywhere near Ronnie Racoon Russo unless I wanted to be dead by dinner, and to absofuckinglutely steer clear of the killer. So I said I'd be a good girl, and he said he didn't believe me, and he was right about that. I was absofuckinglutely not going to be a good girl.

The reason I was on my way to Kenny Cochran's house in Long Beach was because Rick had not fired me. Though he and his stuff were gone, he had not left a note that my services were no longer required, and Shavelson had not called to find out why Rick had canned me. As far as I knew, I was still on the clock as his bodyguard, and if I couldn't guard him from the front, so to speak, then I would guard him from the rear. Meaning I would find the bear from behind and stop him before he tried again.

Or maybe I was on my way to Kenny Cochran's house because I had a score to settle.

Jimmy McCall had been one of the all-time great score settlers. Big score, little score, any score, my father had wanted a clean slate. *"I got nothing on him; he's got nothing on me,"* he'd tell me after a score had been settled. I was my father's daughter in many wonderful ways, and in other ways not so wonderful, including the one about settling scores. I was a champion score settler. Not as good as Jimmy but still damn good.

The bear had been happy to murder me along with Rick. I was what they call a collateral kill. Or would have been if I hadn't turned the tables on the pig. So I was alive, and that was good, but you can't try to kill me and think I'm not coming to settle the score. I'm coming whether or not my client fires me.

It's more or less an hour's drive from the House of Emotional Tics to the city of Long Beach. Located in Nassau County on Long Beach Barrier Island off Long Island's south shore, it's a long, skinny strip of sand bordered by the Atlantic Ocean to the south and Reynolds Channel, which lots of people call the bay, on all other sides. So, yes, water, water everywhere. The City by the Sea, as Long Beach bills itself, is famous for its small-town feel and for its boardwalk but also for its beachy bond to show business, which is why I'd always had a soft spot for the place.

Barrymore, Bogart, Cagney, Calloway, and Valentino had all lived on Long Beach at one time or another, some of them for decades. Billy Crystal has Long Beach roots to be proud of. So does Billy Joel. Mario Puzo put the Corleone family compound in Long Beach. And the late Kenny Cochran had lived here too.

The dead comedian owned a house on Illinois Avenue. A modern, oceanfront showpiece that seemed beyond his financial reach. He'd been in his late fifties—well past his prime—when the bear put a plastic bag over his head and suffocated him to death. Truth was, he'd never really had a prime. He'd always been a fringe comedian, hanging on the edges of the entertainment business, picking up a gig here and a gig there to pay the bills. He'd been around for decades but had never exploded into the national consciousness. Not like Rick, who, after fifteen years in rehab and recovery, was on the fast track again. That's why Kenny Cochran had stolen Rick's jokes, stolen Rick's whole act. To keep his middling-muddling comedy career alive as opposed to dead. Which it now was for good, of course.

There was no way Cochran should have been able to afford this beachfront modern manse. I'd done my research. No family fund for him to tap into. No inheritance coming his way. He hadn't been working anywhere that paid big bucks. Hadn't been working anywhere at all. So where had he found a few mil to drop on his Illinois Avenue abode? That's what I was here to find out. Jimmy used to say, *"Murder is money, honey. If it's not love, it's loot. Though it could be both."*

I sat in the White Whale across the street and down the block from Cochran's house. No yellow police tape. No cop guarding the entrance. His house wasn't the murder scene.

There'd been murders aplenty since the bear had killed Cochran, and the police had their man, meaning Rick. For the cops, this case was closed.

Still, it was possible someone might be watching over or living in Cochran's house. So I'd worn the green contact lenses and blonde wig with heavy bangs that I'd sported in the sporty independent feature film disaster known as *The Horseshoe Murders*. Which was a slasher-drama about a national horse-shoe champion who loses his mind over love and money (like Jimmy had said) and murders all the other competitors during the championship.

The movie had been shot at and around the old horseshoe pits in Central Park with a budget of three hundred dollars all in. I'd played the part of the champion's wife, the hard-drinking, green-eyed blonde with heavy bangs who hated horses and horseshoes and everything equine. I'd been the first to die—a double blessing in disguise because I hadn't had to suffer through day two and because I'd bought my wig and wardrobe for pennies on the dollar when the film collapsed, crushed by the weight of its own incomprehensibility, the morning of day three. You might say *The Horseshoe Murders* had died a suffocating death.

Just like Kenny Cochran.

I got out of the car and walked to his house. The air was cold. I could smell the salt water, practically taste the ocean in my mouth; that's how close Cochran's place was to the beach. Right there. Front row. The long, lean house was wedged between other oceanfront homes on Illinois and Ohio, like it had been built in their backyards. Private and pricey.

The door was locked. There was no one on the street. I took the six-inch restorer's pry bar I'd inherited from my father (one of the items in the cardboard box I'd carried home from Shavelson's office after the reading of Jimmy's will), forced the door open, and stepped inside.

The place was midcentury modern from front to back and top to bottom. Expensive furniture, electronics, and artwork. Drop-dead designer gorgeous. Ready for a five-page feature in *House Beautiful* except for the fact that someone had already been here and left the place a tad untidy.

Probably the police searching for slam-dunk proof Rick was their guy, I thought, *or maybe the bear looking to lift any connection between him and Cochran.*

Whoever had been here, they hadn't tossed the shit out of the place—furniture upside down, contents of drawers dumped on the floor, artwork ripped off the walls. None of that. They'd been careful not to make a mess.

But not careful enough. Cabinet drawers had been left open. Chairs had been moved to where they wouldn't have/shouldn't have been. Just enough of a footprint for me to know they'd already taken the house for a spin.

The ground floor was an open, loft-like space. Foyer to kitchen to dining to living, all of it midcentury marvelous. At the far end of the living room, massive glass doors folded in on themselves until they virtually disappeared, giving access to a fenced and private outdoor area that featured a grill, a dining table and chairs, and, instead of a grassy lawn, a sandy beach with a firepit. Beyond that, access to the actual beach and Atlantic Ocean.

I checked every drawer, every cabinet, every closet, every paper on every table and countertop, searching for I wasn't sure what. A note, a photograph, something that would connect Cochran to the bear or someone who might have hired the bear. Nothing on the first floor.

The second floor offered a laundry room, three full bathrooms, and three bedrooms. At the end of the house, closest to the beach, was the master. The walls were glass and the view alone was worth the two mil Cochran had shelled out for the place. I figured I'd start in Cochran's personal boudoir and work my way backward to the front of the house.

I sat on his bed and opened the top drawer of his bedside table. It was jam-packed with horse-racing publications. Magazines and journals and articles and pamphlets and periodicals and brochures and catalogues about horses and trainers and tracks and trials and times and betting. Including race programs, tons of them. I tried the middle drawer. Same thing. Bottom drawer. Same thing. Overflowing with horse-racing dailies and weeklies and monthlies and program after program after program. Cochran had been heavy into the ponies. Way heavy.

In more than some of the programs, particular races and horses had been circled and comments handwritten in the margins, all signed by someone named Danny Boy Bailey: *Who loves you, Kenny?*; *Tip of the year, Kenny*; *Take it to the bank, Kenny*; *C'mon Kenny, nobody knows the ponies like Danny Boy*, and other annotations along those lines. A recently dated program gave me a mention to go on: *Bad news, Kenny. Call me quick.* Danny Boy's phone number was written beside that dodgy item.

I put that program and some of the other papers in my purse, moved to the long window, and got seduced by the view. It was the shortest seduction in memory.

"What are you doing here?" said an indignant voice behind me. "Who are you?"

I turned to a woman maybe ten years older than me. Not a New Yorker. Midwestern accent. Wisconsin maybe. Minnesota. Indiana. Somewhere like that. Standing in the doorway like she was somehow in charge of things around here.

"I'm Cathy Culver," I said. "I'm an insurance investigator for State Farm. There's a claim on Mr. Cochran's policy due to his untimely death, and I'm doing my job. The real question is who are *you*, and what are *you* doing here?"

Before driving to Long Beach, I'd googled around and learned State Farm insured Cochran's house and Cathy Culver was one of their investigators. The State Farm staff page headshot of Ms. Culver highlighted her blonde hair, heavy bangs, and green eyes, which was why I'd worn *The Horseshoe Murders* wig and the green contacts. If this woman called State Farm to confirm a Cathy Culver worked there as an insurance investigator, the answer would be, *Yes, indeed she does.*

"I'm Lynn Smithson. I live next door," she said. Her indignation had vanished with her cocky attitude. "I saw someone in here—the windows are so close, I couldn't *not* see someone—and I thought, well, I guess, I suppose, I thought maybe I should check on who it was."

I do so love acting, I thought, and snapped a photo of good old Lynn with my phone. "Say your name out loud. For my report."

"Oh no, really, I didn't mean any harm." Her voice trailed off into nothing.

"Listen, Lynn, I'm going to cut you a break this time because I think you're just a nosy neighbor trying to be helpful. But the next time you interfere with State Farm will be the last time you interfere with State Farm. Are we clear?"

"Yes, yes, very clear. Thank you. Very clear."

"Good. Now move out of the doorway before I change my mind and call the police."

Lynn stepped aside, and I left the master bedroom in a confident, all-business huff. I went down the stairs and out the door to the White Whale, where I took a minute to thank Cathy Culver for being as no-nonsense about her investigations as she looked.

12

A WORLD WHERE NOBODY WANTS TO LIVE

I CALLED THE NUMBER ON THE RACE PROGRAM—THE ONE THAT said *Bad news, Kenny. Call me quick*—and a woman's voicemail said, "Thank you for contacting Parties to Remember, your one-stop shop for get-togethers your guests will remember forever. Leave your name and number, and we'll rock your world."

It was a sexy, provocative voice. Definitely not the business voice of the business. I guessed that voice belonged to Danny Boy. I googled Parties to Remember on my phone and discovered the firm was a booking agency for strippers. Bachelor and bachelorette parties, corporate shindigs, retirement celebrations, birthdays, anniversaries, girls' nights out, any occasion that called for strippers of any gender, Parties to Remember would deliver them to your door for an unreasonable fee. Danny Boy took his cut before he paid his dancers, no doubt.

On the drive back to the city, I reminded myself that once upon a lifetime ago, when I'd been a single mother short on cash, a flailing actor in a city filled with flailing actors, I'd danced in a sleazebag topless joint. Had I known about Danny Boy Bailey and Parties to Remember back then, I might have signed on for gigs to make ends meet instead of stripping in a bar. I hadn't been proud at the time. I'd been broke. With a son. The point is people do what they do and then pay for it down the line. All people. Including me. Including Danny Boy Bailey. Including Kenny Cochran.

Thinking about my brief and inglorious career as a topless dancer reminded me of Jimmy jolting me out of that place and rearranging the bar owner's nose on the way out. And thinking about that reminded me of the box I'd inherited at the reading of Jimmy's will at Mel Shavelson's office. And thinking about that reminded me of the manila envelope with my name on it inside the box I'd inherited at the reading of Jimmy's will at Shavelson's office. And thinking about that reminded me of *Jimmy's Rules of Private Investigation for Kate*, a handwritten letter inside the envelope.

There were ten rules. *Rule Number Six* was *Every case has a weak link in its chain. Break that link, you bust the chain.* And thinking about that as I parallel parked the White Whale in a spot that materialized by magic directly in front of the Parties to Remember office made me think that Danny Boy Bailey was the first link in the chain that would take me to the bear. *"One link at time, Katie,"* my father had said a thousand times if he'd said it once.

Parties to Remember was located on the Upper West Side, on the fifth floor of a grimy five-floor walkup on the corner of Broadway and 95th Street, a few blocks from Shavelson's office, it just so happened. The first floor was a Chinese-Spanish restaurant. The kind of culinary mashup you can only find in New York. I went through the door under the exterior fire escape and climbed the five flights of stairs.

There were half a dozen office doors on the fifth floor. The business names had been etched into old-school frosted glass that composed the top half of each door. I felt like I was in a

Dashiell Hammett mystery. I walked to the Parties to Remember door, thought about ringing the bell, decided to screw it, opened the door, and stepped into a world where nobody wants to live.

One-room office. Big square room. Maybe twenty by twenty. It was hard to get my bearings on the size because the place was so impossibly packed with papers. Stacks and stacks, reams and reams, piles upon piles upon piles. An impossible amount of paperwork for a small-time business to generate. Mountains of magazines and newspapers stacked on the floor and on the dozen mismatched file cabinets from various decades. Several large bulletin boards with giant calendars filled with names of events and strippers booked to strip at those events. Headshots of potential clients. Casting couch. Everything cheap and ugly. Nothing had been dusted in decades. Zero decor.

Seated behind a massive oak desk was the one and only Danny Boy Bailey, proprietor of Parties to Remember. Buried in daily racing forms, figuring the odds, charting the charts, computing the payouts. He didn't look up. No need to. There was only one kind of person who climbed the stairs to his shitbox.

"You want to dance, lock the lock, take off your clothes, and show me the merchandise," he said.

He was a rat of a man. A rodent in his midfifties. Thinning black hair—a bad dye job, no doubt. Blue dress shirt, sleeves rolled up. Blue paisley tie loose at the neck. Why he felt the need to wear a tie in a hopeless pisshole like this was beyond me.

I lowered the register of my voice and put on a stern British accent. I was still a green-eyed blonde with heavy bangs. "I'm not here to dance. I'm here for answers."

Now he looked up from his horse-racing resources. "What the hell does that mean? Who are you?"

"Special Agent Louise Harnby. NTRA."

That got his attention. NTRA stood for National Thorough-bred Racing Association, a powerful alliance of race tracks, owners, breeders, trainers, and other related organizations concerned with protecting the popularity and prosperity of the hundred-billion-dollar industry known colloquially as horse racing.

He had small, close-set, ink-black eyes, a little rat nose, a small rat mouth. His whole face came to little rat point. It wouldn't have surprised me if there'd been a block of Swiss cheese on his desk amid the myriad racing publications and stripper headshots. He stood up as if he understood the unspoken seriousness of my visit. He was thin with a pot belly. White on white skin. No sunshine for the rat. Just the inside of his office and whatever OTB outlet was nearby.

"How can I help you, Agent Harnby?" he said.

"Why do they call you Danny Boy?" I said, moving around his mountains of paper, checking out the wall calendars, looking for any piece of anything that would tie him to Cochran's murder.

"My father was Irish," he said. "My mother was Italian. I got her looks and his name. He called me Danny Boy, like the song, to make sure I never forgot my heritage. It stuck to me."

"And what exactly is it you do here such that women have to lock the door and remove their clothing?"

"I'm a booking agent for strippers. Parties and whatnot. I get them gigs. Been doing it thirty years. Started with clowns and guys that spin signs outside convenience stores and tax joints. But they don't make money worth talking about, so I switched to strippers, and now I'm living on easy street."

"The only place you're living, Mr. Bailey, besides this godforsaken sewer you call an office, is the track, or your local OTB."

His little rat mouth fell open. "So I bet on the ponies. So what?"

"So with a single phone call, I can terminate your ability to place a wager on any race at any track or counter in the country for the rest of your sad life."

He gulped a real-life actual gulp with sound effect included. "You can't do that."

"Of course I can. But for curiosity's sake, why can't I?"

"Because I'm the pony pundit to a handful of people who bet on the races like they're hooked in their heart. Except they don't know nothing about the horses, and I do. I follow it close, all day, every day. I go to the track, talk to the trainers, look at the horses, watch them run, read the reports, chart the finishes, stay on top of who's racing where and when and why. People know I'm invested, so to speak, so they call me for advice, help them make their bets. I don't charge a fee for my time. But I take a piece if they win. If they lose, it's on them. They don't got to listen to me. Listening to me is their choice, not mine. But I got lots of friends made lots of money betting with me, so you'd be hurting them too, and they didn't do nothing. For fuck's sake, I didn't do nothing."

"Tell that to Kenny Cochran."

"I feel bad for Kenny, I do. He bet with me for years. But I got no connection with what happened to him. That was between him and that other comedian."

"I beg to differ. What happened to Mr. Cochran had nothing to do with the other comedian and everything to do with you and betting on the horses, which means it has everything to do with the NTRA, whose mission remains preserving the popularity and prosperity of our industry. A man's murder over a wager he made on a horse race is precisely the kind of unfortunate business we must stop in its tracks."

I handed Bailey the program containing his bad-news note.

He gulped again.

"You have sixty seconds to explain that to me, or I will remove you from horse racing and involve the police," I said.

A half minute of internal agony later, Bailey handed the program back to me.

"Kenny made lots of bad bets without my input," he said. "Lost a shit ton of money with some very bad people. I got word that Mad Mike was going to see him, and wrote that note for Kenny to call me, so I could warn him, try to help him."

"Mad Mike?" I said.

"Mad Mike Monroe. He's a debt collector for a few of the local bookies. You don't pay up, you get a visit from Mad Mike."

"And which local bookie reached the end of his rope with Mr. Cochran?"

"Could be any of them. All of them. You'd have to ask Mad Mike."

"Where do I find him?"

"He's a part-time butcher at Shamrock Meat Market."

The phone rang. The sexy voicemail answered the call. Someone left a message that both Danny Boy and I could hear.

"Hi, this is Crystal Jones. I'm a dancer at the Polecat Club in the Bronx, and I want to see if I can sign up with your agency. I got big tits and a great ass in case you want to see them. And I don't do too many drugs. Just enough. Call me at the club. I put on a party you'll never forget. Which is kind of like remembering. Just saying. Thanks."

It was at that moment I fully realized why Jimmy had yanked me hard out of the topless club when I was a young, single mom and made me get my PI license. I wondered if Danny Boy felt the same way about Crystal's call that I felt about it. But he shrugged as if to say, *What can I do? It's a great fucking life* and moved back behind his desk.

"Mad Mike Monroe at the Shamrock Meat Market?" I said, walking through the mounds of papers toward the door.

"It's his day job. My day job's booking strippers. Same thing when you think about it."

I didn't bother turning back to him. "I imagine Mad Mike doesn't tell you to lock the lock and remove your clothing."

As I shut the shitbox door behind me, I heard him say, "Don't matter if he does. You're dead before you get them off."

13

PAMPLONA BULLS IN MY BRAIN

Midtown Manhattan. Nothing like it in a city filled with nothing but nothing like it. The biggest, the best, the greatest, the most expensive, the most exclusive, the most recognized, renowned, and legendary, the most distinguished, the most celebrated, the most of the most of damn near everything is in Midtown Manhattan.

Broadway, Times Square, the Waldorf Astoria, Penn Station, the Museum of Modern Art, Carnegie Hall, Madison Square Garden, Macy's, the United Nations, the Empire State Building, Grand Central, Rockefeller Center—the list goes on and on and on and on. Most of New York's tallest skyscrapers, hotels, and apartment towers are in this district, which stretches across the entire island, from the Hudson River to the East River, and from 34th to 59th. Midtown is so intensely vast in its illustrious density that it includes its own familiar districts and neighborhoods: Flatiron, NoMad, Union Square, Hell's Kitchen, the Plaza, Midtown South, Midtown East, Midtown West, and Midtown Proper, home of Robbie Sloane, Rick's agent.

Sloane's office was located on Eighth Avenue and 55th

Street, on the twenty-fifth floor of a gleaming glass skyscraper, which made me question his trustworthiness even more than the fact that he was a talent agent.

The conundrum was *Jimmy's Rules of Private Investigation for Kate, Rule Number Two: Never trust anyone who lives or works above the twenty-fifth floor*. On its face, the rule was clear. I couldn't trust anyone who lived or worked *above* the twenty-fifth floor. And if that was true, then it naturally followed that I *could* trust someone who lived or worked *below* the twenty-fifth floor. But what if someone lived or worked *on* the twenty-fifth floor? Then what was I supposed to do? Trust them? Not trust them? The holes in my father's rules had holes in them. And those holes had holes. I figured if someone lived or worked on the twenty-fifth floor itself, I would just have to put the trusting part on pause.

I sat in Robbie Sloane's reception room and waited for him to get off the phone. He was on several calls at the same time, so it was anybody's guess how long that would take. Anyway, it gave me time to gather my thoughts, which ran like Pamplona bulls in my brain.

Haughty Nina was pregnant with my son's child, and they were getting married in twelve days. There was so much baggage in that box o' thoughts that I didn't have time to unpack all the various and problematic obstacles, roll around in their many and manifold complications, neatly fold them all back up again, and return them to the box in time to meet Sloane. So I moved on to the next thought.

Which was that one of the twelve Ronnie Russos in the New York phone book would be dead in six and a half hours. I called Al to see if he'd made progress uncovering the clue that would magically link the number twelve to the right Ronnie Russo, which couldn't be and probably wasn't the mobster toward whom Logan was turning his task force. Al said, "The boys are working on it in the background."

The "boys" were his twin mainframes. That Ronnie Russo was working in the background meant Al had other projects computing in the foreground, which meant two hundred dollars had not bought me a seat in the front row, which pissed me off. So I told Al that I was hanging up and calling Fu to see if the Chinese-mob hitman could convince the boys to move me up. Al cursed me like a sailor and said he'd take care of it. I reminded him that time was ticking. He reminded me that time was money. We hung up aggravated, infuriated, and exasperated. There were no happy phone calls when it came Zombie Al Cutter.

Kung Fu Fu and *Psychedelic Sunday* were on my mind as well. LaTanya's movie was a mess. But it was a good way to stay connected in case I needed help finding my father's killer. Forcing Fu to see me more than he wanted to see me, not to mention more than I wanted to see him, wasn't the worst thing that could happen right now—the killer had called me on the freaking phone. Fu would be with me at the end of this road, I felt sure.

And *Psychedelic Sunday* opened Friday night. It was Wednesday afternoon. Put simply, we were screwed. But we always were. That was part of the D-Cup charm.

My last thought was the reason I was in Sloane's office in the first place. Rick was missing in action, and I was responsible for his life.

"Ms. King," Sloane's assistant said. "Mr. Sloane is ready for you."

I'd googled Robbie Sloane while waiting in his reception room. He'd been a rising star at William Morris, then at UTA, CAA, and ICM. Four premium LA agencies in nine years. Big superstar agencies. He hadn't hopped from one to the other to advance his career. He'd been forced out. The issue wasn't his agenting; he was considered to be a phenom in the biz on both coasts. It was sleazebaggery that had precipitated his job jumping. He was a terrible slutbag. Meaning he wasn't simply terrible *for* being a slutbag in the first place, but also that he was terrible *at* being a slutbag, terrible at his own slutbaggishness. Basically, he'd screwed everything in his path—clients, potential clients, wives, mothers, daughters, sisters, partners, associates, and secretaries—and left a trail of rage in his wake. This was who Rick Gotti had landed with. Not all that surprising, actually. Rick was a client no self-respecting agent would touch. Robbie Sloane was an agent no upstanding actor would sign with.

"Ms. King," Sloane said, coming around his desk. He shook my hand and shut his office door. "Pleasure to meet you."

"Dianna, please," I said.

I was Dianna King, the green-eyed blonde with heavy bangs (yes, still wearing *The Horseshoe Murders* wig and colored contacts) in charge of Rick's money. His new accountant. Just signed. Signatures still wet on the paperwork.

"Have a seat," Sloane said, directing me to his plush leather sofa.

He was the sole agent in the company. One-man shop. He had a receptionist/assistant, and that was it. His office was big and bright. Massive windows. Leather and wood interior. Lots of framed movie and TV posters. Plenty of pictures of Sloane with famous folks he'd worked with. And probably screwed. He'd been big-time and slutbagged it all away.

We had a chitchat about the weather and his twenty-fifth-floor view and some other things neither of us cared about, and then I said, "I've been a New York entertainment accountant my entire adult life. This city is home base for me. How are you adjusting to life on the East Coast? It's a significant change, I'm sure."

"Hollywood's idea of purgatory," he said, making half a joke of it. "A galaxy far, far away. Not to worry. I'm still connected. Rick's going to make millions with me at the wheel."

He sat next to me on the sofa, not across from me in one of his fancy leather chairs. Right next to me. Closer than should have been considered professionally acceptable. Closer than I wanted him to be. Uncomfortably close.

"Other than the sand and sun, feels the same to me," he said.

Reading between the lines, the drift was he'd like to celebrate our meeting with some sex on the couch—like he had in the land of sand and sun.

He was handsome. Younger than me—between thirty-five and forty. Gorgeous Hollywood hair. Chestnut brown. Perfectly coiffed. Obedient to the strand. Who had hair like that? Not me. I had New York hair. By midafternoon, whatever I'd done to my hair that morning was long gone. Sloane, I imagined, woke up looking like this. Dazzling smile. Gorgeous skin. Slick and smooth. A shark in the shallows. I could see how he'd seduced half of Hollywood.

"I'm happy for you," I said. "And I'm happy for Rick. Except I don't know where he is today and what deal you've negotiated with Ruby Gold."

"Deal's not done," he said, undressing me with his eyes. "When it's signed and sealed, you'll be the first to know. Second, actually. Rick will be the first."

"That's unacceptable, Mr. Sloane."

"Robbie."

"That's unacceptable, Robbie. If it's Rick's business, it's my business. Now please tell me where he is, what he's doing there, and how much he's making."

He looked into my eyes and smiled, and I knew right then he was smarter than I'd thought he was. And not as smart as *he* thought he was.

"You must know, of course, that Rick never mentioned you to me," he said.

"I'm surprised," I said.

"I'm not. My clients and I are attached at the hip. That's why I make them so much money. There are no secrets between us."

"Very little of anything between you and your women clients, I've heard. Women in general, in fact."

He smiled in a way that made me sick to my stomach. "Cute, Dianna, or whoever you are. I know you're not Rick's accountant because Rick has a longtime business manager, not an accountant. I'm thinking you're the bodyguard he hired. The bodyguard who told him he couldn't do the Ruby Gold pilot or the Victor Vreeland gig. I thought it was you when you called to set the meeting. Rick said you were hot. That's why you're sitting here. And look at that, you *are* hot. Too bad it's time for you to go. Unless you have something else in mind."

He stood up and grabbed my arm in a forceful way I didn't care for, a way that implied my physical submission was expected—in this case, to get the hell out or give the hell in. So I set my feet like I'd been taught and punched him in the nose. He'd been begging for it, like Jimmy had said, and I'd given him what he'd wanted. It was a great shot. A classic right cross. My father would have called it a thing of beauty. Even Raul would have given his approval.

Sloane went down hard. His ribcage smashed into the sharp edge of his coffee table as he fell to the floor. I was sure I'd broken his nose. He'd probably bruised a rib or two as well. Anyway, he was bleeding all over himself.

"Fuck, oh fuck, my nose, you broke my fucking nose," he said, moaning and groaning. "Fuck you, oh Christ, I'm fucking bleeding."

While he was feeling sorry for himself, and straining to breathe because of his ribs, I walked to his desk and looked for his calendar.

"Four agencies and three thousand miles later, and you're still a punk and a bully under all that glamour. Here's what's going to happen, Robbie. You're going to stay down until I'm gone. Then you can call the police if you want to, but I'll say you grabbed me in a physically threatening way, and I defended myself like Raul and Jimmy taught me. I'll tell them to look into your Hollywood history. I'll give them the names of the women who filed complaints and the companies that canned you. That's what I'll say. What will you say? Understand so far?"

"Yes, fuck you, my fucking nose, my ribs, I'm not calling the police, all right?"

"Fuck you too, Robbie. You wouldn't tell me where Rick is because you don't want me to interfere with your commission, a point I wouldn't argue except for the fact that someone's trying to kill our client. See what I did there? Included you in the personal part of the story even though you don't deserve it. Even though you threw Rick's life under the bus to make a buck."

"I'm not telling you shit. Just get the fuck out."

I found his calendar, opened it to today's date, and there it was: Wednesday, four o'clock, Silvercup Studios, Studio 1, Ruby Gold pilot.

I stood over him and made a fist. "I'm never going to see you again, Robbie. Say it out loud."

"You're never going to see me again. Jesus Christ, what's wrong with you?"

"It's a long list," I said, checking my watch and walking out of his office. "And I'm short on time."

14

SOMETHING OF A SUICIDE MISSION

LYING LIKE A RUG IS SOMETHING PRIVATE INVESTIGATORS AND actors have in common. My father wrote it down in black and white for me. *Jimmy's Rules of Private Investigation for Kate, Rule Number Ten: Lying is part of the job. You have to lie every day, sometimes all day. You have to be a champion liar to crack your case. You have to do it, but you never get used to it.* It was one of those lying-all-day days, no doubt.

For actors and PIs, lying through your teeth while telling the truth about something is compulsory behavior. Invariably, ultimately, and always, neither one is telling the whole truth about that thing. Indeed, they might be revealing only the slightest sliver of truth. A scrap of a fragment of truth, in fact, might be the only truth they could find in the thing they're lying about because otherwise the thing is a bag of bullshit for which they have no tolerance. But the art of acting—and of private investigating too, it turns out—is taking that one splinter of a splice of a shaving of a shard of truth you uncovered and making the complete performance about that thin reed of truthfulness while lying your guts out with effortless entertaining energy that is impossible to identify as anything but the truth, the whole truth, and nothing but the truth, so help you God.

It's hard to do it well, even onstage, where an audience has bought into your act—literally purchased tickets to see you play a character who will lie to them about the truth of things in a conjured tale. Even then, when it's applauded, it's hard to make the lie true enough to be real. When it's *unexpected*, when you're out in the world where no one's given you permission to lie to their face, for instance, when you're a private investigator, for instance, it's something of a suicide mission.

I'd fooled Cochran's nosy neighbor and Danny Boy Bailey, but neither had turned any sort of professional acting radar toward me. I'd been truthful and believable and committed in both performances, and they'd each gone for the full ride. I'd have to turn up my energy if I was going to get past Ruby Gold —assuming Rick would even play his part.

Robbie Sloane, of course, had known before the bell that Rick didn't have an accountant named Dianna King, so I'd been dead in the water before I'd even jumped into the pool, so to speak. Sloane was a douche, but he had some acting radar. In the back of my mind, I wanted another chance another day with another role to play to see if I could make him drink the Kate McCall Kool-Aid.

I changed clothes in the first-floor ladies' room of Sloane's office building. I'd worn a blue business suit to play the parts of Cathy Culver from State Farm, Louise Harnby from the NTRA, and Dianna King. But I'd sensed I might need a sexier look a little later in the day, so I'd brought one with me. I'd been right. Even a blind squirrel, as they say in the suburbs.

I drove the White Whale over the Queensboro Bridge, made a right on 21st Street, another onto Queens Plaza South, another onto 22nd Street, and parked in the Silvercup Studios guest lot. I checked my makeup in the mirror, made sure my push-up bra and my cleavage were behaving harmoniously, locked the Toyota, and walked to the guarded entrance gate like I wholly belonged to be here right the hell now.

Located in the converted Silvercup Bakery building in Long Island City, first stop over the bridge in Queens, Silvercup Studios was the big dog for film and TV production in New York. Their huge, red, iconic, rooftop sign was a bold beacon coming across the Queensboro Bridge. Believe me, they deserved every bit of that sign. More or less every important film and television show made in New York had been shot here in some form or fashion since the place opened in 1983, including *30 Rock*, *Mad Men*, *Ugly Betty*, *Gossip Girl*, *Analyze That*, *Gangs of New York*, *Highlander*, *The Devil Wears Prada*, *Sex in the City*, *Meet the Parents*, and *The Sopranos*.

When you're a big damn deal, you get a big damn sign.

As I approached the guard, I reached into my purse because sometimes an actor needs that little something extra to get them past the point of "acting" and into the realm of "being." It could be an accent that does the trick. A certain way of walking. Or perhaps a prop. Yes, sometimes a prop can lead an actor to the promised land.

For me, today, at Silvercup Studios, the prop was a five-carat, hand-cut, hand-polished cubic zirconia engagement ring to make your eyes pop. Unless you were a jeweler, you'd have no idea this thing had set the production company back a whopping two hundred bucks, not thirty thousand. I'd bought it from them for twenty dollars. Not much less than I'd made for the shoot, I'm sad to say.

The gig had been a late-night local cable commercial for a jewelry story in Jamaica Estates. Their pitch: if you were wearing the ring and got murdered, they'd refund your money. I'd played the bride-to-be who got murdered while wearing their ring. I don't know who played the groom-to-be who got his money back. The jewelry store had gone under. No surprise there.

"Hi...Jake," I said, leaning over to read his nametag and giving him a long look at my boobs. I have good boobs, it's true. Not big, just good. People have told me that. Men have not complained. Jake was not complaining.

"Can I help you?" Jake said.

He was twenty-five, maybe twenty-eight. He did not have the sharp eyes of a geek or a wizard or a genius whiz kid making a few extra bucks while he reimagined the internet in his parents' basement. He had the dull look of someone who might be a security guard far into his future. Or, who knows, maybe he was the drummer in a rock band whose break was right around the corner. Either way, I was all in at this point.

"I'm here to watch my fiancé film a pilot," I said.

"Name?" he said, grabbing his clipboard.

"Jennifer Lily Lane. Some people call me Jen. Some call me Lily. Rick calls me JLil. He's a comedian. I don't know which name he gave you."

"I meant name of the pilot. We have more than one project shooting today."

"Oh, sorry. I don't know the name. It's Ruby Gold's show. Rick's in it."

"Ruby Gold. Studio 1. And what was your name? Jennifer Lane, right?"

"Right."

"You're not on the list."

Five of the worst words in the world when said together in that order.

"Well, that's just Rick being Rick. Why should he remember I was coming to the taping? He's only my fiancé." I presented my gorgeous diamond for Jake's approval. "We just got engaged."

Jake was impressed by the ring and my boobs but wasn't budging.

"Like I said, Ms. Lane, you're not—"

"On the list, I know. Please, Jake. He's expecting me, even though he forgot to tell you, and I know you're the boss of the door, and please, Jake, his name's Rick Gotti, and he's famous, and he's in Ruby Gold's pilot, and I'm supposed to be there watching him bring the house down, and please, Jake, let me go see my fiancé, please, Jake..."

I brought a tear to my eye. I'm an actor.

Jake looked at my teary eye and down at my tits and sighed like he was the Boss of the Door and was all of a sudden feeling benevolent, a soft touch under his uniform.

"Welcome-to-the-jungle Rick Gotti?" he said.

The show was in reruns on cable and available for bingeing on Netflix. I nodded, wiping away my tears.

"Sign in," he said. "Follow the arrows to Studio 1. I'll say your name was on the list all along so don't take it out on your fiancé. We'll cut Rick Gotti some slack today on account of your engagement."

I smiled and signed in. He gestured toward the open door like a café maître d' and said, "Welcome to the jungle."

I followed the arrows and entered the arcane world of sitcom TV production. A hundred people scurried around like chickens late for henhouse work. Grips, gaffers, electricians, painters, producers, directors, carpenters, hair, makeup, wardrobe, sound, camera, craft service, crew upon crew dancing a chaotic ballet. Two big sets had been constructed: Ruby Gold's house, a suburban living room, dining room, kitchen, and laundry room, and Ruby Gold's business, a neighborhood bar and grill. *Cheers* meets *The Cosby Show*.

Cameras were in place to shoot the house set. Lighting and decorating and props were being finalized. Stand-ins were standing in. I spotted Rick near the set. Beside him was Ruby Gold. My heart jumped a beat. Ruby Gold herself. Holy shit.

It was the ultimate intersection of private investigating and acting. *"It has to be done, and I have to do it,"* Jimmy used to say. I steadied myself, smiled my best JLil smile, and walked toward them.

"Rick," I said. "Am I late? I tried not to be late. But the bridge was backed up, and I hope I'm not late."

I wrapped my arm around his and kissed him on the mouth. He kissed me back—because if a green-eyed woman with blonde hair and heavy bangs and boobs like mine kisses a man on the mouth, most men kiss her back.

Before he could speak, I turned to Ruby Gold and held out my hand. "Hi, Ms. Gold. I'm Jennifer, Rick's fiancée. I'm so excited to meet you. Rick told me not to ask for your autograph, so I won't, but I want to. I'm really so excited to meet you. Thank you for letting me be here."

She was regal in her bearing. Genuine TV royalty. Had she been wearing a crown, a jeweled tiara, I wouldn't have blinked. She was zaftig, full-bodied beautiful, luminous and larger than life. It was as if all the funniest, most talented Ziegfeld Follies girls had been rolled into one supernova of a woman. She was a tad taller than me, maybe five eight. Her publicly acknowledged age was seventy-five, so maybe she was a few years older than that. But her vibe, her aura, her energy, was many years younger. Decades younger. If I hadn't been lying to her face about, well, everything, I'd have bowed at her feet. She was that freaking famous.

Ruby shook my hand, looked me in the eyes, and turned to Rick. "I didn't know you were engaged."

Rick looked at Ruby and at me and laughed his Rick Gotti laugh. He knew it was me, Kate-me. So this was the moment of Truth. Fired bodyguard or Hired Bodyguard.

"It just happened last week," he said as I presented my ring to Ruby. "And I was thinking about the show and you, and I'm sorry, Ruby. Really. Slipped my mind. Not that I was engaged— sorry, sweetheart—but to tell you about it."

"He did good, didn't he, Ms. Gold?" I said.

"He did, indeed," Ruby said. "Jennifer, yes? Call me Ruby."

"Ruby, we're ready for Rick," an assistant director called out from the set.

Rick nodded, kissed me, and headed to the sitcom house, where hair and makeup and wardrobe waited to guide him to lights, camera, and action.

"Sit with me, Jennifer," Ruby said, guiding me by the arm to a lineup of director chairs near video village not far from the set. "We'll watch Rick steal the spotlight together."

Her chair had been painted gold, and her name was embroidered in delicious ruby-red script on the back. *Ruby Gold.*

She sat me in the chair next to hers and went over to the director, assistant directors, and some of the producers. They spoke for a while, then she spoke for a while, and that was that. Ruby Gold gave the orders on this set. It was her show. Named after her. *Ruby!*

"I think we're ready to roll camera," she said, sitting beside me. "Do you know anything about the show?"

"I'm embarrassed. I don't. Rick just said he was doing a pilot with you, and when he said your name, I kind of blanked out after that."

"I have that effect on people. I'm not sure it's a good thing."

Her timing was impeccable. Her tone was all Ruby Gold.

I laughed. "It's a good thing. Trust me."

She laughed too. "The show is about a bar I own and run, except I have no idea how to own and run it because my husband ran the place before he divorced me and disappeared with his new trophy wife. I didn't even know he owned a bar. He never told me because I don't drink a drop. All our married life, I thought he owned a shoe store. We never meet him or his new wife. They've gone to Tahiti by the time the show opens. Anyway, in the pilot, my bartender is comically shot and killed during a robbery—he and my cook are robbing my house while I'm bumbling around my new business. The cook accidentally shoots him while they're making sandwiches in my kitchen, because robbery builds an appetite, and it's time for lunch, and the bartender's ghost has to stay here and earn his way into the afterlife. That's his punishment from heaven for robbing me. He has to help me run the bar after he's dead. Rick is my bartender. It's a costarring role that requires a wise guy everybody loves. A smartass joker who learns to have a kind heart while he's teaching me to run my business and cracking jokes. Only the cook and I can see him. Of course, the bartender and I become friends despite everything, including his being deceased."

"It's perfect for him."

"Typecasting, I agree. This is the scene where I'm at the bar and Rick and the cook try to rob my house because they know I'm not home, and Rick gets shot while making sandwiches in my kitchen. It takes him five minutes to die. Living room, kitchen, up the stairs, down the stairs, draped on the furniture, rolling on the rug. He has a hilarious soliloquy. Should be a chew-the-scenery showstopper."

Just like that my radar went wild.

15

HOLY NETWORK SITCOM SHIT

THE FIREARM WRANGLER PRESENTED THE GUN FOR RUBY'S approval. It was a Beretta 92F, the most commonly used gun in film and TV production. Of course, it had been modified to fire blank cartridges. But like real rounds, blanks have gunpowder to deliver a believable muzzle-flash and loud report, a big bang for the buck, so there's still some danger involved even with a blank-fire film gun.

So with danger in mind, the wrangler demonstrated all the necessary safety particulars to Ruby, the director, the assistant directors, the director of photography, the producers, the key grip, the best boy, and the actor/cook scripted to shoot the bartender. The actor/cook had already been instructed how to use the Beretta but attended the demonstration for reinforcement—and so everyone could vouch he'd been there.

He was a big galoot of a guy who looked exactly like a cook in a bar. Ruby had told me it was a breakthrough role for him. After many years of struggling through discouraging acting workshops and empty auditions, paying his bills by working as a cook in a bar, his first real role was being a cook in a bar.

The actor-cook was in costume: black pants, black shirt, black ski mask with big yellow fuzzy ball on top for comedic effect. Ruby had chosen the ski mask and wanted to make sure it was still funny. It was. With the mask and the gun approved and all the required paperwork signed, it was time for *places, everyone; places, please.*

I didn't like it one bit. Not the gun or the wrangler or the cook or the cast or the crew or the coffee or the ski mask with the yellow fuzzy ball.

"Do they have to shoot him? I don't like guns. They're loud and heavy and smell like oil," I said to Ruby. Which was wonderful acting on my part because it was true. "Can't the cook stab him or hit him with the toaster? Can't Rick get stuck in the freezer and freeze to death?"

Ruby laughed and told me not to worry, that everything would be fine, that the wrangler was the best in the business, that the gun had been checked and double-checked and triple-checked, that the cook playing the cook had been trained with the actual gun and had also been in the Army at one point so knew his way around weapons. Then the set was hot, the room was silent, and the camera was rolling.

Rick entered, speaking on his cell to his partner, the cook, who was late for the robbery because he couldn't read his own handwriting and so couldn't follow his own directions and so got lost in Ruby's neighborhood. The sitcom cook, we learned quick, was not the brightest light in the night. Rick wore black from head to toe, it turned out, because the cook had convinced him that black was the new black. Rick's exasperation with the cook was funny as hell. Rick guiding the cook to Ruby's house, regurgitating the directions, was hilarious. Rick was Rick, but he was also acting, playing the role of the bartender at the same time he was being himself.

I was impressed. *He didn't become Rick Gotti by accident.*

Since the cook was late and it was lunchtime and the bartender was hungry, he decided to make himself a sandwich. Rick in Ruby's kitchen, making wise-crack commentary on the food in Ruby's fridge, was even funnier than Rick on the phone with the cook who'd got lost in suburbia. Ruby had given Rick freedom to riff, to be the lightning-fast comedian he was, to be true to the cook's character, true to the story world, but also true to his own wiseass, God-given comedic gift.

It was a big-time pilot production that Ruby intended to sell to, well, anyone who'd buy it from her. And whoever wanted the new Ruby Gold sitcom—there would be a bidding war, Ruby told me, because people were already lined up—would have to pay and pay big because Ruby had financed the thing herself. She owned the show.

I was swept up and away in the reality of the moment. Sitting next to Ruby Gold the legend, watching Rick Gotti chew the scenery in a pilot Ruby herself had dreamed and produced and financed, a pilot that would lead to a series that would relaunch Rick's career into the stratosphere. History was happening in front of my eyes. The set was spot-on, the lighting was superb, the crew was best-in-class, the cast had been hand-picked by Ruby herself. She'd spared no expense. The miracle of entertainment success was unfolding before me. This was how they played the game in the big leagues.

Holy shit, I said to myself. *Holy network sitcom shit.*

And then the kitchen door opened and the big galoot of a cook entered the room, wearing black because black was the new black, wearing the ridiculous ski mask with the ridiculous big yellow fuzzy fuzz ball on top of his head. It was funny, the mask. Just the look of it. Ruby had been right about that.

The cook walked through the kitchen into the living room, where Rick sat on the sofa eating the sandwich he'd built from the hilarious ingredients in Ruby's fridge. But instead of playing the scene as written, bantering back and forth a bit about breaking for lunch in the middle of a robbery, instead of that, the cook pointed the Beretta at Rick and shot him point blank in the chest.

Everyone froze.

It was too loud, too real. Nasty and wrong.

It was live fire.

Rick fell off the couch onto the floor, and the cook stood over him and fired two more rounds into his chest. Then he ran off the set into the darkness.

Studio 1 filled with panic and chaos. Cast and crew running all over the place screaming for help or frozen in shock and fear. Ruby Gold was a mess. "What the hell is happening," she said over and over. "What the hell is happening?

I leaped up onto the set, raced across the living room, kicked the coffee table out of my way, and looked down, expecting to see Rick dead on the ground. And he did look dead.

Except for one thing.

There was no blood.

I kneeled beside him. "Rick, can you hear me? Say something. Answer me."

He opened his eyes. "I wore it for you, McCall."

"What?"

"The vest. I wore it for you."

The bulletproof vest Jimmy had given me and I'd told Rick to wear and Rick had said in no uncertain terms he would never wear—that vest.

He'd grabbed it from my closet before skipping out on me to film Ruby Gold's pilot and had put the damn thing on. He'd worn the stupid vest.

"You wore it for me?" I said.

"I did," he said.

I started crying. I couldn't help it. I was overcome with relief and fear and fury. Too many emotions to keep inside, so they came out together as tears.

Ruby arrived beside us, looked down at Rick and me, and said, "Thank you, God. Thank you, Lord."

That wasn't good enough for me by a longshot. I stood, got in her famous face, and said, "What the fuck, Ruby? You shot my fucking fiancé? What the fucking fuck?"

"I didn't shoot anyone," she said. "I would never."

And then various producers and managers and agents pulled her off the set and whisked her out of the studio to someplace safer than Silvercup.

There were other folks around us now—grips and gaffers and set decorators. They helped Rick back up onto the sofa, where he'd taken the first slug in the chest. They brought him a glass of water and called 911 just in case. Other crew members came running back to the set saying the shooter was gone. They'd chased after him but had been too late, too slow to react. Just like me.

It occurred to me that I'd known something was wrong the moment the cook had come through the kitchen door. He hadn't had the same posture, the same comportment, the same sense of situation comedy as the cook I'd met.

That's because it wasn't the cook that shot Rick.

It was the bear.

The question I had to ask myself and did ask myself was, *What the hell is wrong with you, Kate, you stupid, starstruck sap? You're not Rick Gotti's fiancée, you're his bodyguard. So, again, and not for the last time, what the hell is wrong with you?*

I thought I knew the answer, but before I could reply to myself, they found the actor who was supposed to have played the cook. He'd been tied up in a storage room. He never saw who'd hit him in the head, he said, because they'd come at him from behind. Naturally, he had no idea what had happened while the cameras rolled.

We told him some other guy had taken his place and shot Rick three times with real bullets but that Rick was alive because he'd worn a bulletproof vest. It was madness no one could explain.

Except the cook, who simply said, "That's showbiz."

16

WHICH BRINGS US TO RONNIE RUSSO TWELVE

I PULLED MYSELF TOGETHER AND ESCORTED MY FIANCÉ OUT OF Studio 1, out of Silvercup, and out of Queens before the police arrived to take statements and make everyone's life a little less sitcom, a little more *Law & Order*. The police would have to find us if they wanted a statement from Rick.

It was five o'clock. Thirty minutes before the curtain came up on today's *Psychedelic Sunday* dress rehearsal. As ritual, superstition, and theater voodoo commanded, by now I should have been in the dressing room, the second actor to arrive after Roger, as had been our preshow sacrament for a half dozen years. Roger first, me second, everyone else arriving in dribs and drabs after that. But ritual, superstition, and voodoo are fast forgotten when your fiancé has been nearly murdered— even when your *fake* fiancé has been nearly murdered.

If the Queensboro Bridge is light, I thought, *I'll scoot onstage in the nick of time.*

Rick was quiet on the ride to the D-Cup. Had it not been for the vest, he would be dead. Not a little dead. Totally freaking dead. No one knew that better than him. His chest was bruised from the impact of the slugs, but the vest had done its duty.

"Not dead yet," he said out loud, though not to me or even to himself.

The fact that the bear had known where Rick would be and what time he would be there and how to infiltrate the pilot as the actual actor in the scene in which Rick was actually accidentally murdered—wearing the actual ski mask with the yellow fuzzy ball on top, for chrissakes—was the first of many unsettled and unsettling subjects. How had he gotten past Silvercup security? How had he sneaked onto the set? How had he knocked out the cook without anyone being the wiser? How, how, how, and how? I wanted to talk it through with Rick, ask him who'd known he was going to be at Silvercup besides Slick Robbie Sloan, but Rick was lost in his own mortality, so we drove to the theater in silence.

The dress rehearsal was good—good, in this case, being defined as anarchy and madness. With one more dress rehearsal to go before opening night, the Schmidt and Parker Players had, as a troupe, come to realize and accept that at its honest core the show was mainly mayhem and bedlam. And that as long as we sang and danced and acted our theatrical hearts out, the musical's insanity and absurdity would be mystically transformed into pure orgasmic energy exploding off the stage in the form of yet another entertaining evening at the D-Cup.

Rehearsal ended, and Rick told me the two show-stopping orgies were possibly the most sensational song-and-dance crescendos in the history of musical theater. "Not one orgy," he said several times. "Two orgies. In the same show."

While Dennis and Posey gave post-rehearsal notes, Zombie Al texted me he had news I could use.

At seven forty-five, I left the D-Cup for the House of Emotional Tics. Rick stayed in the theater, under the safe supervision of Big Black Bald Bart.

Bartholomew Johnson was six-ten. He'd played basketball

for SUNY Purchase four decades earlier. But he'd never been an athlete in his heart. He'd been and still was a song-and-dance man like his hero Dick Van Dyke. Unfortunately, Bart was atonal and without rhythm. Still, he was a sweetheart, so Dennis and Posey put him in productions that called for a very tall actor in a nonsinging, nondancing role. Otherwise, Bart was part of the stage crew, an excellent set decorator because he didn't need a ladder. He was always laughing, the happiest shit-kicker in New York. Oh yes, and he was Black. And bald. Shaved head. At his first D-Cup audition, he'd started his auto-biographical monologue with *"I'm big, I'm black, I'm bald, and I'm Bart. Big Black Bald Bart."*

"Little Rick not going nowhere," Bart said as I left the theater.

"He's right about that," Rick said.

Rick and Bart were fast friends because Rick had suggested Bart play the part of the strip-club bouncer in the new musical being composed and written just for him and me—and now Bart. Dennis and Posey had loved the idea.

"I'll be back for you later," I said to my fake fiancé. "Don't get killed while I'm gone."

I called Fu from the White Whale, and he was waiting for me in the lobby, which was likely the saddest lobby on the Upper East Side. Soft sad lights, ancient tile floors, a row of depressed mailboxes, a 1960s intrabuilding intercom beside my front door (apartment 1A), and stairs to the upper floors and basement. Nothing extra. Nothing cheerful. No flowers. No furniture. No black-and-white photos of old New York. Just a gloomy amber glow to get you going nowhere. It was always a dreary fall afternoon in the brownstone lobby, even on a sunny summer morning.

"Fu say trap," Fu said as I walked through the door.

No *hello*. No *how was your day*. Just straight into *Fu say trap*.

"You don't know who, where, or anything yet," I said.

"Know one thing."

"What?"

"Know is trap."

"Okay, guess what? I know it's going to be a trap too. I knew that when I was on the phone with the killer. I knew first."

"Fu know first."

"There is no way you knew this was a trap before I knew it was a trap. No way."

"Way."

"How? Tell me how you knew it was a trap before I knew it was a trap when I knew it was a trap when I spoke to the killer before I even told you I'd spoken to the killer?"

"How know?"

"Yes, how?"

"You in trap all time. You in trap before killer call. Fu know then."

"Fu you, Fu."

"Fu you too."

This, in essence, was our entire relationship. Fu torturing me like the most annoying little brother on the planet. Precisely the way my sister had tortured me when we were little girls living in Queens and our mother was alive. There was no one who could get under my skin like Marilyn could get under my skin. Until Fu. It was like Fu and I had shared a room as kids or something. Fu in the bottom bunk, kicking my mattress night after night after night after night.

During his first two years in the brownstone—he'd arrived two days after me—he'd only said six words: *yes, no, Fu, say, you, and too*. Two years of six words only. Since he'd let on his English vocabulary was way more extensive than that, I'd never once had the last word.

We climbed the stairs to the fifth floor, badgering and peppering each other the entire time, and knocked on Al's door. He unlocked all five locks and let us in.

The room was lit only by the lights of his Death Star computer. Six monitors, six towers, multiple modems and printers and scanners and other things doing I couldn't comprehend. Twin mainframes (the boys, Al called them) glowed and blinked and flashed and flickered like they knew all the world's secrets, which they more or less did. Three of the six screens coded and decoded someone else's proprietary property at warp speed. One screen was devoted to eBay, where Al had an international trade deal underway that no regulatory authority was fast enough to follow. Another monitor rifled through databases to locate yet another priced-right, old-model Corolla to add to the fleet. Screen six was dedicated to Ronnie Russo.

As always, it was hard to focus on the business at hand partly because of the overpowering sense I'd somehow stepped through restricted-access portal 5A onto the bridge of a Romulan Warbird and partly because of the Gatorade bottles.

Al's toilet had worked only intermittently for months. Fu had been in the plumbing once a week but couldn't find the fix. The problem was deep in a hidden pipe in an unknown wall somewhere secret in the building. Or maybe it was karma giving Al the shit he deserved.

Either way, Al had taken to buying cases and cases of golden Gatorade, drinking the contents, and refilling the bottles with his own pee. How he differentiated piss from yellow sport drink, I had no idea. I didn't want to think about it. But the bottles were lined up like Stormtroopers demanding allegiance to Al's Zombie Empire, and the whole thing was too much to take for more than ten minutes. So Al got right to it.

"The amount I got paid for the time I put in to program the boys to run your Ronnie Russo records was a pittance of the pay I deserve."

"What you deserve is a pittance of the price I paid," I said. "But a deal's a deal."

"Until there's a new deal," Al said.

"New deal is Fu break zombie neck," Fu said.

"Fu you, Fu," Al said.

"Fu you too," Fu said.

"What's the news, Al?" I said. "It's eight fifty. One of the Ronnie Russos will be dead in forty minutes."

He lifted a printout and reviewed the results. "Ronnie Russo one is a waiter in Washington Heights. Ronnie Russo two works at Best Buy in the Bronx. Ronnie Russo three is an editor in Elmhurst. Ronnie Russo four sells real estate in Rockaway. Ronnie Russo five fights fires in Flatbush. Ronnie Russo six is a dentist in Dyker Heights. Ronnie Russo seven is seventy-seven, which would make him the man if the significant number was seven, but it's twelve, so fuck that fucking Ronnie Russo. Ronnie Russo eight owns a pizza place in Port Morris. Ronnie Russo nine is a bachelor in Bensonhurst. Ronnie Russo ten teaches business at Barnard. Not one of these Ronnie Russos has shit to do with the number twelve, significant, insignificant, or otherwise. Which leaves two Ronnie Russos on the board."

"Ronnie Russo the mobster," I said.

Al nodded. "Ronnie Russo eleven. Connected to number twelve only in the sense he's murdered multiples of that number of people. Otherwise, Ronnie Russo eleven is not the Ronnie Russo you're looking for."

"I agree," I said. "Too obvious. Plus, Logan's all over him."

"Which brings us to Ronnie Russo twelve," Al said, taking a greed-infused pause.

"How much?" I said.

"I had to dig," Al said. "Rewrite the program. Extend the search back in time."

"What's the number, Al?"

"Fifty is fine," Al said.

I gave him fifty bucks just to shut him up, get him going, and save time. The clock was ticking on Ronnie Russo's life.

"Ronnie Russo twelve owns RJM Motors in Jamaica with two partners," Al said, pocketing the money. "He sells used cars by the shit ton to make bank, which he does by the boatload and has a killer garage with the best mechanics money can buy. That business is booming too, but the big bucks, the passion and the prestige, is upfitting stock cars for racetracks and running them up and down the East Coast. Ronnie Russo twelve is a real-deal race-car driver. Know what number he wears? Twelve. Comes from a big family. He's the baby. Know how many kids his mother had? Twelve. Ronnie was twelve of twelve. Know how many race cars he owns? Twelve. The man was married. Know how many years? Twelve, when his wife died six months ago. They had twin girls. Know how old they are? Twelve."

"Jesus Christ," I said.

"Dinner for twelve," Al said.

"Where RJM?" Fu said.

"Queens," Al said. "Jamaica. I told you."

"Where in Jamaica?" I said.

"That's the kicker," Al said, reaching for a bottle of Gatorade I could only hope was Gatorade. "Twelve North 12th Street."

17

—————

SUNSET IN USED-CAR COUNTRY

We got to RJM Motors at nine twenty-five. Five minutes to save Ronnie Russo's life—if he wasn't already dead. I'd called Logan on the way and left a message. There were no police on-site. No sirens in the near distance. No task force in my immediate future. Logan had bet the ranch on the wrong Ronnie Russo.

RJM was an extra-large double lot on a big industrial block in a warehouse neighborhood near the East River. It was jammed from front to back with several hundred used cars, upfitted cars, and flat-out race cars. The three buildings at the back were cinderblock with metal roofs and numbers on the façades. Building 1 was dedicated to standard service and repair —oil changes, tire rotations, spark plugs, filters, fluids—the killer garage Al had mentioned. Building 2 was a specialized garage, where the fancy upfitting was done, where stock cars were turned into hot-rod racers that might not be legal on public roads in certain counties. And Building 3 was sales and management, meaning paperwork and money. Though Ronnie Russo likely spent a ton of time in Building 2, his private office would probably have been in Building 3.

The block was closed for the night. Pitch-black but for RJM, whose lot was lit by flood lights. Not middle-of-the-day bright, more like twilight. Sunset in used-car country.

I parked the White Whale twenty yards down North 12th from RJM. From my vantage point, the lot seemed empty. No one walking the grounds. No one filing or finishing financials in the offices. No one tuning Toyotas or upfitting Firebirds. No one here. Except me and Fu and the killer and Ronnie Russo. I had a plan in place, at least in my mind, turned to tell Fu, and...Fu was gone. As in not in the car with me. As in *What the fuck, Fu?*

Then, *tap-tap-tap*, he was at the driver's window. I hand-cranked it down—Warren's fleet was completely stripped, meaning no frills, meaning no radio, no AC, no electric windows, no electric anything.

"Fu go," he said before I could speak.

Then he ran off like a gazelle, limber and lean. I was struck again for the umpteenth time by his grace, his athleticism, his strength, his agility. It didn't seem possible a man his size could move like that. It was like some special effect in a feature film, where the star is outfitted with futuristic robotics that make him some kind of superman. But this wasn't special effects. This was Fu.

I called after him in my loud whisper voice. "Fu go where?"

"Into night," he said and was up and over the RJM fence, clearing the barbed wire with ease. Lost in the shadows. Gone.

I took a breath, locked the Corolla, and hurried to the lot. My heart pounded and raced and raced and pounded. Ronnie Russo was here somewhere.

I slipped through an opening between two gates on the west side, took the Colt from my backpack, and started down the rows of cars closet to North 12th Street, the front of the lot. Three rows of three sections of thirty cars each. Nine sections total. All lined up nice and neat, like a tic-tac-toe board. There was a two-lane space for driving between each section.

My senses were on red alert. It seemed as likely Russo would be bound and gagged in one of the race cars as in one of the buildings, so I rushed down the first row, keeping low, checking each car, looking, looking, looking.

No Russo. And no sign of the man who'd murdered my father.

I turned right, turned right again, and flew down the second row, time ticking away in my head. Maybe I had three minutes to save his life. Maybe less than that.

End of the second row. Still no Russo. Still no killer.

I turned left and then left again into the third row...and stopped dead in my tracks. On my left were the cars. On my right were the buildings. I was at the end of Building 3.

In the roadway, at the far end of the row, between the last section of cars and Building 1, was an upfit Mustang with its lights on.

There was no sound. Or maybe my heart was thumping so loud in my ears I couldn't hear anything else.

I started for the car, my thoughts a blur. I was terrified but had to move. I had to get to the Mustang before the killer pulled the trigger. Before Russo was shot in the eyes.

The hot-rod headlights were blinding me as I went past Building 2. I gripped the Colt with my right hand and shielded my eyes with my left.

I called out loud enough for him to hear me in the car. "Ronnie is that you? Talk to me, Ronnie."

No answer. *Fuck me. I'm dead. It's a trap, and I'm dead.*

I walked down the row, pointing the Colt at the hot-rod's windshield. If it was the killer and not Russo, I was going to get a few shots off before he murdered me.

I wanted to get the hell out. Run the other way. But I didn't. I kept walking. Step by step into the lights.

When I was twenty feet from the Mustang, the glare of the headlights fell below my eye level. It was an older model, with spoilers and badass pipes sticking out of the hood. I could see through the windshield into the car. It was empty. No one inside. Just sitting in the middle of the two-lane with its lights on.

What the hell is this? What in the world?

An angry car engine roared to life behind me. I spun around.

A souped-up Camaro growled at the other end of the row, lights on, engine revving and revving and revving.

I froze in all the ways a person can freeze. My body wouldn't move. My mind wouldn't move. My heart stopped beating. I was sure I stopped blinking. I didn't know what to think, what to say, what the hell to do.

The Camaro took off down the row like a drag racer.

I felt fury and nothing else.

For reasons I will never understand, I walked toward the Camaro as it gunned for me, shouting *Fuck you* into the night. *Fuck you for killing my father. Fuck you for killing me.*

My eyes filled with tears of rage. I fired once into the windshield. Then fired again. I stopped between Buildings 1 and 2, still in the middle of the roadway, waiting for the Camaro to break every bone in my body.

But Fu came flying from the shadows, lifted me off the ground and onto his shoulder as if I were made of papier-mâche, and ran straight toward the speeding car.

Everything was a blur, but when we were three feet from the Camaro, a blink from a collision that would have killed us both instantly, Fu jumped into the air like a gold-medal Olympic hurdler, hit the hood with his first stride, kept running, hit the roof, kept running, hit the trunk, and then crashed to the ground with me still on his shoulder.

Even though it only was a split second, as we went over the windshield, I saw the driver of the Camaro.

Ronnie Russo.

Tied to the driver's seat, hands taped to the wheel, eyes shot out of his skull.

Fu and I hit the ground, and the Camaro smashed head-on into the Mustang. It was so loud and so violent I thought my head would explode.

In that same second, police cars and unmarked sedans crashed through the RJM gates. Uniformed cops and plain-clothes detectives, guns drawn, surrounded the scene, surrounded me and Fu. *Except Fu was gone.* It was just me on the roadway. Me, the massive head-on collision at the end of the row, and two dozen cops.

"Put your hands on your head," someone yelled. "Hands on your head now."

I realized at that moment I'd lost the Colt when Fu carried me up and over the speeding Camaro. It was somewhere on the ground. I had no idea where.

I raised my arms, and a cop came up behind me, grabbed my wrists and cuffed my hands behind my back.

I was stunned. Head still spinning. I'd been too late to save Ronnie Russo. Close, but too freaking late. I hadn't seen the killer, but he'd seen me and almost taken me out with the late race-car driver already dead behind the wheel, driving toward me at sixty miles per hour without his eyes.

"Are you kidding me, McCall?" Logan said, pulling me back into the moment with just the sound of his anger.

"I called you, Logan. I left you a voicemail," I said in my hapless defense.

"While you were working a case I distinctly told you not to work," Logan said. "A case I manifestly ordered you to stay the fuck away from. A case you patently promised to avoid."

"You were onto the wrong Russo," I said.

"Logan," some detective said. "He's in the Camaro. His eyes are gone. Two shots fired into the vehicle."

"Lew."

It was Jesse, Logan's young partner. He held up the Colt so Logan could see it.

"Oh my fucking God," Logan said, looking at me. "You cannot be serious about this, McCall. The gun? Again?"

"I can explain," I said.

"No, you absofuckinglutely can't," Logan said, "because you are under arrest for the fifth time in three months."

"Don't tell my son," I said as they put me in a squad car.

"Oh, I'm not going to tell him," Logan said. "You are."

Meaning even a shit show like this could get worse.

18

YOU SHOULD CONSIDER HAVING
YOUR MOTHER INSTITUTIONALIZED

THEY FOUND THE TWO SLUGS I'D SHOT INTO THE CAMARO. Neither had hit Ronnie Russo twelve, a fortunate bit of good fortune for me since that meant the Colt had not killed him, but not a big enough bit to spare me the acrimony, disappointment, distrust, and frustration coming at me in waves on the third floor, the homicide floor, of the Thirteenth Precinct on 21st Street between Second and Third.

Logan's desk was in the center of the big, open squad room. It was actually two desks facing each other, forming one massive square desk for Logan and whoever was unlucky enough to be Logan's partner at the time. Since I'd known him —five arrests and counting—he'd had two partners. Harriman and now Jesse. Even handcuffed to the chair by the adjoined desks, I wasn't sure who I felt worse for: me or Jesse. Probably me.

Logan's desk was a sight to see. Layers and layers of newspapers and police papers and magazines and notes and photographs and paper bags and hand-scratched drawings and road maps and candy-bar wrappers and more notes and calendars and stickies in all the colors of the rainbow. Excavating through them to the desk itself would be like an archeological dig in the desert, each level a snapshot of time and place. Occasionally, the papers would shuffle, and visitors and perps alike would get a glance of the corner of Logan's antique Royal typewriter. Or maybe one of his three gigantic Rolodexes might momentarily appear.

It was not a mess, Logan's desk. It was three decades past mess. It was a museum piece.

Matthew sat opposite me. Since Jimmy had left me his PI business-in-a-box and I'd become a private investigator, my son had dialed up the pressure on parenting me, which had been cute when he was five but was decidedly unpleasant now that he was a twenty-eight-year-old assistant district attorney. I'd interrupted an enjoyable evening out for him and Repugnant Nina, his wife in eleven days, the soon-to-be mother of my grandchild. You might think that since Logan had already arrested me four times, Matthew would have become accustomed to his feelings about my being cuffed and in custody by arrest number five. You would be mistaken.

"What am I supposed to do with you, Mom?" Matthew said. "Apparently, there's no bottom for you. Just when I think you've sunk as low as you can sink, you fall off a cliff and descend to a depth I couldn't have predicted."

"At least I called to tell you myself," I said.

It was the best I could do. That's how pathetic I was feeling. I loved my son so much. It hurt my heart to see him this upset with me.

"Because Detective Logan made you," Matthew said.

"Which repudiates the apprehension," Shavelson said. He was sitting across from Logan at Jesse's desk. "My client is entitled to a phone call, and the arresting officer forced her to contact her son instead of her attorney. A blatant disregard of her rights."

"I'm not your client," I said to Shavelson.

"That's what Jimmy used to say," Shavelson said.

I'd inherited Mel Shavelson along with Jimmy's box, and there was no getting rid of him. He was as disheveled a man as had ever been born. Pig Pen from *Charlie Brown*. Or Pig Pen from the Grateful Dead. Or maybe a marginalized Mark Twain character covered with Mississippi mud like Huck and Jim.

Shavelson was overweight in a way that prevented his shirt from remaining tucked into his pants. His belt, obliviated by his bulk, had no say in the matter. He smoked Marlboros, Lucky Strikes, Pall Malls, and Winstons, often at the same time—all four brands burning simultaneously in an overloaded ashtray. I'd seen him do it. He drank Johnnie Black on ice at ten in the morning while eating pastrami sandwiches, drinking rude coffee, and smoking like a chimney. He was incorrigible, irredeemable, unstoppable, unflappable. A cartoon Tasmanian Devil with a bursting blizzard of paperwork in his overstuffed briefcase. Unruly dark hair, small black eyes, a thick neck no tie could tame, and a huge head.

His wife was taking him for everything he had in an acrimonious divorce for the ages because Shavelson had slept with another woman. Which meant miracles were possible. Not that he'd slept with *another* woman, though that in itself was miraculous, but that he'd slept with a woman in the first place, a woman who'd then married him. He was truly one of a kind. When he died, *if* he died—which he might not seeing as how he was probably preserved and petrified by Scotch and tobacco and fatty meats—there would never be another like him.

"Shove it, Shavelson," Logan and Matthew said in unison.

"Shove it, Shavelson," I said. "How did you even get here?"

"Mole in the system," Shavelson said. "Calls me quick when one of my clients is taken into custody."

"Which should never have happened because I didn't shoot him," I said to Logan. "We've been around this block before. Russo was killed elsewhere, probably suffocated. Then the killer shot his eyes out so everyone would know it was him."

"Like Jimmy," Matthew said.

"Like Jimmy," I said. "It was a trap, Logan. The killer was out to get me. Or you. I didn't kill Russo."

"Maybe you did, maybe you didn't," Logan said. "Either way, I can gin up your charges and hold you here until I catch the scumbag myself. Keep you away from me and keep you alive at the same time. Two birds with one stone."

"Ah, yes, the gin-up-your-charges-so-I-can-hold-you-here trick," Shavelson said. "Works well in countries that don't have a constitution."

"The Colt was fired twice," I said to Logan. "You have both bullets. I called you in advance. Which, by the way, gets me gold stars, so can you please take the cuffs off and give me some coffee? Or a beer. How about a beer?"

"You're impossible, Mom," Matthew said.

"But I'm innocent, Matthew," I said.

"Innocent as charged, guilty of everything that matters," Matthew said.

"Exactly," Logan said. "You are the most guilty person I've ever met, McCall. Guilty of obstinance, stupidity, reckless self-endangerment, foolhardiness, unwarranted self-confidence, and bothersome behavior instigating unnecessary exasperation and irritation at every turn, triggering new levels of frustration and aggravation in everyone you meet, especially me."

"And me," Matthew said.

"Not me," Shavelson said.

"Shove it, Shavelson," I said.

"Shove it, Shavelson," Matthew said.

"Shove it, Shavelson," Logan said. "But, yes, as miserable as it makes me, McCall, you are innocent of killing Ronnie Russo."

He nodded at Jesse, who was leaning against a nearby file

cabinet because Shavelson was in his chair. Jesse walked over and took off the cuffs. My wrists ached.

All around us, homicide detectives went about their busy business. There were other murders that needed their attention. Murders that didn't involve the corporate assassin who'd killed my father and Ronnie Russo and a half dozen other people. Murders that didn't involve Logan's task force, which was still grinding it out at RJM Motors in Jamaica. They would be there all night and all day trying to find a telltale piece of evidence that would lead them somewhere significant. It was a waste of time. I knew it, and so did Logan.

"Well, my client is in the clear, so my job is done," Shavelson said, repacking his briefcase with files and folders and more papers than could fit in the thing.

"I'm not your client," I said.

"That's what Jimmy used to say," Shavelson said, leaving like a dust storm.

"Asshole-smokestack-prick," Logan said.

"I'm out too," Matthew said. "There's no point in asking you not to investigate this case anymore, is there? To promise you'll stop and stay home and stay put and stay out of it for your own sake and for my sake and for everyone's sake?"

"No point I can think of," I said.

"Right," Matthew said. "Well, then at least try not to get arrested between now and my wedding, I'd prefer not to do the ceremony in a prison."

"You'll have to talk to Logan about that," I said. "He keeps arresting me for no reason. I think it's because he wants us to spend more time together."

"You should consider having your mother institutionalized," Logan said.

"What makes you think I'm not considering it?" Matthew said.

"Love you, Matthew," I said.

"Love you, Mom," Matthew said.

He nodded at Logan and at Jesse and left the Thirteenth to resume his night with Know-Nothing Nina.

Logan looked at me. "Let me ask you a question, McCall. Does your brain not work in any capacity approaching normal?"

It was just like my father would have said it. Same shake of the head. Same roll of the eyes.

"Works well enough to know what's next," I said.

"No kidding. And what is that? What's next?" Logan said.

"That you and I work in tandem," I said.

Logan sat back and folded his arms. Probably to stop himself from reaching out and grabbing me by the throat. But he drilled me with his eyes, and he could see I was serious, that I had a plan of sorts. He was at his wit's end, and we both knew it.

"Jesse, give me a minute alone with this lunatic," Logan said. "If you see me pull my gun, don't stop me from shooting her."

Jesse nodded and left us alone.

"At the very top of the long list of stupid questions I have asked in my thirty-year career sits this godforsaken beauty: What do you have in mind, McCall?"

"Russo has—had—four partners," I said. "One of them hired the killer to take Ronnie out. It's a power grab. Power and money, Logan. Like Monument Life. Like Superior Press. Like Lowry Lowe. Whichever partner it is, he's not done. He's settling scores and taking control. His other partners are next in line."

"And?"

"And let's work the partners together."

"You and me. That's what you're suggesting?"

"Yes. Try something different. Something new. You did it your way and got the wrong Russo. I got the right Russo but didn't have the team to take the killer down. No task-force manpower on my side. Too big a fleet to navigate the investigation on yours. You said so yourself."

He held his breath and stared off into the cosmos, maybe looking for inspiration, maybe hoping he'd wake up from a bad dream.

"Plus, I don't want to get arrested again," I said. "I think I've been arrested enough. Five times being arrested is my limit, and if you're working with me and I'm working with you and we're working with each other, then you probably can't cuff me for obstruction or intrusion or being a menace to society or whatever reasons you usually cuff me for. Am I right? I am. I'm right, aren't I? Logan? Logan?"

He took an evidence bag from his desk. The Colt was inside.

"I'm going to give your gun back, McCall," he said, "so you can shoot me in the head. Because I'm going to try it your way this one time."

I took the gun and put it in my purse. "You won't be sorry."

"I'm already sorry," he said.

19

PLANTERS-O-PLENTY

It was past midnight when the paper pushers processed me out of the Thirteenth Precinct. Turned out it was as time-consuming to get un-arrested as it was to get arrested. When I got back to the House of Emotional Tics, I went up to the fifth floor and knocked on Al's door because I knew Al would be up. I offered him another two hundred bucks to run research on Ronnie Russo's remaining partners. I would have done the deep-dive due diligence myself, but I was exhausted because Wednesday had been one of those days. Meaning if someone had asked me if I'd pay two bills to sleep right now as opposed to *not* paying two bills and staying up googling for five more hours, my answer would have been: take my money. So Al took my money. Al always took my money. Al always took everybody's money. Anybody's money.

I called Big Black Bald Bart, even though it was one in the morning, to make sure he still had Rick under wraps. He did. They were in the guest room in Dennis and Posey's loft on the second floor of the D-Cup warehouse, eating ice cream and bingeing comedy on Netflix. I heard Rick in the background and realized I was still furious with him for going to Silvercup. I asked Bart to stay with Rick until I got there tomorrow, meaning later today, meaning it was already Thursday. I said I would pay him well for his time and service. He told me it was on the house on account of his getting a role in the strip-club musical.

Like I said, Wednesday had been one of those days.

I slept six hours, then went to Raul's and worked my butt to the bone. Raul busted my chops—while breaking them—by asking me every ten minutes where my boyfriend was. He meant Rick. I tried to explain that Rick was not my boyfriend, that he was my client, but Raul wasn't having any of that noise. *"Maybe he not your boyfriend now, Tortuga, but he be soon."* *Tortuga* means "turtle" in Spanish. That was my nickname in the gym. Raul had called me that for thirty years because that was how slow he said I was. What a comedian. My comeback would have been: *"He's not my boyfriend, he's my fiancé."* But since Raul wasn't biting on the whole client story, I let it go.

I showered, did some brownstone business, and updated my case notes while inhaling a bowl of granola, yogurt, and berries, all fresh, hand-picked, and homemade by the fabulous farmers at the Union Square Greenmarket. Then I drove the White Whale to the D-Cup to collect my client.

Dennis and Posey were running a rehearsal for Chloe Burns, the actor playing the role of Professor Johnny Jedry, the heartsick Columbia art professor who drops LSD for the first time on her way to the Metropolitan Museum, where she hopes the paintings and sculpture will help revive her passion for life and love.

It's a spur-of-the-moment acid trip she inexplicably decides to take when the perfect-stranger cabbie passes her an extra dose he just happens to have on hand. That Jedry has never once done an impetuous thing in her life, meaning not one single moment of spontaneity in her whole time living, had not stopped Dennis and Posey from having the professor accept the drug and do it in the cab. *"Desperation makes otherwise dull people daring,"* they'd told the confused cast at the table read. Such was the depth of character development at the D-Cup. Story logic had suffered a similar fate. For the Schmidt and Parker Players, the plot holes had plot holes in their plot holes.

Nine months ago, Chloe had climbed into her sister's Chevy Malibu in Akron, Ohio, hometown of the Burns family since 1898, the very year the Goodyear Tire and Rubber Company was founded in that very town, and driven to New York, where she intended to become the brightest light on Broadway. Curiously, she'd never been in a musical. Or a play. Or a band. Or a choir. Or a dance company. Never once been onstage. It had been a whispering whim that she could be a star. And her family, who'd worked at Goodyear since, well, 1898, had thought that was just fine. If anyone could make it on Broadway, Chloe had told them, she could. No vulcanized rubber for this Akron gal. Just clear skies and smooth sailing all the way to a bite of the Big Apple.

The problem was she had no talent. Zero. She couldn't sing or dance or act or anything close to it. But she was beautiful. Truly. Supermodel looks. *Playboy* body. Drop-dead, drop-the-mic, drop-everything gorgeous. So Dennis and Posey, big-hearted thespians that they were, had cast Chloe as a lesbian lover of vampire women in *Blood Song and Dance* and as Professor Jedry in *Psychedelic Sunday*, thinking they could teach her to sing and dance and act while making both productions *look* better. It had not worked out as planned. Surprise!

Chloe was rehearsing the scene in which she and Adonis (Roger), who pops out of the Peter Paul Rubens painting with Venus (me), sing and dance a hot-and-bothered romantic song —"Doing the Dirty with Adonis"—in the gallery of romantics. The people in the paintings of Goya, Gericault, Delacroix, and Blake come to life, climb off the canvas, and join them for the chorus.

Roger wasn't here, so Rick filled in, playing the part of Adonis. I wasn't in this scene. It was just Adonis and Jedry getting steamy. I stood at the back of the theater and watched.

Chloe's performance was as awkward and bewildering as it always was. Like Elaine dancing in *Seinfeld*, if Elaine wasn't sure if she was Elaine or Selena Meyer from VEEP or Julie Kavner's character in *Rhoda* or Daryl Hannah with an eye patch in *Kill Bill* or her actual real-life self, the brilliant Julia Louis-Dreyfus. But God bless America, Chloe was stunning onstage. She was so extremely beautiful, in fact, that it was *almost* possible to overlook her off-the-rails portrayal of a heartbroken art professor on acid dirty dancing with a Greek god who's jumped out of a painting on a random Sunday afternoon at the Met. Almost.

Mercifully, the scene ended before Chloe hurt anyone. Dennis and Posey had one-on-one-on-one work to do with Chloe, a Hail Mary to right the ship of the show before opening night tomorrow, and Rick was excused from the stage.

He walked my way, smiling as if he had not a care in the world, like as long as he could eat ice cream and binge comedy all night and have red-hot fake sex onstage with Chloe all day, it didn't matter that he'd disobeyed my explicit instructions and left the safe harbor of the House of Emotional Tics for the hurricane undertow of a Ruby Gold pilot.

"Not sure I'm Greek-god material, but I gave it a go," he said. "Maybe if I was standing in for the Greek god of comedy instead of Adonis."

"Goddess," I said. "Greek goddess of comedy. Thaleia. You were fine."

"You're still mad."

"Why would I be mad? Because yesterday you went to Silvercup after I told you not to and the bear blew three holes in your chest and upon overnight reflection you decided to dry hump Chloe Burns—the kind of young, beautiful starlet, by the way, you have a long, sordid, tabloid history of screwing and then screwing over—and look like you're having fun while doing it live onstage? Oh my, would you look at that. I'm still mad after all. Jesus, grow up, Rick. She's too young for you."

"You're my therapist now?"

"No, but you need one."

"I have one. More than one. They're disposable. Like juice boxes."

He was funny. I tried not to laugh. It was easier because I was pissed at him.

"I'm sorry," he said. "I wasn't trying to get shot. I wore the vest. I went along with you being my fiancée. And overnight reflection is easier said than done with Big Black Bald Bart. And, yes, I was having fun with Chloe. She's gorgeous. But she's also nuts, right? I'm not making that up? She's kind of nuts?"

"Because you wore the vest and played my fiancé, I accept your apology on one condition."

"Name it."

"When it comes to bodyguard business, you do what I say from now on."

"When it comes to bodyguard business, you're the boss."

We shared a look that sealed that deal, and then we watched Chloe.

"You're not making it up," I said after a while. "She's all kinds of nuts. During *Blood Song and Dance*, the show before this show, she lost the line between her real self, the innocent Ohio girl with Broadway dreams, her character in *that* show, a lesbian lover of vampire women, and her character in *this* show, the heartsick art professor who drops acid and dry humps Greek gods that pop out of paintings, which we were rehearsing at the same time we were performing the other show."

"So a full-on mixed bag of nuts."

"Planters-o-Plenty. During *Blood*, we never knew who she was going to be in any given scene. Chloe from Akron, her character in the show we were doing, her character in the show we were rehearsing, or some other character in some other show from some other universe. All bets are off who she'll be tomorrow night."

"What happens if it's the wrong character at the wrong time?"

"We keep doing the show. Chloe comes along for the ride. Like when you take your crazy cousin to the carnival, and she stuffs cotton candy up her nose and in her ears, and it's weird as shit, but she's beautiful, and she's nice, and she's your cousin, and at least you're still at the carnival. It's exciting in a way. Like a rollercoaster live onstage. We're used to it now. The audience likes her too, so that's good. They don't know what the hell she's doing up there, but they like her because she puts her heart in it."

"Champion dry humper, that's for sure."

"As I said, you looked like you were having fun."

"Don't be jealous, McCall."

"I'm not jealous. I'm too pissed off at you for going to Ruby Gold's pilot to be jealous, which I'm not going to be anyway because you're not my type."

"I'm not your type?"

"Not even close."

"That's funny. You're not my type either. So what are we going to do?"

"About us?" I cringed and turned five shades of crimson. "Professionally us, not personally. Professionally."

He laughed. "Yes, professionally us."

"We're going to let the pig go."

"We're what?"

We went to the empty room backstage where the pig had been stashed. He was tied to a chair, gagged, and blindfolded, like we'd left him. Dennis and Posey had fed him bread and water (so he could experience prison, they'd told me), so the pig was ready to run. We untied his ankles, helped him stand, led him across the empty theater to the elevator, and then down to the D-Cup loading dock, where the White Whale waited.

We drove him around the block three times and pulled to the curb one block north of the D-Cup. It was a quiet block to begin with, and today it was quieter still. Rick helped the pig out of the back seat, walked him to an empty building, and sat him on the sidewalk facing the bricks. Then he untied the pig's hands and hurried back to the car.

By the time the pig had removed the gag and blindfold, we'd driven away. Though just across the street, where we could watch him. He had no idea what kind of car he'd been in, so he didn't give us a second look.

He walked to the corner and grabbed a cab. We followed him to the Boulevard Motor Inn on Queens Boulevard, a junky, low-rent, three-story joint in a forgotten Flushing neighborhood. He got out of the cab, went into the motel, and stayed there.

"Now what?" Rick said.

"Death by boredom," I said.

"Every comedian's nightmare," Rick said.

20

I DON'T NEED NO STINKING
SIGNATURES

WE'D BEEN SITTING SILENTLY IN THE COROLLA FOR FORTY minutes, which felt like four hours but was really the equivalent of four minutes in surveillance time. *"Just warming up,"* Jimmy would say after two hours on a park bench or in a greasy spoon or somewhere just off the radar of whoever we were watching.

"How much longer?" Rick said.

"Until what?" I'd been texting back and forth with Al, Logan, and Big Black Bald Bart.

"Something happens."

"First fact of surveillance: nothing ever happens until it does or, more likely, doesn't."

"Who told you that?"

"Jimmy. My father. He was a private investigator. I inherited the business from him."

"Retired?"

"Murdered. This past July."

"Oh, shit, sorry, McCall. I didn't know."

I nodded. It wasn't something I walked around telling people.

"I got my PI license because he made me. It was his way of keeping me close and out of trouble. I sat surveillance with him tons of times. Nothing ever happened until it did or, most likely, didn't. I hated every minute of it."

"Why didn't you quit?"

"Because I loved every minute of it."

"In my normal human life, I would let that go, but since I'm trapped in this clown car with the woman who said it, I'm not going to."

"Spoiler alert. You don't have a normal human life. I loved my father and wanted to spend as much time with him as I could. So even though I hated it, I loved it. Jimmy was my captive audience on surveillance. I had him all to my selfish self. But he had me too, and he liked that as much as I did. My mother died when I was ten, and I had school, and he had work, and then I got pregnant, and Matthew was born when I was seventeen, and Jimmy wasn't always there when I was growing up. He turned around, and I was a single mom working odd jobs to make a buck. Surveillance was like home schooling on the job. He was teaching me the trade and life lessons. Being my dad."

"How old were you when he made you get your license?"

"Maybe twenty-two."

He nodded. Talking about Jimmy had resonated with him somehow. "My father left when I was nine. He was a hard drinker, nasty drunk. One day he hit my mother, and she cracked him in the head with a cast-iron pan. He left that afternoon. I remember him walking down the driveway, bloody bandage on his head, ratty suitcase in his hand. I never saw him after that. My mother had told him if he ever touched her or me or my sister again, she would kill him on the spot. She was definitely not kidding. You'd like her. She's tough as balls and funny as hell."

"Where is she?"

"San Diego. I bought her a house when I was twenty. I bought my sister a house there too. I haven't seen either one of them in more than ten years."

"Surveillance is a good time to reconnect. I pay bills, write letters, make phone calls, answer emails, text people. You have all day until you don't or, most likely, do."

We were quiet after that, watching the Boulevard Motor Inn for any sign of the pig, lost in our own time and space.

After what felt like a long while in surveillance time but was probably only five minutes, Rick said, "So what are we doing here, McCall?"

"What am I doing here, or what are you doing here?"

"What's the difference?"

"You're here because you hired me to be your bodyguard, and I can't protect you if you're not where I am or where I can keep tabs on you. I'm here because I'm going to catch the asshole who tried to kill me and nail him to the wall."

"So we're trying to catch Kenny Cochran's killer before my hearing?"

"If it makes you happy to look at it that way, then sure, we're trying to catch Cochran's killer before your hearing. But mostly, you're tagging along while I nail the pig and the bear and whoever the hell hired them to kill Cochran and you but mostly me. *'You take me down, I take you down harder.'* Jimmy McCall life lesson learned on surveillance. *'Nothing wrong with a grudge if they deserve it.'* That's another one."

"My mother would like you, McCall."

Just then, the back passenger-side door opened, and Big Black Bald Bart somehow folded his long body into the Corolla's back seat. He had a briefcase and a small cooler.

"Ready, Freddy," Bart said to me while shooting Rick a wide smile.

"He doesn't leave the car. Period. You brought bottles to take a leak?" I said.

"Two for him, two for me," Bart said.

"What the hell?" Rick said.

"Get out and come around the car. You're going to sit here and wait for the pig," I said. "Bart's your bodyguard until I get back."

"Where are you going?" Rick said.

"Meeting Logan," I said.

"Why can't I come?" Rick said.

"Because surveillance is your punishment for doing the pilot after I told you not to," I said.

"But I wore the vest."

"Which is the reason I didn't kill you myself."

I climbed out of the Corolla. Rick came around, took my place behind the wheel, and rolled down the window.

"If the pig leaves the pen, call me right away and then follow him wherever he goes. But don't let him see you," I said. "I'll be back later."

"Surveillance sucks," Rick said.

"Come on, Rick, my brother," Bart said, holding up the cooler and his laptop. "I got ice cream and Netflix."

"Don't forget to watch for the pig," I said, walking away to hail a cab.

While we'd been settling into surveillance, Al had texted to tell me the mainframes had landed on the RJM partner most likely to hire a corporate assassin to remove his partners from the business. We'd gone back and forth, redoing the deal we'd already done, meaning Al wanted another fifty for the report, which I'd agreed to because I wasn't there to punch him in the nose.

So he'd emailed me the report. There were four partners. The late Ronnie Russo, Jake Brotherton, Mitchell Joyner—the RJM of RJM—and a fourth partner who's first-name initial wasn't on the logo, Will Duckett.

They'd been three young and ballsy racing buddies, a

rowdy team that had traveled up and down the East Coast grinding out a living on the stock-car circuit. Ronnie was the driver, Jake built the engines, Mitchell ran the crew, facilitated the logistics, and handled the paperwork, and Duckett, a real-estate and business investor in Queens who loved fast cars, wild women, and good times, invested in the boys, controlled the money, and went for the ride.

When they'd burned out after a decade of being on the road ten months a year, Ronnie, Jake, and Mitchell had gone to Duckett and asked him to front the cash for a motor-car company in which Speed Racer Ronnie would be the front man and run the show, Motormouth Mitchell would sell used cars by the bushel, and Two Brake Jake would run a team of mechanics that would tune the cars into tip-top shape. On the same lot at the same time, RJM would upfit stock cars for fanatics and manage racing teams of young studs like they'd been before they'd acquired wives and kids and families at home. Back in the day, Ronnie, the mover and shaker of RJM, had it all schemed out: plans, drawings, numbers, everything.

Duckett had been the partner with dough. He'd made big bucks investing in street-smart ideas, taking a piece of the pie, and owning the land upon which the business did business. He'd made money when the RJM boys were on the road and had thought he could make more money still. He'd purchased a large industrial lot near the East River in Jamaica, signed RJM to a long-term lease, and funded the business Ronnie had devised.

Everything had been wine and roses for fifteen years until Jamaica was ready to join the rest of Queens and build high-rent condos with East River views. Duckett had received an offer he couldn't refuse to sell the land upon which RJM had ruled the racing roost for more than a decade. WD, as he called himself, had wanted RJM to sign a lease-termination agreement so condos could be built where used cars now sat. Who knew how many millions had hung in the balance?

Odds are RJM wouldn't sign, so Duckett made plans to eliminate the reason for their signatures, Al had said in a text. *As in, I don't need no stinking signatures.*

Still in the White Whale waiting for the pig to find the courage to call the bear or the boss, I'd sent Zombie Al's RJM report to Logan and texted with him while I'd texted with Al and reached out to Duckett.

In the Thirteenth, Logan had said he'd try it my way this one time, so we'd decided to meet across the street from Duckett's office, located on Jamaica Avenue near the corner of 164th Street.

This part of Jamaica Avenue was a long stretch of low-end retail, mostly two- and three-story buildings—stores on the street level, offices above. Duckett's building was two stories. A Baskin Robbins, a fabric place, a five-dollar shoe store, and a vape shop occupied the four storefronts on the first floor. Duckett had the entire second. The entrance was in the middle. A blue awning over the doorway helped folks find it. A sign attached to the second floor read, *WD Investments: Business and Real Estate Brokerage, Management, and Development.*

WD. Will Duckett.

I handed Logan a fake mustache, a fedora, and big, black-frame glasses. "Put them on. You're not a cop today."

Logan shook his head in agony. "Then who the hell am I?"

21

DUCKETT'S ON THE DOCKET

AS WE CLIMBED THE STAIRS TO DUCKETT'S OFFICE, LOGAN LOST his patience. Then again, he'd lost it in the '90s and never gotten it back, so nothing new there.

"Stay in character no matter what happens, and follow my lead," I said.

"This is the most moronic thing I have ever done in my entire career as a cop," he said. "Possibly the goddamn dumbest thing I have ever done in my life. Likely the most pointless piece of half-baked, half-witted, thick-headed stupid shit I will ever do going forward because this is absofuckinglutely the last time I ever fucking follow your lead anywhere."

"That's the spirit," I said.

We arrived at Duckett's door. Logan looked like a totally different human. I could hardly recognize him, and he was three feet in front of my face.

To match Logan's suit-off-the-rack look, I'd chosen a red wig with blue contact lenses, blue business slacks with a matching jacket, and a red blouse. I could have been someone named MacKenzie O'Leary, a loan officer at an unidentified Brooklyn branch, and, in fact, had played that very role in the independent pilot *Deadhead Redhead*, which told the tale of a UPS driver murdering red-haired women week after week for reasons no one could explain. On the first day of principal photography, the writer/director/producer was run over by a redheaded woman driving a UPS truck. The project died with him. The good news was everyone in the cast and crew became big believers in karma and kismet, no small feat in that day and age. Plus, I'd taken home O'Leary's wig and wardrobe.

Duckett's reception area was like the lobby of a New Jersey strip club trying hard to go upscale and classy but going garish and tasteless and tacky instead. A large open room in the center of the building. To the right was a hallway that led to a half dozen or more offices, WD's real-estate managers, business brokers, bookkeepers, and so on. There was a copy room and a breakroom, and there were people down that hallway busy as bees. To the left stood double doors with brass plates engraved with the initials WD. Duckett had taken the entire left side of the building for himself. He was that kind of charmer.

"MacKenzie and Harry O'Leary for Mr. Duckett. We have an appointment," I said to Tiffany, the babe Duckett had hired as office eye candy to keep the riffraff at arm's length. She sat at an absurdly large reception desk that could only be described as gaudy. Yes, even the reception desk was gaudy. Gold leaf accents. Don't ask. Tiffany and I had spoken on the phone when I'd called from the cab on my way to Queens to make the meeting. She'd made me want to gag with her elfin sexpot voice, her glamour-girl giggle, and her flirty femme fatale phone facade. My opinion of her was worse in person.

She smiled as she came out from behind her desk, walked to Duckett's doors, and went into his private sanctum.

"Duckett's a dead end," Logan said to me.

"Duckett's on the docket," I said.

"Mr. Duckett will see you now," Tiffany said, gesturing like a *Price is Right* hostess presenting some lucky winner with a two-week Caribbean cruise for sexy singles. She was standing in the double doorway, both doors open. Behind her was a sight to see.

The suite was enormous, ridiculously large for an office on the second floor of a low-rise, low-rent retail building in a junky Jamaica shopping neighborhood. It was also unexpectedly sleek and modern. Also showy and lurid. Not to mention loud and brash. Gold leaf (yes, more) and stainless steel. Black leather and black walnut. Fancy uplighting. A massive desk with four chairs in front, side tables between the chairs. A living-room area with two large sofas and a flat-screen TV. A full freaking bar with six bar stools. Who had an office like this? Maybe some Saudi prince. Or Hugh Hefner in his prime. I expected half naked women to offer me martinis and hors d'oeuvres. It wouldn't have surprised me to see Duckett in silk pajamas and a robe, but he was in Armani from head to toe

WD was in his midfifties. Full head of slicked-back hair. Manicure. Probably a pedicure. Pinky ring. Diamond earring. Pricey gold watch. There were mirrors everywhere. Duckett's biggest admirer was Duckett himself. Nobody loved Duckett more than Duckett loved Duckett.

The man had made millions with nothing but balls and street smarts. He saw himself as classy and cultured, the James Bond of Jamaica, Queens, but was only a flamboyant hustler.

"Mr. and Mrs. O'Leary, please," Duckett said, standing behind his aircraft-carrier desk, gesturing for me and Logan to sit in the chairs facing him.

"MacKenzie," I said, "and this is my father, Harry."

"Nice to meet you both," Duckett said as Logan and I walked across the room and Tiffany shut the double doors behind us. "Welcome to my slice of paradise."

"Nice," I said as we smiled insincere smiles and took our seats.

There was small talk about the weather and the stock

market and some professional sports gambling gossip and some other index rate bullshit I had no interest in and that Logan had less. Duckett used the time to measure us in the same way I (and I'm sure Logan too) used it to measure him. He was sharp in his crude Queens way—he didn't make millions by being a moron—but I had the sense his ego might just get the better of him. He insisted we call him WD and get down to brass tacks. I could hear Logan's jawbone grinding into dust.

"Thank you, WD," I said. "My father and I are silent partners in a chain of laundromats in western New Jersey. Hundred outlets. Nothing fancy. Just machines and vending for detergent and soap and soda and so on."

"I get that your father's silent," Duckett said. "Probably not you, though, am I right?"

He leered at me in a way that made my skin crawl. "You're right about that, WD," I said, flirting back. "I make noise."

Duckett laughed. "Good business, laundromats. Everybody needs clean clothes. I owned a few in my time. Sold the land, made a mint, and moved on. How many partners you got?"

"Four total," I said. "Me and my father own twenty-five percent of the business, and three other guys own twenty-five percent each. They came to us five years ago, and we fronted the money. It's been a great ride."

"What do you think, Harry?" Duckett said to Logan. "Great ride?"

"Stellar," Logan said. "All cash. More coins than you can count."

"Like it," Duckett said. "What's the issue?"

"We have an opportunity to buy another western Jersey chain, but that chain will only sell to our chain, not to me and my father separately, and we have to take the name of the new chain for all the stores. Those are the conditions," I said.

"Money works out?" Duckett said.

"Stellar," Logan said. "Crazy not to do it."

"Then who cares about the name?" Duckett said. "The name of the game is money."

"Exactly," I said. "But our partners don't see it that way."

I could sense the tiniest bit of tightening around his smile. His radar had clicked on. All systems focused on Logan and me.

"Buy them out," Duckett said. "Problem solved."

"They won't sell," I said, "and they refuse to buy the other chain. They had nothing when we started, and now they have houses and cars and lives they like."

"They don't want to rock the boat," Logan said.

I looked at Logan and nodded. Ostensibly to say I agreed with his assessment but really to say *good fucking acting there, Chief.* Logan nodded back. I could tell he was hating every minute of this, but the game was going, and now he had no choice but to play along.

"Then you're stuck," Duckett said.

"Seems like it," Logan said.

"So why are you here?" Duckett said.

"We have a friend in Jersey," I said. "Stock-car racer. Has his cars upfit at RJM."

"We know you own the place. Piece of the place," Logan said.

"Our friend heard from his garage guys that you have an opportunity to sell the land for condos, and that your partners won't sell," I said.

"Our problem in reverse," Logan said.

"So why are you here?" Duckett said again. Except this time there was radar in his voice, and he wasn't trying to hide it.

"Our stock-car friend in Jersey said you found a solution," I said. "My father and I were hoping you could share it with us."

"What solution is that?" Duckett said. He was nobody's fool, even if he was a tasteless scumbag.

"If there's nobody to sign the papers except you, in your

case, and me and my daughter, in our case, then both deals get signed and the world turns," Logan said.

"Ronnie Russo's not signing any deals now," I said. "Or not *not* signing them, in your case."

"One down, two to go for you. None down, three to go for us," Logan said.

"You think I had somebody whack Ronnie Russo? That's what you're saying?" Duckett said.

"We're saying we have a ton of respect for you and your success and your business model," I said, "and that we would appreciate it if you would share the contact information, if you have any, that would allow us to follow in your footsteps. We would compensate you for your time and expertise, of course."

Duckett nodded as if he'd already decided what was to be done, the time and expertise he would offer Harry and MacKenzie O'Leary. He stood and headed to the bar.

"Anybody else need a drink?" Duckett said.

"Just what I fucking *don't* need," Logan said under his breath, barely loud enough for me to hear the incredulity in his voice.

"Name your price, WD," I said. "We'll pay it."

Duckett opened a drawer, removed a .44-caliber Smith & Wesson Dirty Harry handgun, and aimed it at me and Logan. The damn thing could blow a hole in your chest the size of a cannonball.

He came out from the behind the bar. "Do you assholes think you'd be the first fuckers I put down in this room?"

"You got to be shitting me," Logan said nice and loud this time so everyone could hear the incredulity in his voice. For the record, it was Olympic-gold-medal incredulity.

"Who the fuck are you? Because you sure as fuck aren't the O'Learys from buttfuck western New Jersey," Duckett said.

I nodded, reached into my purse, pulled the Colt, and pointed it at Duckett's chest. "You're right about that."

"What in the fucking fuck?" Logan said.

"We're not the O'Learys, Duckett," I said. "We're bounty hunters."

"Fucking bounty hunters. Of course we are," Logan said.

"Your business is your business," I said. "We don't want you. We want the killer you hired to take out your partners."

"Tiffany," Duckett said, calling for his eye candy.

The door opened and Tiffany came in holding a goddamn gun. She aimed it at me and Logan, kicked the door shut, and held her ground. Clearly, I'd underestimated her. She was a cold-stone assassin in a miniskirt and platform heels.

"Not the Barbie doll," Logan said, pulling his gun and pointing it at Tiffany.

Duckett and Tiffany moved their guns back and forth between Logan and me. We moved our guns forth and back between Duckett and Tiffany.

"So we all die in this dump unless you start talking," I said to Duckett.

"I thought you liked my office," Duckett said. "You said it was nice."

"A decor discussion? Are you people insane?" Logan said to all of us.

"Fuck it, Duckett," I said. "This place is *Penthouse* trash. Where's the killer and who's his next hit? Tell me that, and maybe my father doesn't blow your head off."

"What fucking planet are you people from?" Logan said.

"You want to know who the killer is, ask Jake," Duckett said. "If there's a hired gun in the game, it's Jake who brought him in."

"Why Jake?" I said.

"Ronnie and Mitch want to cash in and check out like me. Move on with their lives, for fuck's sake. Or Ronnie did, anyway. Mitch still does. Jake's got no life except RJM, so he won't sign the termination papers. So we got to have an official company vote at an official company meeting at the official company law firm to make the whole fucking thing official, which is going to be tomorrow, and Jake's going to lose that vote. Unless it's just him and me. Then it's a stalemate and the land deal is off."

"So Ronnie's dead yesterday, and Mitch is dead today?" I said.

"Seems like it," Duckett said. "Talk to Jake."

We stood there for five seconds, ten seconds, fifteen freaking seconds, guns still pointed at each other.

"Are you really bounty hunters?" Duckett said.

"Don't we look like bounty hunters?" I said.

"*You* do," Duckett said to me, then turned his attention—and .44 magnum—to Logan. "He looks like a sad sack laundromat man from west Jersey."

"And that, you fucknut fucking fuckwit, is today's last goddamn straw," Logan said, pulling his badge.

22

THERE'S NO SAYING NO TO MAD MIKE MONROE

"I'M OFF YOUR SHIT LIST, LOGAN," I SAID AS WE WALKED TOWARD his unmarked sedan. "You have to take me off the list."

"To the contrary, McCall," Logan said. "Today you have adhered yourself to my shit list with permanent Permabond on top of industrial-strength Gorilla Glue on top of Flex Seal rubberized super glue."

We arrived at his car. He took out his phone and dialed Jesse.

"Because of me and my plan, you now know who hired the killer and who gets hit next," I said.

"Because of you and your plan, I almost got my head blown off by a massive moron in Armani and his Kewpie doll receptionist. *And* I had to wear a fucking fedora."

"I agree, you're not a hat guy. But you didn't get shot, did you?"

Logan put his hand up because Jesse had answered the call.

"It's Lew," he said. "Good chance the next hit is Russo's partner, Mitchell Joyner, and that it happens today. So get everyone going that direction. Full throttle. Seems like the other partner, Jake Brotherton, the mechanic, hired the killer to whack Russo and now Joyner so they wouldn't sell the business out from under him. Yeah, find Brotherton too. I want Joyner and Brotherton on the board ten minutes ago."

He hung up and turned to me without missing a beat. "The only way off my shit list, McCall, is for you to bow out gracefully this very fucking minute and let me handle it from here. Can you do that, please?"

"Depends," I said.

"I said please, for fuck's sake. *And* I had to wear a fucking mustache. Upon what does it depend?"

"I agree, you're not a mustache man. Depends on what you mean by this very fucking minute. Do you mean after today when we save Joyner, arrest Brotherton, and catch the killer in the act? Yes, I can do that."

"There is no *we*, McCall. I tried it your way this one time. Over and done and never again. Jesus Christ, does your brain not work at all?"

Just like Jimmy would have said it.

"Depends."

"On what?"

"On what you mean by at all."

He rolled his eyes, but a hint of smile formed at the wee corners of his mouth. He opened his car door. "Stay home, stay put, stay out of my way. I should have my head examined for saying this, but I'll call you when we know something."

"Will any of that get me off your shit list?"

"Absofuckinglutely not."

"I didn't think so. Hey, if the cop thing doesn't work out, I'll get you an audition at the D-Cup. You played the laundromat man like you were born to be onstage. Or do laundry. One or the other. It was hard to tell. That's how good you were."

"I cannot now nor ever explain the level of loathing I feel for you, McCall," he said. And then he got in the car and drove away.

I grabbed a cab and went straight to the Boulevard Motor Inn. Rick and Bart were right where I'd left them, bored to death in the Toyota.

"No movement?" I said, sliding into the front passenger seat.

"Pig stayed put," Bart said from the back.

"The next time I sit surveillance for you is never," Rick said.

"Then I have good news," I said. "Bart's going to stay with the Corolla and wait for the pig, and we're going to take a field trip."

"What kind of field trip?" Rick said.

"Grubhub delivers to cars," I said to Bart, handing him five twenties. "That should cover your hours and food. If you need more, Rick will pay you when we get back."

"What do you mean *Rick* will pay you?" Rick said.

"Three fifty a day *plus expenses*," I said. "Bart's an expense. You got a problem paying Bart?"

"He brought me ice cream and Netflix," Rick said. "I'll pay any price."

"Yeah, you will, my brother. Now go forth and find your freedom," Bart said, smiling. "Big Black Bald Bart got his eyes on the prize."

We caught a cab to what once upon a time had been the old meatpacking district but was now one of the hippest neighborhoods in Manhattan. Located all the way west by the Hudson River, from 14th Street south to Ganesvoort, only a handful of butchery businesses were still in play from the nearly three hundred packing plants and slaughterhouses that had defined the district during the first half of the 1900s.

Shamrock Meat Market, near Ganesvoort and Little West 12th Street, had come to life in the 1980s, when many of the old meat warehouses were wild sex clubs and bars that serviced all manner of taboo tastes and entertainments. The storefront was retail in nature and size, in look and function. An old-school local butcher shop to be proud of. Anyone from anywhere could drop in and carry home steaks and chops and sausage and bacon butchered onsite. The back end of the business was more of a commercial operation, a butchery and market for hotels and restaurants.

"What are we doing here?" Rick said as the cab drove way.

I handed him the mustache, the fedora, and the glasses. "Finding the fucker who hired the bear and the pig to kill me. And you too."

"Or vice versa."

"Follow my lead."

"Follow it where?"

I was still wearing the red wig, the blue contacts, the blue slacks and jacket, and the red blouse. Rick wore black jeans, a sweet black leather jacket, and now a fedora, a 'stache, and glasses.

"Logan more or less said the same thing," I said as we entered the Shamrock.

It was off-hours, so the place was empty but for two guys behind the counter playing a gambling game of tic-tac-toe using cuts of meat for their Xs and Os and other cuts of meat for their money. It you added up their IQs, these two guys would equal an idiot. It was written on their foreheads in crayon. I had the feeling they were somebody's ne'er-do-well Irish nephews.

It took two minutes to impress upon the nephews that Rick and I were FDA investigators looking for a certain butcher named Mike Monroe, who we knew was working in the back at this very moment. The nephews were told that if they alerted anyone the FDA was in the house, they would go to prison for obstructing meat justice, and so they sent us to the back without a second thought—or really any thought—and returned to their T-bone tic-tac-toe.

The back of Shamrock was considerably larger than the

front. There were several butcher stations with knives galore and a long row of meat hooks, many of which held huge slabs of pigs and cows ready to be carved into commercial cuts. There were walk-in coolers and a few desks and file cabinets. It felt like everything in the joint had blood on it. I couldn't swear that it did, but it felt like it.

Mad Mike Monroe came out of a cooler carrying half a cow. The massive slab of beef had to weigh two hundred pounds, and yet Mad Mike hung it up on a hook—six-plus feet above the ground—with one hand, like it was some kind of dead cow balloon.

"The fuck you doing back here?" Mike said. "Who the fuck are you?"

He moved from the hooks, which were attached to a rolling track system. He was among the scariest-looking men I'd ever seen. Maybe the scariest. Six and a half feet tall and two hundred seventy or eighty pounds. Great big man. Massive arms. Big broad chest with belly to match. Huge hands. Meat hooks in and of themselves. He walked to one of the butcher blocks and grabbed a cleaver the size of an axe. If Mad Mike came to collect money, you were giving it to him. There was no saying no to Mad Mike Monroe.

But the most frightening thing about him was his face. A badass scar ran from the top of his head, across his right cheek, under his chin, and down his neck, like someone had mistaken him for half a cow and cut him open. There were smaller scars —not small but smaller—on the left side of his face and forehead and neck. He looked like Frankenstein's monster. Holding an axe cleaver.

He didn't know who we were yet and was already unhappy to have us in his presence.

"I'm not going to beat around the bush, Mr. Monroe," I said. "I'm FDA Agent MacKenzie O'Leary, and this is Agent Bill Pittman."

"Hello, Mike," Rick said.

"Fuck off," Mike said. "You want to talk FDA shit, call my boss."

There was a full freaking pig on the butcher block, and he slammed the cleaver into it with such ungodly speed and power that he cut clear through the ligaments and tendons and freaking bone and took off the hind leg in one terrifying whack.

"Not this time, Mr. Monroe," I said with as much courage as I could fake. "This time we're going to talk to you, and you're going to pay attention or we're going to take serious action."

Mike looked at me, showed me the cleaver, and said very slowly, so I wouldn't misunderstand the intention behind his words, "Get the fuck out."

His voice was so deep and menacing that it took my breath away.

"Sorry, Mike," Rick said, stepping up to the butcher block. "You have information we need, and we intend to get it out of you one way or another."

"How the fuck you figure?" Mike said. "I ain't saying shit about shit."

"Let's start with what we know," I said. "You moonlight as a bag man for several local bookies. You collect past-due money. This is not open for discussion. This is a fact the FDA is aware of. It will be a fact the police are aware of if you don't cooperate."

Mad Mike said nothing, but his face flushed as if his monster scars were on fire.

"The FDA frowns on illegal activity when it comes to citizens employed in the meat business," Rick said, improvising like a jazz musician. "We identify it and put an end to it, so as not to denigrate the reputation of the FDA. As O'Leary said, we could just as easily call the police."

"Fuck off, you puny piece of shit," Mike said, coming out from behind the butcher block, still holding the damn cleaver.

He took a few steps toward us. The closer he got, the bigger and scarier he was. But one of the first rules of theater is never let the audience see you sweat, meaning act your way through the fear. I was an actor, first and foremost. But, holy moly, my fear meter was in the red zone.

"There's one particular bookie you work for that we're interested in speaking with," I said. "It would go a long way in your favor with the FDA if you would help us locate him."

Mad Mike wasn't having any of it. "Fuck do food agents have to do with bookies?"

His face said he had a bad feeling about authority of any kind. His body language said he was going to do something about it. His scars made it pretty freaking clear what.

Rick and I backed away. The hanging slabs of meat were behind us. Mad Mike was in front of us. We were trapped. The idiots in the front wouldn't step foot in the back because we'd told them not to. We were alone. If Mad Mike wanted to carve us up, there was no one coming to save us. Soon there would be two fewer fake FDA agents asking unwanted questions in the Shamrock Meat Market.

"Food and Drug Administration, Mike. Drugs. The bookie's a dealer on the side," I said.

"We don't think you're involved," Rick said. "But that's up to you."

Mad Mike put one of his meat-hook hands around Rick's throat and lifted him clear off the ground. Rick weighed less than the slab of dead cow, so lifting him off the ground with one freaking hand was no big deal for Mad Mike. But unlike the slab of dead cow, Rick was a living person, meaning he moved—meaning his hands on the butcher's hand that was choking him, meaning legs kicking this way and that. The butcher was thrown off balance and spun around, his back to the hanging meat. He stuttered backward up onto a two-step platform that helped the smaller butchers gain leverage when taking slabs down off the hooks.

With the other hand, Mad Mike held the cleaver up in way that said *death is coming.* "Fuck right it's up to me."

I was frozen. In shock. Our interview had escalated in the blink of an eye. I'd thought we might be able to trick Mad Mike into giving us the bookie's name. Or threaten him with legal action. Or something. It had never occurred to me that Mad Mike Monroe would have two gears and only two gears: violence and extreme violence.

Curiously, it wasn't my life that flashed before my eyes. It was Rick's life. Or rather, my life with Rick. From the time we'd met at the House of Emotional Tics to this deadly moment in the Shamrock, all the scenes ran like film footage in front of my face but got stuck on one particular moment. That time all the way back when to earlier this afternoon when Rick had told me not to be jealous of Chloe.

Was I jealous? I'd made it clear that Rick wasn't my type, so there was no possibility I was now or would ever be jealous of other women in his life. But right now, in this moment, I had to admit I was wrong. Yes, for shit's sake, I *was* jealous. Good fucking God. Really? Yes, really. Why, I had no idea. But I was.

All of this—our relationship playing on the screen in my head, the footage getting stuck on the dry humping, the whole jealous/not jealous/yes, actually jealous flashback—happened in half a microsecond.

In the other half of the microsecond, I remembered that I was the bodyguard and the body I was guarding was being strangled to death by a beast of a butcher who would come for me next.

I jumped onto the platform, grabbed the empty meat hook behind Mad Mike, slid it under the crisscrossed straps at the back of his coveralls, jumped off the platform, and kicked the steps out from under him.

The butcher let go of the cleaver...and Rick, who crashed to the ground, skin a pale shade of cold blue, eyes bulging out of his head. He gulped air into his lungs, shaken but alive.

Mad Mike hung four inches off the ground, legs swinging like a toddler trying to find the floor. Helpless. Though probably not for long. Soon, some other butcher would walk in. Or the idiot nephews. Or maybe Mr. Shamrock himself.

Either way, I had to hurry. I pulled the Colt from my purse and pointed it at Mad Mike's balls. "I'm going to count to five, Mad Mike, and then for the rest of time you're going to be known as No Nuts Mike. Any last words?"

Mad Mike was so enraged, language escaped him.

I pulled the hammer back and focused on the butcher's coveralled crotch. "Five, four, three—"

"The fuck you want to know?" Mad Mike said.

I did not lower the gun. Simply suspended the count. "Kenny Cochran. Comedian with a jones for the ponies. He was in trouble with one of the bookies you work for. I don't think you killed Cochran. I think the bookie got someone else to do it. A specialist. A surgeon. Not a ham-fisted butcher like you."

"Don't know nothing about that," Mad Mike said.

I refocused my focus, tossed in a hefty dose of acting, and put the end of the barrel on his balls. I couldn't have been more serious about blowing Mad Mike's nut sack into bloody oblivion had I been center stage at the Gershwin. "Two, one—"

"Okay, okay, Paulie Crane. Coney Island pawn shop. Cashes checks, loan sharks on the side. Bookie's his big business. Cochran owed him heavy. Paulie asked me to collect, then called it off. Too bad. I hate comedians."

Rick was standing next to me now, still shaky but back in the present.

"Mad Mike hates comedians," I said.

"Comedians hate Mad Mike," Rick said.

"Everybody hates Mad Mike," I said.

"That's what makes him mad," Rick said.

Out of nowhere, I started laughing. Maybe because he was funny. Or maybe because of the way we'd improvised together, sensing each other's vibe, totally in tune, riffing like we'd been doing it for years.

Maybe that's why I was jealous.

23

—————

HOW TO UNPACK ALL THIS

In the cab to Coney Island, I wanted to talk about this feeling I was feeling, but Rick and the cabbie commenced a conversation about the top-ten funniest sitcoms of all time—*The Jungle* was on the cabbie's list, even though Rick was still in disguise—and I wasn't in the mood to join in because *The Jungle* wasn't anywhere near my top ten. So I stared out the window and thought about my father.

Jimmy had been born on the first day of summer, June 20. The summer solstice. The longest day of the year. Sometimes June 21 was the first day of summer. Occasionally, even June 22. But no matter how the astronomers called it that particular year, Jimmy would wake up on his birthday and announce that today of all days there was plenty of time for a ride to Coney Island.

Most years we would pile into the car, but when my father was feeling especially nostalgic, we'd take the subway. Jimmy had told me his father would wake him every June 20, say something like, *"Another trip around the sun, son,"* ride the subway to Coney Island, celebrate at the amusement parks, and eat at the original Original Nathan's Famous Frankfurters on the corner of Surf and Stillwell.

Jimmy, Christine, Marilyn, and I would sit on the beach with our hot dogs and lemonade and watch the waves. I couldn't remember being happier than that. My mother and father sitting side by side in the sand, Christine resting her head on Jimmy's shoulder, all of us eating Nathan's and drinking lemonade. Even my sister would be nice to me on Coney Island. It had all gone weird when my mother died, of course, but, man oh man, Coney Island.

So I thought about my father and my family for a while, and then I thought about what a transcendent Thursday I was having. I'd been arrested and released, let the pig out of the pen, role-played with Lew Logan—and nearly got in a four-way shootout—survived an encounter with the mad butcher from hell, and discovered I was a jealous woman because Rick Gotti had eyes for Chloe Burns, which was what I'd wanted to talk about in the first place.

Had there been something going on between us that I'd missed? We'd been flirting around, but was it more than that? Had I made it up? Or was he feeling it too? Why in the world was I jealous? I'd only known him since Monday. He wasn't my type. I wasn't his type. For shit's sake, we were the diametric opposite of each other's type.

Thankfully, the cab pulled up to Paulie Crane's pawn shop before I made myself completely crazy.

"We go in, we get him to say he hired the bear to kill Kenny Cochran, we get out," I said.

"Who are we this time?"

"Irish mob from New Jersey looking for an out-of-town hitman."

"If Crane has Frankenstein scars, I'm out."

"If he has Frankenstein scars, I'm just going to shoot him."

"That's what my mother would do."

Coney Island Pawn and Cash occupied the corner unit of an eight-unit, two-story strip mall on Coney Island Avenue near the corner of Avenue V. Like practically all pawn shops everywhere, it had a big yellow sign with bold black letters and smaller red letters. The windows were covered with large posters that advertised incredible sales and unbelievable deals on guns and jewelry and watches and guitars and bikes and coins and cards and computers happening right this very minute inside this very store. There were so many posters that there was no way to actually see inside the store and know if the posters were telling the truth about the incredible sales and unbelievable deals.

I was still in my MacKenzie O'Leary getup so when I walked into the shop, no one would say, *"Hey, wait just a damn minute. Aren't you Kate McCall?"* Not that anyone would say that. It was more likely someone would recognize Rick, which would be worse, so he still wore the fedora, the mustache, and the black-frame glasses.

The place was packed with every imaginable thing it was possible to pawn. Long glass display cases wrapped around the room, creating a counter behind which the pawn-shop staff waited to work their funny money magic.

One wall was devoted to guns. Hundreds of hunting rifles and paramilitary semi-automatics hung in locked racks. A bazooka too. Unless someone out to get you owned a tank, I couldn't imagine why anyone would need to buy a bazooka. Row after row of ammunition was displayed in the glass cases with handguns and knives and pepper sprays and tasers, no different than the earrings and bracelets and watches and rings that people pawned for ninety-day cash.

If you had nothing to pawn but *still* needed cash and needed it now, well, Paulie Crane could make that happen for you under the table, in the back room. And if you were here to place a bet on a ballgame or on the ponies, Crane had you covered there too. I imagined you could start a bank with the cash Crane kept locked in his safe.

A handful of customers hawked personal items, trying to get as much dough as they could from the pawn-shop people. Every employee was armed. *Don't fuck around in Paulie Crane's place or we will shoot you in the fucking head* was the company clarion call.

The staff worked behind the counters at the back of the store and to the right. To the left, one man had his own counter. *That's him*, I thought. *That's Paulie Crane.*

Early sixties. Full head of kinky gray hair. Bushy gray mustache. He looked like a Best Buy Geek Squad nerd. Except for his clothes. He was immaculately dressed. Pin-striped three-piece suit—jacket hanging off the back of his chair. Lavender-striped shirt with rose-gold cufflinks. Gorgeous velvet hand-tied bowtie. Bulgari rose-gold-and-alligator watch that had to ring up somewhere in the neighborhood of twenty-five grand. Jimmy would have called him a Dapper Dan. In his spare time, Crane hired men like Mad Mike to break people's legs and arms and necks, depending upon how late and deep they were in debt.

He was working with what looked like two shoe boxes filled with baseball cards. I nodded at Rick, and we walked to Crane's counter.

"Paulie Crane?" I said.

"Yes, indeed," Crane said, glancing up at us.

"We're from South Jersey, Camden County," I said. "I'm Kathy Coonan, great grandniece of Jimmy Coonan. You heard of him?"

He was organizing, labeling, and pricing the baseball cards. They were old and in mint condition. He placed them in plastic baggies like they were made of solid gold. "Anyone who knows their Irish mob history has heard of Jimmy Coonan."

"This is my muscle, Joey Sullivan," I said. "We know who

you are and what you do, and we respect that. We're here to ask you a favor."

"Do you have something to pawn?" Crane said.

"No," I said.

"Would you like to cash a paycheck or purchase an item?" Crane said.

"No," I said.

"*That* is who I am and what I do," Crane said. "I can't imagine the kind of favor you have in mind."

"We know you're a bookie and a loan shark," I said. "We know you hire collectors from time to time to make house calls. We know sometimes these house calls are more final than other times. We're looking for an out-of-state collector to make a more final house call on our behalf. We're prepared to pay you for your expertise."

He didn't flinch. Just kept working on the cards. I looked at Rick. We had anted up. Crane could either keep the bidding alive or call us.

"Clearly, you're not Irish mobsters from New Jersey," Crane said. "Are there even Irish mobsters in New Jersey? It's hard for me to believe there are. And if there were, and if you were, you certainly wouldn't be wearing such an ostentatious wig. Mobsters don't wear wigs, do they?"

I wasn't often tongue-tied, but he'd knocked me off balance in a big way by dissing my MacKenzie O'Leary wig.

"And your muscle? This man is not Irish. There's nothing Irish about him. Maybe on St. Patrick's Day, when everyone's Irish, but even then that would be a stretch for whoever this is. For God's sake, he's wearing a fedora and a fake mustache—I know a thing or two about mustaches, as you can see—and there's no self-respecting muscle in the Greater Metropolitan area that would wear a *fake* mustache. So the question, it seems to me, is who the hell are you and what makes you think I have inside knowledge as to the whereabouts and availability of debt collectors and hitmen?"

Jimmy's Rules of Private Investigation for Kate, Rule Number Eight: Make sure your backup plan has a backup plan for your backup plan.

"You're right," I said. "I'm not an Irish mobster from New Jersey. I'm Liz Cochran, Kenny Cochran's sister. This is my boyfriend, John. We know for a flat fact you hired Mad Mike Monroe to visit Kenny because he owed you big on account of his problem with the ponies. We know Mad Mike never had the chance to collect because you also hired someone else at the same time for the same job. That guy wore a Halloween bear mask of all fucking things. Maybe the bear was only supposed to collect and got carried away. I'll give you that much, but I won't give you more. I want revenge, Crane. You're going to tell me who the bear is because you owe me that."

"How to unpack all this," Crane said, finishing the first box of baseball cards and moving into the second. "Let's start with Michael. You asked him about Kenny Cochran, and he mentioned *my* name?"

"He did," I said.

"And you're standing here?" Crane said.

"We are," I said.

"And where's Michael?" Crane said.

"Hanging around," Rick said.

I tried not to laugh. It wasn't easy.

"The boyfriend speaks. Hello, John," Crane said.

"Hi, Paulie," Rick said, gesturing at the baseball cards. "Let me ask you a question. Are those real?"

Crane smiled. "Completely. I've been negotiating for two years with an ancient man from Manhattan. I paid three hundred fifty thousand in cash for these two boxes not twenty minutes before you arrived."

"Wow," Rick said. "What'll you get for them?"

"This is a 1954 Bowman Mickey Mantle," Crane said, holding up a cherry card from time gone by. "It alone is worth north of one hundred thousand."

"I love Mickey Mantle," Rick said. "Present tense. Hero worship."

"Are you a Yankee fan?" Crane said.

"Big time," Rick said. "You?"

"All my life," Crane said.

"Me too," I said, looking at Rick. "You like baseball?"

"Love it," Rick said. "When I was kid, I lived at the stadium. Scrounged up the money, sat in the upper deck behind home plate, ate Cracker Jacks like crazy."

"Well, certainly this man is not your boyfriend," Crane said, "if you don't know something as basic and personal as his passion for baseball."

"We just started going together," I said somewhat weakly.

"Second date," Rick said.

"And last, I'm afraid," Crane said, gesturing across the room at a large and angry employee who sported both a huge handgun and a nasty knife. The man started toward us, grabbed two other guys on his way over.

Shit, I thought. *Shit and shit.*

I knew I had to pull the Colt, but I was outgunned by a lot. I might be dead before I got it out of my purse. But there was no other play, so I went for it.

Except before I could grab it and point it at Crane's head, Rick reached into the second shoebox, pulled out a card with one hand, and held up a cigarette lighter with the other.

He flicked the flame to life and moved it ominously near the card. "Whitey Ford, 1951 Bowman rookie card. Loved Whitey. What's it worth, Paulie?"

Crane put up an index finger. His men were twenty-five feet from us. They stopped, hands on their guns.

My hand was on the Colt in my purse.

If you were taking the temperature of the shop, your thermometer would have jumped ten degrees. The vibe got thick. Several customers decided it was time to exit stage get-the-hell-out.

"Seventy-five thousand," Crane said.

"I'll burn it if you don't tell me what I want to know," Rick said.

"You'll do no such thing," Crane said.

Rick set the card on fire, put it on the counter, and grabbed another from the box. Crane's eyes went wide. The two remaining customers split. Crane's heavies took a step toward us. Crane held up his index finger again. They stopped on a pawn-shop dime.

"Pete Rose, 1963 Topps rookie card. Nice. What it's worth?" Rick said, holding the flame to it.

"Forty-seven thousand five hundred," Crane said.

"Smoke in one, two—" Rick said.

"I have no idea who Kenny Cochran is," Crane said.

"Three," Rick said. He burned the card and grabbed another.

Crane's men took two more enraged steps toward us. I pulled the Colt, pointed it at Crane, who held up his index finger a third time.

"Sandy Koufax, 1955 Topps rookie card. The rookie cards are the promised land, am I right?" Rick said to Crane.

"Ninety thousand," Crane said.

"You took that old man to the cleaners," Rick said.

"He has money to leave his grandchildren," Crane said.

"Tell me who killed Kenny Cochran or I burn it," Rick said.

"You wouldn't burn Sandy Koufax," Crane said.

Rick burned the card and grabbed another.

"Stop. Stop right now," Crane said.

Paulie Crane had realized he was no longer in control of his shop, of his business, of his money, of his cards.

"Willie Mays, 1953 Topps. The Say-Hey Kid in a New York Giants uni. Has to be worth a fortune, Paulie," Rick said.

"Yes," Crane said. "One hundred thirty thousand for Willie."

"Say goodbye," Rick said, moving the flame toward the card.

"I didn't kill Kenny Cochran," Crane said softly.

"Then who did?" I said.

"Ask Ruby Gold," Crane said. "Kenny introduced her to the horses, and she became enamored. They placed bets together and lost into low seven figures. She blamed him for the losses and was furious he couldn't pay any part of the debt. She had to pay it all. And did. That's why I canceled Michael's collection. You want to know who killed Kenny Cochran, the answer starts and stops with Ruby Gold."

We stood there in silence for what felt like a long time but was probably ten or fifteen seconds.

"Now, card, please," Crane said, holding out his hand for Willie.

Rick gestured me to the door, and we backed toward it. I kept the Colt pointed at Crane. Rick held the lighter to Willie. Crane's men remained frozen, hands on their guns.

"We should go to a game, Paulie," Rick said. "Good times."

He dropped the card, we crashed out of the shop, and ran for our lives.

24

——————

SUPERIOR SURVEILLANCE

WE FELL INTO A CAB AT THE CORNER OF CONEY ISLAND Boulevard and Gravesend Neck Road and took it straight to the White Whale, where Big Black Bald Bart was keeping his eyes peeled for the pig holed up in the Boulevard Motor Inn. We were quiet for a long time, me and Rick, both of us, or at least me, still too blown away to find a corridor into the conversation both of us, or at least me, knew we should have.

"Pete Rose as a rookie, I'll give you," I finally said. "Sandy Koufax, I'll swallow hard and learn to live. But Whitey Ford? Really? You burned Whitey Ford?"

"Hated burning Whitey," Rick said. "Broke my heart."

"Saved our lives."

"Desperate times, desperate measures."

"That's what Ruby Gold probably said when she hired the bear to kill Cochran."

"You believe Paulie Crane?"

"You're down two hundred grand in burned baseball cards, Willie Mays on deck, you don't pull a name like Ruby Gold out of your ass. I don't *not* believe him is what I'm saying."

"That's what I'm saying too. Jesus. Ruby Gold."

"The bear at Silvercup. Has to be her."

We both nodded, then looked out the windows. There was plenty more for us to say, but neither one of us, or at least me, wanted to say it in front of the cabbie, who'd heard names he'd recognized—Rose, Koufax, Ford, Gold—and was busting a gut to get in the conversation.

So the cabbie talked a blue streak all the way to Flushing, where we sent Big Black Bald Bart on his way and sat in the White Whale watching for the pig until our relief arrived. Dennis and Posey had found a few fellow actors from a sister theater company to sit overnight surveillance for spending money, and those fine folks were on their merry way.

While we watched and waited, you might think one of us would have continued the Ruby Gold conversation. How she'd been betting on the horses with Kenny Cochran, had lost a ton of dough, was pissed Cochran couldn't carry his half of the debt, had paid it all herself so Paulie Crane would call off Mad Mike, and then hired the bear to kill the comedian in cold blood. We could have and probably should have been talking about Ruby since Rick's life—and now my life—was part of her deadly calculus. Or how about burning baseball cards worth more than most people make in five years? Or about burning baseball cards worth more than most people make in five years in the freaking lions' den with the freaking lions reaching for their guns? You might think we would at least touch on that topic. Or maybe we could banter a bit about jealousy since that was still front and center in my mind. You would be wrong on all counts.

We talked baseball and childhood, his and mine.

"We're about the same age so we went to games about the same time and sat in the same place, upper deck behind home plate, so it's a distinct possibility we went to some of the same games," I said. "Both of us in the upper deck the same night."

"No doubt," Rick said. "Has to be true."

"I was with my father. He taught me to keep score like a bench coach."

"I drank beer and ate Cracker Jacks. We had fake IDs."

"Who's we?"

"Staten Island kids ditching school, stealing cars, getting in fights, going to ballgames. Park Hill hoodlums."

"You're Italian?"

"On my mother's side. My father was German. He's still German, wherever he is. My mother's still Italian, as of ten years ago, I mean."

"You should call her, find out if she's suddenly Swedish."

"That's funny, McCall. You have skills. And, yeah, I know I should."

I told him about Jimmy and Christine and Marilyn and our life in Queens. He told me about his mother and his sister and their life in Staten Island. As different as our lives had been, there were even more commonalities. The one-parent household—after Christine died, for me; when his father left, for him. The love affair with baseball. The life-defining gravitational pull toward show business. The inability to find and settle into a long-term, loving, monogamous relationship. The bottom line was we were both blue-collar kids from New York who'd lived unconventional lives and were still alone.

We spoke easily, sharing our stories. He was Rick Gotti, so his stories were hilarious. Or at least his delivery was. I laughed a lot. He laughed at me laughing.

"When nothing happened but we'd had a good time together, Jimmy called it *superior surveillance*," I said.

"Is that what this is?"

"What do you think?"

"I asked you first."

"I think you're flirting with your bodyguard."

"I think you're flirting with your client."

So there it was. Finally. Time for the jealousy section of our surveillance tête-à-tête. But just as I was ready to open the floor, our relief arrived in their own vehicle. So we left the pig in watchful hands and drove the White Whale to the D-Cup for the final *Psychedelic Sunday* dress rehearsal. The moment had passed.

Opening night was, holy shit, tomorrow. Were we ready? Not at all. But the show was insanely fun and insanely insane, the Schmidt and Parker Players would spill their hearts and souls all over the stage for the sell-out crowd of loyal D-Cup fans, and a great grand time would be had by all. Two orgies. Not one. Two. How could we lose?

After rehearsal, Rick signed some autographs, and there was talk about the strip-club musical Dennis and Posey were writing for him. Chloe flirted with Rick, wrapping her arm around his arm, casually rubbing up against him, dominating his D-Cup time, all of which, in my current frame of mind, might have made me more jealous than I already was except that Roger had something on his mind that he had to offload on, well, me.

"Years of hard work to become your D-Cup leading man in, what, the last eight or nine shows," Roger said, "and this guy wanders in off the street and gets his own musical for no other reason than he's famous for welcoming people to the jungle."

Roger Platt was a full-time Schmidt and Parker Players leading man and a part-time everything else. Depending upon the phases of the moon and the rising of the tides, he either sold used cars in Queens, worked as a janitor in a Midtown high-rise, or delivered thirty-pound boxes of shrimp to restaurants and grocery stores on Staten Island (maybe even in Park Hill, where Rick had grown up cutting school, stealing cars, getting in fights, and going to Yankee games). He was fifty-two years old and in terrific shape. He had a booming Broadway baritone and danced like Gene Kelly as opposed to Fred Astaire —athletic tap as opposed to balletic ballroom—though he could move almost as powerfully and gracefully as both of those legendary legends.

We'd costarred in quite a few D-Cup productions—leading man and leading lady. That did not make us good friends, exactly, just regular friendly friends who got along fine. In fact, we shared a superstitious addiction to preshow rituals that bound us together on show days. The bottom line was Roger liked singing and dancing with me as much as I liked singing and dancing with him. We had a chemistry onstage that couldn't be denied. Offstage, well, you could deny it sometimes, no doubt.

"It's not a singing-and-dancing role, Roger," I said. "Posey told me you'd be costarring as the strip-club piano player. It's a love triangle. You, me, and Rick. You're still one of the leading men."

"But not *the* leading man," he said. "Sharing a card, as it were. And if there's one thing an actor on my plateau doesn't do, it's share a card."

His tragic flaw, if you haven't guessed, was his ego. Meaning he had one as big as Boston. No one thought Roger was funny more than Roger thought Roger was funny. He'd been every-where and done everything. A man of many hats, all of which fit him perfectly. Whatever task was on the table was his specialty. You didn't even have to ask him. He would volunteer that fact apropos of nothing.

"It's theater, Roger. There are no cards in the credits. Just names in the playbill."

"Still, in all, I can't help but feeling encroached upon. Tres-passed, as it were."

In the same way the freaky folks at the House of Emotional Tics had helped me hunt my father's killer, Roger and the Schmidt and Parker Players, most notably Dennis, Posey, and Chloe, had helped me with whatever other case I was working. So far, in the line of McCall & Company duty, Roger had been "teapotted" in the head, maced in the face, and tased until done. All because of his brash overconfidence in the heat of the moment. In each instance, I'd warned him to tone it down before he got creamed. But once Roger got going, there was no pulling him out of the spotlight. He would be swept up in his performance, lost in his oration, gone with the wind. So while I didn't like seeing him in pain one bit—he was my regular friendly friend, after all—I didn't particularly feel guilty about it either.

"What, may I ask, does he have that I don't?" Roger said.

It was his tone of voice as much as the words themselves. Twice-divorced Roger Platt, deliverer of shrimp, seller of used cars, sweeper of floors, and reigning D-Cup leading man, was jealous of Rick Gotti.

"A hit sitcom in syndication, tour after cross-country comedy tour, fifteen years of drug-and-alcohol rehab, a murder charge, and money," I said.

"Notice that talent is not on that list," Roger said.

Rick joined us just then, Chloe attached to his hip, and it was among the more surreal D-Cup foursomes I could recall—me jealous of Chloe, Roger jealous of Rick, Chloe bitten by the crush bug, and Rick probably wondering if every off-off-off-off-Broadway theater company was as crazy as this one.

That's when Logan called me to say that Jake Brotherton had dropped off the Earth, but that the task force had connected with Mitch Joyner, who'd said that Two Brake Jake had arranged a rendezvous at RJM at eleven o'clock tonight to —and this was Logan quoting Joyner quoting Jake—*settle this once and for all.*

25

YOU NEVER KNOW FOR SURE UNTIL
YOU KNOW FOR SURE

IT WAS THURSDAY NIGHT, TEN FIFTY-FIVE, AND I WAS DOWN LOW in the back seat of Logan's unmarked sedan, waiting for my father's killer to murder Mitch Joyner. Logan's car was parked in the second row of the middle section closest to the buildings, blending in, one of two hundred used cars on the RJM lot.

I'd been sitting here alone for an hour. Logan and his task force were in position, hidden in shadows all around the place, waiting to jump in T-minus five minutes, when Joyner had been told to arrive to meet Two Brake Jake, who, of course, would not be showing up. This time, we all knew, it would be the killer, and Logan would take him down.

I wanted to be there, right there, when it happened, but as far as Logan was concerned, it was a professional courtesy I was here at all. Middle section, second row, back seat was as close to the action as Logan would let me get. He'd made me park the White Whale down the block in case the killer recognized it in the sea of RJM used cars.

So for the past hour, I'd been running my lines, a last-chance all-nighter before tomorrow's *Psychedelic Sunday* opening. I knew my lines, of course, but still, tomorrow night was not a rehearsal. Tomorrow night, the theater would be packed with people expecting exceptional insanity. I had jitters—I *always* had jitters before opening night—and running my lines gave me something to think about besides being jittery.

When I wasn't thinking about my lines and songs and dances and cues and kissing Chloe in front of a full house—my least favorite scene, for myriad reasons that would take an entire musical to explain—I was thinking about my son and my soon-to-be daughter-in-law, Nonsensical Nina, and my soon-to-be-born grandchild. Talk about jittery. Try *grandma* on for size for the first time.

Matthew and Agonizing Nina were getting married at the courthouse in eleven days. Eleven. Days. How would I manage my feelings for Inane Nina once she was Matthew's actual wife? I'd have to change my attitude. I couldn't chase after my grandchild thinking Peeving Nina was an unendurable dipshit, even though, let's be clear, Repulsive Nina was indeed an unbearable bigmouth. It wouldn't be fair to Matthew or to my grandchild or to Intolerable Nina or even to me. It was time to give Inexcusable Nina the benefit of the doubt—an excuse, as it were. To bury the hatchet. Even if Excruciating Nina wouldn't do it, I would.

No, I wouldn't. Who was I kidding? But what I *would* do was be the best grandmother I could possibly be, which meant being a much nicer, kinder, more patient version of myself to Painful Nina, no matter what version of herself she gave to me. I promised myself I would do that for real right there in Logan's car, waiting for the killer to meet Mitch Joyner. I promised. Of course, *promising* and *doing* aren't the same thing. So we would see.

Anyway, thinking about being Matthew's child's grandmother made me think about Jimmy being my child's grandfather. He'd been the best grandfather any kid could have wanted. He'd taken Matthew to the beach and to the Bronx Zoo and to the circus and to Yankee Stadium. He'd bought him a baseball glove and a Louisville Slugger. He'd paid for Matthew's braces. He'd helped pay for NYU. He'd bought us both health insurance because I'd never made enough money or kept a real job long enough for the company to foot that bill. He'd grilled burgers and dogs. He'd taken us to Rizzo's on Steinway Street in Astoria for pizza and to Wo Hop on Mott Street in Chinatown for ribs and dumplings and roast pork chow mein. He'd babysat when I had an audition or a crappy job. He'd held Matthew's hand when Matthew needed a man's hand to hold. He'd been a shoulder for Matthew (and me) to cry on.

And thinking about Matthew (and me) crying on Jimmy's shoulder made me cry in Logan's car at T-minus one minute until the killer came for Motormouth Mitch. I'd never been more grateful to be alone. If Logan had seen me bawling in his back seat, he would have sent me to my room without dessert. Or grounded me for a week. Or taken my car keys. Or—

That's when I saw the killer.

He was in the shadows of the cars to my left. Dark hoodie. Black ski cap pulled low. Hands in his pockets. He was hard to see and in no hurry. It took all my willpower to stay in the car. Every muscle in my body wanted to explode out of the back seat, run down the row, and beat the shit out of the man who'd murdered my father. But I didn't.

As the killer moved through the cars toward the buildings, Mitch Joyner came out of Building 1 and stood in the roadway.

He's waiting for him, I thought. *He thinks Jake's coming to talk it through.*

But it wasn't Jake, and Joyner was going to get his eyes blown out.

Logan and the task force were nowhere to be seen. Jesus Christ, what the hell was taking them so long? Hadn't they seen him coming through the cars? What were they waiting for?

The killer arrived in the roadway, made eye contact with Joyner, and started toward him.

"Hurry," I said. "Go, go, go."

As the killer took his hands out of his pockets, task-force cops swarmed the roadway, tackled him to the ground, and moved Joyner to safety.

Got him.

I jumped out the car and ran down the aisle.

Logan and the task force had the killer face down on the roadway. Two cops kept knees on his back while another cuffed him. From what I remembered, and we'd had several close encounters, it was him. Same size. Same body shape. Him.

Joyner was surrounded by a shield of plain-clothes cops near the front door of Building 1.

My body shook. My blood burned. Anger and pain raged through me. I fought against them. Jimmy would have demanded I keep my wits about me. *"You never know for sure until you know for sure,"* he'd said many times.

They stood the killer up. His back was to me. Yes, same height, same weight. It's all I had to go on. He'd always covered his face and eyes, so I couldn't recognize him that way.

They removed his ski mask. I moved forward, toward Logan and the killer and the task force. Joyner moved at the same moment I did. I was closer now and could see Joyner's face, hear his voice.

"Jake?" Joyner said. "What the fuck?"

Not good, I thought.

"You tell me, Mitch," Jake said. "What the hell is all this?"

Not the killer.

I might not have known his face, but I knew his voice by heart. It wasn't him. Son of a bitch. It wasn't him.

Logan rolled his eyes but not in earnest yet. It was dawning on him that he'd swung and missed, but he hadn't confirmed it for a fact in his own mind.

"Cops said you hired someone to kill Ronnie and then me," Joyner said, "so we wouldn't sign the termination letter and sell the business out from under you."

"What the fuck does that even mean?" Jake said. "Ronnie's murder blew me out. I had to leave town. Think it through. You know what I thought? Life is too fucking short for this shit. I called you and just got back. Came straight here. I wanted to give you the termination letter for tomorrow. It's in my pocket. I signed the fucking thing. I'd show it to you except these idiots have me handcuffed."

And then there was an hour of confusion. The task force had marshaled their men and ambushed the killer and it wasn't him. Things had to be unwound. Dots had to be disconnected and reconnected. There were statements to take. Schematics to reconfigure.

The time ticked past midnight, and my silenced phone vibrated in my pocket. I imagined it was Rick calling from the D-Cup, wondering when I was coming back to fetch him. I'd left him there after rehearsal with Dennis and Posey and Roger and Chloe, figuring that between the four of them they'd be able to keep him entertained. Indeed, with Chloe telling him how wonderful he was, and Roger telling him how wonderful *he* was, and Dennis and Posey telling him and telling him and telling him about his very own wonderful Schmidt and Parker Players musical, Rick might not have had a chance to breathe since I'd split for RJM.

"Kate McCall."

"Hello, Little Engine. You have to admit that didn't go as planned."

His voice took my breath away.

"You're here?"

"Close enough to enjoy the show."

I looked around the lot. Up and down the block. It was dark. I couldn't see a damn thing past the lit-up tarmac of used cars.

"Logan's not smart enough to pass my class," the killer said. "I don't think you are either. But I had higher hopes for you."

"I know your work."

"Yes, you do."

"You killed Russo."

"Yes, I did."

"Fuck you for that. What did he ever do to you?"

"That is the correct question. One point for you, Little Engine."

Tears stung my eyes. That's how angry I was. How filled with rage. We'd thought we were so close, but we'd been nowhere near the game.

"I don't want points," I said. "I want you alone in a room for ten minutes."

"You sound like your father. He'd be proud of you. If he were alive."

"Fuck you," I said, tears rolling down my cheeks. "Fuck you..."

"I understand your frustration. And I admire your emotional commitment to our relationship. So I'm going to give you another chance. Listen carefully. Here's your clue: The king dies at dawn in a day; long live the king at Columbia Cardiology."

"I'm going to nail you, motherfucker."

"I'm going to enjoy watching you try. Send Logan my condolences for his lost pride."

He clicked off the call. I turned back to Building 1. Surrounded by frustrated task-force cops, Logan had confirmed the facts—a swing and a miss—and was shaking his head in livid dismay.

26

THE LIBRARY OF WARREN

SOMEWHERE AROUND TWELVE FIFTEEN FRIDAY MORNING, AS THE task force was dispersing empty-handed, I told Logan about my phone call with the killer. He listened carefully, wrote the clue, word for word, on the back of Two Brake Jake's business card, and said, "Time to turn the fucking fleet." He was in a bad mood, even for him.

"The king dies at dawn in a day," he said. "So not dawn today. Dawn tomorrow. That your read too?"

"Yes," I said. "Meet you at nine at Columbia Cardiology."

"If you show up there, I'll shoot you in the heart so at least you'll be in the right place at the right time," he said.

"Right back at you, Detective Laundromat," I said, wishing I could take those words back so he wouldn't decide to shoot me in the heart on the spot.

Instead, Logan walked me across the lot and down the block to the White Whale to make sure I got there safe and sound. Except his idea of safe and sound was to read me the riot act with such heat that I expected to be sunburned when I got back to the brownstone.

He opened the driver door for me. "Now go home and stay there for a good long goddamn time."

"How long is a good long goddamn time?"

"The rest of my life."

I decided it wasn't the right moment to offer him the killer's condolences for his lost pride. "No problem. See you at nine."

I called Rick on the ride to the D-Cup. He met me downstairs.

"So how was your day, honey?" he said. I think he could tell I was exhausted and down in the dumps and was trying to cheer me up.

I smiled because that's what Rick made you do. "Well, let's see. I infuriated my son at the Thirteenth but got released on my own recognizance, charges dropped until Logan picks them up again later; let the pig run free; went undercover with you and Logan and met three men I hope never to meet again—Will Duckett, Mad Mike Monroe, and Paulie Crane—learned that Ruby Gold killed Kenny Cochran but have no idea how to prove it was her, seeing as how she's got handlers handling her handlers and there's no way to find out where she is, who she's with, or what's she doing; was in the wrong place at the wrong time to stop the killer from murdering a man he had—guess what—no plans to murder; then took a call from the killer, who actually watched us screw the pooch and took pity on me for trying so hard but being so stupid and gave me a follow-up clue for the next poor bastard on his hit list. So I'd say my day was, well, stressful. How about you, sweetheart?"

"Two words. Chloe. Roger."

"You win."

We both laughed but didn't speak after that. Which was fine. It had been what Logan might have called a good long goddamn day for both of us.

The *Kung Fu Fu* call sheet was taped to my door. LaTanya hadn't been kidding about adding Rick's role as the renegade reporter who has a love affair with renegade Detective Cassie Barnett. Rick's call was at eight. I had to be at Columbia Cardiology at nine. It was two in the morning.

My head hit the pillow, and I thought of four things before I passed out. One, the killer had known what was going down tonight at RJM. Which meant, two, there was a leak in Logan's task force. Three, I'd earned a point by asking the correct question: What did he ever do to you? Four, Rick had called me *honey*, and I had called him *sweetheart*, and it had felt...normal. Natural. Comfortable. Like a soft pair of jeans. Like listening to an album that reminds you of your best friend. Like we'd been calling each other those names for a good long goddamn time.

And then it was eight in the morning, and we were shooting in 4B, Warren White's apartment, which was astounding in and of itself because Warren never let anyone in his apartment—ever. I'd been in there exactly once since I'd taken the job as brownstone manager, when Warren helped me with a counterfeiting case a few months earlier. No one else had ever been through the door. Except Al, who was the only one granted access to Warren's domain. Because even though Warren and Al did not like each other, they were best friends and illegal rental-car business associates. The truth was that if Al wasn't a nice man—and he wasn't—then Warren was possibly *less* nice. They were a piece of work as a pair.

I'd told LaTanya that Warren was sort of a mad scientist of stamps and coins and currency in his real life, and that, based on my one time in there, his real-life office might be perfect to play his movie-life office. But Warren had turned LaTanya down when she'd knocked on his door to scout his place. Wouldn't even open his door. So she'd offered him an associate-producer credit like the one Al had for agreeing to let his character be a zombie drug dealer instead of just a drug dealer—Al was sensitive about his zombie-like looks. The opportunity to rub his equal credit in Al's face had been too much for Warren to turn down.

Warren (or maybe some tenant way back when before Warren) had removed the walls in the railroad flat separating the living room, the first bedroom, and the second bedroom, leaving one long, fifty-by-eighteen-foot space. Opposite the front door, floor-to-ceiling hardwood bookshelves painted midnight black ran the entire length of the wall. A black ladder on a rolling track was connected to the bookshelves so that Warren could access the stuff on the top shelf anywhere in the room. And there was more stuff than was possible to take in on first look. Or second look. Or maybe ever.

The world's history, philosophy, sociology, psychology, geography, and politics of coins and currency and stamps in international volumes of magazines and newsletters and pamphlets and books were jammed in everywhere between Warren's vast collections, which were painstakingly catalogued and organized for frequent access and research.

Hanging on the wall opposite the bookshelves were huge maps of the world with colored pins and labels and notes. Box frames of specials coins and bills and stamps. Framed letters of commendation and appreciation from collecting organizations around the globe representing a lifetime of archivist excellence and achievement.

Between the maps were reading areas, leather chairs, wooden end tables, and vintage floor lamps. Three long dining tables were set down the center of the fifty-foot space. The middle one, the largest, was Warren's desk, his personal work surface. On it were a variety of magnifying gizmos, computers, printers, and phones. The tables to either side were piled high with oversized books opened to specific pages denoting whatever the hell coins and currency and stamps Warren was working with.

If you took the office of the Smithsonian Institute Curator

of Coins and the office of the Smithsonian Institute Curator of Currency and the office of the Smithsonian Institute Curator of Stamps and mystically merged them into one wild Library of Congress, then let Hollywood have a whack at it, this would be the result.

The Library of Warren.

I was here to get Rick settled. I wasn't in the scene, which, according to LaTanya's treatment—amended in the margins— was about Rick's renegade reporter meeting Warren's renegade mad scientist to talk about the bomb on the bus but instead talking about renegade Detective Cassie Barnett, who somehow had inside information that would tell the world upon which bus the bomb was ticking. That Cassie had inside information was news to me. And news to her. And news to LaTanya, who had no idea what Barnett's information was, inside or outside. Or inside out.

Warren and Rick were on the set, which was lit and hot and ready to roll. Rick stood across the large center desk from Warren, who was supposed to look like a mad scientist concocting mad-scientist concoctions but looked instead like a Black, short, bald, overweight sixty-three-year-old lifelong coin, currency, and stamp collector busy cataloguing coins and currency and stamps, which is who he was and what he was doing.

LaTanya was doing double duty as director and camera operator. She was on the set, locked and loaded.

"We got a renegade motherfucking mad scientist on the run from the law and a renegade motherfucking newspaper reporter on the run from the IRS, and before fists fly between them, the scientist going to tell the reporter that renegade Detective Cassie Barnett secretly knows the secret of which damn city bus carrying the bomb. But your characters got to call each other by name, as in *fuck you whatever the fuck your fucking name is*, so what are your names?"

"Lenny Pryor. Lenny for Lenny Bruce. Pryor for Richard Pryor. Two of my heroes," Rick said.

"Renegade reporter Lenny Pryor in the house," LaTanya said.

"Warren White," Warren said.

"That's *your* name," LaTanya said.

"Yes, I'm going to use my own name," Warren said.

"Can't use your real name in a movie," LaTanya said.

"No one will expect it," Warren said.

"'Cause no one ever do it," LaTanya said. "Who the fuck you think you are, Elton John making a guest appearance on *Big Bang*?"

"It's outside the box, I admit," Warren said. "But so is this improvised independent feature film. Imagine the reviews: *Renegade actor Warren White, as directed by renegade director LaTanya Bellamy, used his real-life name as his character name to make the case that perhaps he's sort of a renegade mad scientist in his real life as well.* Which, of course, I am."

LaTanya wasn't having it, so Rick slid off the set while they argued.

"It's crazy town around here, the nuthouse of the Upper East Side. You know that, right?" Rick said, gesturing at Warren and LaTanya and the whole House of Emotional Tics.

"If you're here long enough, they suck you in, and you go with the flow."

"If had to guess, I'd say Warren's been here much longer than long enough."

"Four and a half decades. Longer than long enough for his rent-controlled rent to be ridiculously low, which is why he's stayed in the brownstone all these years. Considering the realities of New York City rental rates, it's like Dai Ying, the Chinese real-estate conglomerate that owns the building, is paying Warren to live here. Which, as an aside, is not a problem for

Dai Ying, who uses the brownstone to launder dirty yuan into dollars."

"Is that how Fu ended up here? Dai Ying's with the Chinese mob?"

"Yes, that's *how* Fu ended up here. *Why* Fu ended up here remains a mystery."

Rick nodded, gestured around Warren's apartment. "Like this place. What the hell's going on in here anyway? What is all this stuff?"

"Warren's night job for the last forty-five years has been late-shift doorman in a snooty Third Avenue residential building filled with snooty parents and their snooty kids and their snooty pets living their snooty lives without ever taking the time to learn his name. Not that he cares. His day job, aside from his illegal rental-car company, is collecting coins, currency, and stamps from around the globe. He's been doing it for fifty-plus years and is an honest-to-God expert in all three disciplines. A fact, he tells me ad nauseum, that makes him one of the very few men on the East Coast who's simultaneously a numismatist, a notaphile, and a philatelist. '*Watch your mouth, Warren,*' is my usual response."

"You could be a comedian, McCall. You got skills."

We watched Warren and LaTanya debate the history of actor credits in independent feature films, a subject about which neither of them had the faintest idea. Time was ticking. I had to leave for Columbia Cardiology.

"Lillian Pearl," Rick said, as I turned to the door.

"Who?" I said.

"Ruby Gold's ghostwriter. She told me at the pilot that Lillian Pearl was ghostwriting her life story. Sounded like a big damn deal to Ruby. You said you had no idea how to prove Ruby killed Cochran because she has handlers handling her handlers, and there's no way to find out where she is, who she's with, or what's she doing. Lillian Pearl might be the place to start. The ghostwriter might know where the ghosts are."

I nodded. "I'll pick you up after Columbia Cardiology, and we'll find out."

Before he could answer, Warren and LaTanya turned to me.

"McCall," Warren said. "Can you please explain to Director Bullhead that I am not someone to be dismissed out of hand. That I am, in fact, one of the few men on the East Coast who is simultaneously a numismatist, a notaphile, and a philatelist."

I looked at Rick and gave him my best stand-up grin. "Watch your mouth, Warren."

Rick smiled. "You got skills, McCall."

27

WHAT'S WITH THE CROWN?

Between Morningside and Riverside parks on the way west side of Manhattan is the Ivy League neighborhood known as Morningside Heights. It's primarily a residential area, but there's an abundance of distinguished religious, medical, and educational institutions that also call this uptown West Harlem community home.

Columbia University, the oldest house of higher learning in New York (and the third-ranked university in the country) is here—with its renowned graduate schools and student population of 30,000—and its ten-billion-dollar-endowment footprint is all over the place. The Manhattan School of Music is here too. And so is Barnard College. And Teachers College. Union Theological Seminary. Jewish Theological Seminary of America. Bank Street College of Education. Plenty of brainpower in Morningside Heights.

Plenty of spiritual muscle too. The massive, holy episcopal mountain known as the Cathedral of St. John the Divine, the seat of the Bishop—the largest cathedral in the world—dominates its transcendent West Harlem landscape. But Riverside Church, Church of Notre Dame, Corpus Christi Church, and

Interchurch Center give Morningside Heights religiosity to spare.

New York Presbyterian Medical Center, Mount Sinai Doctors Hospital, and Mount Sinai Morningside Hospital, all renowned health care organizations, are present and accounted for. They intertwine and interact with Columbia University and are surrounded, serviced, and supported by countless private medical practices providing personal, specialized care in every discipline—including cardiology.

Located in a grand old residential building on 116th Street between Amsterdam Avenue and Broadway, opposite Columbia Law School, within shouting distance of the hospitals, Columbia Cardiology comprised the entire first floor of the building. It was sprawling. It was state of the art. It was tastefully decorated—the latest in medical interior design. Everything you would expect from Dr. Gideon King.

King was at the very top of every list of Best Cardiologists in New York, the greater New York metropolitan area, the Northeast, the East Coast...any damn directory that detailed best cardiologists—wherever the hell they named them from. He'd founded Columbia Cardiology three-and-a-half decades earlier when he was just thirty years old. He'd hand-built the practice with his prodigious medical talent—and take-no-prisoners approach to the business of medicine—from one professional (him) to ninety-five cardiologists, two dozen cardiovascular and thoracic surgeons, and two hundred and fifty support staff—medical and administrative—spread across five cutting-edge offices: this one in West Harlem, another in Princeton, New Jersey, a third in Great Neck, Long Island, a fourth in Norwalk, Connecticut, and a fifth in Morristown, New Jersey.

He'd invested in real estate throughout his stellar career and was really rich. Many millions. Double townhouse on the Upper West Side. Mansion in New Canaan. Beachfront palace in Mantoloking. Commercial investment properties all over the tristate area. Apartment buildings in every borough. Sports cars. Race horses. Really rich.

And really ruthless, meaning heartless—a funny word to be associated with when you were also a renowned cardiologist. He'd been married and divorced four times. Multiple children with each wife. *New York Post*–gossip-page alimony settlements. High-society associates. He was larger than life. He knew it. And he liked it.

Logan and a half dozen other task-force detectives were already at work, taking statements, checking files, and reading both practice and private emails when I arrived. Jesse was at the door.

"What's his mood?" I said.

"Somewhere south of kill-anyone-that-talks-to-me," Jesse said.

"He said he'd shoot me in the heart if I showed up."

"Been nice knowing you."

"Where is he?"

"Conference room with Dr. King himself."

There were maybe a dozen doctors doing their cardiology thing, plus thirty or forty physician assistants, RNs, and administrative support staff scurrying back and forth with folders and charts and billing statements and insurance printouts and other medical paperwork particular to cardiologists. Patients filled the waiting area, which looked a lot like a modern, upscale hotel lobby, with flat-screen/touch-screen computer monitors updating weather, news, lifestyle, and sports reports, fancy furniture, and coffee/juice/water bar.

As I made my way to the conference room on the far side of the office, I passed task-force detectives questioning employees in the hallways, offices, and empty examination rooms. There was an unmistakable tension in the air. Bad shit was going down, and everyone at Columbia Cardiology could feel it.

I arrived at the glass-walled conference room. Logan and

several task-force cops were speaking with the one and only Dr. Gideon King and King's attorneys. Without breaking stride, Logan gestured with his index finger in a way that said, *Not the fuck now, McCall. Does your brain not work even a little? If you're still here when I'm done with Dr. King, I will shoot you in the heart.* It was remarkable how much that man could say with his index finger.

But I was here, and I wasn't leaving.

Because though the killer's clue was clear—*the king dies at dawn in a day; long live the king at Columbia Cardiology*—what was even clearer was that the killer wouldn't possibly have made it that easy.

Yes, Gideon King was no doubt the king of Columbia Cardiology. And, yes, the king was slated to die at dawn tomorrow, so early Saturday morning. And, yes, preventing his death would be as simple as keeping King close until the death date was past us.

But—and it was a big freaking *but* for me—there had been nothing simple about the killer so far. Everything had been misdirection. Double entendre. Victims turned on their heads without their eyes. Meaning there was more to the clue than the clue clued in.

I walked through the expansive office, which seemed as large as a football field, past rooms with cardiology gear that had to have cost King millions, past file rooms and breakrooms and exam rooms and doctors' offices, and arrived at the administration wing, at the door of Tammy Bosworth, practice manager.

Large office. Well-appointed. Family photos on the credenza. Walls of cardiology business books and publications. File cabinets. Potted plants. Eight framed inspiration posters on the walls: *Believe and Succeed, Teamwork, Walk the Talk, Affirmation, Attitude, Gratitude, Honesty,* and *Success.* All upscale and nicely done. All business but approachable.

Bosworth was Black, midfifties, sharply dressed. She was the no-nonsense boss around here; that was her vibe. She owed King a flawless practice that ran like a clock, and she delivered in spades or heads rolled. But there was another vibe as well: patience, tolerance, kindness. *Mama Bosworth loves you, child.*

"Ms. Bosworth." I tapped on her open door.

She looked up. "May I help you?"

"I'm Kate McCall. I'm a private investigator working with Detective Logan, trying to help him find the killer who's threatened Dr. King, and I was hoping you could tell me something about the office that might open a door I didn't even know was there."

"You're a private investigator. Not officially part of the task force?"

"Not officially, no."

"Your connection is personal?"

She was sharp as shit. No wonder Gideon King had made her his practice manager.

"Yes," I said. "The same person we think is threatening Dr. King murdered my father."

I hadn't been this truthful in I couldn't remember how long. Actually, I could remember exactly how long. As soon as I'd inherited Jimmy's business and become a PI. *Must be the inspirational posters*, I thought.

"I'm sorry," Tammy said, coming around her desk to me. "Let's walk."

She took me on a tour of the office, giving me history of the place and the people, pointing out who was who and what was what. She was especially proud of what the practice offered its patients.

"We have equipment that allows for the accurate diagnosis of a wide spectrum of symptoms and needs. Cardiac ultrasound and stress; 64-slice low radiation CT; nuclear SPECT CT camera, ankle-brachial index, ABI therapy, vascular ultrasound, enhanced external counter pulsation, EKG, cardiac and pulmonary rehabilitation are among the diagnostic services that—"

I lost focus on what Tammy was telling me because we walked past an administrative office, and the door was open, and the light was out, and no one was home, and I looked inside and saw a picture that tweaked my radar in a way I couldn't ignore.

"Excuse me, sorry for interrupting, Tammy. It's incredible how much gear you've got and how efficient everything is. If I ever need a cardiologist, I'm coming here," I said, making Tammy stop with me at the open office admin door. "But whose office is this?"

She looked into the office, then at me. "Miguel Herradura. Mickey. He's our director of insurance. Manages the filings, forms, coverages, payments, reimbursements, federal laws, state laws, rules, new rules, new-new rules. Medical insurance is complicated and confusing and—"

"What's with the crown?"

There was a framed photograph of a man in some nightclub, on the stage, jamming with a Latino band. He was playing congas and wearing a crown.

She led me in and turned on the light. It was smaller than her office but still nice.

"Mickey owns a little piece of a Latin nightclub in Harlem. It's in a small, converted old church on Frederick Douglass Boulevard, maybe 145th or 146th, a few blocks down from Jacob's. That's a soul food restaurant on the corner of—"

"I've been there. Amazing. Fried chicken, collard greens, pork chops. Thanks, Tammy. Now I'm starving."

We both laughed. But there was something in the back of my mind that wasn't funny.

"You were saying...the crown," I said.

"Mickey plays congas. He's unbelievable. Every Latin band

wants him to sit in. Plus he has his own band. I mean, he's the best. They call him the King of Conga."

"Excuse me?"

"The King of Conga. That's our Mickey."

There was an actual crown on the bookshelf. A freaking crown. And family pics. And dozens of band photos signed by other Latin musicians, some of them household names. Enrique Iglesias, Freddy Fender, Rubén Blades, Trini Lopez, Willie Colán, Gloria Estefan. Most of them writing things like, *To the King of Conga, thanks for sitting in.* And, *Mickey, you are truly the King.* And, *To the one and only King of Conga, love you, Mickey...*

"And he does medical insurance?" I said.

"Steady gig. Health insurance. 401(k). Not a bad choice for a musician with a family," she said. But there was sadness in her voice, just a touch.

"But?"

"He recently lost his wife to breast cancer. He's been taking time off when he can for the last few months. Playing at the club. Doing some grief therapy. He's sixty-four. His children are grown and out of town, living their own lives. They're supportive, but he's mostly alone now. The music helps him deal with the loss. Probably better than the therapy. He's in a group. Or was. Anyway, he's only working if and when I need him, taking time to adjust, to find balance. I'm accommodating when I can be. Especially for something like this, for someone like Mickey."

"The King of Conga."

"Yes."

Bells and whistles were bonging and, well, whistling in my head. This was it. The misdirection. Had to be. *The king dies at dawn in a day; long live the king at Columbia Cardiology.* Not the king *of* Columbia Cardiology. That would be Dr. Gideon King, no doubt. The king *at* Columbia Cardiology. The King of

Conga. Jesus Christ, it could be Mickey, couldn't it? Why not? Although, why the hell would anyone want to kill the King of Conga?

"Any idea how I can get in touch with him?" I said.

"I'll give you his contact information, but you can usually catch him at his club."

"What's it called?"

"Dawn."

Oh my God.

I took Mickey's contact information, thanked Tammy for the tour, and hurried back to the glassed-in conference room, where Logan was still speaking with Gideon King. Except other folks had joined the meeting—a few doctors, maybe another attorney or two, Jesse, more task-force cops—which had turned heated in a way I hadn't expected. There was anger in the room. Frustration. Finger pointing. Someone slapped the conference table with resentment to make a point. King dismissed the guy with a condescending wave of his hand. Raised voices followed, muffled by the glass so I couldn't hear what was being said. It didn't matter. It wasn't good, whatever it was.

Someone saw me standing by the glass and shut the blinds. I took a breath, opened the door, and stepped into the room, though not all the way in.

"Logan," I said.

Everyone looked at me.

Logan growled the words. "Get out, McCall."

"I need to see you right now."

"Are you kidding me? Jesse, get her the hell out of here."

Jesse started to walk toward me. I put up my hand like I meant business. For some reason, and to my amazement, it worked. Jesse stopped.

"It's RJM all over again if you don't listen to what I have to say," I said.

Logan took a defeated breath. It was possible he thought I

might actually have something valuable to add to this cardiology carnival. But it was much more likely he just needed to get the hell out of there for a minute. He rolled his eyes, nodded *excuse me* to the fuming room, and met me in the hallway.

"King's not the king," I said. "I was with the practice manager, Tammy Bosworth, and we went past an admin office, and I saw—"

"I don't give a shit what you saw, McCall. Gideon King has mortal enemies coming out of his ass. There are three raging cocksuckers on the Columbia Cardiology board of directors who have fucking threatened his life directly. They're going for a coup. Trying to get King out of the practice on account of he might be the single biggest douchebag in the field of medicine. Right now, Gideon King is president, CEO, and Chairman of the Board of this money machine that pretends to be a doctors' office. But board member Malcolm Gray, hedge-fund fuckwad, is out to change that. He has a different vision for the practice. Think national chain. Walmart Cardiology. He's got money to burn, friends in dark places, and a history of violent behavior— two arrests for assault and battery. Third wife accused him of hiring someone to kill her. Conspiracy to commit murder. They took him in, but she dropped the charges and got twice the money as the prenup stipulated, so who the hell knows? And oh fucking yes, Gray's one of the three who threatened King's life in no uncertain terms. Plus, he's gone AWOL as the clock ticks toward tomorrow. So please don't tell me what you saw when you were strolling through the park with the practice manager. Don't tell me anything, McCall. Don't talk at all. Just go home, let the big dogs run, and stay out of my way."

And then he went back inside the conference room and shut the door behind him. I stood there for a moment, not knowing what the hell to say. And then I did.

"The king is dead; long live the King of Conga."

28

———

AN INEXPLICABLE, BIZARRO, PERPENDICULAR UNIVERSE

I got back to the House of Emotional Tics in time to catch Rick getting out of the shower. He'd also showered before his *Kung Fu Fu* debut.

"That bad?" I said. "You needed a cold shower?"

"Bad is not the right word," he said. "Inexplicable. Bizarro. Perpendicular universe. Maybe all of them together. Yes, all of them together. An inexplicable, bizarro, perpendicular universe."

"Welcome to my world."

"Improvising in a vacuum of ad-lib lunacy. That's what it was."

"Did you stick to the outline?"

"Who knows? We talked about bombs and buses. We talked about a drug that would imbue whoever ingested it with super-duper martial-arts skills, and we talked about Detective Cassie Barnett being on the take. We talked a lot about Cassie Barnett in general. Warren made up your entire life story. Family history. Dirty-cop career. All of it."

"I'm a dirty renegade cop now?"

"The dirtiest."

"LaTanya was okay with that?"

"The Cinematic Cyclops thought that was the best part of the shoot."

"What did she say?"

He did his best LaTanya voice. *"Detective Peanut not just dirty. She filthy dirty."*

"I should talk to Warren to see what he said so I know who Barnett is and how she got that way."

"Don't bother. He painted you as a deeply troubled, criminally psychotic, sociopathic liar with a badge."

"So whatever I say the rest of the shoot is a lie."

"A blazing lie with nefarious ulterior motives. It was moving faster than I could keep track, but I think you're a drug user too."

"Barnett's an addict?"

"Of all the worst drugs, yes. And an alcoholic."

"So there's no redeeming her?"

"She's irredeemable."

"Good to know."

Rick got dressed, and I googled Lillian Pearl, Ruby Gold's ghostwriter. She had her very own author website and Facebook page. There was much to learn.

She was a poet, a how-to guru for aspiring memoirists, and a ghostwriter to the stars. If you were famous and wanted to claim you'd written your autobiography all by your lonesome but couldn't compose your way around the block, then Lillian Pearl was your ghostwriting girl. She'd ghostwritten dozens of celebrity autobiographies. Book by book, the credit was always the same: Written by Celebrity Name Goes Here with Lillian Pearl. Broadway, Hollywood, Silicon Valley, Wall Street, Washington DC...big names were big names were big names, but none were too big to hire Lillian Pearl to ghost their life stories. With. Lillian. Pearl. According to her website, she was in her midfifties. Her Facebook page confirmed she was working with Ruby Gold. *It's true-blue true*, her post said. *The great Ruby Gold is writing her phenomenal life story with little Lily Pearl.* Another post let on that there was no publisher in place because Ruby wanted a bidding war and, by God, if Ruby Gold wanted a bidding war, then let the bidding begin. There were samples of Lillian's poetry, links to her books on Amazon, reviews to read, and plenty of pictures of her small yappy dog, a Pomeranian named Yo-Yo. I like dogs. I do. But not when they're the size of cats. At least cats don't yap at your heels. I hoped I wouldn't have to kick Yo-Yo into next week for incessant yapping. Lillian had an office on Second Avenue and 53rd Street.

I called Pearl, scheduled an appointment, and Rick and I left the brownstone. We walked to 86th and Second and caught a bus downtown because it was a pretty November day and we felt like seeing the city in something other than a careening cab. Our cover for Lillian was that Rick and I owned a brand-new, niche-focused, well-funded, small-house publishing company looking to make a splash in the biography and autobiography business. Our company name was: High Profile Press.

To look the part, I'd chosen a stylish black wig and blue contact lenses, black business suit, blue silk blouse to match my eyes, and happening black ankle boots. I was as hip a New York up-and-coming publisher as anyone could want to be. Rick was Rick. Jeans, sport jacket, Vans, Life is Good baseball cap, dark shades. For shit's sake, I'd let us publish Ruby's book any day, including today.

We found two seats in the middle of the bus. Rick took the window. His bodyguard took the aisle. We were quiet while we settled into, well, being on a bus. I'd taken buses thousands of times, of course, but hardly at all since I'd become a PI at the end of July, when Jimmy was murdered. After that, I'd had cases to solve and client money for cabs (and Warren's Toyotas) and no time to spare for a slow-rolling bus. Rick hadn't been on a bus in decades. He couldn't remember his last bus ride.

We were only going thirty-three blocks. For the first ten or so, I thought about three things.

First: Matthew's marriage in ten days. I would need a dress. And shoes. And a purse. And probably other mother-of-the-groom things I'd have to study up on in between shopping for shoes and a dress and a purse and the other mother-of-the-groom things I studied up on. Like the rehearsal dinner. Didn't the groom's family handle the rehearsal dinner? They did. Or I did. Or I'd have to. Jesus Christ, when was I going to arrange that? I could see myself being a nervous wreck *at* the wedding because I was a nervous wreck *before* the wedding. I made a mental note to myself to calm the heck down and enjoy the nuptial ride. Oh my God, did I have to throw Doleful Nina a wedding shower? A baby shower? Was that my responsibility? Ten days. Ten.

Second: six voicemails and six texts for Logan since I'd left Columbia Cardiology—and no callback or reply. Logan had blown me off. And while a part of me wanted to blow him off right back, I knew I had to try to alert him about the possibility that Gideon King was the smokescreen and not the target, that there was at least a chance the killer was messing with our heads again, and that the King of Conga was the king in the clue. I couldn't be *sure* if I was right or wrong about that— though I *felt* like I was right—but if Logan would listen, then he'd have the facts on the table and could make the call. Maybe two task-force cops could check out the King of Conga. If it turned out to be a false alarm , then so what? All bases would have been covered, Dr. King would have been saved, and the killer would have been caught. But if it went the other way, then the task force would have kept Mickey Herradura alive to play another gig—and also caught the killer. Win-win. If I made no effort to alert Logan, then I was the poor excuse of a person he said I was. Which was why I'd called and texted him six times each.

Third: jealousy. Mine. Me jealous of Chloe because Rick was rubbing up against her, emotionally and literally. We'd been on the precipice of having that conversation after we'd taken the cab from Coney Island—where Rick had burned Paulie Crane's pricey cards—and were sitting surveillance in Flushing. I'd said, *"I think you're flirting with your bodyguard."* He'd said, *"I think you're flirting with your client."* And the jealousy discussion had been about to begin, featuring questions such as: Why was I jealous? Was I making it up? Had he really been flirting with me? Had I been flirting back? Was that his take too? Were we consenting adults headed toward liking each other because of the case or in spite of it? And what the hell do we do about it now? What was I feeling? What was he feeling? This was where we were about to begin when our relief arrived, and we'd taken off for the D-Cup. So long ago. All of yesterday.

I wanted to talk to Rick about all of that. The wedding. The King of Conga. My feelings about my feelings, meaning him and his case and Ruby Gold and all of that, and so I opened my mouth to start the conversation and something completely different came out.

"Where did you go Wednesday morning?"

"What do you mean?" he said.

"I went for a run, came back, and you were gone. Ruby's pilot wasn't until late afternoon. What did you do all day? Where did you go?"

"Wednesday...Let's see...Wednesday..."

"It's Friday. Yesterday was Thursday. Day before that. Two days ago."

He smiled, making a Rick Gotti joke out of a serious question. "You worried there's another woman, McCall?"

Was I? It was possible, sure. Maybe even likely. Who the hell knew what was happening between my head and my heart at this moment in time? But I wasn't going to fall for it. He wasn't joking his way out of this one. Wondering where Rick had gone Wednesday morning had been on the back burner of my brain for two days, yes, but for reasons I wasn't aware of it had pushed its way to the front, which meant it was more important than I'd thought it was, again, for reasons I wasn't aware of.

"I asked you first, Rick. Where did you go?"

A certain sadness slipped into my voice. Sadness mixed with concern mixed with affection. It was honest. Real emotion. I hadn't consciously put it there. Hadn't been acting. I know Rick heard it because he looked at me, and his smile faded, and his face softened, and he nodded as if he knew it was time to tell me the truth about something he hadn't been truthful about.

"It's not another woman," he said. "There's no one in my life like that. No one special. No one who can put up with me. I'm kind of a mess if you haven't noticed."

"Then what? Where did you go?"

"I meant to tell you. I was going to tell you."

"Tell me what?"

"I have—"

The bus lurched forward.

A jolt of the brakes whiplashed people back and forth. There was screaming all around, which was not a good thing. New Yorkers don't scream when they've been bandied about on a bus. It wasn't that kind of scream.

I got my bearings. Looked up. Three rows in front us, in the aisle seat across the aisle, a big man—*possibly* the bear—had stood up and been knocked off balance like everyone else.

But unlike everyone else he had a gun in his right hand.

The bus jerked again. What the hell was the driver doing? People went flying. Bodies this way and that way. Everyone shrieked because the big man—*probably* the bear—was regaining his balance, turning around, and pointing his gun at Rick.

I had two options, both of which I attempted to review in the time it took to think about blinking. Not actually blink. Just thinking the thought of blinking.

Option one was throw myself in front of Rick and take the bullet. But the big man—*likely* the bear—would simply shoot me first and then shoot Rick. And if he shot Rick first, then he'd shoot me second.

Option one, I thought, *Rick and I both get shot.*

Option two was...I ran out of review time.

I exploded out of my seat and hit the big man—*definitely* the bear—in the waist like a linebacker and whacked his right arm.

The gun went off.

The bullet smashed the window beside Rick's head.

The bus shuddered to a violent stop, and I crashed to the ground on top of the bear, who lost the gun when we—and everyone else—went down hard.

I reached up and punched him, an uppercut to the jaw that only clipped him because of all the other people who'd fallen in the aisle with us. On top of us. Around us. Twisting. Turning. Struggling. Scrambling. Desperate to get up and get off the damn bus before the gun went off again. Shouting and screaming. Running up and down and all around. Panic city.

The bear grabbed me by the shoulder and ripped me off him. Before I could reset myself, he'd gotten to his feet and run off the bus.

I couldn't believe how out of breath I was. It was only just dawning on me what had happened. I turned to make sure Rick was okay.

And Rick was gone.

29

ADONIS TO THE RESCUE

THE BUS HAD DIED ON SECOND AVENUE AND 56TH STREET, three blocks from Lillian Pearl's office. The driver said the engine had seized, the steering gear had locked, the brakes had jammed, the lines had flooded, and whatever other bad bus shit that was possible had happened all at once for reasons no one yet knew.

Every passenger had the same tale to tell: while the bus herked and jerked in the middle of Second Avenue traffic, there'd been a big man waving a gun and a brave woman who'd taken him down and saved the day.

People buzzed about it on the sidewalk while looking at the deceased bus, waiting for a tow truck to move the thing to the bus morgue—where a city mechanic would perform an autopsy and determine its cause of death—and for the cops and news cameras to appear on the scene. Maybe a reporter would interview them live on the street. Maybe they would be on the six o'clock news. Maybe their fifteen minutes had finally arrived.

Miraculously, the bus had not hit anything while in its last violent spasms of operation. No one was hurt. The driver was declared a hero. I was declared a hero.

Rick was not declared a hero. Rick was declared AWOL, as in absent without leave, as in he did not have leave from me to be absent, as in what the freaking hell?

The last thing in the world I wanted was to speak with the police—even though I was the brave woman everyone was gushing about who'd tackled the big man with the gun—so I found a coffee shop on Third Avenue and 56th Street, a world away from the hubbub, bought a cappuccino, took a table by the window, and made some calls.

"Rick, this is Kate McCall, the brave woman on the bus who linebackered the bear and saved your life. Remember me? I called to say you suck. You now need a bodyguard to protect you from your bodyguard. I can't believe you left me again. You better call me in the next five minutes. Did I mention you suck? Because you suck."

"Lillian, hi, it's Barbara O'Rourke. High Profile Press. Bill Bowman and I have a meeting scheduled with you in about thirty minutes, and we've been held up by a conference call with Disney—they're interested in optioning and adapting a ghosted autobiography we represent—and I was hoping we could push our appointment. We're crossing our fingers that you can see us two hours from right now. If you can call or text me at this number as soon as you come up for air, we'll make arrangements on our end and be at your office exactly on time. Thank you, Lillian."

"Roger, it's Kate. Stop what you're doing and meet me at the coffee shop on Third and 56th in one hour sharp. You'll see me in the window. Black wig. I've got a case I need help with. Paying gig for you. You're a bigshot biography publisher named Bill Bowman. I'm your partner Barbara O'Rourke. Bill and Barbara. I'll fill you in when you get here. Dress the part, Roger.

We're hip and happening. Text me back that you got this message and you're on your way. See you in an hour."

Thirty seconds later I got a text from Lillian. *Thanks. Two hours. Perfect.*

Roger texted me one minute after that. *Flattered you need my help but not surprised. My help is exactly what you need. Adonis to the rescue. Your own personal Greek god. You can count on Roger. Side note, you couldn't wait until tonight. Had to see me now. I knew it all the time. Ha!*

Roger had an ego that could choke a—*Whoa...wait. Adonis to the rescue?* Jesus, it was Friday. *Psychedelic Sunday* opened tonight. I knew that—I mean, of course I knew that—but with the bear on the bus and the pig in the pen and Rick ditching me and the King of Conga and Fu saving my life for the fifth or sixth time and Matthew's wedding and Ruby Gold and... Shit, I just hadn't thought about it.

It was almost noon. So in about five hours, Roger and I would meet in the D-Cup dressing room well before anyone else arrived and run through our pre-show habitual ritual, and then the rest of the cast would arrive, and the lights would dim, and the music would play, and the curtain would rise, and I would sing and dance my heart out for a full house and the bear on the bus would be but a memory and—

Whoa...wait. The bear on the bus?

How the hell had I missed the bear getting on the bus? How had he known we were on that particular bus at that particular time in the first place? It couldn't have been serendipity. There were five thousand buses rumbling around the boroughs. It wasn't possible the bear guessed we'd be riding that exact bus at that exact time. Not possible. So how in the world had he—

Whoa...wait. The pig in the pen?

Yes, the pig in the pen. It had to be the pig in the pen. The pig in the pen was the plausible explanation. The pig in the pen was the problem. The pig must have called the bear from the

Boulevard Motor Inn, and the bear had come to see if someone was watching the pig after kidnapping him and letting him go, and he'd seen me and Rick drive away in the White Whale, and he'd followed us to the D-Cup, and he'd waited us out and then followed us to the House of Emotional Tics, and it had been two thirty in the morning—Friday morning, *this* morning for shit's sake—and he hadn't known and couldn't have known what apartment we were in, so he hadn't been able to make his move, so he'd waited all night and followed us to the Second Avenue bus, slipped on behind us without me knowing— Jimmy would rip me for being such a careless bodyguard—and made his move while the bus was puking its guts out and Rick was ditching me and—

Whoa...wait. Rick ditching me?

It wasn't his ditching me that had made me crazy. Well, it was. But it was also his ditching me before he'd finished telling me the truth about something he'd hadn't exactly been truthful about. After the bus had expired and the bear had run off and Rick had vanished, I'd raced up and down the block looking for him. Both sides of Second Avenue. In the stores. Around the corners. Residential entrances. Corporate lobbies. I couldn't believe he was gone again. I was livid but also confused. Had I pushed him away by asking him where he'd been Wednesday morning? Had I reminded him that he'd had somewhere else to be? *"I have—"* he'd said before the bear on the bus cut him short. *"I have—"* What? Tennis elbow that required spur-of-the-moment medical treatment? Midweek pop-up flea markets he couldn't afford to miss? Tickets to see the King of Conga at Dawn and—

Whoa...wait. The King of Conga?

If tonight was *Psychedelic Sunday* opening night, then when was I going to stop the killer from shooting Columbia Cardiology's conga king in the eyeballs in the king's own uptown club?

After the show, that's when. It was Friday. There would be a band playing at Dawn until two in the morning. When the D-Cup curtain came down, I'd head to Harlem. The cleaning crew at the club would be out by four a.m. Since Logan was and would be fully focused on the king *of* Columbia Cardiology, I would keep on the king *at* Columbia Cardiology. Fu and I would be waiting at Dawn between four and seven Saturday morning to catch the killer in the act and—

Whoa...wait. Fu?

I hadn't seen Fu since he'd saved my life (for the fifth or sixth time) at RJM on Wednesday night. I had to thank him for that. Maybe get him a gift. Although I'd already given him a parrot. How do you follow that? How do you top a thank-you parrot? Anyway, I'd go to Dawn by myself if I had to, but I'd feel better about being alone with the killer in a dark club if I was alone with Fu. So I called him to confirm his availability.

"Fu, it's Kate. I broke the next clue. The killer's going to shoot the King of Conga tonight in Harlem at a club called Dawn. I have to stop him."

"Fu say trap."

"Are you kidding right now? You think I don't know it's a trap? Of course it's a trap. I knew it was a trap as soon as I broke the clue."

"Fu know first."

"You did not know first. I can't stand when you—"

I lost the signal before I had a chance to ask him if he'd bake and decorate a dozen tea cakes—his specialty—for one of the multitudinous showers I might have to host for Loudmouth Nina, who would be my daughter-in-law in ten days and—

Whoa...wait. My son was getting married in ten days?

In the middle of the middle of me trying to catch the creep who'd killed Jimmy and keep Rick alive at the same time, Matthew was going to take a wife and become a husband and soon after that become a father. There was something sensationally otherworldly about my little boy being a dad to his own little boy—or girl, of course. If she was a girl, I'd already decided—a grandparent pronouncement that could not be challenged—she would learn to hit like a man at Raul's. Because you never know when Ruby Gold is going to hire the bear to try to kill you and, when it happens, it helps to have an uppercut that connects like thunder and—

Whoa...wait. Ruby Gold?

Ruby had tried to kill Rick three times and then gone off the grid. I'd tried to reach her several times today—using different names and various voices—and each time had been told she was in a meeting or on a call or in transit or out of town or on the set or unavailable or, and this was my favorite, *having a quiet day*. If sending the bear to kill Rick Gotti on a crowded bus in broad daylight was a quiet day for Ruby Gold, then what the hell was a noisy day? What kind of shit was Ruby up to when she was feeling loud?

"Black wig in the window," Roger said. "Mysterious, yet provocative, just like a best-selling ghostwritten biography."

Roger slid into the booth, looking like a million bucks. Blue blazer, blue shirt, blue tie, blue jeans, blue dress loafers, blue pocket square, blue-frame eyeglasses...upbeat and bold. And blue. As an actor, Roger knew how to dress to impress for success.

I filled him in about Rick's case, up to and including today's attack on the bus, and we reviewed Lillian Pearl's Facebook page and website and talked about our goals once we were in the room with the ghostwriter.

"I auditioned for Ruby once upon a lifetime ago," Roger said. "I humbly submit that if she'd cast me at the time, her career would have reached even higher heights."

"Did you hear anything I said about Rick and the bear and Ruby Gold and Lillian Pearl? Or were you thinking about you the entire time?"

"I'm a talented man, Kate. I did both simultaneously."

"Since I'm paying you, can you please focus more on me and my case and less on you and your ancient auditions?"

"Way ahead of you."

"Of course you are."

"Lillian Pearl is only a little older than me. She's single—"

"Don't go there, Roger."

"She's going to be attracted to me, even if I *don't* signal the feeling's mutual. If I *do* give her the Roger signal, and I intend to turn the temperature up, with style and subtlety, of course, like a fine wine that sneaks up on you, she'll be putty in my hands. Prediction? In the first five minutes, we'll find out where Ruby Gold is hiding and how we get to her. You know the drill, Kate. Give Roger five minutes with a single woman of a certain age, and he'll get you whatever it is you want."

"Last time you went overboard—"

"Last times are for losers."

"You got tased."

"And came back electrified, better than ever."

"The time before that you got pepper sprayed."

"Gay man heartbroken I wasn't gay."

"Teapot to the head."

"Old broad distressed I was too young for her."

"Just follow my lead, will you please?"

"Never been a follower, Kate. That's why you love me."

"I wouldn't call it love exactly."

He was never wrong, even if he was wrong. So there was no point debating. And now there was no time. We left the coffee shop and walked to Lillian Pearl's Second Avenue office.

On the way there, I felt the feeling I often felt with Roger— that his ego was the *Titanic*, and I was along for the ride, and we were headed for the iceberg.

30

SHE'S SHOT DOGS BEFORE

LILLIAN PEARL WAS A THREE-TIME DIVORCEE. ALL HER HUSBANDS had been loaded, and she'd emptied their bank accounts. Plus, she was an uber-successful ghostwriter. Bottom line was her bottom line was millions. A massive SoHo loft was home. A Hamptons beachfront cottage kept her cool in the summer. And a sophisticated office on the thirty-second floor of an ultra-modern, Second Avenue office skyscraper said *success, success, success.*

Except for me it said *warning, warning, warning.* Because *Jimmy's Rules of Private Investigation for Kate, Rule Number Two* was *Never trust anyone who lives or works above the twenty-fifth floor.*

"Lillian, I must mention that you're more impressive in person than you are in print, which is not something I say to every writer I meet on the street, and we're here to be your best bid. In fact, and Barb will agree with me, we want to, we intend to, and we're going to take any and all bids for Ruby's book off the table," Roger said.

It was more like the office of a high-powered CEO. Or a too-big-to-fail bank chairman. Or a billionaire bond trader. A charming reception room opened into an extra-large, wide-open space with black-oak floors and huge Persian rugs defining Lillian's writing/reading/library area, living-room area, painting area, and dining-room/kitchen area. Framed, poster-sized versions of her book covers and her own personally painted paintings hung on three of the four walls because the fourth wall was entirely glass.

No wonder showbiz celebrities, titans of industry, and power-punching politicians were comfortable letting Lillian lead the band. She was one of them. Meaning no publishers ever walked in here and thought they could steal a book from Ms. Pearl.

"Flattery will get you everywhere, Bill," Lillian said. "So kindly keep it coming."

She was too impressive, too imposing a person to be charming, which is not to say she wasn't a certain degree of delightful—not to mention entertaining—because she was all that and more. But her captivating charisma seemed more like a consciously calculated thin outer layer of lovely meant to conceal something deeper and darker, something she was practiced at keeping hidden.

She was a substantial woman—big-boned, as some folks say—with a wide smile and grand laugh that she used as a sort of stick to bonk you on the head so you knew that whatever it was it was funny and you should laugh along with her. *Laugh along with Lillian* could have been her tagline instead of *With Lillian Pearl*. Although there was something decidedly not funny about being bossed around into laughing.

She was five-ten, bleached blonde, not at all unattractive. Diamond-studded bifocals on a gold chain around her neck. Expensive business suit with expensive shoes and expensive jewelry. Her teeth were white on white on white on white. Dazzling smile. And she was using it to flirt right back at Roger, who was shamelessly flirting at her.

"You make it too easy, Lillian," Roger said.

"Are you calling me easy, Bill?" Lillian said.

"If it's working," Roger said.

Gross, I thought.

Roger seemed oblivious to whatever bad-beneath-the-surface juju I was feeling, so maybe I'd made it all up in my head. We'd been here thirty minutes, and so far we'd made small talk about the weather, her success, her Hamptons house, her new Ruby Gold book, and her ever-present Pomeranian, Yo-Yo.

Wherever we were, Yo-Yo was. He was incredibly well-behaved for a yappy. Quiet as a mouse but needy. Yo-Yo needed to be loved, demanded to be loved. Lillian was proud as punch of her Pomeranian. She told us Yo-Yo was her best friend in the world, that she wouldn't know how to face the rest of her life without him. There were framed photographs of Yo-Yo all around the office. Yo-Yo in SoHo. Yo-Yo in the Hamptons by the pool. Yo-Yo with a paintbrush in his mouth like it was a stick he'd found in the yard. Yo-Yo in the kitchen sink getting a bath. Plenty-o-Pomeranian.

"So Mo Yo-Yo," Roger said, smiling. No one appreciated Roger's sense of humor more than Roger.

We walked in, sat down in Lillian's office area to get acquainted, and Yo-Yo jumped into my lap. We moved to the kitchen area to get cups of coffee and become friends, and Yo-Yo jumped in my lap. We walked to the living-room area to get down to brass tacks, and brass tacks to Yo-Yo meant jumping in my lap. What can I say? The dog loved me.

Which I decided to use as a negotiating ploy. Meaning it couldn't hurt if Yo-Yo and I were buddies. It wasn't all that hard to act my way through our newfound friendship. Yo-Yo was pleasant and good natured and passive to the max.

If there was a downside, it was that I got stuck on the couch with the dog in my lap while Roger was free to move about and be Roger-being-Bill. No Pomeranian to rein him in. No little yappy to hold him in place and tamp down his ego.

"So what's the number, Lillian? How do we bring you and Ruby Gold into the High Profile family?" I said.

"Before we talk numbers, Barbara," Lillian said, leering at Roger, "I'd like to know who I'm potentially getting in bed with."

So gross, I thought.

"I can tell you with assurance," Roger said, "the High Profile package looks even better between the sheets."

Too gross, I thought.

"Is there an all-cash advance on the table?" Lillian said.

"One point two," I said.

"You have a bank account with that much money sitting silent?" Lillian said.

"More than that, Lillian," Roger said. "And it's not sitting, it's moving around, buying biographies, publishing them to the public, marketing them to the masses."

"It's not that one point two isn't enough money for Ruby, though it isn't. It's that I've never heard of High Profile Press, and agreeing to terms on Ruby's behalf is going to take more than your simple say-so," Lillian said, batting her eyes. "No matter how handsome you are."

Extra gross, I thought.

"How about a bank statement?" I said. "Will that make our say-so less simple?"

Just before Jimmy was murdered, I'd played a rich ex-wife in a failed micro-budget slasher movie who'd flashed her Bank of Cleveland monthly statement of five million bucks in a last-ditch attempt to stop the slasher from, well, slashing her. It didn't work. Not a single one of her five million bucks could save her. Oh well. I'd kept the cool clothes and the fancy faux jewelry and the stylish chestnut-brown wig and the real-deal bank statement. Because I'd never seen five million bucks—

real or otherwise—in one place before. I never imagined I'd be using it to convince Lillian Pearl I was the publisher for her new book. Or that I'd ever claim to be from Cleveland.

"You've never heard of us because we're new, and we're not New Yorkers," I said. "We're Ohio real-estate developers based in Cleveland who've recently been investing in well-told stories of well-known people. The books are presold by the celebrity's fame alone. The investment is minimal. The ROI is considerable. That's just one of our bank accounts, by the way. Money is not the issue."

"One two is a little low for Ruby," Lillian said, passing the statement back to me.

"One five," Roger said.

"I like the sound of one five, Bill. Especially when it comes across your lips."

"I can think of a few other things I'd like to come across my lips," Roger said.

Super gross, I thought.

"Industry-standard contract beyond the advance?" I said.

The Pomeranian was practically purring in my lap.

"Ruby retains all global ancillary rights—movies, TV, theater, novelizations, prequels, sequels, remakes—into infinity. Highest available royalty rate adjusted annually. The rest we'll let the lawyers do," Lillian said.

She'd been her own literary agent for decades and knew her way around a book deal. Her reputation was *shark meets rattlesnake.*

"And the publishing rights belong to High Profile?" Roger said.

"Exclusive for North America," Lillian said.

"We'll take worldwide publishing, thank you. The rest we agree to," I said.

I'd once worked as a receptionist for a fancy publishing company, listened in on some fierce negotiations, and retained some of the lingo. Not that Yo-Yo gave a shit. He was a Pomeranian puddle. I couldn't get rid of Lillian's dog on a bet.

"Let's put it in writing, shall we?" Lillian said. "A letter of intent from High Profile Press to Lillian Pearl representing Ruby Gold with a fully executed publishing Power of Attorney."

She stood and turned to an elegant rolling bar cart that was maybe fifteen feet from the living-room area, perfectly placed against the massive windows that looked east over Second Avenue and beyond. On the bottom shelf was a yellow pad, a pen, and a handsome wooden box. On the top shelf were a half dozen bottles of top-tier booze.

"Before we sign anything, Lillian, we'd like to speak with Ruby," I said.

That stopped her cold. "Why is that, Barbara? I have Power of Attorney. You don't need Ruby's approval to finalize an agreement with me on her behalf."

There was the beginning of an edge in her voice. Wanting access to Ruby Gold had flipped on her radar. Though maybe it had been on the entire time, and she'd been hiding it. I might have missed it, seeing as how I'd been distracted by Roger's over-the-top ego and Yo-Yo's purring.

"Because I'm not giving anyone, including Ruby Gold, a million five if I've never met them, shaken their hand, thanked them in person, toasted our partnership," I said. "So we'll need access to her first, please."

"Ruby is unavailable to you or to anyone. She's inaccessible," Lillian said.

"She's accessible to you," I said. "You're currently ghostwriting her book, aren't you?"

Her face tensed ever so slightly. Her eyes narrowed just enough to signal that her radar was now turned way up, fully functional. She was quite a good actress. If I hadn't been looking, I might not have noticed. But now I *was* looking.

"Well, then our search for a publisher continues," Lillian said with perfectly snide snark I didn't deserve.

For Pete's sake, I was petting her prized Pomeranian, wasn't I? No need to be snide. Or snarky. Unless she was hiding something.

She bent down and returned the yellow pad and pen back to the bottom shelf of the bar cart, and I thought I saw her fussing with the handsome box. But I couldn't focus on that because Roger was tapping his right index finger on his left palm, a cocky gesture that was supposed to mean: *No worries, Kate. I've got her in the palm of my hand.* But it didn't actually mean that. It meant trouble.

He smiled a smile so full of ego it was like looking directly into the sun and walked toward the bar cart.

"Lillian, come on now. We're still talking here. Don't be offended by Barb. She's the numbers gal, just trying to—"

Lillian stood, spun, and cracked Roger in the eye with the butt of the 9mm Glock she kept in the box.

Roger staggered backward. His knees buckled. He must have seen stars, wondering what in the goddamn hell had happened. He must have been in head-banging pain. He wasn't unconscious, just kind of out on his feet.

Lillian didn't miss a beat. She was all over him. Grabbed him by his lapels, dragged him to a chair across from the sofa where I sat with the dog, pushed him down hard, and held the gun to his head.

I was too stunned to move. "What the hell, Lillian?"

"Ruby warned me you would come," she said. "And look at that. Here you are. The bookie's hitmen. It's never enough, is it? Even when she covers the loss *and* the vig. Even then you come and shake down her friends to find out where she's hiding. That's fine. I've shot people before. Bill, or whoever he is, won't be the first to take a Lillian Pearl bullet in the brain."

She was a little nuts, as most writers are. Roger's eye was

already showing evidence of a shiner, but he looked at me with his good eye like he knew who I was and who he was and what had happened, so I thought he was going to be all right—if Lillian didn't blow his brains out.

And what the hell had all that *Don't think this is the first time I've shot people in the head* business been about? First Duckett and now Lillian Pearl. Was I missing something? Were people all over New York shooting other people and I just didn't know about it?

Still holding the barrel of the Glock against Roger's skull, Lillian pulled her phone from her purse and hit a button.

"That's my security-service red alert. The police should be here shortly. So if you move a muscle, if you even breathe in a way that offends me, the police will find you and Bill dead, and poor little Lillian a basket case of self-defense. I'm sure Yo-Yo will vouch for me. He may be cute and lovable, but he's a tough little son of a bitch under all that fluff."

"Yo-Yo's a mofo," Roger said, making himself snicker.

There's a moment in the middle of a shitstorm when the only thing that's real is your own desperation. Roger's eye was turning black-and-blue, the Glock was locked and loaded at his head, the police were on the way, and Lillian held the cards to my unfortunate future.

Out of thin air, for reasons I'll never understand, I pulled the Colt from my purse, held it to Yo-Yo's head, and channeled Detective Cassie Barnett, the deeply troubled, alcoholic, irredeemable, criminally psychotic, drug-addicted sociopath with a badge.

"You flinch, the dog dies," I said, thinking, *Oh, brother, I love acting.*

"You wouldn't dare," Lillian said.

"No mo Yo-Yo," Roger said, chuckling.

"Try me," I said.

"She's shot dogs before," Roger said. "She's a cat person."

"So I'll ask you again," I said. "Where's Ruby?"

"I told you, she's inaccessible. We FaceTime. I don't know where she is. Some Coney Island bookie is trying to kill her. That's all I know," Lillian said. "Yo-Yo, I'm right here, baby. Mommy's here. Don't be scared."

The dog wasn't the slightest bit scared. He was uncannily calm. It was like he had no bones. Completely relaxed at gunpoint. Roger covered fear with humor. Yo-Yo had no fear.

"New storyline. Kenny Cochran got Ruby hooked on the ponies. They were betting buddies. She was pissed about his pissing away her money—low seven figures is the number I heard—and not paying his share of the losses. So she hired someone to kill him, like rich people sometimes do. My client was a witness to Cochran's murder, and now Ruby's hired someone to kill him too. And me along with him. Which is not happening on my watch. The Pomeranian bites the big one before that happens," I said, thinking, *Who loves acting more than I love acting?*

"Don't you dare hurt my Yo-Yo," Lillian said.

"Yo-Yo's a no-no," Roger said, laughing like he was a touch drunk.

"I'll blow his little Pomeranian brains around the room like a damn disco ball," I said, thinking, *I love acting even more than I think I do.*

"Yo-Yo a go-go," Roger said, cracking himself up.

"Ruby didn't hire anyone to do anything," Lillian said.

"How do you know that?" I said.

"Because Ruby is dead broke," Lillian said.

"What?" I said.

"Bad investments on top of gambling debts on top of bad investments on top of gambling debts," Lillian said. "Millions and millions up in smoke. That's why she wants a bidding war. To get as big an advance as she can. Plus, she would never hire anyone to kill Kenny."

"Why not?" I said.

"Because she loved him, of course," Lillian said. "They were seeing each other. Sleeping together. The hottest ticket in town no one knew about."

"Cochran and Ruby Gold?" I said.

"Could have been us, Lil," Roger said.

"She paid off his gambling debts, which were beyond the pale," Lillian said. "You don't do that for someone out of the blue. You do that for someone you love."

I pulled back the hammer on the Colt.

Lillian's eyes went wide. Her jaw fell open. Her bluff had been called. It was time to get the hell out of Lillian Land.

"Toss the Glock on the sofa and tell the police it's a false alarm or say goodbye to your best friend in the world, who'll spend the rest of his days on the streets of dog heaven," I said, thinking, *I love acting more than Lillian loves Yo-Yo.*

"Yo-Yo the hobo," Roger said, belly-laughing.

She tossed the gun on the sofa, called off the red alert, and put her hands on her heart. I thought she might keel over on the spot.

"Grab the gun, Bill," I said to Roger. "Time to go."

I stood, still holding the Colt to the Pomeranian's head, while Roger, wobbly in the knees, lifted the Glock off the sofa.

"This is where we back out of the deal, Lillian. You stay where you are. I'll leave the dog with the desk man in the lobby. Whether I hand him over dead or alive is up to you. If the desk man or the police or anyone is waiting for me, the Pomeranian pushes pansies," I said, thinking, *Nobody loves acting more than I love acting.*

"Poor Yo-Yo," Lillian said, her voice vanishing in distress.

In the elevator down to the first floor, Roger put the Glock in his pocket, and I put the Colt in my purse. We stood side by side facing the mirrored wall panels, Roger looking at his black eye, me watching Yo-Yo lick my hand like licking hands would be outlawed once we reached the lobby.

"What kind of Greek god gets a black eye?" Roger said.

"Ruby Gold paid Cochran's gambling debts," I said.

"No kind of Greek god. Greek gods don't get black eyes."

"Except how did she do that if she was broke?"

"Black eyes are not something Greek gods go around getting."

"Which means someone else paid the bookie."

"No black eyes on Mount Olympus."

"Which means someone else killed Kenny Cochran."

"Black eyes are the forbidden fruit in the garden of the Greek gods."

"Which means Ruby Gold didn't hire the bear to begin with."

The elevator door opened. We walked across the lobby, and I handed the dog to the guy behind the reception desk.

"Found this in the elevator," I said. "It's like a hobbit dog or something."

Roger shrugged, his black eye a piece of modern art, and said loud enough for only me to hear, "Yo-Yo has Frodo mojo." He laughed again, the cleverest, funniest actor anywhere. Just ask him.

We walked out of the building and looked for a Second Avenue cab. *Whoever gave Ruby the money to pay off her and Cochran's debts paid himself back by hiring the bear and killing the comedian*, I thought. *Only one thing I can do. Follow the money.*

"We open tonight, and I look like I went ten rounds with Mike Tyson," Roger said as a cab rolled to the curb.

Cocky, cocky, cocky. He wouldn't have lasted ten rounds with Cicely Tyson.

I opened the cab door. "Who's going to notice? There's two orgies."

31

___

ARE YOU BRINGING A MACHETE?

OPENING NIGHT OF *PSYCHEDELIC SUNDAY* WAS LIKE BREATHING mountain air after sludging through a city sewer. *Blood Song and Dance* had closed Halloween weekend, just seven nights ago, but it seemed like seven years since I'd been in front of an audience fulfilling my destiny. I was never more me than when I was singing and dancing onstage before a live audience. In fact, *fulfilling my destiny* doesn't quite define the emotion I feel when the curtain rises and the band plays and the house is packed and I become one with the music and the moment. It's like the show is life itself. Like there's no other reason for my heart to beat. Of course, there are other reasons, but it never feels like it when I'm singing and dancing and acting for a crowd that's come to experience something special, to stomp their feet and clap their hands, to get lost in the performance, to be transported in time and space by the music and the band, by the characters and the story.

And every time, no one in the theater is more transported than I am, than I have always been. I'm an actor. All of me.

I'd been that way since seventh grade, when I'd played the role of Kim MacAfee in *Bye Bye Birdie*, my first musical. The path of my life had been decided by kissing Conrad Birdie on my middle-school stage. I'd known since my first song and dance that I'd been born an actor in the center of my soul. And after a lifetime of low-paying jobs and truncated relationships, men that had come and gone like the seasons, nothing about me had really changed. I was still an actor.

Psychedelic Sunday was everything we'd expected it to be. Everything the audience wanted it to be. Maybe even needed it to be. You think two orgies in one musical is excessive? Trying telling that to the sold-out, opening-night crowd that gave both of them standing ovations. Turns out theatrical orgies were popular. Go figure.

Roger's eye was too black-and-blue for makeup, so he wore an eye patch. Adonis with a shiner? The crowd shrugged it off. All part of the fun of opening night in the Musical Theater of the Absurd. The D-Cup audience expected the incongruous, demanded the inappropriate, insisted on the illogical, commanded us to deliver the highest level of theatrical energy that was possible to produce. We never let them down. I never let them down. And they joyfully came along for the ride. Was it off-off-off-off-Broadway insanity? It was. So what? Another way to describe it was...heaven.

Matthew had never missed a D-Cup opening night, even though he wanted me to give up musical theater and get a "real" job. In the back of my mind, I'd always thought the next show would be the one he missed to make his point. So seeing him in the third row for the *Psychedelic Sunday* opening performance made my heart soar. Even with Naysayer Nina sitting beside him, I felt my theatrical self ascending.

After the show—and the *three* curtain calls—I met them for a drink at the D-Cup bar at the back of theater. The cast and audience often met there after shows to mingle and share the afterglow. Okay, to get drunk together. Opening nights especially, the bar would buzz. Tonight the buzz was different.

Tonight, something most unusual had created a wacky wave in the greater Broadway biosphere. Was it the musical orgies? Yes, it was the musical orgies. Have I mentioned there were two of them?

"I'm so happy you came to opening night," I said. "It means a lot to me. Especially now. I'm so excited for you both. I really am."

I really was.

Matthew and I drank tequila. Nina drank expensive bottled water. Which she'd brought with her. Because she knew the best water for people to drink. And she knew it better than anyone. Because she knew everything better than everyone. Even water.

"Thanks, Mom. Wouldn't miss it," Matthew said.

"What did you think, Nina?" I said.

"It's not really a show that encourages thinking," she said.

There was plenty of subtle condescension in her voice, covered by a perfectly fake smile and a fraudulently gracious tone of voice. Oh, she was a piece of work, my future daughter-in-law.

"My brain didn't always work when I was pregnant with Matthew," I said. "Hormones and whatnot. It doesn't surprise me that the show went over your head."

Dig and dig back. We both expected it to happen but kept it civil for Matthew's sake.

"We have to run, Mom," Matthew said. "But you were great. I have no idea why a Greek god—even someone's acid trip of a Greek god—would wear an eye patch, but I let it go because the show was so much fun."

"I let it go because I couldn't find a reason to retain it," Scornful Nina said.

"That's because you're retaining water in your ankles," I said. "There's only so much retaining a person can do."

We glared at each other while smiling, as we always did,

then I kissed them both goodbye, finished my tequila, and went back to the House of Emotional Tics.

On the way, I called Fu to make sure he was going with me to Harlem, to the King of Conga's Latino dance club, Dawn, to stop Jimmy's killer from shooting Mickey Herradura in the eyeballs.

"Are you in a car?" I said.

"Fu drive upstate."

"You don't have a license."

"Have parrot."

"I don't know what that means."

"Joe has parrot friend in Finger Lakes. Means parrot playdate."

"There's no such thing as a parrot playdate."

"No tell Joe."

"What are you driving? You don't have a car."

"Fu take Warren Corolla. Black Bull."

"You can't drive to the Finger Lakes tonight, Fu. You're coming with me to Harlem. To Dawn, the dance club. The killer's going to shoot the King of Conga when the club closes. I broke the clue. You said you'd go with me."

"Only thing Fu say is trap."

Shit. It was true. He'd never actually confirmed his availability. "I know it's a trap. Jesus, Fu. You think I don't know it's a trap?"

"Fu know first."

I could hear him smirking. "Stop that. Stop smirking right now. If you're not here, who's going with me?"

"Fu tell Charlie. Charlie go Harlem. Bring machete."

"Charlie's going with me?"

"Bring machete."

"Charlie in Harlem with a machete does not fill me with confidence."

"What fill with?"

"Dread."

It was one in the morning when I got back to the brown-stone. Charlie was doing his laundry. It wasn't hard to find him. All I had to do was follow the freaky fragrance of weed in the lobby down the stairs to the laundry room.

The basement wasn't technically a basement. It was street level, not below ground, meaning you could walk straight out into the backyard, meaning the front steps led up to the first floor. Fu's apartment was down here. Directly across the hall from Fu's front door was the former storage room—now known as Jerusalem Joe's Free Apartment because Fu had moved much of the brownstone storage stuff to who knew where in order to make room for his parrot. Down the hall was the laundry room.

Charlie was smoking weed he'd grown in the backyard. Weed he sold out of the city tow truck he drove during the day.

I leaned against the laundry room door. "Fu said you're going with me to Harlem. Is that true?"

"Pretty sure that happened," Charlie said. "He left town with the parrot. Don't know when. Can't be trusted with time. Could've been yesterday. Or tomorrow. You want a hit?"

Some days he called it product testing. Other days he called it quality control. Either way, with the prodigious amount of asset assessment he did to make sure his weed was worthy, it was amazing he had any reefer left to sell.

"No, thanks," I said. "Are you bringing a machete?"

"You never know."

"You never know if you'll need it, or you never know if you're bringing one?"

"You decide. Sure you don't want a hit? G-13 Haze. Helps the mind return to neutral ground."

Neutral ground was not a place Charlie Nye had visited very often in his life. He was fifty turbulent years old and lived in 2B. Gray hair. Gray eyes. Tattoos. Bullet-wound scars. Knife-fight scars. He'd been to prison three times for various combinations of assault with a deadly weapon, breaking and entering, and grand theft auto—once in Ohio, once in Pennsylvania, the third time in New York. The Big Apple had recruited him out of prison to break into deviant cars and jack them to car jail. The city's early-release pitch had been: *Spend the rest of your life behind bars or the rest of your life in a tow truck and not behind bars.* Charlie had taken the deal. He was an indentured city servant.

Before prison, he'd joined the Army to escape gang life and gone to war in the Middle East as a motor-pool mechanic, where he'd learned to start Humvees under severe duress. Graduate school for car thieves, he called it. He didn't blame the Army for who he'd turned out to be; he'd made it clear he was already a criminal when he went in and that the Army had just taught him to be all he could be.

He was from Scranton, Pennsylvania, and still dreamed of being a professional poker player. He hired hookers, drank whiskey for dinner, and had a violent streak as wide as Wyoming. It was the reefer that kept him calm. Like Al and Warren and LaTanya and Fu, he'd been helping me catch the creep who'd murdered Jimmy.

"So we'll get there at two, when the club closes, and scope it out," I said. "When the cleaning crew leaves, you'll pick the lock and get us in before the killer kills the King of Conga. Then we'll take him down, and everyone will live happily ever after."

"Fu has no license."

"Charlie—"

"He'll have to kill any cop pulls him over. That's what I'd do. Ergo, the machete."

"Charlie, focus."

"Two o'clock. Harlem."

"Right. I know you've got guns and knives and brass knuckles. But what's with the machete?"

"My mother gave it to me. It was her backup. Believe me,

she's the one with the temper. I'm like Lake Placid. You know, a placid lake."

"Okay, then."

I went upstairs to my apartment, ate something, and changed my clothes. The whole time, all I could think about was Charlie chopping the killer's head off with his machete.

Full confession—it didn't bother me one bit.

32

JUDGE, JURY, AND EXECUTIONER
PRESENT AND ACCOUNTED FOR

Near the corner of 145th Street and Frederick Douglass Boulevard was a small, old church that over the course of its long and colorful Harlem life had been home to several different congregations, survived a fire, stood empty and boarded up for years, then become a Gap, a Borders bookstore, a jazz bar, a punk rock joint, and, finally, a Latino nightclub called Dawn.

Columbia Cardiology's Mickey Herradura had bought a little piece of the club with the money he'd made decoding the cryptic vagaries of medical insurance and played his heart out until his heart broke when his wife died. Now he was about to follow her into the grave—without his eyes.

Why someone, anyone, would want to hire a professional assassin to kill the King of Conga was a murderous mystery I couldn't begin to unwind—though I would have to. Because that was the question: *What did he ever do to you?* I had no idea, so the best I could do right now was try to stop the murder before it happened, which was why Charlie and I were in the White Whale at three thirty Saturday morning, parked across the street, waiting for the nightclub cleaning crew to call it a, well, night.

At three thirty-five, two Hispanic men and two Hispanic women carrying vacuums and mops and buckets of cleaning supplies exited the service alley on the far left-hand side of the church, locked the chain-link service gate behind them, and went about the business of loading their gear and themselves into a van parked in front. It was a messy orchestration that took ten minutes. Then they drove off into the night.

"Anybody fucks with us, I machete the shit out of them," Charlie said.

For a stoned dude, he was crazy violent. "I'm counting on it."

He wore his everyday tow-truck clothes: blue jeans, blue work shirt, shit-kicker work boots. The only difference was that tonight was apparently tow-truck-pirate-night because he'd tied a bandana around his head like Jack Sparrow. He carried a gym bag in one hand and the machete in the other. When I tell you that Charlie Nye was a badass not to be fucked with, I'm not kidding. If he wasn't stoned out of his mind most of the time, he'd beat the brains out of someone every day.

I wore my usual breaking-and-entering outfit: black running shoes, black pants, black jacket, black baseball cap, and small black backpack, which held my phone, wallet, flashlight, keys, and the Colt.

We crossed the street to the service gate. Charlie unwrapped his professional lock-picking tools from a soft towel and unlocked the gate. We went to the side door at the back of the church, at the end of the alley, and Charlie clicked that lock open too.

"Never gets old," he said with stoned nostalgia.

"Stay in the alley, in the shadows. If someone sees us and calls the cops, come get me. If I'm not out in five minutes, come get me. If you get a bad feeling about this, come get me."

"I get a bad feeling about everything, so that's probably not the best barometer."

"I don't know how to respond to that."

"Nobody does."

I nodded and went into the club. I was in the back of the house, in a service hallway that, obviously, opened out to the side alley where Charlie waited with his mother's backup machete. It was dark and darker. No lights back here. I grabbed the little flashlight from my backpack and moved slowly, quietly, down the hallway. Boxes of club stuff lined both walls. Racks of extra glassware. Locked doors to the liquor rooms and offices.

I turned a corner and went through a doorway, turned another corner, and was in the restroom lobby. Ladies to my left. Men to my right. Again, no lights. Pitch-black but for the narrow beam of my flashlight.

I went through the restroom lobby, down another hallway, and stopped at the double-wide doorway into the club itself.

He's in here, I thought. *He has to be.*

Oh man, it was dark. I killed my flashlight and let my eyes adjust. Big square space. Raised stage to my right. Bar running the length of the long wall opposite the stage. I was at the back of the building, so the front door was opposite me, all the way at the other side of the club. The entire middle of the room was dance floor. Several hundred people could shake it to the King of Conga's band.

In what little light the red exit signs gave off, I saw that a balcony wrapped around three sides of the building—above my head, over the bar, and over the front of the club. Not above the stage. I could barely make out tables and chairs along the balcony rail all around the dance floor. Great view of the band and dancers. I couldn't be sure, but it looked like a sound-and-light booth was positioned on the balcony over the bar, dead center.

I focused on the main floor. Where would the killer be? With an oversized ego like his, there was only one logical place. The stage.

I got low, hugging the wall, and slipped toward the bar, where I would have a straight-on view of the stage. About halfway across the room, I glanced back.

A silhouette sat on a chair in the middle of the stage.

He's waiting for me, I thought. *He knows I'm here, and he's playing with me. Either that or...*

I grabbed the Colt out of the backpack, stayed low, and started straight across the floor, from the bar to the stage.

"You move one inch, I shoot you," I said, hoping the fear I was feeling hadn't slipped into my voice.

No response. Zero. That's when I knew it wasn't the killer.

That's when I knew it was the king.

I stopped in front of the stage, dead center, Colt in my right hand, flashlight in my left hand, and put the beam on the body.

Mickey Herradura. Tied to the chair. Dead. Congas quiet forevermore. Eyes shot out of his head. Grim, hideous holes looking out at his empty dance floor.

I was too late.

I stepped onto the stage to...I don't know what exactly. Look for clues I knew weren't there?

As he'd done with all his other victims, including my father, he'd murdered Mickey somewhere else, transported him into the club, and positioned him in the chair while Charlie and I waited for the cleaning crew to pack their van and vamoose.

There would be no clues. No evidence whatsoever. No blood. No fingerprints. No fibers. No nothing.

I'd been right about the King of Conga but too slow to make a difference. I knew I should call Logan—who'd positioned his task force to protect Dr. Gideon King from hedge-fund fucknut Malcolm Gray—and tell him to turn the fleet toward Harlem. I reached around for the phone in my backpack.

And a white-hot spotlight blasted me, and a voice came through the sound system.

A voice I knew by heart.

"Chug, chug, chug, Little Engine. Day late, dollar short."

The killer.

He'd been on the balcony, in the sound booth, waiting for me to show up and admire his handiwork. I hadn't been able to see him in the darkened club, and now I was blinded by the spotlight and still couldn't see him. Couldn't see anything but the light. Couldn't hear anything but his voice. He was up there, watching me like I was some kind of puppet on a string. *His* fucking puppet. Talking to me through the sound system so I'd be intimidated by his voice alone.

"Matter of time, asshole," I said with as much obstinance and courage and confidence as I could find.

"I'm afraid you're going to run out of time, Little Engine. Off the rails and into the Great Gorge for you."

"I'm taking you down you with me."

He laughed into the mic. The sick sound filled the club. I hated hearing it.

"Your bravado is refreshing, I'll give you that," he said. "The King of Conga was wearisome. Weeping and whimpering, pleading and praying, beseeching and begging to the end. Whatever fight he once had in his heart left him long ago. Not like you, Little Engine. Battling insurmountable odds. Challenging an unbeatable opponent."

"You're just another low-life fucking bully. He was a medical-insurance guy who played congas. If you look up 'harmless' in the dictionary, that's the damn definition. What kind of scumbag would have Mickey murdered?"

"You don't get points for asking the same question in a different way. And I'm not a bully. I'm a person. This is personal."

Same question in a different way, I thought. *What did he ever do to you? That's what he means. What did he ever do to you?*

"Killing innocent people is not business," I said.

"In my courtroom, innocence is a figment of the imagination, guilty is the only verdict, and the sole penalty is execution."

"The signature on the death warrant is shooting out the eyes."

"Judge, jury, and executioner present and accounted for."

My index finger pushed on the Colt's trigger.

And Charlie stepped onto the stage and into the spotlight.

"Charlie," I said, whispering, "you should be watching the alley."

"Been five minutes."

He must have seen the emotion in my eyes—the anger, the frustration, the fear, the rage—because his voice was as quiet as mine. Somehow he knew to match my volume.

"I was expecting your Chinese friend, Little Engine," the killer said. "But once again you've surprised me."

"He couldn't make it. Parrot playdate," I said.

"What does that mean exactly?" the killer said.

"Nobody knows," I said.

"Be that as it may, it must be said that as a secret backup security officer, your new friend is not your Chinese friend. Your new friend, in fact, is an abject failure. Still, as a machete man, I'm sure he's top-notch."

"That's him up there?" Charlie said softly, pointing with the machete to the middle of the balcony above the bar.

"Sound booth. That's him."

"Scumbag."

"The scumbaggiest."

"I confess to curiosity," the killer said, voice booming like a cruel god from on high. "What are you going to do with your machete?"

"Stick it in your throat and twist it back and forth until your fucking head falls off," Charlie said loud enough to reach the balcony.

"Anger issues," the killer said. "Too deep to deal with now, what with the limited time we have left together. Still, I'm guessing born with fury and rage at the world."

"That's what my mother says," Charlie said.

"Wise woman," the killer said.

"She was here, she'd cut your balls off and shove them down your throat," Charlie said.

"I have no doubt," the killer said.

"Do you have a gun?" I said to Charlie, whispering again.

"Fuck right I do," Charlie said for my ears only. "Browning Hi-Power. Service pistol. Stole it from the Army."

"There are stairs to the balcony on either side of the club. Only way up or down. On three, I take the front, you take the back, we meet in the middle and blow this asswipe away. Only one thing—we may get shot."

"Six years since I been shot," Charlie said. "Kind of miss it. Don't matter. I'm good. I'd take a bullet to rip this guy's throat open."

"I can smell the smoke up here, Little Engine. Overloaded brain gears burning up the track. You've settled on a plan, then? Machete man good to go?"

"One, two, three..."

Charlie and I jumped off the stage, out of the spotlight in different directions.

My heart pounded out of my chest. I pushed through the fear, through the hesitation, and bounded up the stairs. The killer was waiting. He was armed. Bullets would fly.

I reached the top of the front stairs, pointed the Colt toward the middle of the balcony, where the sound booth was set, and stayed low, ready to shoot the shit out of the killer.

It was dark as night. I couldn't see him.

I moved toward the sound booth, held my breath, heart in my throat, finger on the trigger, squeezing it just to the point of firing off a shot.

I reached the sound booth at the same time as Charlie.

No killer. Not on the balcony.

"Oh, that was special," the killer said, his voice still booming through the speakers.

I looked down. He stood on the stage next to the King of Conga, a wireless mic in one hand and some kind of remote device in the other.

He'd never been on the balcony. He'd stood in the shadows on the main floor. The spotlight had distracted me from seeing him, sensing him. His voice amplified through the sound system had covered his actual voice emanating from the darkness of the dance floor.

Charlie lifted his Browning, aimed it at the stage.

The killer hit the remote, and the spotlight began to strobe like crazy. It was hard to see the killer clearly. Hard to focus on the stage at all. Hard to look straight at the strobing spotlight. Charlie didn't pull the trigger.

"A for effort, Little Engine," the killer said. "One gold star for the machete man, and one for you. As a reward, here's your next clue: someone else will have to draw the beach house because this pen runs out of ink tonight."

And then he held the mic straight out in front of him and dropped it on the stage. As it hit the ground, he turned out the spotlight, plunging the club into utter darkness. He was gone.

I'd had him and lost him.

"That smug son of a bitch is a maggot motherfucker," Charlie said.

I nodded. "The motherfuckiest."

33

THAT'S WHY YOU HAVE ULCERS AND MIGRAINES

I DIALED LOGAN—MY *SEVENTH* CALL TO HIM REGARDING THE KING of Conga—got him on the line (he was guarding Gideon King), told him what had happened, and sent Charlie home before the police arrived in Harlem. Despite the jangling of my nerves, the racing of my heart, and the rush-hour traffic in my brain, I knew it probably wasn't the best idea for Logan to find me at the scene of the crime, dead man on the stage without his eyeballs, standing next to a tow-truck driving, machete-wielding, pot-dealing, three-time ex-con with a predisposition for belligerent violence. It was bad enough Logan would find me here at all.

Anyway, Logan and his task force arrived at Dawn before, well, dawn. The club filled fast with cops and forensic specialists, who turned up the lights and proceeded with their hopeless search for evidence. Meaning both Logan and I knew no matter how many specialists he threw at the club, they wouldn't uncover clue one.

We sat in the balcony by the sound and light booth, looking down at the busy hive of task-force bees going about their investigative business, Logan chewing me out to beat the band, a nonstop diatribe about police work being a lot like Vegas and me being a bad-luck albatross wrapped around his neck. The gist of it was another innocent man was dead, the serial contract killer was still on the loose, the task force had been in the wrong place at the wrong time watching the wrong King, and somehow all of this was *my* fault. Somehow, *I* had bet the house and lost.

Meanwhile, Mickey Herradura sat on the stage, tied to the chair, while a team in white jumpsuits took skin samples and blood samples and hair samples and scraped under the King of Conga's fingernails and checked his teeth and every fiber of his clothing. One of them spent an inordinate amount of time investigating the holes in Mickey's head where his eyes used to be. Maybe there was gun powder residue around the dark, horrifying, empty sockets. Maybe the killer had left a rogue fingerprint while tying Mickey to the chair. Maybe a shred of his shirt. Maybe a thread from his sweater.

Maybe when pigs fly.

"...so the killer's cashing his chips, I'm crapping out at Columbia Cardiology, all bets on Gideon King, a true-blue blazing shitbag, and you're counting cards with the King of Conga in some hokey Harlem nightclub, making me look like a rookie who can't follow a Clifton clue to New Jersey."

"I reached out and reached out and reached out. You blew me off."

"Nobody hates to hear *I told you so* more than I hate to hear *I told you so*."

"It was never *I told you so*. It was me rolling the dice. You weren't interested, so I followed the signs."

"Which pointed to Gideon King."

"Except everything's misdirection with this guy. Words behind the words. What he says isn't what he means. He means something else."

Logan shook his head. One part furious at himself, one part

furious the killer had played him for a fool (again), one part furious I'd figured it out and he hadn't, and one part furious because he was Lew Logan.

"If it makes you feel better," I said, "I can hide my gun behind the bar, let Jesse find it, and you can arrest me for old-time's sake."

"That *would* make me feel better."

Frustration filled his words with the stink of stale coffee. Although, that might have been from the cup of stale coffee he was actually drinking.

"There's no evidential connection between Ronnie Russo and Mickey Herradura," Logan said. "They exist in different orbits. Got any idea why someone would hire a psychotic contract killer to terminate these two disparate people?"

"Three. Third one's tonight."

"Read me the clue again."

I'd written it on a bar napkin. "Someone else will have to draw the beach house because this pen runs out of ink tonight."

Jesse arrived on the balcony and took a seat on the sound-board side of Logan. I was on the light-board side. Both Jesse and I knew Logan well enough to give him fire-breathing room. Sitting directly beside him would have been a mistake.

"I want a list of every architectural firm in the city currently designing beach houses," Logan said to Jesse. "Hamptons, North Shore, Long Beach. Every goddamn beach house being drawn in New York. And then I want the names of each architect in every one of those firms who's working on those houses. Money issues, political issues, legal issues, corporate issues, family issues, power issues...any name with a potential problem gets a red flag. It's Saturday, five a.m. Some fucking architect somewhere in the city dies tonight."

"On it, Lew," Jesse said, standing again.

"We're lost at fucking sea here, Jesse."

Jesse nodded and was gone. Logan and I were quiet for a moment, then he shook his head in disgust and disappointment—at himself this time, not at me.

"You think I know who the killer is?" he said.

"He knows you, so, yeah, I think he exists in your orbit, to use your phrase."

"I got a thirty-year orbit filled with dealers and douchebags and criminals and cocksuckers and killers and creeps and assholes galore."

"Can't be one of them. Has to be someone you'd never suspect, never consider. The opposite of whatever task-force profile you've put together."

He nodded as if he'd searched his mind, found something he wasn't especially fond of, and come to terms with it all in a split second.

"My father was a homicide detective in Pittsburgh," he said.

"I didn't know that."

"Of course you didn't know that. Why would I tell you anything about my father being a homicide detective in Pittsburgh? Why would I tell you anything personal or important to me?"

"Because you secretly like me."

"I do not surreptitiously, furtively, or stealthily like you. I don't like you out in the open or hidden in the shadows or anywhere in between."

"So your father was a homicide cop, like father like son, and my father was a private investigator, like father like daughter. I get it. We're having a breakthrough, sharing something special."

"We're sharing nothing. I'm telling you a story for my own intellectual, physical, and emotional benefit. You have no role here except to shut the hell up and listen to the story."

"I still say we're having a breakthrough. It's kind of sweet."

"Zip it, McCall. My father had a wannabe snitch, an annoying, irritating, exasperating moron he could not shake to save his life. And there was one particular case, someone killing addicts in the shooting-gallery slums of Homewood. Not exactly a high-profile case—who gives a shit if someone's murdering addicts in the slums?—but my old man did give a shit. *'Murder is murder,'* he used to tell me. *'And I'm a cop.'* Anyway, in addition to being annoying, irritating, and exasperating, the wannabe moron snitch was also a complete fucking idiot."

"This is me, right? I'm the annoying, irritating, exasperating moron idiot in this parable?"

"The moron idiot wouldn't let it go. He attached himself to my father and would not let the case drop. So after a string of unsolved drug-addict murders, my father had ulcers and migraines and finally gave in and listened to what the moron idiot had to say."

"So he could solve the murders and his ulcers and migraines would get better?"

"Of course not, McCall. He listened because the moron idiot was *causing* the ulcers and migraines in the first place, and he hoped hearing him out just that one time might alleviate his torment and pain."

"Ah, that's why you're talking to me. Got it. Still kind of sweet in a way."

"It's my head he's fucking with, so it has to be somebody I pissed off."

"Shouldn't be too tough to narrow that list," I said with just enough sarcasm to make my point that I was one of them. "How many could it be?"

"Thousands," he said, somehow matching my sarcasm but leaving out the irony. "Probably everyone in this club more than once." He exhaled hard. Not a sigh exactly, but close to it for Logan.

"Has to be someone smart enough to stay two steps ahead," I said.

"And sick enough to kill people for money."

"Not just for the money. Also to prove you can't catch him."

"*You* meaning *me*?"

"You meaning you, me, anyone. Everyone."

"Thinks he's the smartest guy in the room."

"So far he is."

One of the white-jumpsuit forensic folks looked up at Logan, shook her head, and called up to the balcony. "Nothing, Lew. It's like Mr. Herradura blew his own eyes out somewhere down the street, walked into the club, and tied himself into the chair. No blood, no hair, no prints, no skin, no fiber. No evidence."

Logan nodded, and the forensic team began to break their gear down. All around the club, cops dusted for prints they wouldn't find, looked for clues that weren't there. Logan got himself ready to stand up and move on.

"I realize you don't want to have this conversation," I said.

"What conversation?"

"The reason he's two steps ahead. You have to consider the possibility that there may be, might be, could be a leak on your task force."

"You're right."

"I am?"

"I don't want to have this conversation."

"Thursday night at RJM with Two Brake Jake and Motor-mouth Mitch, the killer was there, watching us swing and miss, enjoying himself."

"And?"

"And he wasn't planning to kill Mitch or Jake or Duckett or any other RJM partners. Russo was dead. He was already moving to Mickey."

"So what was he doing there?"

"Gloating. Watching you whiff. Giving me the next clue. All of the above. But *what* isn't the question. *How* is the question. How did he know we'd be there that night at that time? I didn't tell him. You didn't tell him. So who told him?"

"You think I haven't considered this question? You think this question doesn't keep me up nights?"

"I think it gives you ulcers and migraines because the answer is someone from the task force told him."

Logan sat back, shook his head. "I hand-picked everybody here."

"I'm not saying they crossed the line intentionally. I'm saying someone on the task force is speaking to someone who they don't know is the killer. Another cop. Or someone close to the cops. Someone getting advanced task-force information fed to him from the source. The killer's been in on the game plan since day one. That's why you have ulcers and migraines."

"For fuck's sake, McCall. Either you're not listening or your brain doesn't work. I have ulcers and migraines because thinking about *that* leads to thinking about *this*: if no one on my task force *told* the killer, then someone on my task force *is* the killer."

He left me with that thought, and I sat there feeling like an annoying, irritating, exasperating moron idiot private investigator who'd had the killer in her sights and let him get away.

34

HOLY HOT SHIT KISSING

I GOT BACK TO THE HOUSE OF EMOTIONAL TICS AT SIX THIRTY, Saturday morning. I was too exhausted to do anything but pass out on top of the covers, in my clothes, dead to the world. My last thought wasn't the King of Conga tied to the chair on the stage or Charlie Nye with his mother's machete or Lew Logan reaming me out on the balcony or some psychotic, task-force killer cop shooting innocent people in the eyes. It was that I didn't have anything to wear to Matthew's wedding. *I have to go shopping*, was the last half-conscious thing I said to myself before I fell asleep. *I'm the mother of the groom, for God's sake. Must...go...shopping...*

I opened my eyes at eleven forty-five and found Rick Gotti making French toast in my kitchen. He must have shown up after I'd conked because he sure as shit hadn't been there when I'd gotten home. I'd forgotten how pissed off I was at him for ditching me yesterday—holy shit, was that yesterday or three weeks ago?—after I'd saved his butt from the bear on the bus to Lillian Pearl's place.

"What are you doing, Rick?" I said, still in the clothes I'd worn to Harlem.

"Making French toast. You were wiped, and I'd stopped for sourdough from Orwasher's, and—"

"I mean what the hell are you *doing*? Where have you been? Are you out of your fucking mind? You ditched me. Again. I saved your life on the bus, and you ditched me. What were you thinking? What *are* you thinking? What the hell, Rick?"

"You can't yell at someone while they're making you Orwasher's sourdough French toast. That's an unspoken kitchen rule. I'm surprised you don't know that."

I heard Jimmy in my head. *Katie, some people go begging for a good punch in the nose, and it's your job to give them what they want.* I made a fist—that's how upset I was. Naturally, I was conscious of being angry and frustrated, but I was also conscious of another emotion I couldn't put my finger on.

"My kitchen. My rules, Rick. I couldn't care less if you're surprised. I asked you what you're thinking. Give me a goddamn answer, you little Staten Island shithead," I said.

I heard the sound of my own voice. It wasn't all irritation and exasperation. There was relief in my emotional mix. Relief that he was here and alive and not dead in a dark alley.

"I'm thinking if I should add more cinnamon to the eggs," he said with sarcasm, anger, and impatience. He was trying to control himself but losing the battle.

I'd hit a minor nerve by calling him a little Staten Island shithead because that's exactly what he'd been all his life. And he was proud of it. It was a badge of honor for him, and I'd used it as degradation, a mark of disgrace and embarrassment. And I wasn't done. Not by a long shot. That's how pissed off I was.

"You are the most arrogant, most immature man I've met in a long damn time," I said. "What are you, twelve? Why can't you just listen to me?"

"Because you're inflexible, unreasonable, and irrational."

"Inflexible because I won't let you act like the fucking teenager you are? Unreasonable because you hired me to save your life and that's what I'm doing? Irrational because it makes sense to stay away from the people trying to kill you?"

He lowered the flame under the pan and turned to me. He'd jumped from frustration to resentment to anger in the time it had taken me to call him a fucking teenager.

He took an angry step toward me. "Because only a small-time, bad-tempered, short-sighted, bullshit bodyguard would make a man watch months of *Animal Planet* on her flea-bit sofa when the smart move would be to help him prove his innocence *before* he gets to his pretrial."

I took an aggressive step toward him. "Really? Because from where I'm standing only a juvenile, self-important, asshat with his life on the line would risk a public appearance knowing bad actors were waiting in the wings to take another shot at him."

I was as hot as he was. And he was pretty flipping hot.

"Juvenile?" he said.

"Infantile," I said.

We were ten feet from each other.

"I should never have hired you."

"Then fire me."

"Fire you?"

"Fire me."

"You're fired."

He took another step toward me. I took another step toward him. We were six feet from each other.

"Good luck out there," I said.

"I'm fine on my own," he said.

"On your own—you got that right."

"Look who's talking."

"What's that supposed to mean?"

"It means there's no man in your life for a reason."

"Look who's talking now."

"What's that supposed to mean?"

"You can't have a real relationship because you're so wrapped up with yourself there's no room for anyone else."

"And you can't have one because you're too fucking bossy."

"I'm not bossy."

"You can't go five minutes without giving orders."

My face flushed. I took another step toward him. He took another step toward me. We were three feet apart.

"Is that why you've spent the whole week flirting with me?" I said.

"I'm not flirting with you. You're flirting with me."

"I don't flirt with clients."

"I don't flirt with employees."

We both took a half step toward each other. Two feet between us.

"I'm an employee now?"

"I'm paying you, aren't I?"

Another half step. One foot away now. Feeling each other's heat. Face-to-face.

"You were until you fired me, you smug, smartass son of a bitch."

"Should have done it days ago, you arrogant, wiseass bigmouth."

And then we kissed. Really kissed. Holy hot-shit kissing.

I'd done some pretty good kissing since I'd become the McCall in McCall & Company. Harriman had kissed like a house on fire. Peter Mills had been strong and gentle at the same time. And Blue had swept me off my feet—professional athlete kissing.

But kissing Rick Gotti was a different kind of kissing. It took me by surprise. And it took my breath away because we fit just perfectly together. I didn't know how or why or what the hell made it so perfect, but we kissed perfectly. I'd never kissed anyone like that before. Nobody had ever kissed me perfectly.

The kissing ended. We stayed in each other's arms. I think we were both a bit blown away.

"Wow," I finally said.

"Yeah," he said.

"Did you feel that?"

"All of it."

"Good."

And we stood in the middle of my kitchen and kissed again. And it was even better the second time. The kissing ended. We held each other and let the warmth wash over us.

"I'm putting you back on my payroll," he said.

"I'm hired?" I said.

"You're hired."

"Bodyguard?"

"Guarding my body."

"Okay. But my sofa's not flea-bit."

"I know. I like your sofa."

"My sofa likes you."

"I sleep on it, so it's good to know I haven't pissed it off somehow."

"You're all good with my sofa."

We were still embracing, but I could feel him smiling. I was smiling too, and I imagined he could feel it like I could feel it. I didn't want to break the moment, but if any of this was real, then the question that had been on my mind since Wednesday had to be addressed.

"Where did you go, Rick? The first time you ditched me, last Wednesday, where did you go? On the bus to Lillian Pearl's office, before the bus died and the bear pulled his gun, you were telling me you had something. And then all hell broke loose, and you ditched me again, and I have to know where you go. I'm sorry. It's important to me. I don't know why, but it is."

He nodded and loosened our embrace so we were looking into each other's eyes.

"I have nieces," he said. "That's where I go. To see them."

"You have nieces?"

"A few."

"A few nieces?"

"Six. Maybe seven. Possibly eight."

"I want to meet them. Can I meet them?"

"If you're not bossy about it."

I laughed, and we kissed again.

35

MAYBE I'M LYING THAT I'M LYING THAT I'M LYING THAT I'M LYING

As if I needed more emotional goo to gum my gears, now I had to carry kissing Rick Gotti around in my overburdened baggage. Not just kissing. Major-league making-out. Romantic and embarrassing and tender and confusing and passionate and maddening and adoring and complicating all rolled into one overthinking ball. News flash: I tend to overthink my romantic entanglements. Which is one of the reasons they don't last long. Anyway, Jimmy would have ripped me a new one if he'd caught me kissing a client. What the hell was I thinking? What the hell was I doing?

At the moment, I was putting it behind me because Warren White was on today's *Kung Fu Fu* call sheet, and it was hard to secure a slot on his calendar between his doorman duties and his do-not-disturb collecting marathons and his under-the-radar rental-car company, and I needed his special skill set to keep up with the killer.

So LaTanya called *action*, and Warren held a gun in my back and said, "How the mighty have fallen."

LaTanya had refused to let him use his full real-life name for his character, so Warren had chosen to use his first name twice. All things considered, Warren Warren seemed as good a name for an evil, renegade mad scientist who hides a bomb on a city bus while creating a drug that imbues those who ingest it with super-duper martial-arts aptitudes as any other name.

"How the tables have turned," Mo Einstein said. Charlie had named his renegade drug-dealer character after Mo Howard (of *The Three Stooges*) and Albert Einstein because he believed Mo was right to bash Larry, Curly, and Shemp and because, as Charlie had explained, *Theory of relativity? You shitting me? Einstein was smoking something sweet in that pipe. I should know. I'm a professional.*

"One day you're putting drug dealers in a cage," Robert the Bruce said. "The next day they're doing it to you. Ain't life grand, Barnett?"

In today's scene, Warren Warren, Robert the Bruce, and Mo Einstein had captured Detective Cassie Barnett, the alcohol-soaked, drug-addicted, serial-lying renegade cop, and were walking her down to Warren's laboratory dungeon to lock her in the mad scientist's jail cell. Because all mad scientists had jail cells in their laboratory dungeons—right next to their laundry rooms, apparently. In LaTanya's original outline, the bad guys were supposed to capture Fu, but Fu was still out of town with Jerusalem Joe on a parrot playdate in the Finger Lakes, so the outline was adjusted on the fly. Barnett alone would suffer the indignity of being locked in Joe's parrot cage.

Somehow—no one knew how—they'd captured Barnett and were escorting her from the fifth floor to the brownstone basement. But LaTanya had decided simply walking down five flights of stairs wasn't cinematically gripping enough, so today was the day the renegade drug dealers had swallowed Warren's magic medicine, which would take effect as they descended the stairs, changing their physiology by the time we reached Joe's Free Apartment, recast as Warren Warren's laboratory dungeon jail cell.

"I propose a trade to make it grander," I said.

I could say literally anything because, A, we were improvising every line of dialogue out of thin air with virtually no story context looking forward or back and, B, Warren had established my character as a psychotically lying cop. So if it came out of Barnett's mouth, it probably wasn't true anyway.

"What kind of trade?" Robert the Bruce said.

For today's shoot, Al had worn the oversized, audaciously boxy, garish gray suit he'd bought as a Halloween costume a decade ago so he could attend parties as David Byrne, the beloved Talking Heads front man. It was virtually the same suit. Shoulders two full feet wide on either side of Al's zombie head, which seemed one third its normal zombie size, like some head-shrinking medicine man had made him drink his head-shrinking potion bubbling over his head-shrinking campfire.

"You help me solve the killer's clue, I hand you Fu on a silver platter and give you a hundred bucks each," I said.

"Cash on the barrel?" Robert the Bruce said.

I knew the mention of money would get Al's attention. Charlie's too. Although, Charlie was stoned, so I wondered whether he knew we were shooting a movie or if he thought this was somehow his real life now. He'd worn a black suit with a white shirt and black tie and black sunglasses and looked like Elwood Blues of the Blues Brothers.

Warren had purchased a long white lab coat from a medical-uniform store and adorned it with an honest-to-goodness stethoscope around his neck and a tongue depressor in the top pocket. He looked less like an evil mad scientist and more like a small-town pediatrician who collected stamps, coins, and currency as a hobby.

"Rat out your partner?" Mo Einstein said.

"I'm not just dirty, Mo," I said. "I'm rat-bastard dirty."

"Rat-bastard dirty Detective Peanut," LaTanya said. "Don't you forget it."

She was in front of us, directing and shooting, walking backward with the camera as we descended to the fourth floor.

"You can't talk, LaTanya," I said. "And don't call me Peanut."

"What if we don't solve it?" Warren said.

"No Fu, no Franklins," I said. "I got three of them in my pocket. They're yours if you help me solve the clue."

"Why can't we just take the money, put you in the cage, and fuck the clue?" Robert the Bruce said. "You're the prisoner."

"For the time being," I said. "But this moment will end before lunch, and I will become your landlord, allegorically speaking, and cancel your lease. On life, I mean, if you get my drift. That goes for all three of you."

"Let me guess. You got this clue from some psycho serial killer," Robert the Bruce said, making sure we were all on the same page—*doing* the movie but also *not doing* the movie, doing real life.

"A psycho serial killer who's trying to steal your bomb on the bus. Exactly. This guy lives for the lead and thinks if your bus blows up, you'll knock him off the front page, so he's out to stop you in your tracks. If I catch him first, your bus detonates in a blaze of glory, and you guys get famous fast. If I don't, your plan goes up in a puff of smoke, and no one knows your name. He's hogging your headlines. So help me nail his ass to the wall and secure your super-villain future," I said. "The clock is ticking."

"She's lying," Warren said. "She's a dirty, no-good, lying cop, and she's lying through her dirty, no-good, lying teeth. No way she lets the bus blow if we help her."

"He's right. I'm lying. I'm Detective Cassie Barnett," I said. "Or wait. Maybe I'm lying that I'm lying. Or maybe I'm lying that I'm lying that I'm lying that I'm lying. The only thing you can be sure about is the three bills in my pocket."

"She's right about the clock," LaTanya said to Al and Charlie as we arrived on the fourth-floor landing. "It's tick-tock ticking. Your internal chemistry is burning in your bodies. You turning into kung fu freaks before our cinematic eyes. So start turning."

On the fourth-floor landing, Robert the Bruce and Mo Einstein began to shimmy and shake as Warren Warren's martial-arts drug did its number on them.

As if keeping in character with their respective wardrobe choices, Al twitched and danced like David Byrne doing "Girlfriend is Better" in the brilliant Talking Heads film *Stop Making Sense*—if Byrne, of course, was also a zombie.

And Charlie, looking like Dan Aykroyd playing Elwood doing "Soul Man" on *Saturday Night Live*, shook to a rocking blues band only he could hear.

Surreal didn't begin to describe it.

We started down the stairs to the third floor. LaTanya led the way, going backward, shooting up at us. Then came Al and Charlie, still shaking and twitching and changing into kung fu fighters. Then me and Warren.

"What's the clue?" Robert the Bruce said while transforming. "I been here an hour and haven't made a dime yet."

"Someone else will have to draw the beach house because this pen runs out of ink tonight," I said.

"All clues have context," Warren said.

"NYPD thinks some New York architect is next on the hit list," I said, "so they're checking every New York architect drawing a beach house on every beach in New York."

"Makes sense," Robert the Bruce said.

"That's what I'd do if I wasn't a drug dealer being a drug dealer," Mo Einstein said, blending realities for a moment.

"Except nothing is what it seems with these clues," I said. "It's been misdirection after misdirection from day one."

We reached the third-floor landing. Al and Charlie added some karate chops to their jump-jive-jump transitions.

"Then perhaps the beach house isn't a beach house," Warren said.

"And the pen isn't a pen," Robert the Bruce said.

"And the ink isn't ink," Mo Einstein said.

"Then what are they?" I said.

We started down to the second floor.

"One must begin with the obvious and most likely," Warren said, "and assume for the sake of argument that they are names."

"Why obvious and most likely?" I said.

"Because the killer plainly tells us *someone else will have to draw*," Warren said, "and it follows that that someone must have a name."

A big part of being a coin, currency, and stamp collector was tracking the history and mystery of the coins, currency, and stamps you collect. So we were in Warren's wheelhouse, which was why I'd brought it up in the first place.

"So the architect idea is still in play?" Robert the Bruce said.

"In the context of the clue, the word *house* is unlikely to represent anything other than a house," Warren said. "So, yes, moving forward, one must assume that whoever's been drawing the house is likely an architect."

We reached the second-floor landing, Al and Charlie shaking and baking, adding kung fu kicks to their kooky karate chops and herky-jerky dance moves as the drug transformed them into martial-arts madmen. We started down to the lobby.

"But the house is not necessarily a beach house," I said.

"If misdirection is the killer's game, then, yes, it's probably something other than a beach house," Warren said.

"If it's about names," Mo Einstein said, "maybe beach is the name of the house."

"As in The Beach House, yes, that's certainly possible," Warren said.

"If the killer's going to whack the architect drawing The

Beach House, then maybe the architect is named Pen," Robert the Bruce said.

"And maybe the guy he's going to whack is named Ink," Mo Einstein said.

A bright-white light bulb went off in my head as we reached the lobby, and I pulled three hundred-dollar bills out of my pocket and gave one to each bad guy.

"Not maybe," I said. "Now let go of my arm and get out of my way."

"What about Detective Fu Steinburg on a silver platter?" Warren said, tying it all back into the movie. "That was part of the deal."

"He's in the Finger Lakes playing patsy with a parrot," I said, starting for the door. "He'll be back Monday. If you're not still martial-arts masters by then, or even if you are, good luck getting him in the cage."

"Where are you going?" Warren said. "The outline says *you* get in the cage."

"Rewrite," I said. "Cassie has a killer to catch and half a day to catch him."

"No one called *cut*, Peanut," LaTanya said, camera still rolling.

"You can't talk, LaTanya," I said. "And don't call me Peanut."

36

—————

ALSO THE PRESENCE OF A GRADE A ASSHOLE

THERE JUST SO HAPPENED TO BE A NOTORIOUS, ILLUSTRIOUS, infamous, scandalous, and outrageous boutique residential architecture and design firm in New York City that obliterated the line between art and architecture, fame and fortune, war and peace, decency and decadence, and decorum and recklessness. And while they were at it, fit the killer's clue. The founding partners had reimagined an old loft factory in SoHo and repurposed it as the hippest, most understated, and most jaw-droppingly beautiful office building anywhere in Manhattan. It was a small, exclusive firm that specialized in prestigious waterfront properties in New York and around the world, beach houses in particular. Budget-busting beach houses.

Someone else will have to draw the beach house because this pen runs out of ink tonight.

The name of the firm was Penn and Ink. The founding partners were scandalous genius warrior artists. Hyper-competitive, rage-against-the-machine, madmen of Borneo.

Phillip Penn and Lucas Inklaar.

The two of them had spent as much time in the society pages as in the architecture and design pages—and not an insignificant amount of time in the police pages. Arrest reports, anyone? Their disputes were legal and legendary. Also physical. They'd sent each other to the hospital a dozen times over the years, drawing blood during battles. Young architects who'd done time at Penn and Ink hoping some of the rarified genius air filled with mystic architect pixie dust might land on them instead recounted tales of breaking up fistfights while dodging chairs and framed photos and crystal glasses and marble mementos hurled across the room —and, on two occasions, ducking bullets. Yes, twice on the record, Phillip Penn and Lucas Inklaar had fired guns at each other in the office while arguing the design direction of a waterfront *objet d'art*.

Their work was the envy of architects everywhere. The ultra-high-end beachfront, lakefront, and riverfront homes they designed were featured regularly in *Architectural Digest* and dozens of other prestigious international architecture-and-design publications. They were winners of the AIA Gold Medal, the Kahn, the Pritzker, the Good Design Award, the American Prize for Architecture, and manifold design medals and honors and commendations too numerous to mention.

Their client roster read like a global A-list Dream Team that couldn't even be possible. A high-powered intersection of political heavyweights, financial titans, technology billionaires, Texas tycoons, superstar athletes, jet-set royalty, Hollywood royalty, royalty royalty, and other stratospheric spenders with twenty to forty to sixty million to drop on a house on a beach or a river or a lake somewhere glorious.

After Warren and Al and Charlie had cracked the clue to the point where I could connect the dots to Penn and Ink, I called Logan and told him I'd scheduled an emergency meeting with the firm's partners. Telling the truth for a change, I let Logan know I'd said I was a private investigator working with the police to catch a killer and that Mr. Penn and Mr. Inklaar were *Persons Connected with the Investigation*.

"Bring your father's Colt," Logan said.

"Why?" I said.

"Because when I see you," he said, "I'm going to shoot you in the face with it, put it in your hand, and tell people you killed yourself out of abject stupidity."

Logan met me in SoHo, kicking and screaming and cursing me out for inserting myself into official police business despite the fact that the killer had himself inserted me into the official business of the police by making me the middleman between him and whatever psychological voodoo he had going on with Logan.

When Logan was out of steam and I was covered with a caustic coating of his repugnance, we went into the building and were escorted to the third floor—the top floor, the partners' floor—where Lucas Inklaar himself was waiting for us.

To say the renowned architect was larger than life was to vastly understate the words *larger* and *life*.

Inklaar was working, imposing by force of artistic will his vision for a home in the Hamptons on a five-foot-by-three-foot sheet of drafting paper taped to a wall, using charcoal for the outline of the structure—for the bones—and paint for the flesh and blood. More images of the same house, other angles and viewpoints, were taped to the same wall, above and below and beside the piece he was currently creating.

Without turning to us as we crossed the five-thousand-square-foot art studio/architectural office, without stopping his impassioned painting, Inklaar said, "You have unalloyed nerve to interrupt my work with pointless police procedure, Detective Logan...and whoever the hell you are, McCall private investigator something or other."

"Kate McCall," I said.

"I don't care," Inklaar said. "Don't speak again without my permission."

"I've been telling her that since summer," Logan said. "Never sinks in."

The entirety of the third floor was the domain of Penn and Inklaar—and only Penn and Inklaar. Penn occupied the northern half of the space, Inklaar the southern. Massive floor-to-ceiling sliding glass doors/panels/walls that mystically folded in on themselves, virtually vanishing at the touch of a finger, separated the partners when one or the other required privacy or, when open, created one huge shared loft. I wondered whether this was where they'd had their gunfights. I surreptitiously looked for telltale bullet holes.

Whether one office or two, the space was off-the-charts fabulous. Immense factory windows. Sixteen-foot ceilings. The world's most expensive yet most tasteful custom-designed office furniture.

On Inklaar's side of the building, near one wall of windows, was a gorgeous drafting table cut and crafted from some rare breed of exotic African wood. Whatever wood it was, Inklaar's massive desk was made of it too. His conference table was hand-carved and complemented the desk and drafting table. The fourteen chairs around the twelve-foot table had been individually bench-built, all different, all beautiful. The space was masculine but soft. Bold but subtle. Every inch, every piece of furniture, every rug on the loft floor had been designed by someone with taste and talent. Oh, that's right. Designed by Inklaar.

Penn, of course, had designed all the furniture and accoutrement on his half of the loft. Although, I couldn't ask him about it. Penn was out of the office.

We walked to the drafting area where Inklaar was working, a space defined by a beautiful, twenty-by-twenty, Inklaar-designed, handwoven rug. Nearby, the complex architectural plans in progress were spread out on his drafting table. They were intricate works of art unto themselves. Different than but wholly part of the dozen or so charcoal drawings taped to the wall, which gave the loft an art-gallery vibe. I had the unmistakable sense I was in the presence of greatness.

Also in the presence of a Grade A asshole.

"To what investigation are Phillip and I *persons connected*?" Inklaar said with condescending impatience.

He kept working. Beside him, beyond him, all around him, framed architectural honors and awards and medals and letters of commendation along with dozens of framed photographs of him and Penn and their famous clients covered yet another long section of wall space. Three-dimensional models of houses-in-progress and houses-completed were displayed on modern sculpture pedestal stands. It was like being in the office of the Curator of Architecture and Design for the MoMA.

At the other end of the loft, Penn's office was similar to Inklaar's in scale and grandeur. Different stylistic approach, yes. But the same brilliant, tasteful, appealing palette, absolutely.

Inklaar was sixty-three years old. Maybe six-five or -six. Trim. Clean-shaven. Long brown hair going gray tucked stylishly behind his ears. Designer glasses. He radiated impatience, anger, violence, power, and, yes, artistic genius. He was intimidating and terrifying. Domineering. Authoritarian. Controlling. No one denied, disputed, refuted, or refused Lucas Inklaar. Except Phillip Penn, who was in every way his fierce, intense, short-fused egotistical equal and who, by all accounts, denied, disputed, refuted, and refused Inklaar just for the simple fuck of it.

And, of course, Detective Lew Logan, who denied, disputed, refuted, and refused anyone he damn well pleased.

Logan told Inklaar about the killer, starting the story at the end of July, when Jimmy had been found murdered in an insurance-company elevator, and ending yesterday—three in the morning today—with the murder of the King of Conga and the latest clue.

Inklaar never once looked at Logan or me. Never stopped working. Bold, definitive, striking charcoal strokes for the structure—the lines, the bones of the house. Strong yet soft colors for the sand and sky. Handsome shades of gray for the exterior walls. Metallic white for the roofing.

"You believe I hired this assassin to murder Phillip?" Inklaar said.

"Or Penn hired him to murder you," Logan said. "Yes. I believe it's possible."

"More than possible," I said.

"Where's your partner?" Logan said.

"Suffering, I hope," Inklaar said. "Suffering is my wish for him. I hope he's suffering wherever he is."

"Suffering from what?" Logan said.

Inklaar's hands were black from the charcoal. Gold and blue and gray and metallic white from the paint. "In specific? Grief. His wife passed eight months ago, and he's been unable to carry on, to create anything of value since her death. Grief counseling has been in vain. In general? Defeat."

"Defeat?" I said.

"Phillip and I began our dissolution two months after she died. He went out the door with half the architects, half the administrative staff, half the clients, and half the houses. It's been a spiteful, rancorous legal war since that moment. Reconciliation has been suggested by the court but is futile. Largely because Phillip believes he's entitled to half the monetary value of the working projects."

"And you believe otherwise?" Logan said.

"Projects for which *I* was the creative fountainhead, the artistic inspiration solidifying client commitment, the guardian guiding the design and construction processes, belong to me," Inklaar said.

"I understand," I said. "The nerve of your partner thinking half the money is his. It's not like *he* won all these accolades and awards *with* you and—oh, wait, he did, didn't he? That's his office right over there, isn't it? Damn, I can see it from here, and it looks just like...just like...just like what? Oh, I know. It looks like half of all this belongs to him."

Inklaar turned to me, burned me with his eyes, melted me with the disdain and quiet rage in his voice. "The war between us is decades long. The court has recently awarded me a forty-million-dollar waterfront home that Phillip attempted to steal upon his exit. If I have to battle him project by project, I will reclaim what is mine. Whatever it takes. You, whoever you are, know nothing."

"I've been telling her that since summer," Logan said. "Never sinks in."

Inklaar's artistic flow interrupted, he moved to a nearby work sink and washed his hands. "If you're quite done, you can see yourselves out before I lose my temper."

Both Penn and Inklaar were renowned for their titanic tempers. Not that Logan gave a shit.

"Or you can answer the question before I lose mine. Where's Penn? Second time I'm asking. Don't make me ask again."

Inklaar sighed. "Most likely working. Completing checklists on any one of the eight or nine projects he unlawfully took from me. I don't know where he is. He went missing several days ago. No one's been able to communicate with him since Thursday."

Logan looked at me as if to say, *Not fucking good*, and then looked back at Inklaar. "I'll need a list of those projects."

Inklaar walked to his drafting table, surveyed the plans. "I think not, Detective. Those are private clients, all of whom take their confidentiality to heart, and all of whom have no personal involvement in my dispute with Phillip."

Logan crossed to Inklaar and grabbed the pen right out of his hand. "Pay attention, Inklaar. From my perspective, it's entirely possible you hired a psychotic corporate killer to whack your partner or that he hired him to whack you. This murder is meant to happen tonight. The state of New York says it's my responsibility to protect you from Penn and Penn from you. I don't need to find you because my scumbag radar tells me you're right in front of me. To that end, I'm assigning a task-force officer to sit on your arrogant ass for the next few days. But I do need to find Penn. So unless you'd like me to bring my task force in full into your office and rip the place to fucking shreds in order to compile the requested itemized inventory of projects Penn walked out with, I suggest you print me the list in the next sixty seconds."

I stepped to the drawing table and stood beside Logan. "Make two copies, Inklaar."

Inklaar glared at me and locked his jaw in anger. "Rarely do I have such an instinctive feeling of deep animosity for a person I don't know."

"I've been telling her that since summer," Logan said. "Never sinks in."

37

TUMBLEWEEDS IN THE WIND

AND THEN THE SON OF A BITCH DIDN'T PRINT ME THE LIST.

Inklaar printed one copy for Logan, who said he'd give me a copy *after* his task force had analyzed, scrutinized, dissected, inspected, evaluated, and extrapolated the shit of out the thing. After they'd taken "a deep dive into the details." If he remembered, if he wasn't too tired, if his hemorrhoids calmed down and his headache went away, then and only then would he email me the list of houses where Penn might be hiding out.

For Logan, finding Penn was important, of course, but it was downstream from protecting Inklaar because Logan believed Penn had hired the killer to whack his partner. That's why Penn was off the grid. He was hiding until Inklaar was dead and he could return to town and reclaim his throne.

I thought Inklaar had hired the killer to whack Penn. My reasoning was that even if Penn was as vicious and vindictive as his partner, which he probably was, he was too distracted—by sadness, rage, pain, whatever—to pay someone to murder his maniac-genius-douchebag partner, to summon the energy for that kind of dark emotional commitment, to make the arrangements and see it through. Inklaar, though, was focused like a laser. Just the kind of maniac-genius-douchebag who would hire someone to shoot Penn in the eyes while Penn was otherwise overcome with grief due to the death of his wife. Just the kind of maniac-genius-douchebag who at precisely the time his partner's life was crumbling would decide that *that* was the moment to pay an assassin to finish him off.

Penn was possibly-probably-likely at one of the beach houses he'd taken from Inklaar on his way out the door. One of the beach houses on the list. The list I didn't have.

Any other day, Inklaar's list would have been Item Numero Uno on my hit parade. But this wasn't any other day. This was the day I was waiting on the sidewalk across the street from the Greenwich Village brownstone home/office of Oscar K. Ricci, Ruby Gold's bookkeeper and accountant—12th Street between Fifth and Sixth, five blocks north of Washington Square Park.

I'd gotten Ricci's name and address from Robbie Sloane of all slimeballs. Lillian Pearl had reset the scene with the news that Ruby was dead broke, and it had become clear—at least to me—that whoever had paid Ruby's gambling debts had hired the bear to kill Cochran and then Rick (and me). Given that I had no idea what else to do, the next step—my only step—was to follow the money.

Sloane had spoken with Ruby's money man regarding Rick's sitcom cash, so after Rick and I had kissed like crazy, Rick called Sloane and put him on the speaker without telling him I was in the room—and definitely without telling him we'd been making out like teenagers. Sloane had sounded congested, like he had terrible allergies. But he didn't have allergies. He had a broken nose. Anyway, Sloane had gone off on me, telling Rick what an out-of-control, lunatic bodyguard freak I was. How I'd slugged him out of nowhere and stolen the Silvercup information right out of his date book while he was bleeding on the ground. He'd demanded Rick fire me. Rick told him he already had, which was true. He didn't tell him he'd hired me back a minute later. Happy to hear I'd gotten sacked, Sloane gave Rick the name and address and hung up to ice his nose.

I wanted to keep thinking about kissing Rick Gotti, but Dennis, Posey, Chloe, and Roger arrived dressed in their theatric versions of IRS agents on the job, and every other thought in my head went *poof*.

I'd called them with a plan—or something that passed for a plan—after I'd read about Ricci. And because I was pressed for time, I'd allowed them to make up their own code names. Dennis had said the names would be tied to a theme. I'd known I was in trouble at the word *theme*. But I'd let it go. Another in a long line of McCall mistakes.

Roger wore a black suit with fancy cowboy boots, ten-gallon hat, rhinestone bolo tie, and eye patch, seeing as how he was still black-and-blue from when Lillian had clocked him with her gun what seemed like decades ago but had been only yesterday. Dennis, I kid you not, wore a full-on denim three-piece suit with blue snakeskin cowboy boots and a cowboy hat that was less than ten gallons. Maybe seven gallons. Possibly five. Posey and Chloe had gone for Western-looking business suits and cowboy boots. No hats.

We all had IRS lanyards that identified us as special agents. They were realistic props from the D-Cup madcap musical *Tax Dancing from the Grave*, two hours of unadulterated absurdity. It was set in the early 1920s and told the tale of married IRS agents—me and Roger—who were enthusiastic tap dancers in their spare time. In the show, Roger died during an IRS raid but somehow stayed on the tax team and participated in the takedown of the bootlegger who'd shot him dead. The bootlegger went to prison for assorted atrocities. Roger and I tap-danced to the cemetery where he tapped down into his grave until the next case, when he would rise to *tax*-dance again.

Yes, Dennis and Posey either had fabulous drugs in the

present or technicolor flashbacks from fabulous drugs in the past.

"I don't want to ask," I said.

"Guy's name is Oscar K.," Roger said.

"His initials got us thinking," Dennis said. "O.K."

"As in O.K. Corral," Posey said.

"It's the Wild West, Kate," Chloe said. "We're IRS gunslingers who shoot corrals to shit and ride off into the sunset."

"You understand he's Italian," I said. "From Bensonhurst. Not Tombstone."

Aside from gunslingers shooting corrals to shit, Chloe was right about the plan, the log line for which was: *Flashing an official search warrant, a tight team of IRS agents raid Oscar K. Ricci's office, find out who furtively funded Ruby Gold, and get the hell out before Ricci realizes the agents are frauds and the warrant is bogus.*

Point of interest: The warrant itself wasn't bogus. It was a true-to-life search warrant made bogus because I'd forged the signature of an actual New York City judge who was conveniently out of town for the weekend.

What was I doing with a true-to-life search warrant? Jimmy had gotten his hands on a stack of the things and left them to me as part of my inheritance—he'd never told me the specifics of how he'd come to possess them, just said something about a cop friend who'd gotten screwed by the system he'd sworn an oath to uphold taking a moment to give the system the finger on his way out the door. *"Not for everyday use,"* Jimmy would tell me when he'd peel one off for an uncommon case. *"Special occasions only."*

I should say I wasn't proud of breaking the law like this. But I was doing it for my father, so I was well within the rules, specifically *Jimmy's Rules of Private Investigation for Kate, Rule Number Seven: Don't break the law for just anyone.*

"Wherever he's from," Roger said, gesturing at Ricci's place, "he's still a bookkeeper. No way he makes this kind of dough. He's got to be cooking the books."

"Fudging the figures," Posey said.

"Rigging the records," Dennis said.

"Nuking the numbers," Chloe said.

Correct on all counts. Ricci was a money man for the mob, for Wall Street hedge funders, for mighty media moguls, for Broadway shooting stars, for anyone who needed bookkeeping and accounting services that were below the radar, behind the scenes, in the background, off the grid, and on the sly. He lived and worked in a drop-dead gorgeous, three-story brownstone that had to have cost seven mil or more.

Ricci's cash came from somewhere criminal, but he was so far under the table that not only had the police never been able to make any charges stick, they'd never been able to make any charges, period. None. Ricci wasn't clean, and everybody knew it. But he was untouchable. Hush-hush clients paid him huge money to do their dirty work and keep his mouth shut about it. About them. And he'd done just that. As a result, Ricci was rich.

I'd googled him. There was lots to learn. Ricci had no front-door access, so to speak. If he didn't know you, you weren't getting in. No way he'd see me on such short notice. And no way he'd spill the name of Ruby Gold's sugar daddy even if he did. This was a back-door job. Which was why I'd called my personal Pinkertons and given them two hours to pull it together and meet me in the Village.

"What we're doing is wildly illegal," I said. "Last chance to beg off."

"We'll be gone before he realizes we're as crooked as he is," Dennis said.

"Ghosts in the machine," Posey said.

"Smoke in the night," Roger said.

"Tumbleweeds in the wind," Chloe said.

My plan was nuts, and my team was nutsier. I also knew I

was the nutsiest for thinking this was a thing I should do. But I was doing it.

"In and out," I said as we started across the street. "We have to be at the D-Cup by five so Chloe can drop acid in a cab, Roger and I can pop out of a painting, and two orgies can do whatever it is orgies do. What I'm saying is follow my lead."

"Follow it where?" Chloe said.

"To the O.K. Corral," Posey said.

"Boots, chaps, and cowboy hats," Dennis said.

"Yippee yi-yo-ki-yay," Roger said.

"IRS," I said, holding both my prop lanyard and fraudulent warrant up to the front-door security camera. "This is a search warrant. We have reason to suspect unlawful financial behavior on the part of one of Mr. Ricci's clients. Open the door or we'll huff, and we'll puff, and we'll blow your house in."

The buzzer buzzed, the lock clicked open, I turned the knob, and we went into the brownstone.

38

SHOULD BE EASY TO GET THE CUFFS ON HER

IT WAS LIKE STEPPING BACK IN TIME. THROUGH THE IRON GATE and into the Corleone family's 1940s compound. Everything heavy and dark and vintage. Spotless, but from another era. Expensive antique Italian furniture. Classic, turn-of-the-century lighting fixtures. Priceless rugs handwoven in the Old Country when the Old Country was young. Handsome silk draperies. Ornate gold frames featuring portraits of the Ricci family tree stretching across the Atlantic to Sicily, before air travel, when ocean liners carried Ricci relatives to Ellis Island and New York City, the Statue of Liberty welcoming them with her eternal flame and the promise of justice for all.

An upstanding American life might have been possible for the Ricci family upon their arrival, but fate and fortune turned them down a darker road, and they'd made their mark in the cutthroat construction business as plumbers, electricians, carpenters, masons, and union bosses—bosses being the key word as far as the unions went.

Oscar K.'s union boss father—with deep mob ties—had died (been murdered) when the boy was but one year old. He'd been raised by his mother, Maria, who'd married in her later thirties, given birth to Oscar K. when she was forty, and decided right there in the hospital to never remarry, to dedicate herself to the only child she would ever have—her pride and joy. Oscar K. would be her life's work. Her reason for living.

I'd read about her online on my way to the Village because like the wives of other union mobsters who'd died in a hail of bullets, Maria's story had been part of her husband's story, part of the bigger Ricci picture. So there she was on the internet.

Of course, she'd been fifty-odd years younger then. Now, she stood before us in the large entrance foyer, ninety years old if she was a day. Closer to midnineties. Elegant, yes, but eyes cloudy with age and more than a touch of confusion.

"I'm Mrs. Ricci," she said in a pleasant elderly voice that matched her pleasant elderly smile. "You're here to play with my Oscar?"

"Yes, Mrs. Ricci," I said. "We're the IRS."

"That's nice, dear," she said, gesturing at a massive oak door carved, no doubt, by Ricci craftsmen a hundred years ago. "He's waiting for you in the office. Have fun."

An ornate wooden stairway with a carpeted runner led up to what I imagined was the family's living space above. Mrs. Ricci started up the stairs, leaving us alone in the large foyer.

We took a moment, nodded that we were ready to rumble, and went through the impressive door into Oscar's office. Longer than it was wide. Taller ceilings than expected. One wall, from the front of the building to the back, was entirely exposed brick, most likely laid by Ricci masons many decades earlier. The other walls were oak, custom paneled with beautiful built-in bookshelves created back when carpentry was art. File cabinets and electronics were the only things keeping Ricci's office in the twenty-first century. Otherwise, it looked and felt like a private upscale Italian men's club for mobsters with money and power, a swanky Prohibition supper club with thick steaks, illegal bottles of booze, and Cuban cigars.

Oscar K. sat behind his desk, most unhappy indeed that a team of IRS agents had shown up with a search warrant looking for mafioso financial mischief that would put him and his boss and his underboss and all the rest of the capos behind bars.

He was a wiseguy in a five-thousand-dollar Armani suit. Silk tie. Crooked nose. Pockmarked skin. Thinning dark hair going gray. Meaty hands (but manicured nails). If he wasn't cooking your books, he was choking you to death. That was the vibe he put out in spades. He was a five-foot, ten-inch square block of Italian granite. Not to be fucked with. He had friends who would shoot you in the back of the head without blinking, and he was not afraid to ask them for such a favor. I wondered how many IRS agents were dead at the bottom of the East River because Ricci had made a phone call.

He closed the ledger and looked up at us. Since I seemed to be the one in charge, he directed his opening comment to me.

"The fuck you want, Agent Whoever the Fuck You Are?" he said.

His voice alone could kill. Scary dude, no doubt about it. And yet, a CPA. A numbers guy. How was that even possible? Everything about him—other than the suit, the diamond pinky ring, the manicure, and the Rolex—said mob gravedigger. That he'd graduated high school would have been shock enough. That he'd matriculated at Fordham and gone on to graduate school for accounting was entirely incongruous.

"Shaw," I said, flashing my D-Cup IRS ID and forged search warrant. "And these fine folks are..."

"Agent Holiday," Roger said.

"Agent Earp," Dennis said.

"Agent Oakley," Posey said.

"Agent Calamity Jane," Chloe said. "Yeehaw."

As if I needed reminding, I realized again what a bad idea it had been to let the Schmidt and Parker Players develop a theme and name themselves after it.

"Do what you got to do and get the hell out before I get angry enough to make a phone call," Ricci said.

A phone call? I thought. *East River here we come.*

"You shouldn't talk to the IRS that way," I said, covering my fear with bravado like any good actor. "We tend to hold grudges."

"In case you forgot, Ricci, we're the financial law in this town," Dennis said.

"An IRS posse of gunfighters," Posey said.

"Both barrels blazing," Roger said, blasting Ricci with his index fingers, then blowing the imaginary smoke away.

"Shootin' for the whole kit and caboodle," Chloe said, putting on the worst Western accent I might ever have heard.

It took every ounce of facial control I could muster not to cringe. All I could do was hope Ricci wasn't a fan of cowboy history. Agent Calamity Jane? Jesus Christ.

"What Agent Jane is trying to say," I said, "is the IRS is aware you've been cooking the books for decades. So far, no one's been able to tag you. But that changes today. So you can tell us what we want to know, or you can watch us turn this fancy funeral home upside down and inside out. Your call."

I was hoping he'd say, *"What is it you want to know?"*

But instead he said, "I call fuck you."

Then he stood up. Jesus Christ, he was a beast. How he'd become a dapper bookkeeper instead of a hitman was the mystery of the day.

"Gloves, please," I said, turning to my team.

Dennis, Posey, Roger, and Chloe put on latex crime scene gloves.

I did too. "Have it your way, Mr. Ricci."

The posse moved to the file cabinets and began their search, almost but not quite looking like the real thing. Ricci killed them with his eyes. I imagined them dead on the floor, Harvey Keitel coming in to clean up the bloody mess.

There was no possibility, none, that Ricci would crack and tell me who'd given Ruby Gold the money to pay off her debt with Paulie Crane. No chance he'd even ask what we wanted to know, what we were here for in the first place. Failure was inevitable. The whole crazy charade had been a dangerous waste of time.

What the hell was I thinking? What the hell am I doing here? I thought. *Oh wait, I know, I'm impersonating an IRS agent with a fraudulent search warrant, a full-blown felony on top of a full-blown felony. We should leave now before any of us get hurt or arrested or dropped in the East River with a block of cement chained to our legs.*

And then Roger started to sing.

"Oh, give me a home where the buffalo roam, where the deer and the antelope play, where seldom is heard a discouraging word..."

Being musical-theater people to the center of their souls, Dennis and Posey couldn't help themselves from joining in with a three-part harmony. "And the skies are not cloudy all day..."

Chloe, who could just about carry a tune, added her weird Western twang to the chorus. Somehow, it didn't sound bad at all.

"Home, home on the range..."

Ricci's jaw fell open. I couldn't begin to imagine what he was thinking. It was tough enough to imagine what *I* was thinking.

While my cowboy agents sang the song and worked the room—and Ricci stood there burning—I checked out the dozens of framed family photos on the bookshelves.

Ricci's life story. Birthdays. Communion. Graduation. Little League. All the many milestones. But it was what *wasn't* here that was even more telling.

No pictures of a marriage or a girlfriend. Or boyfriend. No wife and children. No pictures of family vacations. No Mr. and Mrs. Oscar K. Ricci and their Oscar K. Ricci kids in Disneyland or camping in the mountains or swimming at the Jersey shore. No shots of Ricci hunting or fishing or playing golf or tennis with his friends. No friends anywhere. Lots of photographs, mind you. All the life landmarks. Just no one in the pictures but Ricci and his mother.

The two of them, and the two of them, and the two of them.

Ricci and his mother on a trip to Sicily. At Niagara Falls. In front of Mount Rushmore. Looking out at the Grand Canyon. Celebrating New Year's Eve with champagne. Trimming the brownstone Christmas tree. Filling an Easter basket with painted eggs and chocolate rabbits. Carving a turkey at a Thanksgiving dinner for two. Buying Oscar K. his first car.

The two of them, and the two of them, and the two of them, and the two of them.

What the hell? I thought. *What the freaking hell?*

"Attention, attention. Hello, hello. Time for a snack," Mrs. Ricci said, coming into the office with a tray of milk and chocolate-chip cookies.

The IRS cowboy chorus got quiet.

I froze in front of a photograph of Maria and her son on top of the Grand Coulee Dam when Oscar was about ten years old.

Ricci rushed round his desk and helped his mother put the tray on the coffee table between the leather sofas in the sitting area in the center of the room.

"Mama, what are you doing?" Ricci said. "Let me help you. Be careful. Why didn't you call me? I would've come upstairs. I would've helped you."

The tone of his voice had transformed in the presence of his mother. The murderous tenor he'd blasted at us like a flamethrower was replaced by a gentleness that was...juvenile?

Adolescent? Youthful? Yes, youthful. Like he'd been transported, body and soul, to days gone by.

When I say *body and soul*, I'm not kidding. Not just his face, but his entire demeanor, his total physicality. Eyes, mouth, shoulders...his spirit. Everything about him softened as if he'd somehow physically regressed from a fifty-five-year-old murderous mob bookkeeper to a boy playing with Matchbox cars on the living-room carpet, Mama surprising him with a sweet snack in the middle of the day for no reason other than she adored him with all her heart.

It was astonishing. And made even more profound by the accompanying realization that failure in Ricci's office was no longer a fait accompli. Ricci could be cracked. How did I know? Because if I was one thing above all others, even above being an actor, I was a mother. And a mother knows what a mother knows. And what I knew now was that Oscar K. was a hopeless, helpless mama's boy. He was drowning in mama's boy. Had already drowned in it long, long ago.

But it was more than that. Maria wasn't just his doting mother, righteous best friend, and saintly divining rod. She was his connection—his *only* connection—to a life of innocence, where he wasn't a criminal manipulating money for mobsters, drug dealers, con men, and thieves. His lone link to the clean life he'd lived as child, the life his mother had wanted for him, dreamed for him, worked for, prayed for, guided him toward.

Oscar K., Maria's honest and forthright CPA son.

Except it had never happened. And he couldn't live with the guilt. So he'd made a deal with himself. So long as he loved her, devoted himself to her in the way she'd devoted herself to him, he was not an irredeemable man. In her spiritual embrace was forgiveness. In her transcendental adoration, he was not consigned to the bowels of hell for crimes committed. They would be dutiful and faithful to each other in a way that was too deep, too creepy for Hallmark. She was and would be his savior.

There was one and only one way to beat him.

"Officer Jane, cuff Mrs. Ricci," I said to Chloe. "She's an accomplice to every financial crime her son's committed in the last thirty years. If her son won't talk, then she will. We'll take her to the office and interrogate her until she cracks like an egg."

Chloe had honest-to-goodness handcuffs for reasons none of us wanted to know. She took them out and froze. Roger and Dennis and Posey froze too.

Ricci's face filled with shock and horror.

"Officer Jane," I said.

"She's ninety-five years old," Chloe said.

"Then it should be easy to get the cuffs on her," I said.

Chloe moved to Maria and cuffed her wrists.

"Stop," Ricci said. "Oh my God...please...you can't do this..."

He was torn between wanting to wring someone's neck and cry like a five-year-old. He moved to Maria, but Roger and Dennis stood their ground between him and his mother. I imagined the tough-guy cowboy theme had given them courage they might not otherwise have had, given the circumstances.

"We can do anything we want, Mr. Ricci," I said. "We're the IRS. Holiday, Earp, Oakley, let's ride."

Roger started singing again. "When I was walkin' one mornin' for pleasure, I spied a young cowboy just ridin' along..."

"*Git Along Little Doggies*"? I thought. *Oh, why the hell not?*

"Oscar, what's happening?" Maria said. "Why am I being arrested?"

Dennis and Posey joined Roger. Again in western three-part harmony. "His hat was throwed back and his spurs were a jinglin' and as he approached he was singin' this song..."

"You're not being arrested, Mrs. Ricci," I said. "You're being detained by the IRS for questioning because your son refuses to cooperate with our investigation. You can blame your boy for this one."

I wasn't proud of using an elderly handcuffed woman as a wedge, but there are times when I'm not a nice person, and this was one of them.

Chloe joined in for the chorus. "Yippi ti yi yo git along little doggies..."

We moved slowly through the office—I mean creepy crawling—toward the massive oak door, Chloe led the way with me and Mrs. Ricci next, Posey behind us, and Dennis and Roger bringing up the rear, keeping Oscar K. away from his mommy.

"Fat Frankie Petrillo," Ricci said. "Owns a string of dry cleaners. Literally launders ten thousand dollars a day."

The IRS posse sang, "It's your misfortune and none of my own..."

"Not what we're looking—" I said.

"Greasy Gary Fortuna," Ricci said. "Runs a protection racket in the Bronx. Deducts his expenses through companies he doesn't own in exchange for not burning their businesses to the ground. Tax fraud for fifty years."

Jesus Christ, I thought, *he's confessing to save his mother*.

"Yippi ti yi yo git along little doggies..."

"No thank you, Mr. Ricci," I said.

"Big Balls Bobby Benvenuto," Ricci said, panicking as we went through the carved oak door and into the foyer, spitting out names and crimes like a slot machine spits out nickels, tears in his eyes, for Pete's sake. "Pyramid scheme. Takes money from investors and spends it on cars and boats and booze and broads. There's no business, no product, nothing to invest in except Big Balls Bobby."

"You know that Wyoming will be your new home..."

"We don't want them, Mr. Ricci," I said, "and we don't want you, and we especially don't want your mother."

We reached the front door. Ricci was practically crying. "Then what the hell do you want?"

"Language, Oscar," Maria said.

"Sorry, Mama. What the heck do you want?" Oscar said.

We were all at the door, Chloe's hand on the handle.

The IRS posse stopped singing.

"Ruby Gold is your client?" I said.

"Ruby Gold?" Ricci said, suddenly confused. "Yeah, she's my client."

"Who gave her the cash to pay back the money she lost betting on the horses with Kenny Cochran?" I said.

"What?" Ricci said.

"Agent Jane," I said. "Open the door."

Chloe opened the door.

"Victor Vreeland gave her the fucking money," Ricci said. "Straight gift. Vreeland gave her six mil to pay off her debt and fund her sitcom."

"Language, Oscar," Mrs. Ricci said.

"Sorry, Mama. Freaking money," Ricci said. "Victor Vreeland gave her the freaking money."

"Calamity, take the cuffs off Mrs. Ricci," I said.

Chloe unlocked and removed the cuffs.

For some reason, an old Gene Autry tune popped into my head. "Saddle up, posse. It's time to say goodbye to the prairie."

Of course, all that did was move Roger to sing the last chorus, with help, naturally, from Dennis, Posey, and Chloe.

"When the purple sage blooms in the springtime, memories and dreams will come to me. I hate to say goodbye to the prairie, the land that is a part of me."

We were through the door and down the street before Oscar K. could figure out what the heck had happened.

39

I'VE GOT NOTHING AGAINST ALPACAS

WE ARRIVED AT THE D-CUP FOR THE SATURDAY-NIGHT performance of *Psychedelic Sunday* with no time to spare for Roger and me to honor our longstanding preshow routine. This meant Roger went up to the theater with Dennis and Posey—the first actor to arrive—I stayed on the sidewalk outside the entrance (giving Roger ten minutes to settle in), and Chloe went for a cup of coffee so as not to screw up our solemn theatric ceremony.

While I waited, Logan surprised me with a text. It was Inklaar's list of projects Penn had walked out with, projects, Logan thought, where Penn was likely to be hiding after hiring the killer to blow Inklaar's eyeballs out of their sockets and through the back of Inklaar's head. There were half a dozen on the list. Logan had starred the four he said I should stay away from because his task force was going to raid each one of them and take Penn down. At the same time, Logan said he would sit on Inklaar all tonight and tomorrow so the killer couldn't access him, kidnap him, murder him, shoot his eyes out, and gloat about it.

All four starred projects were New York beach houses—

houses being an inadequate word for oceanfront manors, palaces, estates, and castles. Logan had eliminated the projects that weren't beach houses because the killer's clue had specifically stated: *Someone else will have to draw the beach house because this pen runs out of ink tonight.*

I still didn't think Penn had hired the killer to whack Inklaar. The guy was grieving his late wife for pity's sake. I still thought Inklaar had hired the killer to whack Penn. And I imagined Penn thought so too, which was why he was hiding. Logan didn't buy into the misdirection theme the killer had established. I did. But I knew him up close. Of course, I could have been wrong about that, but that's what my gut was saying.

So I focused on the two that weren't starred. One was a penthouse on the Hudson River. Six thousand square feet. Breathtaking views of the George Washington Bridge. The other was a hundred-acre farm in Katonah, an exclusive, Westchester County hamlet within the town of Bedford, about an hour north of the city. One hundred acres. In Katonah. The land alone had to be worth ten mil.

I disregarded the penthouse and focused on the farm, five acres of which was a fenced pasture for alpacas. An alpaca farm. Now, I've got nothing against alpacas—they look like mischievous 1960s British rock stars to me—but they weren't the reason for my focus.

The reason was the farm's owners. Julian and Martha Montgomery, adventuring billionaire philanthropist daredevils, fixtures in the society pages for giving millions and millions to charity and for scaling unscaled mountains and bungee-jumping into deep canyons and running with the bulls and making expeditions to distant wild jungles and climbing into smoking volcanos and traveling to the freezing poles and taking tiny submarines to the bottom of the sea and so on and on and on around the world. But audacious Montgomery thrill-seeking wasn't the reason I focused on the farm.

The reason was that Julian and Martha's billions had come from her family fortune. And her maiden name was Beetch.

The hundred-acre Katonah estate had been in Martha's family for generations. She'd inherited it—and everything else—when her daredevil parents were killed (eaten) while free diving with sharks. She'd sold the family business, a global construction wholesale company, for seven billion and most every other Beetch asset for another three billion. But she'd held on to a few prime properties, including the Katonah estate.

Martha, basically, was her mother reborn, an untamed mustang running wild around the globe. Plus, she'd married her father reborn—Julian was an indefatigable madman thrill seeker like Barry Beetch. Martha and Julian were both adrenaline junkies. And they both loved alpaca sweaters—as soft as cashmere but stronger—and so they'd repurposed five acres in Katonah as an alpaca farm they called Wild Wooly Ranch.

None of that was the point. The point was the stunning, massive thirty-thousand-square-foot mansion on the grounds that Julian and Martha were redesigning from stem to stern with Phillip Penn, who'd taken the project with him when he vacated Penn and Ink.

It was called The Beetch House.

Someone else will have to draw the beach house because this pen runs out of ink tonight.

The killer had chosen that undefined timeframe for a reason. Not seven tonight. Not nine thirty. Not ten forty-five. Just *tonight.* He was waiting for me to get there.

Fu would be on his Finger Lakes parrot playdate until Monday, so I called Charlie and asked him to go with me after the show. But Charlie said, and I quote, "Can't make it. Got a poker game and a hooker on tap."

So I called Zombie Al Cutter, and he beat me up for three hundred bucks. "An hour there, an hour back, crazy killer in the middle of the night, lost money I could've made on eBay if I wasn't wasting time with you in some foreign fucking land called Katonah. Three bills is a fucking gift, McCall."

Then I went up to the theater—second actor in the house—did my hair and makeup, put on my skintight, flesh-toned leotard, became Professor Jedry's tripped-out version of Venus, and took the stage for a sold-out shit show—I mean performance—of *Psychedelic Sunday*.

Once the music started, every other thing in my head dissolved into mist. There was singing and dancing and acting and orgies. There was laughter and joy and applause and a curtain call. And then Al was waiting downstairs in the White Whale, and we were on our way to Katonah.

40

FOUL PLAY, DEAD BODIES, THAT KIND OF THING

We took Saw Mill River Parkway North through Yonkers and Tarrytown and Mt. Kisco, got off at Girdle Ridge Road in Bedford, and worked our way to rustic Upper Hook Road in Katonah. There was no traffic to speak of. It was ten fifteen when we'd left Manhattan. Eleven thirty when we parked the White Whale deep in the dark shadows across the woodsy way from The Beetch House.

You couldn't see the house from the road, which was saying something since the thing was thirty thousand square feet. But we knew we were here because there was a hand-carved sign on a custom-made, extra-wide entrance gate that read: *Wild Wooly Ranch*.

The sign also read: *By appointment only*.

Define appointment, I thought.

One hundred acres of rolling hills, thick with trees colored by autumn. The property had a picturesque ten-acre lake somewhere out of sight. For generations, the Beetch family had left the land wild. But Martha and Julius had tamed five acres for thirty-two alpacas, who were also in there somewhere out of sight.

I'd told Al to wear black from head to toe. I'd done the same. I had my little black backpack to hold my wallet and keys and Colt. We looked like criminals, and to the extent that trespassing was a crime—I mean, we didn't have an appointment—that's what we were.

A cedar split-rail fence ran from the entrance gate for what seemed like miles in both directions, meaning one hundred acres is a big piece of property. The gate was latched but not locked because, I imagined, who the hell would ever be out in the middle-of-Katonah-nowhere wilderness that you had to lock your gate?

Me and Zombie Al, that's who.

I unlatched the gate, and Al and I started up the long, winding entrance road toward what I hoped would be The Beetch House and Phillip Penn.

Al didn't talk for a while. This struck me as amazing. Either he was in awe, or he was terrified, or he'd never seen woods before, or he was in such disbelief that he'd agreed to come with me for a measly three hundred bucks that words escaped him.

"You're not paying me enough, McCall," he finally said.

We went up and down a few winding hills, came around a bend, and there, in the near distance, atop the next hill, in a gorgeous glade, was the largest, most magnificent rustic house I'd ever seen. Several flood lights on tall posts were spaced around the immediate grounds, illuminating construction equipment—backhoes and dump trucks and scaffolding and several foreman trailers—all around the house, which was in the midst of a phenomenal transformation. Make no mistake, the original design was impressive, but the work Phillip Penn was instituting—with Julius and Martha's blessing and blank check—would have made Frank Lloyd Wright proud. The lines, the materials, the glass and steel and wood and stone, were out of this world. Midcentury rustic glory. And thirty thousand feet. Jesus Christ, it was overwhelming. Penn was every bit the genius Inklaar was…plus some extra genius.

We walked down one hill and up another into the glade, which was more or less the size of a football field, and arrived at the front of the massive house. I had two thoughts. One, Julius and Martha really were billionaires because normal, run-of-the-mill rich people could only dream of a house like this, a project this size. Two, what was wrong with the world when two people needed a thirty-thousand-square-foot house?

"We'll walk the perimeter first, then go inside," I said. "I'll go this way, you go that way, we'll meet in the middle in the back. We're looking for lights or open windows or unlocked doors. Signs of life. Or death. Foul play, dead bodies, that kind of thing. Put your phone on silent but leave it on. Call me if you see something."

It was eleven forty-five.

Someone else will have to draw the beach house because this pen runs out of ink tonight.

"Be careful, Al," I said.

On the one hand, I felt guilty for dragging him into the Katonah woods. For asking him to come with me to find Phillip Penn, who was under threat of grisly death. Not because we were friends. Al and I weren't friends. We didn't like each other. We were more like family. Stuck with each other. That's why I felt guilty. No one wants to be responsible for putting a family member in a compromising position, not that a compromising position was waiting for Al around the corner. But even if you don't like someone in your family, you care about them on some subatomic level. You don't want to see them hurt on your watch.

One the other hand, Al was a grownup of sorts and had said yes, had even negotiated a fee for making the trip. On some arcane level of his own, he'd *wanted* to be here. Maybe the adrenaline made him feel alive in a way that eBay trading and illegal rental cars did not. So he'd said he was all in for three hundred bucks. *He'd* said it, not me. Anyway, I still felt responsible for him being here. Responsible for him, period.

"I fucking hate alpacas," Al said as he started around the house.

"Why?" I said, heading the other way.

"Because they look so fucking happy."

It took a few minutes to work my way around the building. Believe me, thirty thousand square feet is even bigger than you think it is. Wing after wing after wing. Construction gear everywhere. Pitch-black inside.

If Penn was in there, he was sleeping. Or he was dead.

I turned one more corner and arrived at the rear of the house. A sliver of moon was the only light back here. I walked across a huge flagstone courtyard. I say courtyard because patio is too puny a word. Courtyard doesn't do it justice either. It was more the size of a town square. Massive outdoor stone fireplace. Matching stone outdoor kitchen. Two hundred people could have had a barbeque out here.

I waited for Al. And waited. And waited. Five full minutes. Either his side of the house was bigger than mine or I didn't know what.

Shit, I thought. *Where the fuck are you, Al?*

I grabbed my phone to call him, and instead he called me.

"Al, did you find something?" I said.

"Not Al, Little Engine."

A dozen very bad images shot through my head. All of them featuring Al Cutter dead in some terrible way.

"If you hurt him—"

"Your friend is alive and will stay that way so long as you follow my easy instructions. Can you follow instructions, Little Engine?"

"I followed you here, asshole."

"Yes, you did. Come down the stairs to the pool. Al and I will hold."

Grand flagstone steps led down to what looked like an Olympic-sized pool, gorgeously landscaped, surrounded by dozens of chaise lounges and tables, like an exclusive hotel. I came down the stairs and stopped beside the pool.

"Now turn right and walk to the diving boards," the killer said.

There were three, set at three different heights, as if some summer a surprise Olympics might break out in Katonah and Julius and Martha wanted to be ready for the divers to descend.

I walked the length of the pool and saw a dark mass on the lowest board, the one closest to my side of the pool. I had a bad feeling about what—or who—it was.

"You son of a bitch," I said into the phone as I approached the diving board.

It was Phillip Penn. On his back. Barefoot. Dead. Terrible dark empty holes where his eyes should have been.

Of course, I thought of my father in the Monument Insurance elevator, tied to a chair, dead without his eyes. But I had no time to be sad.

"Inklaar hired you?" I said.

"Of course not. But don't tell Logan. The fact that once again he's moronically mismanaged his task force, pointed them in precisely the wrong direction, might well push him over the edge. On second thought, yes, go ahead and tell him. Few things would please me more than knowing I've pushed Logan over the edge. Do you see the field on the far side of the pool?"

"Yes."

"Open the gate and walk across the Wild Wooly Ranch to the fence at the far end. The alpacas will follow you. They're good-natured and curious. But they'll grow weary of you, as I have, and fade into the night. Leave your gun on the diving board next to Phillip. If you don't, I'll shoot Al in the eyes, which would be a merry bonus for me but sad for you. And for Al. So sad for Al. We'll hold."

I took the Colt out of my backpack, placed it next to poor dead Phillip Penn, walked around the pool and down more flagstone steps, opened the gate, and started across the fenced five-acre field.

At which point, things got even weirder than they already were.

Out of the shadows came thirty alpacas. They meant me no harm. They were domesticated, accustomed to being around people. Maybe not in the middle of the damn night, but they recognized me as a person and not as a bear or a wolf or a mountain lion, so none of them were freaked at my presence.

They followed me across the field. It was like being a surreal part of the 1960s mop-top British Invasion. Walking across the fruited plains with the Dave Clark Five, Herman's Hermits, The Hollies, Kinks, Stones, Beatles, and Animals.

They were curious and pleasant and drifted away as I approached the tall chain-link fence at the back of the field. Maybe twenty yards from the fence, I saw silhouettes of two figures. I could tell they were on the other side of the fence. Outside the field. Beyond my reach.

Al and the killer.

I arrived at the fence. Al was gagged and blindfolded. His hands were tied behind his back. There was a leash around his neck. Talk about a compromising position. The killer held the leash in one hand and a gun in the other. He was dressed in black from head to toe, including the ski mask that covered his face. I'd been up close to him several times since he'd murdered my father. I still wasn't used to the feeling.

"A goddamn leash?" I said.

"He's fine. Well, fine may be a tad strong. But he's not overly injured. Apart from his pride, that is."

We looked at each other for a long moment. I wanted to kill him with my bare hands. He was five feet from me. But on the other side of the fence.

"If Inklaar didn't hire you, who did?" I said.

"No one."

"You just killed him?"

"I wouldn't say *just*. It's a high-end kill, you must admit. But, yes, I did."

"Why would you do that?"

"I can't tell you everything, Little Engine. You have to work for it. That's the only part of this exercise that interests me. Without your plucky stumbling and bumbling, you'd have no relevance to me whatsoever."

He walked along the fence line, leading Al like some fucking alpaca on a family trek. I kept pace on my side.

"You should know I alerted the local police and also Logan's task force. If I've timed it correctly, they should arrive simultaneously at any moment," the killer said.

"Then you'd better get on with it."

"*It?* Be specific, Little Engine."

"Another clue."

"Yes, another clue. Well done."

"You could have called me."

"I think we're beyond that, don't you? We're involved."

"Fuck off, you sick piece of shit."

"You sound like your father when you talk like that."

I could feel my heart ripping apart in my chest all over again. I refused to let him break me, to see me break.

"You sure you want to give me another clue? Next time, I'll be there before you and, I swear on Jimmy's grave, I'll take you down hard."

"So spunky. I almost want to keep playing beyond this next clue."

I was too filled with rage to concentrate. And then a rogue

alpaca wandered over. He had a belligerent, though smiling, look on his face that said, *What in the hell are you still doing here?* which tagged him as more of a 1960s *American Bandstand* kind of guy as opposed to a genuine British mop-top. Maybe Paul Revere & the Raiders. Yes, that was it. This particular alpaca was one of the Raiders. Anyway, thinking about an alpaca on *American Bandstand* with Paul Revere calmed me down in time for the clue.

"A mystery man widowed and dreary; on safari through grief became leery; of his guide, who felt funny; with lawyers, guns, money; and turned hunter to hunted, in theory," the killer said. "Ah, look. One minute past midnight. Sunday. You have one week from today."

I reached the end of the rear fence, which turned right and ran back to the house. The killer clipped Al's leash to the links and walked off into the woods.

In the distance, I heard the police. They'd found Phillip Penn on the diving board, my gun next to his head.

41

I KNOW WHOSE HOUSE IT IS

WE TOOK CARE OF AL FIRST—UNHOOKED HIM FROM THE FENCE, removed the leash from his neck, got rid of the blindfold, ripped off the gag, and freed his hands. By "we" I mean me and the cops who'd crossed the field with guns drawn and flashlights blazing. The alpacas must have thought Julius and Martha had planned an afterhours surprise party. With the guns, I imagine some of them were worried it might be a hunting party.

When Al regained his composure—not altogether different than when he'd lost his composure—he said one word: *bonus.* I nodded because the least I could do was pay him for wearing a leash. He said nothing else until we were halfway across the field, dutifully followed by a dozen alpacas.

Then, he stopped, turned to them, and said, "What the fuck is so fucking funny?" Then he clammed up. Sat on a chaise lounge beside the pool, arms folded.

Logan, on the other hand, had plenty to say.

He was apoplectic that my gun had been found next to Phillip Penn's dead body. Furious that the killer had embarrassed him again. Enraged I'd figured out the Katonah estate of

Julius and Martha Montgomery was actually The Beetch House and not simply the Wild Wooly Ranch. Incensed I'd once again crossed the line into his investigation. Infuriated when I told him the killer had said Inklaar hadn't hired him to whack Penn. Enflamed when I shared the next clue. Exasperated Al wouldn't say one word that might help the task force get a feeling for the killer's mindset or motivation.

All of this was bad news, so I held out my hands to make it easier for Logan to slap the cuffs on. But he didn't.

Instead, he gave me the Colt and said, "If you shoot that fucking zombie in the head right now, we'll call it even."

"I can't shoot him, Logan. He has to keep me awake on the ride home."

"You're not going home. You're sitting your ass down next to the zombie until you're dismissed. Somebody around here might have a question for you. But not me. I can't even look at you without my ulcer burning a hellhole in my guts."

He shook his head and sent me off with a wave of his hand that contained more loathing than a foul paragraph of four-letter words.

As I walked away, he said, "I hate limericks."

No one on the task force wanted to touch me with a ten-foot pole, but Logan made us sit there until three o'clock Sunday morning. We got back to the House of Emotional Tics at four fifteen.

Rick was asleep on my sofa. I slipped past him and fell into bed with my clothes on, determined to reassess what I knew, what I didn't know, what I'd never know, and what I had to know. But I passed out before any such assessment could begin.

The smell of coffee brewing accompanied by the clang and bang of pots and pans woke me at eleven. Rick was baking bread pudding with fresh strawberry sauce for brunch. The number one trick to preparing the best bread pudding, he told me, was to serve it with mimosas. Unless some kind of comedian was on the wagon. In which case coffee was the number two trick. So Prosecco and OJ chilled in an ice bucket on my little kitchen table, and the coffee brewed, and the point is the pudding hadn't gone in the oven yet, so I had time for a run. Which was good because my head was filled with shit my heart couldn't get a handle on, and vice versa in spades.

Bad weather was threatening, but I went twice around the reservoir without getting rained on. Also, without clearing the fog in my mind. I thought I'd talk things through with Rick over brunch, especially the parts about him—making out like hot-to-trot teenagers for one; Victor Vreeland giving Ruby Gold six mil for another; his many mysterious nieces for a third—but somehow none of that happened.

Instead, it poured down cold November rain all afternoon and night, and we ate bread pudding with strawberry sauce and drank mimosas in my kitchen and talked about nothing impor-tant and played Monopoly afterward. Then Rick read a maga-zine and took a nap. And I balanced my checkbook, looked online for something to wear to Matthew's wedding, and took a nap too. We ordered Chinese food for dinner and watched TV and went to bed without having sex.

God knows I wanted to. I was pretty sure he did too. But somehow we silently and simultaneously decided to take it slow, to become friends first. It had been a long damn time since that had happened to me, with me, for me. I'd been swept off my feet and dumped at the curb (or done the dumping) more often than I cared to recall. It felt warm and fuzzy to share a lazy Sunday with a man who was funny as hell—even if that man was under arrest for a murder he hadn't committed and I was his bodyguard.

We did, though, kiss each other good night, which was warm and lovely, but he slept on the sofa, and I slept in my bed. Monday morning we took the White Whale to Queens Boulevard in Flushing to see if I could get the pig to bolt the Boulevard Motor Inn.

Thanks to Dennis and Posey and Big Black Bald Bart (and on Rick's dime), multiple teams of way-off-Broadway actors had been taking turns watching the hotel since Thursday, when we'd followed the pig here. He hadn't left the building since. Licking his wounds and letting his face heal, sure, but also letting the dust settle before chancing his exit. No way he was getting nicked twice.

There was a metered parking spot across from the hotel on Queens Boulevard with a view of the main entrance. I slid the Corolla into the spot, left the engine running, and called the Boulevard Motor Inn. The front-desk girl, who identified herself as Olivia, answered with a tired, dispassionate voice that might as well have said, *Boulevard Motor Inn, this is Olivia at the front desk. I hate this job more than anything in the world and will probably quit before we hang up so make this easy or fuck right off.*

"Olivia, this is Detective CM Rogers with the NYPD," I said. "Listen carefully or you'll find yourself involved in a criminal investigation from which it will take many years, multiple lawyers, and thousands of dollars to unravel yourself. Are you listening, Olivia?"

I'd put her on speakerphone so Rick could hear the conversation. He nodded his approval of my performance and mouthed, *You've got skills.*

"I'm listening," Olivia said, perking up for her own good.

"This past Thursday, a man checked into your hotel. I don't know what name he used—he has several aliases at his disposal—but his face was battered and beaten, and he hasn't left the building since he got there. Do you know the man I've just described?"

"I know him. I checked him in. I thought he was fishy."

"What name did he use?"

"Howard Beckman. Room 206."

"Your cooperation is duly noted. You just saved your own ass, Olivia."

"What do I do now?"

"Nothing. Don't do or say anything. You never spoke to the police. Trust me, Olivia. You don't want to interact with this piece of garbage. He traffics in sick and perverted crimes beyond human tolerance and specializes in women who work in hotels."

"Gross."

"He has no idea we're onto him, and we intend to keep it that way. Surprise is man's best friend."

"I thought it was a dog."

"We'll handle it from here, Olivia. Is someone else working the front desk with you?"

"Joaquín."

"Good to know. Stay on the line until I tell you it's safe to disconnect the call."

I put her on hold and called the hotel again.

"Boulevard Motor Inn. This is Joaquín at the front desk. How may I help you?"

"Room 206, please."

"Connecting you now."

The pig's phone rang in his room. Rick nodded and mouthed, *Badass.* I couldn't help but smile. Rick thinking I was a badass was all the motivation I needed.

"What?" the pig said.

"Mr. Beckman, this is Detective Kathy Webster of the NYPD. We're on our way to your hotel. ETA is fifteen minutes. We have questions. We think you have answers. My official advice is to stay where you are. See you in fifteen."

I clicked off that call and switched back to Olivia.

"Okay, Olivia. Good job. If hotel work gets old, you've got a career in law enforcement."

"You think so?"

"You're a natural." I hung up.

"That was awesome. Your father taught you how to do that?" Rick said.

"He taught me how to do everything."

"Wish I could've met him."

"Me too. He would've liked you after a while."

"I'm a person who comes with a disclaimer, it's true."

"Jimmy, this is Rick Gotti. You're not going to like him much at first but give him time. He'll surprise you."

"Did I?"

"What?"

"Surprise you."

"Too soon to tell."

"Work in progress?"

"Under construction."

I was behind the wheel. He was riding shotgun. We were leaning toward each other—consciously, unconsciously, whatever—to kiss.

"I haven't made out in a car since I was sixteen," he said.

"I was pregnant when I was sixteen. Blew right by the making-out-in-a-car part."

"Never too late."

"I'm forty-five. Feels too late."

"I'm forty-eight. Feels like perfect timing."

I wanted to kiss him at that moment more than anything just because he thought I was a badass, but before my lips touched his the pig rushed out of the hotel and hailed a cab. So no kiss. Instead, I put the White Whale in gear, and we followed the pig.

Grand Central Parkway over the Robert F. Kennedy Bridge onto the FDR. South to 97th Street, through the park to Columbus Avenue, right on 87th Street, and two thirds of the way down the block toward Amsterdam to a beautiful brownstone on the north side of the street.

A thirty-five minute drive during which Rick and I talked about the weather (remarkable how today could be so much nicer than yesterday), about bad traffic (unreasonably congested for a Monday morning), about the worst traffic we'd ever been in (him on the 405 in LA; me on the Long Island Expressway), about Jimmy, about the D-Cup and the strip-club musical being written just for Rick, about the House of Emotional Tics and *Kung Fu Fu*, and, finally, about something I'd been trying to discuss since he'd split on me not once but twice during my tenure as his bodyguard.

"I have a question," I said. "Why do you have so many nieces, and when do I get to meet them?"

"That's two questions."

"Pick one."

"You get to meet them Friday."

"I do?"

"I told them about you, said I wanted to introduce you, we checked our schedules, and they'll all be in the house Friday for lunch."

I was excited and, for some reason, nervous. Why was I nervous? What the hell was I nervous about? I would have to ponder that later.

"Why do you have so many?" I said.

"He's stopping."

"What?"

"The pig, the cab. In front of that brownstone."

Like I said, it was a beautiful building. Four floors of classic, handsome, West Side panache. Custom-built, craftsman-style, glass-paned double front doors ten steps up from the street. Subtle street-level door tucked beneath the front steps, accessed via a small, iron-fenced entrance patio. Artistically designed iron bars on the street- and main-level windows. Elegant architectural features on the exterior face—arched stones, balustrades—made me think the inside could only be sophisticated, cultured, and timeless.

Whoever lived here had money to burn.

The pig got out of the cab, climbed the steps, and rang the buzzer. Ten seconds later, the door opened, and the bear let the pig into the brownstone.

Rick and I were silent, double-parked in the White Whale on West 87th Street, letting the bear and the pig and the brownstone wash over us. It was only last Tuesday when those Halloween-masked assholes had tried to kill us at Rick's place in Brooklyn.

"It was them," Rick said.

"Definitely," I said.

"What do we do?"

"We find out whose house that is because it sure as shit doesn't belong to those loser scumbags."

Rick took a breath and nodded. "I know whose house it is."

I wasn't sure I'd heard him right. "What?"

"I know who lives here."

"Who?"

"Victor Vreeland."

42

LET ME CHECK MY POCKETS AND GET BACK TO YOU

THE REST OF MONDAY CAN BE SUMMED UP LIKE THIS: TWO HOURS of Raul melting my muscles; checking out a few of my favorite vintage stores for a mother-of-the-groom ensemble; food shopping like a New York snob; cleaning my house—Rick kindly lifting his legs so I could vacuum under his feet—preparing Jimmy's famous linguini with red clam sauce for Rick (with a bottle of Barolo...for me, not him); and researching the life and times of Victor Vreeland.

Rick had known it was Victor's house because he'd been there—at an all-night, drug-and-alcohol-fueled after-party—twenty years ago, when he was a star stand-up comedian touring the country's best comedy clubs. He'd played Victor's Vreeland's Comedy Camp way back then and had not played it since, which was what Victor had told Robbie Sloane when he'd called to invite Rick to host this year's Comedy Camp Cornucopia.

I'd said no to that gig on the grounds of it being too crazy dangerous for Rick to be on a public stage with hitmen on his heels but was now soul-searching that response.

Victor had given Ruby Gold the money to pay off her Kenny

Cochran gambling debt and fund her sitcom. We knew that for a fact because Oscar K. had handled the transaction for Ruby (possibly while his mother served milk and cookies). And now we knew—not for a fact but close to it—that Victor had hired the bear and the pig to kill Cochran and then Rick, a hit that went so far south the pig had been on ice at the D-Cup, been followed to the Boulevard Motor Inn, and then been followed to Victor's Upper West Side brownstone, where the bear had welcomed him home.

I knew the pieces. What I didn't know was *how* and *why* they fit together.

"Call Sloane," I said while chopping fresh Italian parsley. "Get him to set up a lunch with Victor. Tell him you changed your mind and want to discuss the gig. I'll go with you as your fiancée, and we'll see if we can get him to crack in the restaurant."

"You told me we're not dating because it's unprofessional and Fu will hold it in his top pocket for the rest of time. Now we're engaged?" Rick said. "Make up your mind, McCall. Am I top-pocket material or not?"

I laughed. "Let me check my pockets and get back to you."

While Rick reached out to his sleazebag agent and the clam sauce cooked on the stove, I went online to learn everything I could about Victor Vreeland, who was larger than life in all possible ways, meaning there was information aplenty available for anyone with working Wi-Fi.

Just nothing I needed.

Nothing deeper than his career in comedy. Nothing wider than the width of his club. No *there* there. Victor Vreeland's history was a mystery by design. He had a gargantuan public persona, but his personal life was buried under a big burning pile of mind-your-own-fucking-business. Other than his comedy-club accomplishments, no one had anything to say about Victor Vreeland, who, I thought, had been a public sphere in the public sphere for too many years to have no dirty laundry online. Yet everything I read was common knowledge. No one knew where Victor was from or how he got to where he got to, which was not what I'd been hoping for.

What I'd been hoping for was a clue behind the clue, a reason Victor would pay off Ruby's substantial debt and fund her sitcom; a motive for him to have Cochran killed; an intention for him to offer Rick the coveted MC spot in the Comedy Camp Cornucopia; an inner-circle associate I could target for inner-circle secrets. If I was going to break Victor Vreeland at lunch, I would need inside information, a way to get past his Death Star force field. But it wasn't here, there, or anywhere.

And then, in a tiny, toss-away Paramus publication, six or seven screens deep, there was a tiny, toss-away news item about Victor putting his father in a local retirement community. The father's name was August Vreeland. Everyone called him Augie.

The article was eight years old. Augie had been eighty-eight when Victor set him up in Paramus, so he'd be ninety-six now. A phone call confirmed Augie was still alive and kicking in that same community. It was a twenty-five-minute drive from the House of Emotional Tics to the Belvedere Health and Rehabilitation Center on Fairview Avenue. I was at the kitchen table writing down directions when Rick walked in.

"I found Victor's father in Paramus," I said. "If anyone has inside dope that can help us hack Vreeland into bite-size pieces, he does. So we'll be at his door bright and early tomorrow morning. Did Sloane have any luck with lunch?"

"Better than lunch. I used to be Rick Gotti. We're booked for dinner on Thursday at Oxbow Tavern."

"Oxbow Tavern? Rick Gotti was primo in his prime, no doubt."

"And...I accepted the gig in advance so we'd be celebrating instead of negotiating because, if memory serves, when Victor celebrates, everybody celebrates. So we'll get him good and drunk and see if he cracks. Robbie confirmed you could come too. Victor told him the more the merrier. So that's a table for four."

"Four?"

"You, me, and Victor. He takes two seats. Always gets a table for four, even if he's alone. Orders half the menu. Multiple bottles of champagne and wine. Cognac. Flaming desserts. The man needs space. As in outer space. Like a planet. Bite-size pieces of Victor are the size of an orbiting moon. You may have to adjust your metaphors."

Then he took me in his arms and kissed me with energy and passion and excitement. I kissed him back with more of the same, and the kiss got heavy, meaning I thought we were headed for an X-rated rendezvous before dinner, which, with half a bottle of Barolo in my brain, was fine by me.

But instead he smiled and moved away. "Don't lead me down the path of dirty dancing, McCall. Not when I have to get up early and go to Paramus. I'm not that kind of man anymore."

I laughed. "What kind of man are you?"

"Primo in my prime."

He smiled again, and I swooned. *I'm falling for Rick Gotti, and he's falling for me*, I thought.

Jimmy would have killed me...if somebody hadn't killed him first.

43

FU SOLVE NOW

First thing Tuesday morning, still in my New York Football Giants pajamas, I went to check my mailbox—seeing as how I hadn't checked it Monday—and found Fu mopping the lobby floor, earbuds in place, Italian opera blasting as if the Turin Philharmonic Orchestra itself was live at the House of Emotional Tics. He was supposed to have been back Monday but had stayed an extra day for reasons I couldn't imagine. I mean, what could possibly prolong a parrot playdate?

Watching this banished, Chinese-mob killing machine mop the dreary lobby floor on a Tuesday morning made me surprisingly sad. An expatriated superman assassin working as a janitor in a beat-down brownstone on the Upper East Side of Manhattan. No life other than mundane building maintenance, parrot playdates, and helping me find my father's killer.

Maybe it was that I hadn't seen him in four days. Four days! Maybe that was it. Fu and I had been together basically every single day since we'd both arrived at the House of Emotional Tics more than two years ago. Not to mention he'd saved my life on five or six occasions (one in dispute). When I'd needed him most, Fu had been there for me. Until this weekend, when he'd taken his parrot to the Finger Lakes because he'd had nothing else to do but drive Jerusalem Joe four and a half hours to squawk with another damn bird, which was depressing in and of itself.

Seeing Fu in this gloomy amber lobby light, I thought I might work harder at getting along with him. Maybe stop competing for the last word in every argument. Yes, that's what I would do. Stop fighting for the last word with Fu.

"Watch Fu mop all day or ask Fu help?"

Or screw all that, I thought, hearing the smirking smirk in his words. *How does he do it? How does he open his mouth and get under my skin with just the sound of his voice? How did he even know I was here? He never turned around. Never saw me. Couldn't hear me with the music blasting. What the hell, Fu? I should have known by the smug look on the back of his head that the first thing he said was going to piss me off. No one pushes my buttons like he does. Last word, here I come.*

"What makes you think I need your help?" I said, crossing the lobby.

He turned to me, kept mopping. "Catch killer in Harlem?"

"Obviously, you spoke to Charlie, so you know I—"

"Catch killer in Katonah?"

"And you spoke to Al too, so you also know that—"

"Fu go Harlem, killer no drop mic. Fu go Katonah, Fu no wear leash. Fu catch killer. That what happen if Fu go Harlem and Katonah."

"Yeah, well, you didn't go. You took Joe to play with his friend."

"Girlfriend."

"What?"

"Joe in love. Fu romantic at heart. So Fu take Joe Finger Lakes."

"First of all, you're not a romantic at heart, you're a mob hitman. Second of all, parrots don't fall in love, and even if they did, there's no girl parrot anywhere, not in the Finger Lakes or any lakes, that would fall in love with Joe, who is the rudest parrot in the history of rude parrots. Third of all, I don't have to ask you for help because I don't need your help. Why do you think I need your help?"

"Solve next killer clue?"

Shit. "Not yet."

"Fu solve now."

I could feel my blood pressure rising. "What? Now? Right now? You're going to solve the clue right now? No way. You understand, Fu? No. Way."

"Fu solve now."

No one in the world but my sister could infuriate me like this. "It's a limerick. You know what that is, a limerick?"

"Fu poet. Fu know limerick."

"Fu poet? Really? Fu poet? What does that even mean?"

"Fu poet in China. Write many book of poem. Million people read Fu poem."

I believed him. In addition to every other improbable life Fu had lived on top of being a shifu-trained assassin—circus bareback rider, for shit's sake; filmmaker of bird movies—it was entirely plausible he'd written a book of poetry that a million people in China had read.

"Okay, fine," I said, and I took my phone from my pajama pocket, opened my notes, and read it out loud. "A mystery man widowed and dreary; on safari through grief became leery; of his guide, who felt funny; with lawyers, guns, money; and turned hunter to hunted, in theory. That's it. That's the next clue. Not just the next clue, the *last* clue. The killer said he almost wants to keep playing after this next clue. You understand? *Almost* wants to. If I don't catch him this time, I may never get another chance."

"Fu understand. What victims have in common?"

"I don't know."

"Think more. What victims have in common?"

"What do you mean *think more*? All I do is think more. And more and more and more. I don't know what they have in common. Do they have *something* in common besides the killer shooting their eyes out? Yes. Do I know what it is? No. That's the problem, Fu. I can't even find square one."

"Fu know problem. Problem is you not think more. Killer put in limerick. What victims have in common?"

"Don't do this, Fu. Stop doing this. I've asked myself that question a thousand times."

"Ask more time. What victims have in common? Killer put in limerick."

"Jesus Christ, Fu. You're making me crazy right now."

"Killer put in limerick. What victims have in common? Say again."

"Okay, okay. A mystery man widowed and dreary; on safari through grief became leery; of his—oh my God..."

It hit me like a wrecking ball. Fu was right. The killer *had* put it in the limerick. *Grief*. That's what they had in common. Ronnie Russo, Mickey Herradura, and Phillip Penn. All three of them. *Grief*. I had no idea what it meant, but it was a place to start.

Fu could see it on my face. "Tell Fu what square one."

"They'd all lost their wives. They were all grieving."

"What else know?"

"The killer said on Sunday, one minute past midnight, that I had one week. So the next victim, the guy in the limerick, whoever it is, dies this Sunday."

"Or not die Sunday."

"Yes. If I can stop him."

He was still mopping. I was still in my pj's. It was still early Tuesday morning. I hadn't had my coffee yet. I walked back across the lobby to my apartment, put my hand on the door, and realized something. I wasn't sad because Fu was working as a janitor in the House of Emotional Tics. I was sad because I knew one day he *wouldn't* be working as a janitor in the House of Emotional Tics. One day his banishment would end, the mob would call him back to China, and I would never see him again. I was sad because he was the closest thing to a little brother I'd ever had, and I knew it wouldn't last. Just four days in the Finger Lakes on a parrot romantic weekend and I could feel his absence in my heart. What would that feel like when he was out of my life for good?

"You weren't here," I said, looking back at him. "What if something had happened to me? What if I'd been in trouble?"

He kept mopping, put his other earbud back in. "Fu know trouble not start yet. Trouble start now. Fu here."

44

TALK ABOUT POTS CALLING
KETTLES BLACK

DRESSED IN BUSINESS ATTIRE, RICK AND I WERE AT THE
Belvedere Health and Rehabilitation Center by nine thirty
Tuesday morning. We introduced ourselves to the harried
woman at the front desk as estate attorneys dispatched by
Victor Vreeland himself to dot and cross the final i's and t's as to
how and who and where and when Victor's comedy money was
to be dispersed, dispensed, and disseminated to the vast Vreeland family, including his father.

Augie Vreeland, the front-desk woman told us, was in the
courtyard enjoying some brisk morning air before art class. She
was too distracted to deal with us—some kind of ruckus in the
game room—so we signed her guest book, and she gave us
visitor stickers and buzzed us into the Belvedere inner sanctum.

The center was a large, two-story square with a courtyard in
the middle. Once we were through the locked doors, we were in
an oversized lounge area, like a hotel lobby, with sofas and
sitting areas and floor lamps and coffee tables and magazines
galore. A comfortable room the elderly residents utilized to
meet with family and friends should the visiting crowd be too
large to congregate in the upstairs two-room apartments.

Across the lounge was a wall of French doors that opened into the courtyard, a pleasant garden space with various patio areas. There was only one person outside. A man in a wheelchair smoking a pipe. Augie Vreeland. Rick and I went through the French doors, walked across the courtyard, and sat on a bench across from him. It was immediately evident Augie's pipe was filled with pot.

Did I mention he was ninety-six and getting stoned at nine thirty in the morning?

"Augie, I'm Claire Thompson, and this is Robert Green," I said. "We're estate attorneys representing your son, Victor. We'd like to ask you some questions regarding the disbursement of Victor's will, but before we start, I'd like to clarify that we're aware you're smoking marijuana."

"Get it from the kid who cooks," Augie said. "His food is shit, but his reefer is madness. Get it? *Reefer Madness*? You think my son got his comedy chops from his mother? No way. All me, Claire. Or whatever your real name is."

"Excuse me?" I said, thinking, *Sharp as a tack, good to know.*

"My legs don't work," he said, "but there's nothing wrong with my bullshit meter. So if you want me to talk crap about my son, you should start by telling me who the hell you really are. Because Victor cut me out of his will a couple decades ago, if you catch my drift."

I looked at Rick, Rick looked at me, and in my head I thanked my father for *Jimmy's Rules of Private Investigation for Kate, Rule Number Eight: Make sure your backup plan has a backup plan for your backup plan.*

"I'm Jessica Dean, and this is Jeff Bryant," I said. "We're tax investigators for the city of New York. We can't seem to account for a six-million-dollar gift Victor bestowed on a woman named Ruby Gold. We thought if we led with that, you'd dismiss us. I can see now that was a mistake on our part. We apologize."

"Sorry, Augie. Won't happen again," Rick said.

"Damn right it won't," Augie said. "Wasn't born yesterday. Want to hit my pipe?"

"Yes," Rick said.

"Except we're working and the courtyard walls are made of glass, if you haven't noticed," I said.

Augie laughed. "Comedian tax investigator. I would introduce you to Victor, but he doesn't talk to me anymore. Card for my birthday. Cheese log for Christmas. End of story."

It wasn't the end of the story by a longshot.

Once Augie got rolling, it was like someone had positioned his wheelchair at the top of a tall hill and given him a push.

Here's what he told us while smoking a bowl of some sweet-smelling grass.

Augie and Vanessa Vreeland had lived in a small Washington Heights, low-rent apartment building with their only child, Victor. Residing in the same building, one floor down, was the Goldmacher family—Chester, Patty, and their only child, Robin, who everyone called Ruby.

Ruby and Victor had met when they were both five years old and quickly became each other's best friend, soul mate, and one true love. They'd become even closer than that as time ticked by but were never lovers because that wasn't what they'd needed.

Victor was gay and so had no desire for what the conventional world called a "girlfriend." As he got older, there'd been boys aplenty to satisfy that secondary itch. But his natural sexual preference was dwarfed by his main motivator, his primary driving force: the incontrovertible fact that he was insatiable in all ways for all things—toys, candy, cake, pizza, ice cream, and soda pop when he was young; gourmet cuisine, money, fame, power, drugs, and alcohol as he grew older. Plus the toys, candy, cake, pizza, ice cream, and soda pop that had followed him into adulthood in large quantities to this very day.

Victor's ravenous appetites set him apart from the other

children. Made him the odd boy out. No one felt-it-saw-it-knew-it more than Victor himself. His self-awareness of his ostracization had been a tough pill to swallow. He couldn't do it alone. To combat his inner demons, his self-destructive gloom, he'd needed someone to make him laugh, to see and appreciate the dark humor of his own gluttonous existence. He'd needed that, of course, and also someone to love him for who he was.

Augie told us it was Victor's greatest stroke of luck, God's special gift to him, that he'd lived in the same building as Ruby, an indefatigable comedian, a perpetual jokester in constant trouble for her inability to live in the serious world seriously. An infinite class clown cold-shouldered for her uninterrupted comedic routines at inappropriate times. An unrelenting, ridiculous girl separated from her peers by her incessant search for an audience. Her search for that, of course, and for someone to love her for who she was.

Victor and Ruby became codependent in the sense that in his very building, one floor down, he'd found someone who made him laugh, kept him grounded, and loved him for who he was; and in her very building, one floor up, she'd found someone who laughed at her jokes and hijinks, kept her grounded, and loved her for who she was.

Meanwhile, Augie had been a traveling salesman unafraid to cross the line, bend the law, or take a risk if crossing the line, bending the law, or taking a risk was part of the deal. Because of that, he'd been in and out of jail for embezzlement, fraud, and other white-collar crimes throughout Victor's life.

"Victor crossed lots of lines to get where is," Augie said. "Learned it from me. Got his appetite from Vanessa, who killed her liver, which then killed her."

He took a vial of blood-pressure pills from his pocket. But instead of pills, he pulled a pinch of weed from the vial, put it in his pipe, struck a match, and toked it deep.

"Would Victor give Ruby six million dollars to pay off her gambling debts and fund her pilot?" I said.

"If he had it, sure," Augie said. "He'd hang the moon for her. They swore an oath as kids. Blood brothers, sisters, both, whatever. Had a whole ceremony with a Swiss Army Knife and Band-aids and whatnot."

"What do you mean *if* he had it?" Rick said.

"Could be broke, I don't know. Got involved in a real-estate deal couple few years back," Augie said. "Piece of property in Yonkers. Full acre. Big money. Sunk millions in some pie-in-the-sky apartment fantasy. Still just a pile of dirt. Lost it all is what I think. But what do I know? I'm just a ninety-six-year-old ex-con stoner stuck in New Jersey because he embarrasses his son. I mean, imagine that. *I* embarrass *him*. Talk about pots calling kettles black."

"Who would know, Augie?" I said.

Augie blew a cloud that would give me a contact high for the next four hours. "Who would know what?"

"Who would know about the pie-in-the-sky land deal?" I said. "Who would know if Victor was broke?"

Augie nodded, took another hit off his pipe. "I thought we'd end up here. Bruce Bailey. Real-estate broker. Seller of pipe dreams."

"Why did you think we'd end up here?" Rick said.

Augie blew a big cloud of weed. "Pipe dreams."

45

WHO'S THE BUYER?

JIMMY HAD A THING FOR JOINTS. BURGER JOINTS, BEER JOINTS, bourbon joints, and old diners. Especially old diners. One of his favorites was in Dumont. The Dumont Crystal Diner on Madison Avenue. One of the oldest diners in New Jersey. Near the old railroad tracks, it had been built from a Victory Dining Car somewhere around 1930. Long and narrow, curved metal roof, counter from one end to the other, stools bolted to the floor, booths opposite the counter, photos of customers and Dumont Crystal history everywhere, grill behind the counter in plain sight of the crowd. Jimmy just loved the old-school atmosphere, the food, and the way the place smelled the minute you walked through the door.

Once or twice a year, back when my mother was still alive and my sister and I were young, he'd pile us in the car, tell us it was past time for a "great, big, beautiful Bergen County breakfast," and drive us across the George Washington Bridge to the Dumont Crystal. *"That's what real food smells like,"* he'd tell Marilyn and me when we walked through the door. He'd hold hands with my mother while we read our menus.

Dumont's not all that far from Paramus, and I was hungry

after breathing in great gusts of Augie Vreeland's wacky weed, so I took Rick to the Dumont Crystal.

"That's what real food smells like," I said as we walked in.

"Damn right it does," Rick said.

We sat at the counter so we could watch the show at the grill, ordered eggs and bacon and home fries and rye toast and pancakes and waffles and orange juice and coffee. Turned out Rick was as contact high as I was and had the munchies as bad as I did.

While we inhaled breakfast, I realized I'd left the Belvedere Health and Rehabilitation Center even more confused than when I'd arrived. Like Dumont Crystal pancakes, the case was too big to swallow all at once, so I broke it down into *what I knew* and *what I didn't know.*

What I knew was Ruby Gold had bet and lost the horse farm with her comedian lover boy, Kenny Cochran, who couldn't pay his part of the damage done. What I knew was Ruby had covered Cochran plus paid her share, a total of seven figures, meaning lots of zeros. What I knew was after paying Paulie Crane, Ruby had then funded her own sitcom pilot, meaning zeros on top of her zeros. Which would have been fine because she was freaking Ruby Gold. Except Lillian Pearl had told me Ruby was dead broke. What I knew was Oscar K. had verified Victor Vreeland's gifting Ruby millions. What I knew was Augie Vreeland had told me Victor and Ruby had been childhood soul mates, bound by blood ceremonies that required Swiss Army knives and Band-aids. What I knew was Augie said his son would bend the law like he had.

What I didn't know was if Victor had hired the bear and the pig to kill Kenny Cochran—and then Rick, who the bear thought had seen him murdering Cochran backstage at The Joke Joint. I had a *feeling* that was true—we'd seen the bear and the pig in Victor's brownstone—but I didn't *know* it. What I didn't know was if Victor had been broke when he'd given Ruby all that dough. What I didn't know was if Victor *was* broke, where had *that* money come from? Maybe *that* person had hired the bear and the pig to kill Cochran. What I didn't know was how the hell I was going to tie any of it together. And even if I *could* tie it together, what I didn't know was what in the world to do then.

We drove straight back to the House of Emotional Tics because Rick wanted to work on his act hosting Victor Vreeland's Comedy Camp Cornucopia—which was this Sunday night—and found Wednesday's *Kung Fu Fu* call sheet attached to my door. My call was eight in the morning. We'd be shooting the scene where Detectives Steinburg and Barnett arrest Warren Warren, the renegade mad scientist. Rick was listed as cameraman. It was impossible to figure out where we were in the story—beginning, middle, end—for good reason. LaTanya had said she wasn't thinking about things like time and place and meaning and motivation when she'd made it all up.

"All the real writing's done in the editing room," she'd said.

"Don't tell the real writers," I'd said.

While Rick wrote new material, I googled Bruce Bailey and discovered he was a land broker—buying and selling and trading raw acreage all around the boroughs and beyond. I called his office and made an appointment for later that afternoon as Jennifer Wilson, real-estate agent representing a developer client looking for land.

I'd once worked as a receptionist for a real-estate brokerage on the West Side, and one of the agents there had specialized in land. She would often come into the office wearing work boots and hiking clothes, and she regularly smelled like tequila in the middle of the day. I'd learned a lot about land brokerage from her, including that it was perfectly fine to do tequila shots at lunch. Her name was Jennifer Wilson, and she'd been a wild woman. Fifty-some-odd years young. Married and divorced four times. An avid spelunker.

Explorer of caves. A caver. She'd spent her free time diving deep into dangerous caves around the world. She'd been rough, rowdy, and riotous. Eventually, she'd moved to Mexico because, she'd told me, it was like the Wild West with an abundance of raw land to broker, caves to explore, and, well, tequila.

To become real-estate agent Jennifer Wilson, I chose a short blonde wig with bangs and green contact lenses because she'd had short blonde hair with bangs and green eyes; put on jeans with a nice blouse and sport jacket because that's what she'd worn to work; and decided on flats because as Jennifer once told me as she changed out of her work boots, *"You never know when you might have to run, and who the hell can run in heels?"*

I checked myself in the mirror and thought, *Thank you, Jen, wherever you are in Mexico.*

I was pretending to be Jennifer Wilson because Bruce Bailey had something of a lawless reputation—not so much a shark in the shallows as a bull in a china shop—and I thought personifying Jennifer could inspire me to hold my own. Bailey, the internet informed me, made deals happen—good deals, bad deals, big deals, small deals—by the sheer force of his will. By bravado. By outrageous behavior and unbearable energy. He was pushing sixty and over the years had made and lost hundreds of millions for himself and his clients. He was respected and admired while concurrently despised and condemned. For Bailey, that was the whole point of the exercise. The adrenaline rush of the unknown—just what the hell was hiding in the dirt, a fifty-story skyscraper or an environmental disaster—was what he loved about the business. *"Win, lose, draw, who gives a good goddamn?"* he'd been quoted as saying. *"If you're not in it for the ride, get out of the land business before you get hurt."*

Despite his brash and eccentric online persona, which painted a portrait that was loud, animated, unconventional, and aggressive, I was not prepared for Bruce Bailey in actual living color.

His office was in Willets Point, an industrial neighborhood in Corona, east of Citi Field near the Flushing River. People in Queens called it The Iron Triangle because of its abundance of car shops and junkyards.

The office itself was in a former auto-body shop abandoned decades ago and then condemned by the city. An eight-thousand-square-foot, one-story building with twenty-five-foot ceilings. Bailey had renovated the place, an odd choice for his company headquarters seeing as how he was a one-man band.

All he needs is a room, I thought as I walked through the front door. *What's he doing with eight thousand square feet?*

Bailey's office manager, a fifty-five-year-old picture of bemused self-control, sat behind a massive desk in a huge outer office/waiting area that had to be eight hundred square feet. Enormous framed vintage carnival art covered the walls as they were designed to, seeing as how these were the actual classic posters plastered on sides of buildings when carnivals came to towns all across the country back in the '20s and '30s and '40s and '50s and '60s and '70s. Hung between the posters were giant vintage circus flags. Exposed ceiling and HVAC ductwork. Industrial lighting. Disparate rugs and carpet covering much of the concrete floor.

Old-school carnival ticket booth. Original jumbo Funhouse mirror. Actual merry-go-round horses from who knew how long ago.

The woman came around her desk and shook my hand. "You must be Jennifer. I'm Marybeth, the reason Bruce doesn't implode or explode or blast off into orbit. You can tell him I said that. It's why he pays me the big bucks. To keep him grounded. Nice to meet you. Come on, I'll take you in. The trick with Bruce is to relax and enjoy the ride. If you can do that, there's money in the dirt."

Above wide double doors hung a huge circus entrance sign. Blue border. Red and white stripes. White cloud in the middle with the words: *Come one, come all!*

Relax and enjoy the ride? I thought as we went through the doors. *What the ever-loving hell is that supposed to mean?*

I took two steps in and stopped flat on the floor. It was too much to take in all at once. Too much to *ever* take in. Too much of too much of too much.

"Jesus Christ," I said out loud instead of in my head.

"He's here somewhere," Marybeth said. "I saw him last week."

Let's start with the sheer size of the place. Seven thousand-plus square feet with twenty-five-foot ceilings. Big freaking space. Bruce Bailey had an airplane hangar for a private office. And everywhere, in every corner of the vast building, were huge pieces of vintage circus and carnival memorabilia. Parts of real rides. Entire rides. A train car that once held circus tigers. Honest-to-God carnival booths from half a century ago. A sideshow tent. Trophy case after trophy case after trophy case packed full of smaller items. More giant posters. More flags. More and more of everything. It simply wasn't possible to acquire and assemble this much carnival and circus stuff in one place. As creepy as it was cool. As off-the-rails nuts as it was off-the-charts extraordinary.

In the middle of the room, Bruce Bailey was, I swear to God, throwing knives at a naked woman strapped to a wooden wheel that was spinning round and round like at a carnival or a circus or *America's Got Talent*. And for shit's sake, Bailey was blindfolded.

"Bruce, Jennifer Wilson is here to see you about a piece of land in Yonkers," Marybeth called out as we crossed the crazy crowded warehouse.

"You want in on this action, Wilson?" Bailey called back.

As we got closer, I realized it wasn't an actual naked woman.

It was a naked mannequin woman. If it had been an actual naked woman, I think I might have cracked.

Relax and enjoy the ride. "No thanks, Bruce. I don't trust myself with sharp objects after I've had a shot of tequila."

He laughed, took off his blindfold, pulled a small remote-control clicker device from his pocket and pushed a button. Throughout the cavernous space, a loudspeaker system blasted what sounded like a crazed, Springsteen Madison Square Garden concert crowd screaming: *Bruce, Bruce, Bruce, Bruce...*

I had never seen or heard or experienced anything like it.

Bruce, Bruce, Bruce... Bailey let them scream for a bit, then clicked off the crowd and put the remote back in his pocket.

"Thanks, MB. You're doing a great job. You should ask me for a raise," Bailey said as Marybeth started back to her domain.

"Stop giving me raises," Marybeth said, walking away. "You'll break the bank."

"I'm feeling soft and sentimental," Bailey said.

"You're throwing knives at a naked mannequin," Marybeth said.

"She makes half a mil," Bailey said to me. "Worth every dime. Does all the paperwork. All the work. I'm buying land on Mars without her. Come on, I'll show you the place, and you can tell me what kind of land you're looking for in Yonkers."

He put the knives down and escorted me through the building, pointing out pieces of carnivals that had faded into history, circuses that had bitten the dust. Sharing carnival lore of days gone by, circus legends of yesteryear. He populated his stories with autobiographical information so I'd know how impressed I was supposed to be. But I hardly heard a word. I'd learned everything I needed to know about Bruce Bailey when he'd hit his clicker and the crowd cried: *Bruce, Bruce, Bruce, Bruce...*

"My client has his eyes on a one-acre, apartment-building

development site," I said. "Mclean Heights. Used to be a muffler shop or an oil-change place or some kind of chemical plant."

"On the elbow of Mclean Avenue?"

"How did you know that?"

He laughed, hit the clicker in his pocket. *Bruce, Bruce, Bruce...*

He's out of his mind, I thought. *Total crazy man.*

He hit the clicker again, and the crowd went silent. "I know it because I sold it. It's not available. Under contract, closed, gone, goodbye."

"There's nothing on it. Nobody's building. No action at all. One acre, fifty thousand buildable. Twenty-five thousand-square-foot footprint. Two-story, seventy-unit building. Twenty thousand square feet for parking. If someone owns it, why aren't they building it? And if they're not building it, why aren't they selling it? To my client, for instance."

He led me to a large office area visible behind a big piece of Palisades Amusement Park rollercoaster. Slick office. Modern. Expensive. Tasteful. Striking models of buildings on pedestals. Huge maps of the boroughs on vintage artist easels. Living-room area, conference area, kitchen area. Top-of-the-line everything.

"Wow. Impressive," I said.

He reached into his pocket—*Bruce, Bruce, Bruce, Bruce*—and sat behind his mahogany desk. I sat across from him in a sleek leather chair.

"Jennifer, you're going to have to trust me here. That project went so far south, you couldn't find it in Cape Horn."

"What happened?"

"You mean what didn't happen."

"Bruce, I have a buyer with money to burn who's interested in this particular piece of property. Maybe it's available, maybe it isn't. But given the premise everything's for sale at the right price, if you know what went down and who it went down with,

I'd like to hear it. Maybe there's an opportunity for my client. Plus, what self-respecting broker doesn't love a good real-estate story? Especially one with you in the middle."

He hit the clicker. *Bruce, Bruce, Bruce, Bruce, Bruce...*

"Let's start with the seller," he said. "Ever hear the name Tommy Tariccone?"

Jimmy had once been hired by Tariccone's ex to take compromising pictures of Tommy with another woman. Jimmy caught Tariccone with his pants down—literally and figuratively—and Tariccone's ex moved to Miami with money to spare.

"Sure. Contractor with mob-boss ties."

"More like mob boss with contractor ties. He's the silent partner in a company called Yonkers Land Group. That group owns the land. So Tariccone's the seller."

"Who's the buyer?"

"I'll get to him. Tariccone has architectural plans but no approvals; engineering specs, but no environmental-impact studies, just an official-looking letter with an attached report from some geologist who says the land looks clean to him. Based on the letter and the report and the plans and the specs, Tariccone's offering an 'as is' deal no one in his right mind should make. But the price is low, and the buyer's not in his right mind."

"Who's the buyer?"

"I'll get to him. The deal is one acre, four and a half mil like I said, as is. Ten percent down. Balance—four mil and change —is a balloon due on Tariccone's schedule. Which is buyer has one year to start the build. You already got the plans and the specs, so hit the bank, get your money, and start moving dirt. If you start by the end of year one, you owe four mil and change. Which you'd have on hand because—"

"Because the buyer's in business with a bank covering the construction cost, including the cost of the land."

"But if the buyer doesn't build by the end of year one, price goes to five mil."

"So now the buyer owes Tariccone four and a half mil on top of the four fifty."

"Gets worse. If the buyer doesn't build by the end of year two, the price goes to six. Lost opportunity cost is what Tariccone calls it. Says he could have built it himself or sold it to someone else at the increased price point at that moment in time. That's why it was such a low price to begin with. Either way, if you haven't started building by the end of year two, all the money's due. You heard of pay-or-play? When Tommy Tariccone makes that deal, it's called pay-or-die. I just made that up."

He hit the clicker. *Bruce, Bruce, Bruce, Bruce, Bruce, Bruce...*

"You let the buyer make that deal?"

"Sometimes buyers make the bad deal because it's the *only* deal, and they have to make a deal for whatever reason they have to make a deal. There's no stopping them. Land makes people loopy. It's the dream of what it could be. The promise of a rich and famous future. Bottom line is seller wants to sell. Buyer wants to buy. Commission's happening with or without me."

"So who's the buyer?"

"I'll get to him. Buyer takes the project to the city. City says the geologist's letter and accompanying report would be useful as toilet paper, and orders a full environmental-impact study that comes back in bold letters that say: *Bad Dirt.*"

"How bad?"

"Worst anyone's ever seen. No way anybody approves the property without a cleanup that's going to take three full years and millions of dollars. Extremely bad dirt. Chemicals no one's ever heard of. Pure poison going down fifty feet.

"So the buyer's screwed."

"That's an understatement. He doesn't have six million

dollars on the Friday it's due, so Tariccone gives him until Monday morning. At that time, Monday morning, lo and behold, the buyer pays Tariccone five mil, five hundred fifty thou, six million total, for the land. Buyer owns the acre outright, saves his life at the same time, and needs three years and millions more to do anything with it. Is that a great story or what?"

Bruce, Bruce, Bruce, Bruce, Bruce, Bruce, Bruce...

"You're still in touch with the buyer?"

"Could be. What's your client's offer?"

"Six two. Buyer's out with a profit, my client does the cleanup and puts a seventy-unit building on the elbow of Mclean Avenue."

"I'll let him know."

"I'd like to make the offer myself."

"Split commission?"

"Of course. Time to get to him, Bruce. Who's the buyer?"

"Victor Vreeland."

Son of a bitch. "Where did he get the money?"

"It's a mystery."

"Who could solve it?"

"Maybe his ex-wife."

"Victor Vreeland has an ex-wife?"

"Doesn't everybody?"

46

CAN'T BE NOTHING, SO IT HAS TO
BE SOMETHING

WEDNESDAY MORNING, EIGHT A.M., RICK AND I WERE ON THE SET of *Kung Fu Fu*, which today was the front steps of the House of Emotional Tics. The shoot went as expected, meaning insane from the moment LaTanya called *action* to the moment she called *cut*.

The scene was Detective Steinberg (Fu) and Detective Barnett (me) walking out of the brownstone with mad scientist Warren Warren (Warren), who we've arrested for reasons so arcane that neither Steinberg nor Barnett can describe them.

Fortunately, the actual arrest would be filmed another day. Today, LaTanya was picking up the action right after the arrest. So we came through the front door and Warren improvised the following line: "You can dance me down the street to jail, but I'll never spill the beans."

I had no idea where that line had come from—there'd been no discussion of dancing in any of the scenes we'd shot so far— or why he'd felt compelled to say it, but once he had, it was floating in the atmosphere all around us and had to be acted on.

So Warren started to dance down the steps. And then Fu

started to dance down the steps. And then I started to dance down the steps. And from there, me holding one mad-scientist arm and Fu holding the other, the three of us danced down East 83rd Street toward First Avenue.

We ran out of time, and LaTanya called cut and told us there would be no reshoot. The dancing was in. I imagined she planned to fix it in post.

The rest of the morning I worked the phones and the internet and updated my case notes at the kitchen table while Rick wrote jokes in the living room. I heard him running through joke after joke, trying it this way and that way, pairing it with other jokes, building an act, then tearing it down and building it again. When he made himself laugh out loud, he'd tell the same joke again to see if he still found it funny. If he did, it stayed in the act. If it didn't, he went back to the drawing board.

I realized that, yes, Rick had been born with an absurd amount of natural comedic talent and a special kind of charisma that lifted his career to the top of the game before his attitude and addictions crashed the whole thing down, but the real reason Rick Gotti had become Rick Gotti was that he'd worked his ass off to be fresh and funny.

I laughed to myself all morning while I did research and made calls and revised my case notes. Not every PI gets a private Rick Gotti comedy show in their living room.

Neither one of us felt like cooking, so we ordered a pizza, washed it down with A&W Root Beer, then he went back to the living room, and I went back to the phones.

Ronnie Russo had been married twelve years when his wife had died six months ago. They had twelve-year-old twin daughters. Ronnie was the youngest of twelve siblings. Twelve of twelve. Since no one caring for the Russo daughters would let me near them—I wouldn't let me near them either—I went looking for a brother or a sister who would speak to me about Ronnie's late wife and his struggle to cope with his grief.

Seven of the Russo siblings lived in the Midwest, where they were originally from. One lived in Oregon, one lived in New Mexico, and one lived in Florida. Ronnie was the lone Russo who'd moved to New York, where he'd become a successful race-car driver, father, husband, and business owner. It took hours to find them all. I called the first ten Russo siblings. Left voicemails for four and spoke to six. For each call, I invented a short story about who I was and why I was calling about their late, murdered brother. Each conversation was short and not-so-sweet: *My brother's sad business is none of your business.* But then I found a sister in Cleveland, where my sister lived, and my luck changed.

Her name was Barbara Russo Jessup. She told me she was nine of twelve, six years older than Ronnie. He was her favorite brother. She was his favorite sister. They were close until the end. Close enough that she was going to raise Ronnie's twins. That's close in my book. My sister wouldn't raise my cat, if I had a cat.

This time, I told the truth. I wasn't an NYC coroner or a life-insurance agent or the owner of a local crematorium. I was a private investigator working her brother's murder because I knew for a fact the same corporate killer had murdered my father too. I wasn't exactly working with the NYPD, I said, but I also wasn't working against them. We were working in parallel. But it was personal to me and just a case to them. (It was personal to Logan too, but not like it was to me. Anyway, I left Logan out of the story.)

Barbara told me it was true Ronnie had taken his wife's passing hard. She'd been his rock, the love of his life, his reason for breathing. His grief was insufferable, so he got help. Group therapy. She had no idea what group or where they'd met or anything about it. Just that he'd needed help and found some.

She started to cry on the phone, and, for shit's sake, I started to cry too. Thinking of poor Ronnie Russo tied behind the wheel of a Camaro with his eyes shot out made me think of Jimmy in the Monument Insurance elevator, tied to a chair, dead forever. Thinking of how hard Ronnie had taken the death of his wife made me remember how hard I had taken—was still taking—Jimmy's death. Anyway, Barbara and I had a good cry together. Then she had to go because she had a life, and I had to go because I had more calls to make.

On my private tour of Columbia Cardiology—while Logan grilled Dr. Gideon King—I'd found the King of Conga, Mickey Herradura, and practice manager Tammy Bosworth had told me Mickey's wife had passed and his children were grown and living out of town. In the framed photos in Mickey's office, I'd noticed the King of Conga had three kids, all girls. It turned out one was living in Costa Rica (so, yeah, out of town), one was living in Tampa, and one was living in Hartford. The Costa Rica daughter was beyond my reach. I tried a number I found online, but it was no longer in service.

I connected with the Tampa daughter, who was still very sad about her father's death but had nothing new to say about her mother dying or her father's violent murder. She was still in a state of shock, which was to be expected. Shock is what you're supposed to feel when you've lost both your parents. I felt horrible for her.

And I felt horrible for me. I mean, I lived a more or less normal life—for a way-off-Broadway actor, single mom, brownstone manager, private investigator—but a part of my soul would always be in shock. For me, that feeling started when Christine, my mother, died and had been cemented in place when Jimmy was murdered.

While the Hartford daughter's phone was ringing, I remembered something else Tammy had told me. Mickey Herradura had been doing group grief therapy.

Just like Ronnie Russo.

Coincidence? Possibly. Not likely. Both murdered men had lost their wives and been overwhelmed with sorrow. Both murdered men had joined a grief-therapy group. The same group? Like her sister in Florida, the Connecticut daughter had no details about the actual group. Mickey had mentioned something about it, so she'd known her father was getting help, but that's all.

I felt funny about calling the Russo and Herradura families. Those murders were still fresh and present. Grief-stricken scabs still raw and bleeding. Disturbing their privacy filled me with guilt. I called them anyway because I was doing it for Jimmy, but I didn't enjoy pouring salt on their wounds. I mean, for Pete's sake, Ronnie Russo had been murdered a week ago. The King of Conga had died at Dawn four days ago.

I hung up with the Hartford daughter and thought, *No more. I can't call Penn's kids. It's only been three days. I can't do it.*

But I had to do it. I had to know if Penn had participated in a grief-therapy group.

Can't be nothing, I thought, *so it has to be something.*

Penn had two sons and a daughter, all of them living in the tristate area. Daughter on the beach in Cape May, New Jersey. Son on a lake in the Berkshire Mountains. Other son on the Lower East Side in the city. All three were architects like their father. But not one of them had landed at Penn and Ink, which, by all accounts, was like working in the middle of a war zone. Maybe they'd decided it was better to love their father as their father than have him throwing chairs at their heads as their boss. Penn's kids were smart. Penn's kids blazed their own trails.

Cape May and Berkshire Mountains either couldn't or wouldn't talk to me. Who could blame them? Like the Russos and the Herraduras, in the last year, the Penn siblings had lost both their mother and their father (found murdered—by me— on a diving board in Katonah). I hadn't been able to turn feelings into words three days after Jimmy's murder. All I could do was sit on my sofa and weep. I felt their pain.

But Lower East Side heard me out and told me, yes, his father had joined a grief-therapy group to deal with his overwhelming loss.

My heart started to pound. Not a coincidence, definitely something.

"I know this is hard," I said to Lower East Side, "and I'm sorry to ask, but do you know or remember anything about the group, when or where they met, how often he met with them, who he was meeting with?"

"First of all, it's not that hard," Lower East Side said. "My father was a genius in every way a person can be a genius, including being an asshole. He was an absolute genius at being an asshole is what I'm saying. So, of course, he was a genius at grief too. Out-of-control madman genius grief. So same as always except substitute grief for asshole. But still plenty of asshole in there because he didn't share any group-therapy specifics with me or with my brother or sister. We weren't important enough to know the details of his suffering. We were only his children. All the therapy engagements went through Penn and Ink insurance. Lucas took care of it."

"I'm sorry. Did you say Lucas Inklaar handled your father's grief-therapy group?"

"Organized, made the arrangements, authorized the insurance payments, yes. My father was a volcanic mess at the time —well, he was always a volcanic mess, not unlike Lucas—but he wasn't professionally functioning after my mother died, so Lucas found him a group to try to ground him and save the business. You'll have to ask Lucas if you want to know more."

I thanked him for his time, told him again how sorry I was for his loss, and clicked off the call.

Fu was right.

Trouble start now.

47

A FISSURE IN HIS VOLUMINOUS TOPOGRAPHY

WHEN SUPERSTAR CHEF TOM VALENTI CLOSED HIS BELOVED neighborhood bistro, Quest, it felt like a prized piece of New York food heaven had come crashing to the ground, like every food junkie in town was asking the same question: *Where the hell are we going to eat when we need an intravenous infusion of miraculous modern American food?*

Fortunately, Valenti opened Oxbow Tavern on Columbus Avenue near 71st Street before anyone jumped off the Brooklyn Bridge. Featuring coq au vin, linguini with lamb Bolognese, braised duck ragout, Australian lamb chops, and a simply grilled brace of quail that made your brain melt in your head, Valenti's larger-than-life Oxbow seemed like the perfect place to experience Victor Vreeland up close.

Although *close* was a relative term when referencing one's proximity to Victor Vreeland.

Valenti's Oxbow was rustic West Side sophistication taken to its fashionable zenith. Rick and I arrived on time, but Victor was already at a table for four by the windows. And already eating and drinking. He had four appetizers in front of him—black soil beets, deviled eggs, steak tartare, salmon gravlax. He was more than halfway through a bottle of Pinot gris. Two more bottles waited in the wine bucket on the table. He stood as we walked toward him, my arm wrapped around Rick's, and I was rendered speechless by his gargantuan charismatic presence.

Victor Vreeland was six feet tall and six feet wide. He had to weight four hundred fifty pounds. Maybe more. Probably more. He was freaking enormous, yes, but somehow carried it like weighing four hundred fifty-plus pounds was fine for him. He was solid, not flabby. His skin was flawless, which made him appear younger than seventy-eight, the same age as Ruby Gold. (I remembered they were five when they'd first met in Washington Heights.) He had a full head of long salt-and-pepper hair and wore blue-framed glasses that matched his silk scarf, which matched the three-step folded silk square in his suit pocket. Twenty-thousand-dollar diamond Cartier watch. Multiple diamond and emerald rings. Armani from head to toe. Every stitch custom tailored from the ground up. Let me say that again. Custom-tailored Armani from head to toe. The amount of fine Italian fabric required to cover a body that size was astounding. Thousands and thousands for just one ensemble.

I remembered Augie saying his son's insatiable appetite included a ravenous need for men, money, power, fame, drugs, alcohol, and food. I made a mental note to add clothes and jewelry to that list.

He was, bottom line, a human planet, and everything and everyone in the Oxbow Tavern operated in his orbit. I had the sense that everyone and everything everywhere operated in his orbit.

"Rick, long time," Victor said. "Your agent tells me we're a done deal. That makes me happy as hell. And if Victor's happy…" He paused to let Rick finish the sentence.

"Everybody's happy. Hi, Victor. Great to see you again. Can't thank you enough for this opportunity."

"Let's get past all that, Rick. You're awesome, I'm awesome, we deserve each other, we've got each other, now introduce me to this beautiful creature, and let's celebrate like we own the world, which we very nearly do."

Rick introduced me as Jennifer Lily Lane, his fiancée for all of two weeks. I used the same name I'd given Jake, the Silvercup security guard (and possible future rock-star drummer), and Ruby Gold the day the bear shot Rick in the chest on the set of Ruby's sitcom. I wore the same blonde wig with heavy bangs, the same green contact lenses, and the same five-carat, hand-cut, hand-polished cubic zirconia engagement ring in case Ruby and Victor had a little chat about his Oxbow dinner with Rick and Rick's fiancée.

The four appetizers sitting in front of Victor were not for sharing with the table. They were for Victor. I learned this when Victor asked us if we (me and Rick) were having anything to start. Same with the wine. *"Will the lovebirds be drinking?"* All three bottles in the bucket were for Victor. Augie's description of his son's insatiable appetite had been the understatement of the year.

Victor ordered two salads, three entrées, five sides, four desserts, and three double espressos with three double sambucas. He drank all three bottles of wine. I got a glass of Cabernet. Rick drank a nonalcoholic Heineken. I ordered the quail. Rick had the striped bass. We drank coffee but skipped dessert. The food was blissful. It was to Valenti's culinary credit that I could focus on my meal at all because I had never in my life seen a human being consume the volume of food and beverage in one sitting that Victor Vreeland devoured.

It was astounding, yes, but it didn't seem freakish or bizarre. Quite the opposite. Victor Vreeland eating three full entrées all by himself seemed conventional. Victor Vreeland drinking three entire bottles of wine seemed commonplace. Victor Vreeland downing three double espressos with three double sambucas and four desserts seemed natural. A normal night on the town for the comedy-club impresario. Maybe it was how effortlessly he did it, how happily, how gracefully, without a moment of regret or shame or embarrassment. It was not the slightest bit freakish to *him*, meaning he was completely comfortable in his own skin. Having a ball because this was who he was. This was how he lived. This was how much he ate and drank and laughed and joked and opined on all manner of subjects. This was Victor Vreeland. And it was impossible not to get sucked into his aura, to become captive to his planetary gravity. If you were near him, you were inevitably pulled into his orbit—like everyone and everything else.

He was funny and smart. Well-read. Articulate. Interesting. And he was, of course, famous. Not famous like Rick and the hundreds of other comedians who'd become household names in part by playing Victor Vreeland's Comedy Camp but every bit as famous in the New York entertainment social scene. Victor Vreeland was a big damn deal in every way a person could be a big damn deal.

Which reminded me again that New York City was the one place in the world that someone like Victor Vreeland could and did exist. Granted, Los Angeles had its own unique eccentrics— I'd been there for pilot season four or five times over the years and had met some crazy original folks, no doubt—but Victor Vreeland was only possible in New York City.

He was the consummate conversationalist, the host with the most, guiding us through one long, seamless tête-à-tête that encompassed, among other things, the decades-long saga of Victor Vreeland's Comedy Camp; Rick's fall from grace, recovery, and comeback; the state of the Knicks (Victor loved basketball and knew quite a bit about it); how constant freeze-thaw cycles contribute to road damage in all the boroughs but worst of all in Queens, which had the highest number—twenty thousand—of pothole complaint reports; and Rick's upcoming court case. Victor, of course, proclaimed his belief that Rick hadn't killed Kenny Cochran but admitted Rick's circumstance was fabulous publicity for his Cornucopia, not that that was the reason he'd reached out to Rick, Victor said, finishing the pan-roasted halibut and moving on to the grilled double-cut pork chop.

I wasn't kidding when I said consummate.

Victor was so good at guiding the conversation I nearly forgot I was Rick's bodyguard looking for a fissure in his voluminous topography, trying to maneuver him into casually letting it slip he'd hired the bear to kill Kenny Cochran.

I almost had him at one point. He was telling us about his custom-built Mulsanne Bentley, how it could comfortably hold two very large men—him, obviously, and his six-foot-four-inch full-time chauffer, and I was sure it was the bear and somehow finessed the conversation to Halloween masks of my youth. I loved animal masks, I said. *Lions and tigers and bears, oh my. And pigs.*

But Victor was too slick to fall for any funny fissure business. Slicker than me by a ton. Pun intended. He smiled in a way that made me think his radar was now pointed my way and deftly directed the discussion to the story of my engagement to Rick.

I'm an actor, so I didn't let on I was aware Victor's radar was aimed at me. Instead, I embraced the tall tale of my romance with Rick. And Rick embraced it too. Together, having the time of our lives at Oxbow, we told Victor the love story of Rick and Jennifer from the time we'd met—literally bumping into each other at Whole Foods two years ago—until he'd proposed under the 59th Street Bridge, both of us soaking wet because it had started raining cats and dogs, and we'd been kissing along the river and had run for cover a little too late. Rick down on one knee under the bridge in the middle of a thunderstorm, trying to discern the difference between the rain dripping down my face from my drenched hair and my tears of joy. We were perfect together, me and Rick. I told one part of our fabricated history, and he picked up the story from there until I picked it up again. Back and forth and forth and back. Passing the story baton between us like we were born to spend our lives together.

We were acting, but it was no act. It was as real as it was fake. There was something wonderful between us that I could feel in the heart of my heart.

And then we were having coffee and Victor was on his third double espresso, third sambuca, and fourth dessert, and I allowed myself to breathe and relax in his orbit, mesmerized by the power of his personality, hypnotized by the immensity and intensity of every aspect of him.

I had the sense that Victor was at the center of Cochran's death and the attempts on Rick's life—he'd given the money to Ruby; the bear and the pig were in his brownstone—but I also thought he wasn't whacking Rick tonight in the Oxbow Tavern. He wasn't doing the whacking himself. Period. He was the center of attention just being who he was, eating dinner at a table in the window. No possibility he was going to kill Rick in public in the Oxbow. None. He had the bear and the pig to do his dirty work when dirty work needed doing. Tonight was a touchy-feely decoy to gain Rick's trust, to gather information so Victor could kill him later.

He must know I'm Rick's bodyguard, I thought. *He has to have figured it out by now.*

That's when my napkin slipped off my lap and landed on the floor. I bent down under the table and saw Victor's Glock 43 in an ankle holster.

I gave it a good look but still thought Victor wouldn't pull it out and shoot Rick (and probably me too) on a random Thursday night in November. So I sat back in my chair, still in character, Rick's fiancée, Jennifer Lane, intent on enjoying the rest of the evening, when a waiter showed up with the check.

A waiter.

Not *our* waiter.

Some *other* waiter who had not been *our* waiter.

All my bells and whistles went off. *Wake up*, I thought, pushing the Cabernet to the back of my head. *Pay attention.*

Victor and the waiter flubbed the check exchange, and the check and the little check tray and the pen dropped to the floor —right beside Victor's ankle holster.

Right beside Victor's Glock 43.

It's happening, I thought. *The waiter's grabbing the gun. He'll take Rick out and run for the door. The whole thing will be over in a second, Victor will get off scot-free, Rick will be dead, and Jennifer Lily Lane will be lost and alone with no wedding to plan.*

As the waiter came up with the check—and Victor's gun—I stood and flipped the table upside down onto the waiter and pulled the Colt from my purse.

Table crashing, glasses and plates smashing, people gasping and shouting and yelling. Incredibly loud. Shockingly loud. Desperately loud.

So what? I'd saved Rick's life.

Except the waiter didn't have Victor's gun. He had the check. Which he handed to me—from his knees—with trepidation, since I was still pointing the Colt at him.

"I'm sorry," the waiter said. "I thought Mr. Vreeland was paying."

The entire restaurant stared at me, everyone dead still and silent. Rick was looking at me like I'd grown another head.

And then Victor laughed, a booming bass of a sound that filled the Oxbow Tavern and echoed up and down Columbus Avenue. "You're marrying this wild woman, Rick? Let me tell you something, boy-oh. You're going to get your ass kicked. Talk about arm wrestling for the bill."

Here was the truth of Victor Vreeland, who was as famous for comedy as anyone in New York: when he laughed, everybody laughed. And so everyone in the restaurant started laughing. First they started breathing, of course, *then* they started laughing. Even Rick and I were laughing, though I was sure neither of us thought it was funny.

I put my gun away and held the check up for Victor to see. "Our treat."

"But I invited you," Victor said. "Can I talk you out of it?"

Fat chance, I thought.

Pun intended.

48

WHEN WEAR DISGUISE, ALWAYS GO TROUBLE

RONNIE RUSSO, MICKEY HERRADURA, AND PHILLIP PENN HAD nothing in common except their wives had died, which had sent each man into an emotional tailspin that drowned them in heartache and misery, and they'd participated in a grief-therapy group to cope with their devastating losses. (That, and they'd all been murdered by the corporate assassin who'd killed my father.) But the same group? Different groups? No one in their respective families knew any details about the grief groups in question. Which is to say that knowing what I knew was just a half step above knowing nothing. To get a full step above knowing nothing, meaning to actually know something, I would have to convince Lucas Inklaar to share some confidential information.

Good luck with that, I thought as I exited the House of Emotional Tics.

Fu was standing on the front steps.

It was eight thirty Friday morning. Too damn early for a fight with Fu. But I could tell he was looking for a confrontation. Several times since Jimmy had been murdered at the end of July, Fu had met me on the front steps and not let me pass until he'd gotten what he'd wanted. Today was not going to be one of those times.

I went left. Fu went with me. I went right. Fu went with me. I faked right and went left. Fu blocked me. I faked left and faked right and went left, and Fu was standing there. I hit him in the chest with a frustrated punch. It was like whacking concrete.

Shit. It was going to be one of those times.

"What?"

"Where go?"

"You're not the boss of me, Fu. I don't have to tell you where I'm going."

"No need tell. Fu know."

"Oh, really? You're a mind reader now? Okay, smart guy, where am I going?"

"Trouble. When wear disguise, always go trouble."

He was right, of course. I was on my way to see Lucas Inklaar, pretending to be Nancy Silverman, insurance investigator for Rialto Health, Penn and Ink's health-insurance company. Once upon a lifetime ago, I'd played the role of an insurance-company investigator named Nancy Silverman in a late-night local cable TV commercial selling the services of a fly-by-night injury-insurance outfit that promised to *investigate your accident until the other side begs for mercy.* That was their honest-to-goodness tagline. They'd gone belly up before the commercial even aired. I'd bought Nancy's outfit for pennies on the dollar. Black business slacks, gray blouse, black jacket. I chose a red wig pulled back in a ponytail, blue contact lenses, and red-frame eyeglasses. The Colt was in my purse.

"So why are you blocking me?"

"Fu go trouble."

There was no possibility I could change his mind. He was coming with me. Plus, he was most likely right about me heading into trouble.

"Fine. But we're insurance agents, so check your closet and dress like one."

Incredibly, Fu's closet contained a gray pin-striped suit, a blue dress shirt, a blue bowtie, and beautiful black dress shoes. In the two years we'd been living at the House of Emotional Tics, I'd never seen this outfit. And those shoes? No freaking way.

"This is from *your* closet? Are you kidding me with these clothes?" I said.

"Fu businessman in China. Own five men store. Have many suit. Fu haberdasher."

"*Fu haberdasher?* Did you just say Fu haberdasher?"

Believe it or not, I believed him. *Of course* Fu owned five menswear stores in China. Between making bird movies, riding bareback in the circus, and being a poet mob assassin, he was a freaking haberdasher. Of course he was.

"Well, you look handsome," I said.

"Fu handsome man. Many women tell Fu."

"That's the end of this conversation. Understand? No more talking about how handsome you are or the many women who've told you that. No more. Zip it."

We took a cab to SoHo. The Penn and Ink building was even more impressive than I remembered. I'd been here with Logan last Saturday. It was Friday, midmorning. So more or less a week ago.

I explained to the receptionist that we were independent insurance investigators representing Rialto Health, that we needed to examine the documents surrounding the late Phillip Penn's grief-therapy treatment, and that she should immediately call whoever she needed to call to facilitate our investigation or perhaps lose her health care—not to mention every Penn and Ink employee's health care.

The receptionist, a temp filling in for the week, called

Inklaar, who had issued a company-wide directive that any and all Phillip Penn inquiries be routed directly to him.

Inklaar told the temp to inform us that he was working, was not to be disturbed, and that we could make an appointment for next week or we could go to hell. The temp struggled with that last bit, but I could hear Inklaar saying it himself, since he was yelling loud enough for his voice to bleed through the temp's headset.

Next week, of course, would be too late. The killer's clue—*A mystery man widowed and dreary; on safari through grief became leery; of his guide, who felt funny; with lawyers, guns, money; and turned hunter to hunted, in theory*—had been impossible for me or Al or Logan or anyone to crack, but the killer had been clear about one thing: *You have exactly one week from today.*

Since I'd been given the clue at the Wild Wooly Ranch at one minute past midnight, last Sunday, victim number four was slated to die the day after tomorrow, this Sunday. I had to see Penn's group-therapy information now.

I scheduled an appointment with Inklaar for next Thursday—like a cooperative little independent insurance investigator—and asked if I could use the ladies room, which was around the corner and out of sight of the lobby. Right beside the elevator.

"Screw Inklaar," I said to Fu as we rounded the corner. "We're going up no matter what. I need—"

I stopped dead.

An armed security guard stood beside the elevator. Expressly there, I felt sure, to keep everyone and anyone from accessing the third floor. Inklaar's floor.

"Need elevator?" Fu said to me.

I looked at the guard. The guard looked at me. I considered all the options—none of them good—in the blink of an eye.

"Yes, please," I said.

Fu walked calmly to the guard, who probably thought he

was some kind of tough guy but was really just a lost soul guarding an architect's elevator in SoHo.

"Help you?" the guard said.

But before he could actually put the question mark on that question, Fu grabbed the back of his head, pulled him forward, and smashed foreheads with him at five hundred miles per hour. The guard was out on his feet in a flash. Fu caught him before he hit the floor, and pushed the button. The elevator door opened. He pointed up at a security camera that had filmed the assault.

"Fu hide guard, wipe tape. You go third floor. Fu find."

There was no time to argue. It was a better plan than I had. Especially since I didn't have one.

I stepped into the elevator and hit the third-floor button. As the door closed, I saw Fu carry the unconscious guard down a hall that led to who the hell knew where.

Inklaar looked up from his drafting table as I crossed the loft office toward him. He was decidedly unhappy to see me.

"You're the insurance investigator who can't take no for an answer?" he said.

The good news was he didn't recognize me. Not yet, anyway. I hadn't been in disguise last Saturday when Logan and I asked him for the list of properties Penn had walked out with.

"Nancy Silverman, yes. Time is of the essence, Mr. Inklaar. Mr. Penn's children have initiated a claim that demands immediate attention."

The mention of Penn's children turned Inklaar's temperature way up. If he was angry in his natural state, he was now rising fast toward fury.

"Pathetic, ungrateful, small-time, no-talent, bullshit architects," he said. "Worthless human beings. I detest them. What claim have they commenced?"

I arrived at the drafting table. Inklaar stood. I'd forgotten how tall he was. Six foot six. Wiry. Strong. Eyes blazing. More intimidating than I remembered. And he'd been pretty freaking intimating last week. However, I was an actor. No way I would let him see me sweat. Even though with his size and his temper on his turf, I was sweating bullets.

"They blame you for their father's death. They don't believe you arranged for Mr. Penn to join a grief group. They're claiming you falsified the insurance information regarding Mr. Penn's therapy, and his untreated grief forced him to make decisions that led to his untimely passing. If I could simply confirm the therapy documents, the location of the group and so on, I'll terminate the claim and—"

He flew into an all-out rage and stormed violently around the drafting table. Jesus Christ, he was a terrifying man.

"Fuck Phillip Penn and his goddamn children. And fuck you, Silverman. Get out of my office before I physically remove you."

"That's fine, Mr. Inklaar. If you insist on acting like a child, then I'll treat you like one. I'll start with Mr. Penn's files. If I don't locate the group-therapy documents there, I'll continue with yours."

I turned toward Penn's half of the loft. The massive sliding glass panels were open. I started across the office, on a direct line toward Penn's file cabinets, but the truth was I was stalling because I didn't know what the hell else to do. Unbridled anger like Inklaar's can throw you off balance. Maybe that's why he'd done it. Intentional or not, I was way off balance and needed time to regain my composure. It was a simple request. A no-brainer. *Show me the group-therapy papers, and I'll terminate the claim.* How hard could that be? I'd thought he'd consent just to get rid of them—and me. But Inklaar hated Penn's children, and they hated him even more than they hated their own father —and probably each other. The moral to this sad story is there are no simple requests when the animosity between parties is off the charts.

Shit-shit-shit. Now what?

I didn't have to wait long to find out. Inklaar caught me by his conference table. Grabbed my arm and spun me around like he meant to hurt me. And he *did* hurt me.

If Jimmy had driven one lesson home above all others, it was this: *if someone grabs you in a way you don't want to be grabbed, break their fucking nose.*

And Raul had taught me how to do just that.

I punched him as hard as I could. But he was tall and agile, so I only clipped his chin.

He felt it. But not enough to make a difference. Only enough to send him over the edge.

Blind with rage, he wrapped his left hand around my throat and bent me back onto the conference table. Choking me. I had no leverage. He was too big. Too strong. Too filled with hatred and adrenaline and violence.

A small, heavy, glass sculpture of the Earth was near my face. He grabbed it with his right hand and lifted it into the air behind his head, like a pitcher in fastball windup, ready to smash my skull open.

I couldn't breathe. Couldn't close my eyes. Just watched the glass Earth, waiting for it to spill my brains on the table.

But Inklaar's arm stopped midair.

A look of surprise and shock filled his face.

Still choking me, he turned his head.

Fu had grabbed Inklaar's right wrist and was holding his arm in place.

"What the hell?" Inklaar said.

"Mother not teach no hit girl. So Fu teach," Fu said.

Inklaar's rage did not subside despite his shock at being unable to move his right arm. He released my throat and raised his left fist.

But before he could throw the punch, Fu smashed him in the throat with some kind of brutal martial-arts thrust of death.

Inklaar's eyes bulged out of his head. He couldn't breathe. Couldn't speak. He dropped the glass Earth.

I was still on my back on the table, regaining my senses, realizing I wasn't dead and should be standing up, when Fu slammed Inklaar face first into the table—his head right next to my head.

Inklaar's nose was shattered to shit. Blood went everywhere. I was amazed his head didn't go through the freaking table.

Inklaar didn't scream out in pain, probably because his vocal chords had been rendered inoperable, but I saw fear in his eyes. He was in trouble and he knew it. His face filled with terror. No one could do this to him. He was Lucas Inklaar. Douchebag Superman.

No one but Fu, that is.

Fu reset his grip on Inklaar's right wrist and pinched a pressure point. Inklaar fell to his knees and released an inhuman groan.

Fu leaned down and said into Inklaar's ear, "No hit girl. That lesson of day."

He was defending me. Not just saving me, which he'd done six times, including now, though maybe seven, since one was in dispute. *Defending* me. Defending my honor. I wanted to tell him how much he meant to me, but he spoke first.

"Know what need?"

"Yes."

"Go get. Fu teach more lesson."

I leaned into Inklaar's bloody face. "Will I find what I'm looking for in your file cabinet?"

Fu applied additional pressure to Inklaar's wrist. The genius architect gasped and nodded.

I left Inklaar with Fu and rifled through Douchebag Superman's file cabinets.

Under "I" for insurance was a folder labeled *Meridian Counseling Associates*.

49

A WOMAN AND A CHINESE BLOCK
OF GRANITE

Fu had wiped the security footage of him head-butting the elevator guard into oblivion followed by me stepping into the elevator the guy had been guarding. But what to do about Lucas Inklaar? He'd originally assumed we were health-insurance investigators, though I doubted he'd thought that by the time our visit ended. Meaning, he would no doubt call Logan—when his vocal chords became operable—and inform him of our little chat, since Logan had previously demanded he report any suspicious behavior that involved his missing (and now dead) partner.

But Inklaar didn't know who we *really* were, so the question on the table was: *How much and when did I tell Logan about Meridian Counseling Associates?*

That was what I was thinking as Fu and I walked into the House of Emotional Tics lobby at ten fifteen Friday morning. Fu went down the stairs to his apartment to change out of his swanky suit—the man was a haberdasher, after all—and I went to check yesterday's mail.

As I turned the key in my mailbox, the front door to the brownstone opened and Edie and Ray blew in with the breeze.

"Hello, Kate," Edie said. "We're back from the market, and we've brought this nice young man with us."

"Says he's getting married in three days," Ray said. "But when you're nice, who knows what the hell you mean."

The nice young man was Matthew. He'd forced a smile for Edie and Ray and was keeping it there, but I could tell he wasn't happy about something. Edie had her arm wrapped around his arm, so he couldn't get away. And Ray was on his other side, carrying two bags of groceries from the Korean place around the block. In other words, Matthew was boxed in. I could see the invisible smoke coming out of his ears—like all mothers can see the invisible smoke coming out of their sons' ears. What I didn't know was if Edie and Ray had done something to irritate Matthew or if that honor belonged to me.

I doubted it was Edie and Ray, who were certainly odd enough to illicit raised eyebrows but probably not peculiar enough to piss anybody off.

Edie and Ray Mazzone had moved into apartment 2A immediately after their wedding fifty years ago. They'd taken their honeymoon money and purchased a dry-cleaning business on First Avenue and 63rd Street rather than spend some sexy week in the sun. They'd promised each other they'd take a proper honeymoon one fine day in the future, but unfortunately, they'd worked themselves to the bone six days a week, fifty-one weeks a year, for the next five decades. They'd always taken a break during week fifty-two, between Christmas and New Year's, and driven to Pittsburgh to visit family, but they'd never had that honeymoon.

Instead, cleaning clothes was their world. Until two years ago, when Fu and I moved into the building. That's when they'd sold the business and retired into their abnormal nuthouse life—which, since summer, had included swinging— that often left me shaking my head. It's not that I didn't like them. I did. Especially Edie, who swung in protest. I liked Ray too, but his special charm usually wore off in forty-five seconds.

"I mean I'm getting married on Monday, in three days," Matthew said. "It's not that complicated."

"Trust me, Matthew," Edie said. "There's nothing *more* complicated than getting married in three days. Isn't that right, Raymond?"

"Three days, fifty years, that's why I bought the Viagra," Ray said. "If you got wood, you got everything."

For the past four months, Ray had been telling anyone who'd listen about his escapades with the little blue pill. No one wanted to hear about them. Especially Edie.

She was seventy-five. He was seventy-seven. She'd handled the customers and the counter and the tailoring. Front of house. He'd handled the cleaning and the pressing in the back. Fifty years of sucking in hot steam and dry-cleaning chemicals had done a number on Ray's brain cells.

He was thin as a pipe cleaner from top to bottom. Razor mustache above his skinny upper lip. A Bony Maroney of a man whose special kind of crazy presented itself in the clothes he wore.

Today's outfit was skintight leopard-print leather pants that maybe Mick Jagger once wore many decades ago, zebra-striped sweatshirt, and beekeeper hat and veil. Dress shoes. No socks. Not kidding about the beekeeper hat and veil.

"Are there bees buzzing around out there I should be worried about?" I said.

"African killers," Ray said. "You can't be too careful."

"I'm afraid the buzzing is inside your head, Raymond," Edie said, winking at me.

She was a bleached blonde with huge hair and heavy makeup. Elegant clothes you don't see every day. Glamorous ensembles you would never wear to the Korean market around the corner, for instance. Today, she'd chosen a vintage, 1980s purple prom dress with a heart-shaped neckline, extra-puffy sleeves with a great big bow on each one, matching magenta 1980s pumps, and enough faux jewelry to open a store.

"I think the buzzing is inside my pants, if you know what I'm talking about, Matthew," Ray said.

"Matthew has no idea what you're talking about, Raymond," Edie said, releasing Matthew's arm and starting up the stairs in her prom gown. "He's a nice young man."

"He'll figure it out in three days," Ray said, following Edie. "I think it's the African killers, Edith. That's what's going on down there. Not a safe situation for a prom girl."

I winced. I think we all did.

"Don't worry about me, Kate," Edie said as she reached the second floor and turned the corner. "I'm a nature girl. I know how to keep bees at bay."

Ray said something else, but thankfully he was already around the corner and we didn't hear him.

I took five seconds to let the African bees buzzing in Ray's pants evaporate in my mind and finished opening my mailbox.

"Three days. So exciting, Matthew."

Like me, he was still shaking Edie and Ray out of his head. "Yes, but that's not why I'm here, Mom."

I could hear it in his voice. It *was* me. I was the source of the smoke coming out of his ears.

"What else could possibly be on your mind? In three days, you'll be a married man. That's all you should be thinking about."

"In a perfect world, maybe."

"It's not a perfect world?"

"Not for Lucas Inklaar."

That was fast, I thought.

There were two trash cans near the bank of mailboxes. One for garbage, one for recycling. I stood by the recycling can and tossed the junk, kept the bills. Matthew followed me.

"Logan and I went to see him," I said casually. "He gave us a list of projects Penn walked out with. He's not a pleasant man, Inklaar. His anger issues have anger issues. No surprise it's not a perfect little Inklaar world."

"The surprise is he has a bad concussion, a broken nose, and a cracked jaw."

"Was he in a car accident?"

Matthew laughed. It was ugly. I hated that laugh. It was the laugh that said, *I know you're lying, Mom. You're always lying now that you're a PI. You're a professional liar. That's what you are now. A liar by profession.*

"This is how we're going to do this?" he said.

He was right, of course. I was a lying liar telling lies. Too late to turn back. There was nothing I could do except tell the truth later.

"How we're going to do what?"

"Logan called me this morning. I'm minding my own business. Thinking about my wedding. Drinking coffee. Watching Nina do prenatal yoga on the living-room floor."

"Yes, good, let's talk about you and Nina and the baby and prenatal yoga on the living-room floor and the wedding, and let's not talk about Lucas Inklaar with a bad concussion, a broken nose, and a busted jaw."

"And Logan tells me Inklaar called him from the emergency room and said two people who claimed to be health-insurance investigators trespassed into his office and demanded information. He told Logan it was a woman and a Chinese block of granite."

"I understand yoga is good for pregnant women if you know what you're doing, and no one knows more about yoga than Nina. Just ask her."

"He said at one point the Chinese block of granite said something like, '*Your mother never taught you not to hit girls, so now Fu's going to teach you.*' The exact quote was, '*So Fu teach.*'"

"She's a yogi, isn't she? I remember her telling me that. Certified, she said. Two hundred hours or two thousand or some big number. That's a great deal of Downward Dog. Give me a heavy bag any day and—"

"Stop it, Mom. There's a Chinese block of granite living in the basement whose name is Fu."

"Fu is a common Chinese name, Matthew. I'm sure there are dozens of large Chinese men named Fu in this city. Dozens. Any one of them who'd met Inklaar would want to break his nose."

I finished tossing the last of the junk mail. Matthew stood on the other side of the recycling can, trying to look like he didn't want to be annoyed. But he was.

"What are you doing here, Matthew?" I said. "Why did Logan call *you*?"

"Because he thinks it was you and some Chinese block of granite you know, and he didn't want to come here himself because he knew he'd arrest you for—let me read this so I get it right; I wrote it down—*intolerable stupidity beyond the pale*, and he didn't want to ruin my wedding. Unlike you."

"I would never intentionally ruin your wedding."

"Oh, well then, that makes me feel so much better. You wouldn't *intentionally* ruin it. Unintentionally, that's another story."

"Did Logan say what they wanted, the health-insurance investigators? What were they doing there? Inklaar didn't tell him that?"

"Inklaar couldn't remember. Said he wasn't paying attention because it was absurd. Something about Penn's children suing him over their father's health insurance. So Logan called Penn's children. They're not suing Inklaar or anyone. So, no, Logan doesn't know what the health-insurance investigators were after. He asked me to ask you. So I'm asking you. What were you and Fu doing there, Mom?"

"How am I supposed to answer that?"

My son was much smarter than me. He rolled his eyes to let me know he was well aware I hadn't said, *"I don't know, it wasn't me."*

"I have to be in court," he said. "Stay away from Logan. Stay out of trouble. Three days. That's all I'm asking. Three measly days. Can you do that, please?"

I kissed him on the cheek. "Does Logan know about the block in my basement?"

Which meant *Have I crossed a line I can't cross back?* He shook his head in dismay and walked toward the door. "No, Mom. Logan doesn't know about Fu."

Which meant he hadn't told him. Yet.

"Love you, Matthew."

"Three days."

As soon as the door shut behind him, I remembered the question on the table: *How much and when did I tell Logan about Meridian Counseling Associates?*

Knowing what I knew now, the answer was: *Nothing until I sort out what the hell it means.*

50

NO CROSSING SWORDS IN THE GRIDLOCK OF GRIEF

Twenty minutes later, Al Cutter met me in the lobby wearing a black suit, a black tie, black shoes, and a black fedora.

"Grieving widower, hundred bucks an hour," he said.

He looked more like a zombie undertaker than a grieving widower, but he was the only one available on short notice, so I paid his price.

"Try not to scare anyone, will you, please?" I said. "You're grieving the death of your wife, not hunting human flesh."

To be safe, in case Logan followed up, I wore the black wig, black jeans, dark-dark brown contact lenses, and black leather jacket from the D-Cup musical *Jane on the Brain*, a dark romantic piece about a psychologist (Roger) who literally can't get his new patient, Jane (me), out of his head. Jane has issues, which is why she's seeing a psychologist, but it's never clear what those issues are. Stress and anxiety? Habits and addiction? Phobias? Loss? All of the above? It didn't much matter because it was the D-Cup and singing and dancing inside Roger's character's head that was the point of the production. Story logic? The crazy folks inside Roger's head—ex-wives, old bosses, nasty teachers, sadistic dentists, vicious dogs—were far more fun than story logic. Sadly, the romance with Jane didn't work out for poor Roger's character, who jumped off a bridge at the end of every performance. Jane, however, was cured. So there was that.

Anyway, that's why I'd chosen Jane's wardrobe. So that later no one could tell Logan it was me snooping around for information. Plus, maybe Jane's luck would serendipitously rub off on me at Meridian, which was where Al and I were headed.

I drove the White Whale down Second Avenue to 73rd Street, and parked in a garage. We walked west toward Third Avenue. It was a pleasant, tree-lined block with stately, six- and seven-story brick residential buildings, awnings stretching from the front doors to the street. Uniformed doormen greeted guests and tenants and delivery folks and patients seeking psychological absolution at Meridian Counseling Associates.

Meridian had taken the entire first floor in one of the pricey brick buildings in the middle of the block. There was no signage. None. If you didn't already know there was a counseling center here, there would be no way to find them.

A uniformed doorman with a visor cap stopped us at the entrance. I explained we were here to see a Meridian counselor but didn't know which one because today was our first day. The doorman had heard it all before. He pointed us toward double doors on one side of the large lobby, took a second look at Al because, well, Al, and then turned his attention to an arriving UPS delivery guy.

The guest lobby was clean and comfortable. No expense had been spared to give people the feeling that while Meridian was in business to make money, they weren't bleeding their patients dry, meaning their design budget had limits because they were careful and thoughtful folks. Pottery Barn casual was the psychological motif. If there'd been a kitchen and a bed, I'd have moved in.

"Hi, my name is Jane Bailey, and this is my brother, Chase," I said to the administrative receptionist. "He recently lost his wife and is adrift in an ocean of sadness, caught in an undertow of grief, and needs help to get clear of it. I had a friend who lost his wife and was in a widowers' grief group here, and it did wonders for him. I'd like to get Chase in that same group. Can you help me do that?"

The woman's name was Cheryl. She was pleasant and kind and sympathetic while letting you know it would be business before pleasure as far as she was concerned. She looked at Al, who was too distraught to speak. Thank God. The pain on his face, however, was palpable. Though it wasn't clear if he was suffering from the loss of his wife or kidney stones or irrepressible horniness.

"Does your brother have insurance to cover the cost of counseling?" Cheryl said.

"Our family has money," I said. "We'll be paying with cash. I understand there's an initial intake session. How much will that be? Poor Chase can't wait another day."

"Three hundred dollars," Cheryl said. "Let me see if Sandra is available to register your brother and find him a group."

I gave her three hundred dollars, and we waited in the Pottery Barn living room for five minutes. Al told me he didn't mind waiting because as soon as the clock ticked past one hour, I would owe him two hundred bucks.

"I'm not prorating shit," Al said.

"Whatever, Al," I said. "Just stay in character."

"Projecting pain when I'm in your company is a rope of piss," he said.

"Project without talking," I said.

Cheryl appeared at the window. "Sandra will see you now."

We left the Pottery Barn living room and went into a cozy Ethan Allen office. Cheryl sat us at a charming round conference table at which I hoped they'd serve lunch later. After a minute, a pretty, professional woman, maybe thirty-five or younger, came in, smiled kindly, took a seat across from Al and me, and introduced herself as Sandra Owen, licensed psychologist and Meridian's administrative manager. She placed an iPad on the table in front of her, intending to take notes, register Chase into the system, and assign him to a grief group tout de suite.

Sandra gave us some Meridian background—founded by Karen Weissman, PsyD PhD JD and Ross McGowan, PhD MD twenty-three years ago; forty-seven independent licensed therapists, counselors, and coaches working as an association for the betterment of individuals and families suffering from various mental and emotional challenges; awards and accolades out the wazoo; unparalleled compassion and experience; accepting all major insurances, credit cards, and cash, but no checks.

We went through the basic intake process, Sandra entering Chase's information into her iPad. As instructed, Al stayed silent. He was suffering the death of his wife too deeply to speak, I explained. Indeed, he hadn't spoken a word in weeks. It had been my idea for him to join a group because he was resistant to help while suffering in silence. It was past time for him to grapple with his grief. That was my story.

"I'm so sorry for your loss, Mr. Bailey," Sandra said when she'd finished typing. "I'd like to guide you into a group that will offer a stable emotional platform where you'll find clarity and kindness, a compassionate place for you to pursue peace with your wife's passing. I have some recommendations I'd like to share with you and your sister. Is that all right with you?"

She smiled—wow, gorgeous sexy smile—to let me know she was speaking to me but trying to connect with my brother too. Al nodded in a way that signaled a change in his comportment. Meaning the pain in his eyes turned from grief to some kind of zombie leering lust. It was not a good look on Al, who hadn't looked all that good to begin with.

"Call me Chase," Al said.

"Oh, look at that," I said. "It speaks when it's not supposed to."

"All journeys begin with a first step," Sandra said to me, still smiling at Al.

"I got a first step in mind," Al said.

Shit, I thought. *Irrepressible horniness. I should never have let him choose his own grief manifestation.*

"What Chase means is there's a specific group we'd like to join," I said.

"Small group," Al said to Sandra. "Just me and you."

"I'm sorry, Mr. Bailey, but I don't facilitate a men's grief group," Sandra said.

"Say my name," Al said. "I want to see me on your lips."

"Excuse me?" Sandra said.

"Of course you don't facilitate a men's grief group," I said. "We weren't suggesting anything of the kind. What we *are* suggesting is joining the group that includes a friend of ours who also lost his wife. Mickey Herradura."

"I can't help myself," Al said. "I'm overwhelmed with arousal."

"Al," I said, hoping to stop him in his lewd zombie tracks.

"I thought his name was Chase," Sandra said, checking her intake notes.

"I call him Al. Like the Paul Simon song," I said.

"I don't understand," Sandra said.

I had two choices, neither one good. I could end the fiasco now and walk out embarrassed and emptyhanded before Sandra called security. Or I could go with Al's flow—however painful and disgusting it might be—and take a shot at what I'd come for.

"It's a bawdy grief, Sandra," I said. "There's no other way to explain it. My brother's been lewd, crude, and rude since he lost his wife, and only a men's grief group can save him. So if you can just tell us the name of Mickey's group, maybe share the names of the other widowers, it's possible that knowing them, knowing who Chase will be opening his titillated heart to, sharing that group with us, those names, might go a long way toward helping my brother get past his grief-caused concupiscence."

"I got something long I'd like to share," Al said.

"Keep it in your pants, Lance," I said to Al.

"Sandra knows what I'm talking about," Al said.

"I'm sorry, I really don't," Sandra said. "I thought it was Chase. Or Al."

"Everybody grieves their own way," Al said. "I grieve with sex. And I got a big grief, if you know what I mean. You got to see it to believe it."

I threw up a little in my throat.

"What?" Sandra said.

"Mickey Herradura," I said. "What was the name of his men's group again? I missed it the first time."

Sandra lifted the phone and hit a button. "Can you come in here, please?"

"And the other widowers," I said. "That would be swell."

"I'll give you something swell," Al said. "Something swelling as we speak."

"Gross," I said.

"My grief is growing, sis. I don't deny it," Al said. "Since my wife died, I got no one to be with in the biblical sense. Nothing gross about that. The horizontal mambo is a beautiful thing."

The door opened and another woman walked in. Maybe my age. Stunning. Long legs. Big chest. Stylish gray hair. Beautiful smile.

Jesus Christ, was every goddamn therapist in this practice a supermodel?

"This is Rebecca Howard," Sandra said. "She's a senior

associate. She approves all patients registered into the practice. This is Chase Bailey, or maybe Al or Lance, and his sister, Jane."

"Threesome. Cool. Let's get groovy with some grief, girls," Al said.

"Mickey Herradura?" I said. "The names of the men in his group?"

"Mr. Bailey claims he's lost his wife and is grieving his lack of sex in her absence," Sandra said to Rebecca. "He would like his therapist to offer him some relief."

"If you could just share the names of the men in Mickey's group," I said, "we'll sign right up. Pay cash on the barrel."

"Is that true, Mr. Bailey?" Rebecca said. "You believe the therapy you need to assuage your grief is sexual in nature?"

"It's a case of carnal knowledge. A round of rumpy pumpy. I got enough grief for both of you, if that's what you're asking," Al said.

A security guard appeared in the doorway. He was larger than the doorway, so his whole self didn't actually appear in it, just his chest and head.

"He's not invited," Al said. "No crossing swords in the gridlock of grief."

"I'm sure there's a brothel on Broadway your brother can visit," Rebecca said to me. "Perhaps they'll have a group more suited to his needs."

The guard turned sideways and wedged himself through the door and into the room.

"So no names today?" I said, already standing.

51

____

HIS HEART WAS HERE IN THIS DINING ROOM

I'D PAID AL FIFTY UP FRONT, AND THE MERIDIAN WOMEN HAD seen to it we hadn't clicked past an hour, so I handed him five tens, put him in a cab, and told him I never wanted to hear him say "rumpy pumpy" again in any context ever for the rest of time.

Then I found a pharmacy on the next block and changed my look in the ladies room. I lost the black wig and contacts, lightened my makeup so I wouldn't look like the sad sister of a grieving sexual predator, exchanged my pumps for navy blue Chucks, and drove the White Whale to Ditmas Park, a historic district in the Flatbush neighborhood of Brooklyn.

Rick had given me an Argyle Road address. That's where his nieces lived, he'd said. They were making us lunch. Had been planning it all week. Shopping. Prepping. Decorating. It was all they could talk about. *Kate is coming! Kate is coming!*

I was a nervous wreck.

What in the world? Why was I nervous about having lunch with a group of girls?

Because I wanted to make a good impression on them. That was why.

I liked Rick. Really liked him. He made me laugh, he made me think, he was a romantic kisser, and we'd been on the same wavelength since the moment we'd met. That didn't happen every day, the same wavelength stuff. At least not to me. Finishing each other's sentences, thinking each other's thoughts, feeling each other's feelings. Nope, not every day. Up until Rick Gotti, in fact, I'd been the queen of Not on Anywhere Near the Same Wavelength.

Argyle Street was lovely. Beautiful Queen Anne–style single-family homes set close together on both sides of the street. Tree lined. Sidewalks. Lamp posts. If my life had gone one way instead of another, I could have been hellaciously happy here.

The house where Rick's nieces lived was charming with a capital C. A great big brown Queen Anne between Ditmas and Dorchester. Three stories. Wraparound front porch. Adorable architectural details. Plenty of windows.

Rick had said to park in the driveway, so I pulled in behind a Chevy pickup, killed the engine, checked my makeup in the mirror, and took yet another nervous breath, my mind racing.

I want Rick's nieces to like me. That's what this is about. I'm forty-five years old, and I want my boyfriend's nieces to like me. Like I'm a college girl being presented at Christmas. A gift-wrapped girlfriend introduced for the first time to the parents and the brothers and the sisters and the uncles and the aunts and the nephews and the nieces. Especially the nieces. If the nieces don't like the girlfriend, then there's no hope for the—Whoa, are you out of your mind? You're not Rick Gotti's girlfriend. You're his bodyguard. As in on the payroll. Snap out of it, Kate. Get your shit together and—

"She's here!"

Three girls between the ages of twelve and fifteen came flying down the stairs and sprinted toward the Toyota. They dragged me out of the White Whale and up the steps, across the porch, and into the house, introducing themselves in a whirlwind of excited laughter. Julianne was white. Claudia was Black. Choko was Asian.

From the beginning, when Rick had told me he'd ditched me to visit his nieces, I'd thought that sounded a bit off because he'd also told me his sister lived in San Diego with their mother—Rick had bought them houses at the height of his fame and fortune. So unless he had brothers and sisters he hadn't told me about, what were his nieces—his sister's daughters—doing in a quaint Queen Anne on Argyle Road in Ditmas Park? And why was one of them Black and another one Asian? I mean, families came in all shapes and colors, of course, but three girls born within three years of each other who looked utterly unrelated made me think.

Not that I had much time to think.

Julianne, Claudia, and Choko whisked me into the dining room, where I was overwhelmed with yet more energy. Two girls were setting a big table. One was sixteen or seventeen, Hispanic. The other was younger, maybe fourteen, white. They yelled their names out as I was push-pulled toward the kitchen.

"I'm Isabella."

"I'm Allie."

The house was gorgeous. Tall ceilings. Crown moldings. Wood floors. Light streaming in. And beautiful furniture. I had a feeling Rick had built piece after gorgeous piece for the place. For his nieces.

There were two more girls in the kitchen. One (Hispanic and maybe twelve) was preparing a salad with a woman, fifty-five or so, who had a kind but official air about her, and the other (Black, the youngest, possibly ten) was working with Rick by the stove, putting slices of lasagna on plates and carrying them into the dining room.

"Hello, Kate," the woman said. "This is Maria and that's Monique. I'm Dee, nursemaid, babysitter, house mother, butcher, baker, and candlestick maker."

"Dee's the bomb," Rick said. He wore an apron that read: *Uncle Rick's House.*

"Don't worry about that deer-in-the-headlights feeling, Kate," Dee said. "We're used to seeing it around here. Aren't we, girls?"

"Hey, I still feel that way sometimes," Rick said.

The girls groaned just exactly like their Uncle Rick had made yet another cornball Uncle Rick joke.

Lunch was a raucous affair. Rick sat at one end of the table, Dee sat at the other, I sat next to Rick, and the girls sat everywhere else. There were seven of them, for Pete's sake, so when I say everywhere else, I'm not kidding. They definitely *sounded* like they were everywhere else. Competing for airtime like unruly talk-radio hosts. Asking me countless questions about being a private investigator and being an actor and being a boxer and living in the city and having a son who was getting married and being a grandmother in the spring and... Holy crap. Rick had told them all about me.

Dee refereed the meal as best she could, coordinating the inquisition with a gentle touch, which meant mostly letting the girls have at me to their heart's content and laughing right along with them. Somehow, she made sure everyone was eating and not just shouting out questions and laughing like hyenas. I sensed respect and affection going both ways. I sensed something else as well, something more profound, but couldn't put my finger on it because the tsunami of life and laughter ripping around the table left no time for deeper contemplation.

Rick was the punchline of many jokes, meaning the girls had great fun teasing him mercilessly about all manner of things—his looks, his truck, his cooking, his corny jokes, and especially his love life. Which, as you might imagine, meant me. He enjoyed every minute of it. But it was more than that. It was as if he'd found the center of his life. That this house, these girls, these moments were his reason for living. His connection to the girls was palpable. For all his wild history—hit sitcom bad-boy superstar, sold-out king-of-comedy tours, fame, fortune, addiction, rehab, arrested for murder—his heart was here in this dining room.

I barely got a word in edgewise. No sooner had one question been rifled my way, than another followed right behind. *Let her answer. Give her a chance. Hold the phone. Put it on pause,* Dee told them with little success. I found myself swept up in the joy of lasagna for lunch in Ditmas Park with Rick and a roomful of his animated nieces.

I was on the witness stand, it was true, but they were so happy to have me there that I didn't want to be anywhere else. The cross-examination only ended because we ate all the food and Dee announced it was time to do the dishes, straighten up the house, get back to their schoolwork, and let Rick and me have a moment to ourselves.

That, of course, led to a full chorus of catcalls and whistling. I expected an impromptu version of *Rick and Kate sitting in a tree*, but Rick took me by the arm and led me onto the front porch, shutting the door behind him.

"I don't know where to start," I said.

"Start here," he said, and he kissed me.

It was gentle and heartfelt, and I didn't want it to end, but it did, and we smiled and moved to the porch rail and looked out over Argyle Road. It was a crisp and clear November day. Blue sky. Leaves falling. Breath hanging in the air. Ditmas Park so many light years away from the city.

"When I got into rehab, the second time, I had the feeling the only way to save myself was to save somebody else," Rick said. "I don't know where that feeling came from. Maybe God, if you believe that sort of thing, but I couldn't shake it. So I bought this house and fixed it up and started a nonprofit and put some money in—a lot of money—and raised other money with grants and government funds and hired Dee and went looking for girls who were broken by abusive families and gangs and drugs and alcohol. Girls who had nowhere to else to go, nowhere to turn, no one to help them straighten it all out."

"I had no idea."

"No one does. Because it's not about me. That's why it works. For me *and* them. Whenever it's been about me, it's been a fucking mess no matter what it was. Because *I* was a fucking mess. I still am, but I'm getting better. That's what I want you to know, McCall. That's why I brought you here. I want you to know I'm getting better."

I couldn't find any words. Rick Gotti, incurable selfish smartass creating a house where lost girls could come and find their footing. I was profoundly moved.

"Been about ten years," he said. "Lots of girls in and out since we opened the doors. The social system helps me find them. Some stay a year, some less, some longer. They can live in the house until they're eighteen, then we help them take their next step—job, school, something solid."

"Dee lives here with them?"

"Yes, she's a saint. Licensed RN. Licensed therapist. Credentialed social worker. I met her for coffee a decade ago. Her husband had just died. She was realizing that with all her education and training and experience, the system stood between her and the people she wanted to help. She told me she wasn't looking for a job. She was looking for a life where she could touch people's souls and lift them up."

"Saint. Yes."

Tears in his eyes. "She touched my soul and lifted me up too. I'm so lucky, McCall."

I put my arm around him and rested my head on his shoulder. "You're a pussycat, Uncle Rick."

"Don't tell anyone."

"My lips are sealed."

He turned to me and smiled. "Since we're talking about lips..."

We kissed again, and I thought, *This is the way I always wanted to be kissed.*

52

BRING YOUR DUMP TRUCK

On Tuesday, Bruce Bailey had told me Victor Vreeland had pulled six million bucks out of his backside and purchased the one-acre elbow on Mclean Avenue in Yonkers from Tommy Tariccone. Victor had been broke at the time, of course, and Bailey had no idea how his comedy-club client had come up with the dough. To the prerecorded cries of *Bruce, Bruce, Bruce, Bruce,* Bailey had told me the one person who might be able to solve the mystery of the miracle money was Victor's ex-wife.

Victor's ex-wife? Say what?

So on Wednesday, while I'd been digging deep in the internet earth to uncover the kids of Ronnie Russo, Mickey Herradura, and Phillip Penn, I'd also clicked around for Victor's ex. And found her in Forest Hills.

Her name was Wendy Bell.

She wasn't exactly a she.

It had been a whirlwind romance for Victor and Wendy, who'd met in March, married in June, and annulled in October, the seven months more or less encompassing the one-acre elbow, the explosion of Ruby Gold's and Kenny Cochran's horse-gambling debts, Cochran's murder, and Rick's arrest.

I'd called Wendy on Wednesday and introduced myself as Emma Rose, a freelance gossip-magazine reporter specializing in the fabulous follies of famous folks. I'd said I would love to feature her in a piece I was planning for *Hollywood Life* or *Us Weekly* or *In Touch* or *Close Weekly* or *Cosmo* or *Star Magazine* or *Life & Style Weekly*, all of which were bidding for the boffo story I was about to put to paper. It was an ex-wife exposé, I'd said. A where-are-they-now-and-what-dirt-do-they-know sort of saga that millions and millions of readers would devour on commuter buses and trains, drinking Americanos in coffee shops, passing the time under salon dryers, and waiting their turns in doctors' reception rooms across the country and around the world. I'd explained there would be a glamorous full-page photo shoot of the famous exes and a substantial paycheck for their participation—so long as they had enough dirt to cover the cover, so to speak.

"Oh, Emma, honey," Wendy had said. "Bring your dump truck."

Forest Hills is not generally the kind of place you find a Wendy Bell. It's among Manhattan's most sedate suburban neighborhoods. Nothing too terribly terrible going on in Forest Hills, which offers neat and narrow curvy streets, green and lush, with tidy single-family Tudor homes sharing the block with handsome Tudor-style apartment buildings, all tastefully maintained. Charming. Pleasant. Agreeable. All systems go for a normal life in a normal neighborhood. Nothing to see here, people. Move along. Nothing unusual lurking around the corner in Forest Hills.

And while its amiable residential vibe is overwhelmingly underwhelming in terms of jazzy hipster funk, Forest Hills is not without its claims to fame. Indeed, there were four that Jimmy had said put the place up there with any burg in any borough.

The West Side Tennis Club, home of the renowned Forest

Hills Stadium, is in this affable neighborhood. For years and years, this was the home of the United States Open Tennis Championships. The US Open. One of the great global Grand Slam tournaments. In other words, big freaking tennis deal. Well, for all those years, even though it was officially called the US Open, no one actually called it that. They called it Forest Hills. That's a claim to fame in anybody's book.

Simon and Garfunkel had both graduated from Forest Hills High School. They'd first taken the stage of the legendary Forest Hills Tennis Stadium as part of the Forest Hills Music Festival in 1966. They'd played there several times over the next few years. It was home base. Whatever music floats your boat, that's a claim to fame.

The Ramones originated in Forest Hills. The Ramones. In fact, there's a Ramone's Way at 67th Avenue and 110th Street in front of Forest Hills High School. That was Jimmy's favorite claim to fame for Forest Hills. That The Ramones started here. My father loved The Ramones—before someone shot his eyes out.

And Dale Carnegie, though born on a farm in Maryville, Missouri, once lived on Wendover Road in Forest Hills. That's right, the penultimate self-improvement guru had Forest Hills roots. Among many other accomplishments, Carnegie had created and written *How to Win Friends and Influence People*, published in 1936. It's been a best seller since day one. If you'd been trying to win friends and influence people any time in the last century or so, Dale Carnegie was your Forest Hills man of the moment.

I would need his spiritual guidance today if I was going to get the inside skinny from Wendy Bell.

She lived in a delightful white Tudor home on Tennis Place, an easy walk to the tennis club. The neighborhood was so peaceful, so serene, so far from the madding chaos of the city, that you could fall asleep walking down the sidewalk to your house. Wendy's white Tudor had to be worth two mil.

I parked the White Whale in the driveway behind Wendy Bell's Range Rover and checked my look in the rearview mirror. I'd changed back into the black wig, dark contact lenses, and black leather jacket from *Jane on the Brain* because I imagined any gossip rag reporter worth her salt would have issues on her issues—like Jane did.

But Jane had been cured, and Dale Carnegie had my back, so I knocked on the door and waited for Wendy to let me in.

"Oh dear God, you're wearing black, Emma. Black is the old black. The new black is diamonds," Wendy said. "Give me diamonds or give me death."

She was too much to take in at one time. For one thing, she was six foot seven. For another thing, she was thin as a flag pole. For *another* another thing, she was a man. But her blonde wig put my black wig to shame, her makeup was fashion-model gorgeous, and she wore an eight-thousand-dollar Dolce & Gabbana short lace dress with marabou trim and rhinestones that made her look like some kind of exotic wild bird—a Fifth Avenue ostrich, perhaps. Custom-made shoes from who knew where that had to cost who knew what. She drank a martini from a massive martini glass.

Diamonds? Oh hell yes. Earrings, bracelets, necklace, ring. Dazzling. Too many carats to count. Maybe Wendy Bell was why Victor Vreeland was broke.

I mentioned she was a man, didn't I?

There'd been no obvious surgeries. No sense that her gender was in transit. She was all man and yet all woman. Wildly beautiful in a way nobody thinks of beautiful because there simply aren't that many people running around the world like Wendy Bell. I wished I had skin as smooth and clean and clear as hers.

The exterior of the house may have been charming timeless

Tudor, but the interior was modern Hollywood Regency, a delightful blend of art-deco-inspired silhouettes with a grownup sense of unabashed, unrelenting, unforgiving high-polish glamour. French furnishings; clean lines; vibrant, nearly blinding colors; high-shine surfaces and finishes. It took a minute for my head to stop spinning.

She led me—by the hand, as if I were her girlfriend, or maybe her daughter—to the living room, where she made me a martini without asking if I wanted one, and then sat next to me on the sofa, which she'd apparently purchased from the future.

"Let's gossip, gossip girl," she said.

No need for Dale Carnegie today, I thought. *We have gin.*

"But I'd like to set the stage before we begin," she said. "I'm a woman in a man's body, attracted to men who like men. There's a name for that. Would you like to know what it is?"

"I would."

"It's called *I need another martini.*"

She moved to her Hollywood bar cart and made an ocean of a martini while letting me get to know the real her.

She'd been born Benjamin Bell, the only child of Harvey and Irene Bell. Both parents had been bigwig bankers and left her the house and a whopping pile of insurance money after they'd died tragically in a Swiss Alps avalanche while on a skiing vacation to celebrate their fortieth wedding anniversary.

Benjamin had known he was Wendy since age five or six but hadn't fully blossomed until after her parents' death five years ago. She was now in her midforties. Same as me. Much prettier. Much richer. Way more out of bounds.

She'd met Victor at an after-party at the club back in March, and their mutual attraction had been seismic.

"So much man," Wendy said, returning to the sofa, "I hardly knew where to start. We couldn't keep our hands to ourselves. There were bodily fluids flying all over his office. I lost track of whose was whose."

Too much information, I thought, trying to push the visual of Victor Vreeland and Wendy Bell doing the dirty in Victor's office out of my mind.

"We got married in the heat of the heat of passion, and when I say hot, I mean there was lava between us, Emma. Every day. Twice a day. Lava."

"Lava, got it," I said.

"I was a June bride. So romantic. And then a hurricane summer of love."

"And then?"

"Even a volcano cools down after it blows. And we were ice cold. I repulsed him. He repulsed me. Our marriage was annulled. But the judge said I could keep the ring. Which infuriated Victor because he needed the money."

Here comes the dirt, I thought. "This is what my readers want to know, Wendy. Why in the world did Victor Vreeland need the money? He's rich."

"Once upon a punchline."

"Didn't he buy a piece of property from a mob boss for six mil right around that same time?"

"He did. In Yonkers."

"While he was broke?"

"In debt up to his ding-dong."

"So where did he get the money? Ruby Gold? I know they were close friends."

"That's so funny I need another martini," she said, heading to the bar cart. "Ruby had less money than Victor."

"How do you know that?"

"Because we were double-dating. Victor and me and Ruby and Kenny. They loved the horses, those two. Victor and I went to the track with them a few times. They lost a fortune. Her fortune. And by *they*, I mean Kenny. Kenny lost it all."

She told me all about Ruby and Kenny and her and Victor. I sipped my martini and took notes.

"When I tell you the dirt was dirty," Wendy said, circling back to the elbow on Mclean, "I mean it was filthy rotten moldy crud."

Victor Vreeland would double-cross and triple-cross any legal line, any friend, any business associate, his own mother, his own father, to gain an edge, to hold power, to get what he wanted. Which was, she also told me, *everything*. His appetite for every single thing was insatiable. Unfortunately, he lost his appetite for his wife almost immediately after they were married.

"It's all about the chase for Victor. The game. The capture. The power. The conquest," she said. "Once he had me, he didn't want me. Which was fine because I'm a big girl and can take care of myself."

It wasn't long before they were at each other's throats. Victor had wanted access to Wendy's insurance money, which was seven million smackers. Wendy wasn't having any of that action.

"I told him I didn't care how good the sex was," she said. "But you can tell your readers it was Certified All-Star Porn Star. With a man like Victor and a girl like me, the possibilities are obscene."

Jesus, that image again, I thought, suppressing the filthy vision of a four hundred-plus-pound impresario and his six-foot seven-inch string-bean man/wife naked and triple-Xing it up.

"Did he want you to pay for the Yonkers land?" I said.

"He did."

"You told him no?"

"I told him *hell* no. What man in his right mind comes between a girl and her money?"

Good point. "So where did he get the cash, Wendy? Imagine me backing up my dump truck at this very moment."

She polished off her martini and put her hand on my knee.

"We were well on our way to annulment, so I was in and out of the picture, meaning I won't swear to this on a motel Bible, meaning I didn't actually see him do it, but Victor made a mountain of money at the Cabaret in May."

"His famous fundraiser?"

"One man's nonprofit donations are another man's cash flow. There's a name for that. Would you like to know what it is?"

"I would."

"It's called *I need another martini.*"

She moved to the bar and made a martini you could swim laps in.

"Is there a way to check, to confirm that Victor donated the donations to Victor and not the nonprofits?" I said.

"Oh, Emma, honey. You're talking turkey with the corroborating queen. Mommy and Daddy were big-boss bankers. They made me get an MBA from MIT. Business analytics for Benny before he was Wendy. Not only *is* there a way to vet Victor, it's something we can do together while we mix martinis and talk like teens."

She grabbed her laptop from a writing desk and carried it to the sofa with her drink. I had no idea a person could consume that much gin and live to tell the tale. She sat and patted the cushion beside her. I slid over. Her legs were longer than my whole body. And they were gorgeous. If I'd had legs like that, I would have been Chita Rivera.

She opened her laptop and typed like the wind. Her hands were huge. She could easily palm a basketball. But they were soft and elegant too. Beautiful hands. The hands of a slender, graceful, elegant, woman concert pianist—who was six-seven and a man.

"Here's the list of nonprofits Victor had designated as this year's Cabaret donation recipients," she said. "It's still on his Comedy Club website. Whoops, Victor. And this is GuideStar, the website where nonprofits list their annual reports and other financials, which are publicly available to make sure there's no nonprofit funny business. So let's drink a martini and see what we can see."

There were more than two hundred nonprofits on Victor's list, which was a lot, of course, but not so many when compared with the thirty-five thousand nonprofits registered in the city. We checked the financial records of the first fifty on the list. They'd each received either a pittance of the pledged amount— just enough for them to keep their mouths shut in the hope more was coming soon—or none of it.

"Not a good look for Victor Vreeland," I said. "Very bad look."

"There's a name for that," she said. "Would you like to know what it is?"

53

NOTHING WORSE THAN ANGRY GRIEF

I WAS IN A HURRY BECAUSE IT WAS THREE THIRTY, FRIDAY afternoon, and I had to be at the D-Cup in two hours—the second actor in the house—for this evening's performance of the orgiest shit show in town: *Psychedelic Sunday*. So I backed the White Whale out of Wendy Bell's driveway, pointed it at Manhattan, and hit the gas. Then I picked up the phone and called Charlie Nye.

"Yo," Charlie said.

"Charlie, it's Kate."

"You calling me?"

"Yes, I'm calling you. Your phone rang, you answered, and now we're talking."

"That's what I thought."

He was in the tow truck, hauling cars across the city to lots so far-flung no one could recover them without also purchasing an airline ticket.

"Can you call it a day and meet me at the brownstone?" I said. "I need you to help me."

"Should I bring my machete?"

"Depends on the depth of your grief."

Back at the House of Emotional Tics, I changed my look from gothy *Jane on the Brain* to Doris Day meets Jennifer Aniston, wholesome, caring girl next door. Blue contact lenses, blonde wig, brown tortoise-shell glasses, white sweater, tight brown cords tucked into brown Fry boots. Charlie met me in the lobby looking like Hugh Hefner after an after-after-party. Full-blown tuxedo, bowtie untied. Dark shades covering blood-shot eyes. Not a bad look after an after-after party at the Playboy mansion, but possibly not the best look when portraying a grieving widower at Meridian Counseling Associates.

I drove the White Whale to 73rd Street and parked in a lot on Lexington. We walked a few blocks to the brick building between First and Second, and I told the very same doorman that we were here to sign up with Meridian. The good news was the doorman didn't recognize me from this morning, when I'd been here with Al. The bad news was he did a double-double take at Charlie, who, it turned out, was a Dean Martin doppelganger.

On the drive down Second Avenue, I'd told Charlie the game plan—he was Dean, a grieving widower looking to join a specific men's grief-therapy group, and I was his sister-in-law, Georgia. I also told him Al's sexually deviant grieving-widower act had failed miserably, and there was a bonus in it for him if his act succeeded.

"What's my grief look like?" he said as we walked across the lobby to the Meridian front doors.

"Up to you," I said. "As long as it's the opposite of Al's."

"Not a problem."

"And let me do the talking."

"Don't worry about me. I'll cry in my beer."

Cheryl was still behind the reception desk. She tilted her head at my story as if she'd heard it just this morning, but it was different enough to throw her off—my brother-in-law (not my brother) was grieving the loss of his wife, my sister, and was looking for a certain men's grief-therapy group. And I'd changed my name, my look, the tenor, tone, and range of my voice, my posture, and my gestures, so she didn't physically recognize me. Or Charlie, for that matter. I was paying cash, and it had been a long day, so she let the similarity go and escorted us from the Pottery Barn reception room into the Ethan Allen intake room, where Sandra Owen, licensed psychologist and Meridian's administrative manager, placed an iPad on the table in front of her, intending to take notes, register Dean into the system, and assign him to a men's grief group lickety-split.

In the middle of her Meridian backstory—founded by Weissman and McGowan twenty-three years ago; forty-seven independent, licensed therapists, counselors, and coaches; awards and accolades out the wazoo; compassion and experience—in the middle of all that, Charlie took a bottle of beer out of his pocket, twisted it open, and cried while he drank it.

I was too stunned to react. Every bit as stunned as Sandra.

"I'm sorry for your loss, Dean," Sandra said, "but we don't allow alcohol in the office under any circumstances."

"It's part of his grief," I said, trying to pull myself together. "Crying in his beer, I mean. It's cliché, I know. But in this case, it's true. Dean literally cries in his beer."

"Cliché or not, either he stops drinking or the meeting is over," Sandra said.

To which Charlie pulled a gun—a Smith & Wesson .38 Special—out of his other pocket and said, "Either you give me the group I want or more than this meeting is over."

"Jesus, Dean," I said. "Not what I had in mind by a longshot."

Charlie shrugged in a way that made me think he was playing Dean Martin for real. "This is what my grief looks like. Up to me, you said."

"I know, but Jesus. Is it loaded?"

"No idea, Georgie. Could be. Forgot to look. Too broken up about my dead wife. I'm guessing loaded."

"Is this a robbery?" Sandra said.

She was terrified. I didn't blame her. Charlie with a gun that might or might not be loaded? I was terrified too. And *Georgie*? Pretty good acting, I had to admit.

"No, Sandra," I said, deciding to play it out instead of bolt. "It's not a robbery. But if you don't put Dean in the group he's asking for, someone's going to get hurt. And by the looks of where he's pointing that gun, I'm thinking it's you."

"I don't understand," Sandra said. "What group?"

"It's a men's grief group," I said. "We heard about it from a conga player named Mickey Herradura."

She looked at me funny. It was the second time today someone had asked for that particular group. Coincidence? Sandra though not. "I can't share the personal information of our clients no matter how many times I'm asked in the same day. First your brother, now your brother-in-law. You look different and sound different, but you're not different. It was against the law this morning. It's against the law now."

"I'm about to rewrite your definition of against the law," Charlie said. "Nothing worse than angry grief. Time bomb in the brain. Mine's about to blow."

"Angry grief sounds like bad news for you, Sandra," I said.

"He's bluffing," Sandra said.

The thing about bluffing, Jimmy once told me, is that when you're in, you're in. There's no changing the bluff midbluff.

"Are you bluffing, Dean?" I said.

Charlie had been a poker stud since his army days and knew all about the bluff. He stood, walked around the table, put the barrel of the gun on the side of Sandra's head, and pulled back the external hammer. "My wife's dead, and this broad won't let me cry in my beer. She wants to see my hand, she can go right the fuck ahead and call."

"Oh, look at that, not bluffing," I said.

Bluff or no bluff, loaded or not loaded, there was a gun to her head.

"What group was that again?" Sandra said.

"Men's grief group with Mickey Herradura," I said.

Sandra tap-tap-tapped on her iPad and called up a file. I came around the table and stood on her other side so that she was seated and sandwiched between Charlie's snubnose and me.

"What am I looking at?" I said, bending down so my head was next to her head. If Charlie pulled the trigger, he'd murder us both with one shot.

"Mr. Herradura's grief-therapy group," Sandra said.

There were four men on the list. Mickey Herradura, Ronnie Russo, Phillip Penn, and Stewart Sinclair. Three of them were dead. Sinclair was next. Had to be.

"Who runs this group?" I said.

"No one," Sandra said. "It was discontinued several months ago."

"Why?" I said.

"I don't know," Sandra said. "You'd have to ask the psychologist who ran it."

"Really, Sandra?" I said. "You going to make me ask every question?"

"Dr. Marcus Moore," Sandra said. "He's no longer associated with the practice. I don't know why. Psychologists come and go. It's not unusual."

"Too bad. Maybe he could've helped me," Charlie said. "I got issues besides my wife's death. I didn't even know I *was* married. That's a fucking issue right there."

And with that, it was time to get the hell out of Dodge. We left Meridian in a hurry—Charlie threatened to visit Sandra at home if she called the cops, which scared me half to death, and I wasn't the one being threatened—raced to the garage, and sat in the White Whale for few minutes, both of us—or at least me —phasing back into real reality.

"You can't go around pulling guns on people, Charlie," I said.

"That's what my mother says. Except she does it, and she's got a sawed-off."

"You're the most violent stoner I've ever met."

"She says that too."

With Charlie, sometimes all you could do was shake your head. "Was it loaded?"

"What?"

"The gun."

"Like I said. No idea. Forgot to look. Too broken up about my wife. Wish I'd known her better before she died."

"Can you check?"

"Pretty sure I never met her."

"The gun, Charlie."

"Right, yeah. The gun. Better not to know," he said, firing up a joint of homegrown happy hemp. "Better to let it fade away."

I nodded, turned the engine, and drove us home. On the ride back, I had plenty to consider. Rick's nieces, Wendy Bell's martinis, Matthew's wedding, *Psychedelic Sunday*, Lew Logan, Victor Vreeland, *Kung Fu Fu*, Wild Wooly Ranch, and all the chutes and ladders that sprang and sprung from every one of them.

But all I could think about was Marcus Moore and Stewart Sinclair.

54

SMART AS SHIT BUT TWISTED AS TWINE

I called Logan while driving Charlie to the House of Emotional Tics. I called him again in the cab going downtown to the D-Cup. I called him a third time from the dressing room, me and Roger running through our preshow rituals. And I called him a fourth time ten minutes before curtain.

Each voicemail had the same general vibration. *Logan, are you freaking kidding me? Answer your phone. I know who the next victim is. I mean, I don't know who he is, but I know his name. And I have a lead on the killer. A name. The killer's name. Listen to your voicemail and call me back. I have a show tonight, so call me now or after the show. But freaking call me. Where's a cop when you need one, Logan?*

By the fourth message, I was more melodramatic than was necessary to make my point, but I'm an actor. Sue me.

Logan never called me back, and the curtain rose, and the lights came up, and the band played, and there was singing and dancing, and the house was full, and just like every single solitary time before, I lost myself in the show.

Or maybe I found myself again.

The two-hour block between curtain up and final curtain was where my soul lived. Time stopped, the real world faded from view, and I became who I was born to be. The joy of the show, the thrill of the stage, the glare of the lights, the thunder of the band, the roar of the crowd, all of it fed me, nourished me, sustained me, filled my tank, restored in me the energy that made me who I was and who I would continue to be. I was the theater, and the theater was me.

Like *Rocky Horror Picture Show*, D-Cup musicals had somehow osmosed into participatory theatrical events. Actual audience involvement was not unexpected. Maybe not at every performance of every show, but often enough for us to be trained to keep on keeping on with the play when the crowd sang the songs or spoke the dialogue or dressed in costume or danced in the aisles—all of which happened somewhat regularly, often all at the same time. But what did not occur regularly was the ticket-buying public storming the stage and joining that cast in the actual play when the actual play was being an actual play.

But that's what happened tonight.

A half dozen audience members took the stage during the second orgy and danced with us as if they themselves were in the middle of a swirling psychedelic trance, playacting and pantomiming sex with the actors, who were playacting and pantomiming sex with each other in Professor Jedry's lovesick acid trip.

So...bizarre on top of bizarre on top of bizarre.

We went on with the show, but I couldn't help but be amazed by how badly people, just regular folks living their regular lives in the regular city of New York, how badly, how deeply, they were craving an orgy. And if they couldn't have a real one, then by God, they were going to have one on the D-Cup stage with George Washington, who wasn't even the real

George Washington *in the play*, but instead was the George Washington who'd stepped out of a painting while the professor was tripping.

Who doesn't love theater?

I removed my makeup, changed my clothes, and found Logan at the D-Cup bar. He was drinking Scotch. I thought to ask him if he'd only just arrived or if he'd seen the show, but the incredulous trainwreck of a disaster of a fiasco of an otherworldly clusterfuck of a look in his eyes gave it away. Oh yeah, he'd seen it.

"What did you think?" I said.

"I'm considering season tickets," he said.

I knew he wasn't. Of course he wasn't. "Why's that?"

"Because when I'm feeling like my life is a crazy kaleidoscope of fucking fucked up, you folks are going to make me feel fine by comparison."

"Because we're entertaining?"

"Because you're even more fucked up than me."

"Right."

He bought me a tequila, and we clinked glasses.

"You have names," he said.

I told him about the three grieving widowers who'd already been murdered, about the bereavement group they'd been involved with at Meridian, about the list Charlie and I had procured at gunpoint—though I left out the gunpoint part.

"Stewart Sinclair is the fourth and last name on that list," I said.

Logan called Jesse. "Stop what you're doing and find out everything you can about Stewart Sinclair. He's the next victim. We need to find him yesterday."

I heard Jesse through Logan's phone. "On it."

"Why do you think you know who the killer is?" Logan said as he clicked off the call.

"Because the only thing the victims had in common was this group and the guy who ran this group, Dr. Marcus Moore."

I thought Logan was going to pass out. "Fucking fuck me."

He called Jesse again. "Put a pin in Sinclair and find me Dr. Marcus Moore. I want both, but give me Moore first."

He clicked off the call and downed the rest of his Scotch.

"You know him," I said. "He told me you did, and you do."

"Forensic psychologist. Criminal profiling, testifying in court, helping solve crimes. Specialized in homicide. Worked in my precinct. With me. Smart as shit but twisted as twine. Too deep and dark for his own good. Darker than the killers we were trying to catch. Arrogant, genius, scumbag shrink. So I got him canned from police work for the rest of time. He didn't take it well."

"Jesus, Logan."

"He runs that group?"

"Ran. Past tense. Terminated it for reasons I don't know. Disassociated himself from Meridian. Again, don't know why."

"I'll bet Russo knows. And Herradura. And Penn. Except they're all dead."

"Sinclair's alive."

"Dead Sunday."

"So what do we do?"

"*We* do nothing. *I* am going to circle my wagons, find fuckface Marcus Moore, and see if he's shooting people in the eyes for money. *You* are going home with my sincere appreciation for a job well done and my equally sincere warning to stay out of my way from this point on. Do you understand me, McCall?"

"As well as anybody."

He laughed. "That's probably true."

His phone rang. It was Jesse. Logan listened, wrote Moore's address on a cocktail napkin, grunted several times, and hung up.

I snatched the cocktail napkin off the bar. "He murdered my father and put me in the middle of you and him. I'm not going home, Logan. I'm going with you. Do you understand me?"

"As well as anybody," he said. "And what I understand best is your brain doesn't work worth shit."

Just like Jimmy would have said it.

55

I DIDN'T TELL LOGAN MY PLAN
BECAUSE, WELL, LOGAN

Jesse had found Moore's address with a simple search, which didn't surprise me because Jimmy had said many times that hiding in plain sight was the best place to hide.

So I went with Logan to Dr. Marcus Moore's house to kick corporate-killer ass. The former forensic psychologist lived in a handsome prewar building on 88th Street and Riverside Drive, one block south of the Soldiers' and Sailors' Memorial Monument, the white marble kissing cousin of the Choragic Monument of Lysicrates in Athens, near the Acropolis. Other than its look, there was nothing Greek about the Soldiers' and Sailors', which commemorates Union Army servicemen of the Civil War. Because it's *all* the way west, not many New Yorkers know about it or venture here, but I knew and had because in addition to the many Memorial Day celebrations held on the monument grounds—this had been Jimmy's favorite spot to spend Memorial Day—summer performances of Shakespeare on the monument's back steps were a thing, as were dance concerts and featured location gigs in films such as *The Odd Couple* and *Godspell* and TV shows like *Law & Order* and *Sex in the City*.

Anyway, Marcus Moore had moved into the prewar ten

years ago—so said the doorman to Logan. Moore owned a four-thousand-square-foot apartment with breathtaking views of the Hudson River and the Palisades. *Penthouse Palace*, the doorman called it.

He was a rotund, way-too-white guy with totally fake teeth that were also way too white. He wore a doorman uniform with a doorman hat. Under the hat, his hair was, yes, way too white. Of course, his nametag read, *Whitey*.

"I don't want to tell tales out of school, but the super said Dr. Moore paid cold cash for the place. Never knew psychologists made that kind of scratch. Must be a hell of a head shrinker."

Psychologists *didn't* make that kind of scratch. Not even when they moonlit as forensic psychologists. But when they moonlit as six-figure corporate assassins, then, well, yeah, that's the kind of scratch they make.

It was eleven thirty, Friday night. Way Too Whitey's shift had just started, so he didn't know if Moore was home or out on the town. So what? He could buzz up there and find out, couldn't he? Or we could skip the buzzer, bust down Moore's door, and blow his brains out on the spot. That's the choice I voted for.

But Logan voted otherwise—and he was the only one who got a vote.

"For all his doctoral degrees—*three* that I know of—and narcissist genius bullshit, Moore's just another scumbag sewer rat," Logan said on the way back to his car. "If we buzz him this time of night and he's home, he'll read it like a book and be gone before Whitey says word one. Meaning, we have to assume he has an escape plan in place. Secret basement door to hell or wherever sewer rats run. He'll leave New York and shoot people in the eyes for money somewhere else. Chicago, maybe. San Francisco. Another country. Another continent. Ghost off the grid. If we break down his door and he's *not* home, some kind of hidden alarm will alert him he's fucked forever in this town. Hello, Argentina. Don't cry for me and all that shit."

So we sat in Logan's unmarked sedan (so gratuitously a government vehicle that its unmarked-ness made it more marked than unmarked). Most of the task-force cops were parked up and down West 88th Street. Only a handful were trying to locate Sinclair, even though Sunday was his day to die. Logan's plan was to anchor the task force and catch Moore on his return home or, if he was already home, clip him when he left the building in the morning.

But everything Moore had done to date (*if* it was Moore, which I knew it was, but, okay, *if* it was) had been misdirection after misdirection. So catching him at his house was just another arrow pointing down the wrong road. Maybe he knew we'd find him and had *given* us this address to get us out of the game. My gut told me waiting for Moore to come to us was what he wanted us to do. *His* plan. So *my* plan was to find Stewart Sinclair and let Moore come to me.

I didn't tell Logan my plan because, well, Logan.

I left at two o'clock Saturday morning and grabbed a cab across town to the House of Emotional Tics. Rick was sound asleep on my sofa. Still in his clothes. Pages and pages of jokes for his Sunday-night Cornucopia gig at Victor Vreeland's Comedy Camp on the coffee table. He'd passed out writing jokes. If there was a real Rick Gotti, this was probably him. This...and the guy with all the nieces.

I went to the kitchen, made a pot of coffee, and opened my laptop. Stewart Sinclair's life story would be here somewhere. Everyone's was.

Everyone except him, it turned out.

Sinclair had no social media presence whatsoever. None. Zero. No physical addresses. No phone numbers. No email addresses. No contact information of any kind except for his business, Sinclair Electric. Five screens in and all I'd found was an article and interview he'd done with Forbes.

He was, the article made clear, an extremely successful electrical engineer, the reclusive president and CEO of a multimillion-dollar engineering company that designed the grids and panels and wires and whatnot for commercial projects—apartment buildings, office complexes, shopping malls—in New York, New Jersey, and Connecticut. He was the only child of only children. Married once—then widowed and devastated several years after the interview—to a woman who'd also been an only child of only children, a commonality that had bound them together in love and life. Both sets of parents were deceased. Sinclair and his wife had no children of their own, not even an only child. No family for me to find out where he was hiding. No brothers or sisters or uncles or aunts or cousins. No one to call. Nowhere to reach out. If Sinclair didn't want to talk to anyone, then no one was talking to him.

Except for his business. Though I imagined he'd left strict instructions with his staff to intercept and handle with unrelenting discretion any and all communications that involved him. Bottom line: no one at Sinclair Electric was telling me shit about where the boss was hiding. I was beaten. Either Logan would find Moore or we'd be reading about the late Stewart Sinclair in Monday's paper.

And then, at five fifteen Saturday morning, on a screen so deep I'd lost count of my clicks, I found a lifeline. Armory Hunt Club had published a public relations piece in *African Safari Magazine* praising the accomplishments of one of its premier members, Stewart Sinclair, who'd done a stint as a special guest guide for a top-tier tour company and exceeded all expectations, meaning happy hunters in the jungle.

It was my only lead. I did some reading about Armory Hunt Club and African hunting safaris, made some notes, couldn't keep my eyes open, and fell into bed.

I woke up at eleven. Rick had left a stickie on my bed table. *Didn't want to wake you. Went to see my nieces. Back after lunch.*

I hated the idea of Rick out in the world without his body-guard, but put it out of my head, reached for my phone, and called Armory Hunt Club.

"Armory. This is Carol. Can I help you?"

"Hi, Carol. Yes, I hope so. This is Abigail West of Wild Africa Safaris." There really was an Abigail West of Wild Africa Safaris. "We've heard nothing but superlatives about Stewart Sinclair and would like to offer him an all-expenses paid hunting trip as a special guest guide. Can you put me in touch with Mr. Sinclair directly? His cell phone number would be ideal."

We went back and forth about the safari specifics—I regurgitated the information from the press release and Wild Africa Safaris website—and Carol said it was a generous offer but—

"But Mr. Sinclair is adamant that we don't give out his direct contact information to anyone for any reason at any time."

"Can you get word to him this morning, Carol? I'm afraid we need to move fast on our end."

"Mr. Sinclair has been out of town and unavailable the last few weeks but has a personal appointment at the Armory scheduled for tomorrow at noon. I can certainly leave word for him."

I thanked Carol for her help, left her the real Wild Africa Safaris number and Abigail's real email, and clicked off the call.

What a coincidence, I thought. *Stewart Sinclair and I both have personal appointments at Armory Hunt Club scheduled for Sunday at noon.*

56

SWELL TO HELL

THE GENERAL MANAGER OF PINNACLE EVENTS, THE CATERING company providing fine food and impeccable service at tomorrow night's Comedy Camp Cornucopia, was a former Schmidt and Parker Player. Jimmy used to say he'd rather be lucky than good. That's what he'd meant.

Before she got married, got pregnant, and got the Pinnacle GM job, Melissa Kinneman had been a peripheral player on the D-Cup stage, primarily singing and dancing in the chorus while working her way up the Pinnacle corporate catering ladder. She was leaving her D-Cup life behind as I was signing on, so I'd only known her for a short time—we'd done one show together—but Dennis and Posey knew her well. They were friends socially as well as professionally. So I called them after I hung up with Carol. They took my call together on speaker.

"I need a PI favor," I said. "Related to Rick."

"We're on the clock," Dennis said.

"Bodyguards 'R' Us," Posey said.

"Bodyguards and Beyond," Dennis said.

"Bodyguards in the Box," Posey said.

"Bodyguards To Go," Dennis said.

"Are you done?" I said.

"All ears," Posey said.

"He's hosting Victor Vreeland's Cornucopia tomorrow night," I said, "and Pinnacle is catering."

"Big gig for Melissa," Dennis said.

"It's an upscale Thanksgiving feast for three hundred fifty fancy folks," I said, "so she'll have forty or so servers in the club. I can't watch all three fifty at the same time and still keep an eye on Rick."

"Say no more," Dennis said.

"Mum's the word," Posey said.

"Zip the lip," Dennis said.

"In the bag," Posey said.

"Are you done?" I said.

They were done. So I hung up and went looking for Fu. I found him in the basement, in Jerusalem Joe's Free Apartment. Joe was on his perch. The cage door was open, and Fu was cleaning out the mess.

"Who invited you, Sad Sack?" Joe said as I entered what had been the House of Emotional Tics storage room until Fu brought Joe home from the Finger Lakes.

"He's the meanest bird that's ever been," I said to Fu.

"Kiss my ass, girlfriend," Joe said.

Before Fu became his caretaker, Joe, a fifteen-year-old, drop-dead beautiful Amazon parrot, had belonged to a bitter and abusive Brooklyn middle-school gym teacher (who'd retired to the Finger Lakes with his bird). The gym teacher had taught Joe to say a half dozen or so wiseass, mean-spirited put-downs that Joe saved for me and me alone. The bird would say nothing all day, then let me have both barrels whenever I arrived. I gave him shit right back. That I was bantering with and losing to a parrot did wonders for my self-esteem, let me tell you.

"Joe not mean. Joe feisty," Fu said.

"I'm not here to talk about Joe," I said.

"Good luck with that," Joe said.

"What talk about?" Fu said.

"Sunday," I said. "I set something up but don't know how it's going down."

"Heck of a job, Brownie," Joe said.

The bird had only six or seven phrases in his kit bag. How the hell he knew which one to say when was a mystery to me. An irritating, infuriating, exasperating mystery. My sister, Fu, and Joe...the people and parrot who could get under my skin in two seconds flat.

"What saying?" Fu said.

"I'm saying this may be my last chance to catch the killer," I said.

"You got no chance," Joe said.

"Better chance than you," I said to Joe.

Stop arguing with the fucking parrot, I said to myself.

"What really saying?" Fu said.

"What I'm really saying is I'm not fast enough to watch my own back," I said.

"Ten laps, lard ass," Joe said.

"Your bird hates me," I said to Fu.

"Joe not hater. Joe lover," Fu said.

"Sunday noon, Fu. That's what I'm *really* really saying," I said, and I glared at the parrot and turned to leave. "See you next time, asshole," I said to Joe.

"So long, sucker," Joe said.

I went back to my apartment, updated my case notes, paid some personal bills, did a pile of House of Emotional Tics paperwork, realized it was one thirty out of nowhere, and discovered I was hungry.

There was chili in the fridge—from JG Melon, the classic Third Avenue pub that had been famous for burgers and chili for five decades—and it was a brisk November Saturday, so chili sounded about right. I made myself a side salad, opened a beer, sat down at my little kitchen table, and had an honest-to-God epiphany as to why I had not yet found a wedding dress for Matthew's wedding on, Jesus Christ, Monday.

The unexpected flash of insight was that I hadn't found a dress because *I didn't want to find a dress*. And I didn't want to find a dress because Matthew's wedding to Ball-Breaking Nina was more sentiment than I could internalize, too much emotional current moving too swiftly for me to safely navigate.

How could my son be old enough to get married? Hadn't he just been born on my seventeenth birthday like a week ago? Playing Pee Wee soccer in Central Park last month? Going to his first day of school? How old was I anyway? Where had the years gone? And why *her*?

I didn't want to be related to Abominable Nina. Not even as an in-law. I didn't like her, and she didn't like me, and now I had a lifetime of that to look forward to.

"Swell to hell," as Jimmy used to say.

And speaking of Jimmy, there was no way Matthew could get married without my father in attendance, blessing his grandson's marriage with strength of character, hard-earned wisdom, and unconditional love. No. Way.

Except Jimmy had been brutally murdered back in July and was gone forever.

I'd thought I was over the deep, unforgiving grief of losing my father, but I wasn't. Over JG Melon chili and a cold beer, I cried like a lost little girl, sobbing like it was the end of the world, which is what Jimmy's death was for me. Total emotional meltdown that lasted fifteen minutes. I hadn't wept like that—*power weeping*—since, well, the last time I'd wept like that. But this was it. No more. I wouldn't lose my shit like this again until, well, the next time I lost my shit like this. That's the thing about grief. In the end, there's no end. You just press on with it in your back pocket forever. No matter where the hell else you go in your life, your grief goes with you.

I rinsed my face at the kitchen sink, blew my nose, finished my chili, drained my beer, and called Rick to make sure he was okay, meaning safe, meaning not doing something stupid, meaning not dead.

He was still at the quaint Queen Anne on Argyle Road with his nieces. I could picture him in his *Uncle Rick's House* apron, doing dishes and lifting lives back up into the light. He sounded happy to hear from me, said he'd stay with the girls all day, and see me tonight at the brownstone after my show.

Then I took a deep breath, faced the facts, and set off to West 14th Street, to Screaming Mimis, a vintage-clothing store that owned a piece of my heart. I think I'd been subconsciously saving it for the last minute, after I'd had my very own personal Come-to-Jesus meeting about Matthew's marriage to Maddening Nina and knew I had no choice but to buy a dress. If there was a shop that had one waiting for me, it would be Screaming Mimis.

So I tried on a dozen dresses and then found a coffee place I'd never been to and had a latte and emailed friends I'd been out of touch with, all the while trying not to think about Sunday, trying to be Zen about the danger that day promised, the uncertainty, the not knowing who would live tomorrow and who would die. Rick? Sinclair? Me?

I was being pretty good about redirecting those thoughts to the back of my mind, but then I went to the D-Cup—second actor in the house, of course—and Roger wanted to talk about Sunday night's Cornucopia while we ran through our preshow paces. The problem was I couldn't wrap my mind around Rick and Victor Vreeland and the bear and the pig and Sunday *night* until I wrapped it around Stewart Sinclair and Marcus Moore and Sunday *noon*, which was when Sinclair was set to meet my father's killer at the Armory Hunt Club.

And then some other Schmidt and Parker Players wanted to talk about it too, and I felt cornered, and then *Psychedelic Sunday* saved me. Until the second-act orgy blew all thoughts of everything else out of the water.

Just last night, a few rowdy audience members had joined George Washington's orgy onstage. But tonight, when George and the other colonists popped out of their paintings and stripped off their clothes and cavorted like rakes and debauchees and hedonists, it was like some kind of communal bell had gone off in the first three rows, stage right.

Apparently, a New Jersey nudist swingers club had bought that block of tickets with a plan in place. And the plan was to have their own orgy in the audience while we had one in the play. Or maybe there'd been no plan. Maybe they'd simply been swept away with the music and the singing and the dancing and been moved to move. Either way, the first three rows stage right got nearly naked in a hurry and had a dancing orgy in the seats while George and the colonists were getting jiggy with it on the stage.

So from then on I wasn't thinking about anything except that until I got back to the House of Emotional Tics, where Rick was waiting up for me.

And then there was something else to think about.

"Long day?" he said.

"Long day," I said.

He was watching *Animal Planet*, something about how deadly hippos could be if they were in a nasty mood, which, apparently, they always were. He muted the TV, came around the sofa, put his arms around me, pulled me close, and kissed me the way I always wanted to be kissed.

"Me too," he said. "I missed you today."

I'd been swept off my feet before and knew what that felt like. It wasn't this. This was something deeper. This was connection like I'd never felt.

"Shut up and kiss me again," I said.

He did. It was even better. It was so good and warm and real and loving that I thought we might kiss our way to my bed and make love. But I was just too blown out. Emotionally, physically, and intellectually exhausted.

"I want to make love to you," he said. "More than anything. But I'm too tired."

"Me too," I said.

"You want to make love to me or you're too tired?"

"Both."

"We have to promise each other this will never happen again," he said, and because he was Rick Gotti it was funny.

"I promise," I said, laughing.

"Me too," he said.

We kissed again, and I went to my bedroom and got ready for bed, brain bouncing from Victor Vreeland to Ruby Gold to the bear and the pig and three hundred fifty people in Victor's darkened club with the spotlight on Rick and wished I had a plan—some plan, any plan—so that we could live through the night and not be too tired to make love. But I had nothing. No plan.

And then just before I fell asleep...I did.

57

GET INSIDE, SAVE SINCLAIR, CATCH THE KILLER

IN THE 1940S, A ZILLIONAIRE NEW YORK INDUSTRIALIST NAMED Sheldon "Shelly" Cotter purchased a massive West Side armory from the National Guard with the express intent of founding an exclusive hunt club. Cotter had been known for his take-no-prisoners business style and for turning intentions into realities. He'd called it the Armory Hunt Club. The membership fee was sky high, the dues were backbreaking, and members had yearly hunting benchmarks that would make most manly men melt in the African sun.

Annual African hunting safaris were mandatory for all members, who were required to return with their trophies and deliver them to the club's in-house taxidermist. The animals were then artfully displayed throughout the armory, which had been redesigned, reconstructed, and redecorated with Cuban cigars and Kentucky whiskey and leather furniture and Tiffany lamps and mahogany floors and guns galore.

It was as west as west could be—28th Street and Twelfth Avenue. Right on the Hudson River. An impenetrable fortress. Restricted access at all times. Members and guests only. And guests were discouraged. Decades and decades of exclusivity.

Hundreds and hundreds of hunting trips. A macho display of countless wild African animals throughout the club that was rumored to leave the Museum of Natural History's vast taxidermy exhibits in the Saharan dust.

I say *rumored* because the Armory Hunt Club didn't advertise or publicize. Other than its members, no one had ever actually been inside. Interior photography was prohibited lest the pictures leak to the press and the public. The privacy of the club and its members was paramount. Big bucks to burn and a principled, professional passion for African big-game hunting were the only measures of membership. Race, creed, color, and religion were irrelevant. No matter who you were, if you were a member, if you were hunting for the club, your personal particulars were safeguarded like money in the mint.

No wonder Stewart Sinclair was comfortable here.

It was eleven o'clock in the morning. I parked the White Whale on 27th Street, and Fu and I walked north on Twelfth Avenue, passing in front of the enormous armory, which was locked and alarmed and shuttered on Sunday, the Lord's Day even for multimillionaire hunters. We passed the club's impressive double-doors entrance—thick, heavy, massive slabs of hardwood carved in and imported from Africa. There were security cameras and a sophisticated digital keypad. No code, no entry. At the corner, we turned right, heading east on 28th Street. There were iron doors on this side of the building that were for exit only, so no door handle, no lock, no nothing. Just a block of solid iron. Also on 28th was a huge metal loading-dock door for safari deliveries and whatnot. Same digital keypad as the front door. Same security camera. Unless you were a dead animal or a case of bourbon or a shipment of Cuban cigars, you weren't getting in this way.

"What plan?" Fu said once we were out of camera range.

"Get inside, save Sinclair, catch the killer," I said, making a

U-turn and walking back toward Twelfth Avenue, past the loading dock and iron exit doors, now on our left.

"That not plan. That dream. Plan mean *how* make dream happen."

"I know the difference between a plan and dream. I make plans all the time. I made one before I fell asleep for Rick's show tonight, as a matter of fact."

"What plan make for now?"

"You mean how do we get inside, save Sinclair, and catch the killer?"

We reached the corner and turned left, heading south on Twelfth, walking back toward the double African entrance doors. I was stalling because I had nothing beyond the dream. I'd gotten us here early to case the place and make a plan. So my plan for today, for now, was to make a plan as soon as I could make a plan. Probably not the best plan in terms of making plans. Definitely not something I could say to Fu.

"No have plan," Fu said, smirking like a younger brother who happened to be a banished Chinese-mob assassin who'd saved my life six (or seven) times since the summer. "Fu know whole time. No have plan."

"It's not like I have *no* plan. I have *some* plan. You have to give me that."

I was still stalling. And lying. Lying and stalling. Because if I had to admit I had no plan at all, then I also had to admit that Logan's plan—to nab Moore on his way out of or into his Penthouse Palace on the Upper West Side was better than my partial plan to find Sinclair and let Moore come to me. Plus, I would have to admit I'd failed Jimmy by not nailing his killer to the wall. And that was an admittance I just couldn't make.

"Fu no give. Tell Fu *some* plan."

And then right there on Twelfth Avenue, heading south, I sighed the sigh of someone who knew the game was over. I opened my mouth to admit I had no plan...

And then I saw him.

He was coming toward us, heading to the hunt club. Black pants, black shoes, and a black overcoat that came to his knees. Baseball cap pulled down low. But I still knew who it was.

Stewart Sinclair.

I recognized him from the Forbes interview photo. It was him. And just like that I had a plan.

"Mr. Sinclair," I said when we were ten yards apart.

He didn't like that he didn't know us, liked it less that he'd been recognized on the street, and swerved to avoid us. I moved with him and stopped him face-to-face. He tried to push past me, but Fu put a hand in his chest that stopped him dead in his tracks. It only took one Fu hand in the chest to know you'd better stay put.

"Who are you, and how do you know who I am?" Sinclair said.

"I'm going to tell you all that," I said, "but right now what you need to know is Marcus Moore murdered my father, who you don't know from Adam, and also murdered Ronnie Russo and Mickey Herradura and Phillip Penn, who you know from your Meridian grief group. Right now what you need to know is today, at noon, Marcus Moore is going to murder you too."

He was in his mid to late fifties. Maybe an inch taller than me. It was hard to tell what he looked like under his big coat, but I had the sense he was trim and strong and wiry...like the life he lived. He was an African big-game hunter who'd built a business and made a fortune. He was smart and tough and daring. I could see it in his eyes. Stewart Sinclair was used to getting what he wanted when he wanted it. Whether it was a multimillion-dollar electrical engineering contract in Connecticut or a two-thousand-pound Cape Buffalo charging him with bad intent. But I saw something else in his eyes too. Something behind his fearless big-game hunter glare. Pain.

Loss. Sadness. I knew it when I saw it because I'd been feeling those emotions since Jimmy was murdered.

He'd been sturdy and strong until I'd said Meridian. Until I'd mentioned Marcus Moore. Then he'd thought of his wife, who'd died and left him to live out his life alone. And thinking of her had brought with it a wave of emotions he couldn't hide or keep at bay. A state of mind I knew by heart.

"I'm meeting him here at noon," Sinclair said.

"I know," I said.

"I don't understand," Sinclair said.

"Get us inside, and I'll explain everything," I said.

He was hesitant. Actually shook his head. Not *fuck no*. More *I'm not sure what's happening here*.

"Please, Mr. Sinclair. He could show up any minute," I said.

He looked into my eyes and registered nothing but honesty and truth. He looked at Fu too and figured Fu was my muscle, and he was right about that. He nodded, and we hurried for the African doors.

It was eleven twenty. My heart pounded, and I wasn't sure why.

"He has the code," Sinclair said. "He could already be in there."

Right, I thought. *That's why*.

58

THIS WAS THE END, RIGHT HERE, RIGHT NOW

"THE KEY CODE IS DIGITALLY PROGRAMMED TO CHANGE EVERY Sunday at midnight," Sinclair said. "Members get an automated text at two a.m. with new numbers for the week. So today is the last day for this particular sequence. Passing the code is forbidden, of course. But of all the days, Sunday is the safest. Least possible harm done."

Except to you, I thought. "But that's not why you gave it to him."

"No. I gave it to him because he has compromising information about me and my late wife and threatened to share it with the *New York Times* and *USA Today* and *Sixty Minutes* and so on if I didn't meet him to discuss the lawsuit."

"Lawsuit?"

"He wants us to drop it."

"Us?"

We were in the bar, which was magnificent, elegant, rugged, and macho to the max. Dark wood and bamboo. Plush leather furniture. Massive black-and-white framed photos of Africa and Armory Hunt Club safaris. Guns on the walls. This was where big-game hunters, for whom confidentiality was sacrosanct, felt comfortable drinking expensive bourbon and telling tales of their adventures. A secret society, no doubt.

Fu was checking to see if Moore was already here. It was just me and Sinclair and the elephant in the room, so to speak.

"Ronnie, Mickey, Phillip, and me," Sinclair said. "We were jointly suing him for malpractice and extortion. He stands to lose a significant amount of money, his various board certifications and licenses, his reputation, and quite possibly his freedom."

"Jail time?"

"Phillip was insistent that Marcus go to prison for what he did, was doing, and intended to do to us."

"They're all dead."

"Yes."

"Why, Mr. Sinclair? What did he do to all of you?"

He shook his head as if to say, *Sorry, this is not something I'm comfortable talking about.* A deeply private man with profoundly private pain. I imagined these were feelings he'd never shared with anyone but his friends. Not friends. Fellow grievers who'd probably shared their secrets as well. And Dr. Marcus Moore. It took a moment for Sinclair to decide to tell me. He started to speak, but Fu stepped into the bar, interrupting him midbreath.

"Fu hear loading-dock door. Killer come now."

It was eleven thirty-five. I'd imagined Moore might get here early to settle himself before Sinclair arrived, and I'd been right.

"Get him out of here, Fu. Put Mr. Sinclair in a cab and come back for me. I'll be on the second floor."

Fu took Sinclair by the arm in a way that left no question as to whether or not the man was getting in a cab. I'd swapped my jacket for his overcoat and baseball cap, my hair tucked up and under. I'd been right about his general size and shape. He was slender and fit and not much bigger than me.

Fu moved Sinclair to the door but stopped and turned back to me. "Have gun?"

I held up my father's Colt. "Yes."

"Shoot killer before killer shoot you."

"Good idea."

Then Fu and Sinclair were gone, hurrying to an exit at the back of the building.

I should call Logan, I thought. But I knew I wasn't going to. It was too late for that—literally and emotionally. It had been me and Moore from the beginning, since he'd murdered my father at the end of July. Me and Moore at Stony's Tudor. Me and Moore on Joe Shepherd's boat. Me and Moore at Jack Lowe's Connecticut horse farm. Me and Moore in the subway. Me and Moore in Harlem at Dawn. Me and Moore at the Wild Wooly Ranch. It had to be me and Moore at the Armory Hunt Club. One way or the other, it had to be me and him at the end. And if *women's intuition* meant a goddamn thing, mine was screaming this was the end. Right here, right now.

I moved into the main room of the club, the Great Hall. Sinclair had turned on only a few lights so it was dusky, just enough light for me to see what I was dealing with, what kind of place it was. One word came to mind: *breathtaking*.

The Great Hall, the heart and soul of the Armory Hunt Club, was the general size and shape of a professional hockey rink. Oval. Wide. Long. There were many rooms off the hall— bar, kitchen, offices, storage, taxidermy, security, operations— but it was hard to concentrate on them because the Great Hall itself was so overwhelming, so commanding. Half a dozen thoughtfully positioned sitting areas (as if the cavernous space were a huge, swank, masculine hunting lodge lobby) surrounded on all sides by countless big-game trophies, *hundreds* of wild animals on display.

If it could be hunted in Africa, it was here in the Great Hall in multiples. Not one African buffalo but ten. Two thousand pounds apiece. Massive, majestic creatures. A herd. Facing off with a pride of lions. Leopards. Cheetahs. Tigers. Black panthers. Rhinos. Elephants. Hippos. Giraffes. Zebras. Wildebeests. Warthogs. All shapes and sizes and species of apes and monkeys. A clan of hyenas laughing at the irony of a hunt club such as this existing in the city of New York, home to eight million of the wildest animals anywhere.

Antelopes of all kinds, a hundred or more—kudu, sable, nyala, roan, impala, gemsbok, springbok, waterbuck, bushbuck. Such elegant animals, with their glorious horns, gracefully spiraled and curved, or straight as swords and sharp as razors. I was taken by a dozen or more gemsbok positioned midway in the hall and toward the far side. Horns three feet long. Deadly, resplendent spears.

The second floor was an interior balcony with many more trophies and guns and such on display. It went around the oval like a running track, the center wide open, so that members standing by the rail could look down onto the first floor or up to the domed armory ceiling, which rose sixty feet from the Great Hall floor.

And that's where Moore had instructed Sinclair to wait for him. On the balcony. In front of the silverback.

I pulled Sinclair's baseball cap down low, put my hands in his overcoat pockets—my right hand gripping Jimmy's Colt—and walked across the Great Hall as if I was the grieving, reclusive, big-game hunting, electrical engineer about to sue the shit out of Dr. Scumbag Marcus Moore.

I was a professional actor. I'd watched how Sinclair walked, how he held his hands in his pockets, the bend of his elbows, his posture, the jut of his jaw. I knew his pain, his sense of loss. Not exactly, of course, but enough to internalize it, to make it a physical part of his presence in me. From the bottom of my feet to the center of my soul, I was Stewart Sinclair.

There were two sets of stairs—one at the top of the oval

(twelve o'clock) and one at the bottom (six o'clock). The bar was closer to six, so I took the twelve o'clock stairs so I could cross the Great Hall. In this dusky light, if Moore was watching me wind my way through the leather armchairs and sofas, the bamboo coffee tables, the Tiffany lamps and wild animals, he would think nothing was wrong with this picture. Sinclair was on his way to the balcony to die. That's what he would think. I knew otherwise. So I would have the advantage.

The silverback gorilla stood midway on the south side of the building (three o'clock), so I turned right and walked a quarter of the way down the balcony. All around the fifteen-foot-wide track were smaller, more private, more secluded sitting areas—perhaps for hunters planning their next African expeditions. But just like the Great Hall main floor, there were trophies everywhere, artfully posed and positioned.

I arrived at the silverback. An extraordinary male. Enormous. Six and a half feet tall. Close to five hundred pounds. Regal in stature. Impossibly powerful. One of nature's most imposing creatures.

I hate hunting, I thought. What could possibly possess someone to kill an animal this magnificent? What joy could be found in the moment of its death? What sense of accomplishment could there be? Armed with high-powered hunting rifles and long-range scopes, the animal would have no chance. The hunt was fixed. Fish in a barrel.

I hate guns, I thought. I couldn't imagine shooting another living thing. Except Marcus Moore. I would make an exception for that murdering son of a bitch. I would shoot him in the fucking face without blinking.

If it was Moore.

He would announce himself—*Thank you for coming, Stewart*—and I would know the voice in a heartbeat, know he was the one who'd shot Jimmy in the eyes.

In one sweeping motion, I'd pull the Colt from Sinclair's overcoat pocket, spin around, and blow him away.

I gripped the gun. I'd been chasing my father's killer for four months. He'd been taunting me, mocking me, daring me, using me, belittling me the entire time. I'd nearly had him on the subway platform. Hit him solid in the jaw. But I'd lost him then. I'd lost him every time since the end of July. He'd always been a step or two ahead. But not this time. This time I'd shoot *his* eyes out.

See how he likes it, I said to myself and felt tears coming. I took a breath. *Get your shit together, Kate.*

"Take your hands slowly out of your pockets, Stewart, and hold them straight out at your sides, like Jesus on the cross. Hold the gun by its barrel. Yes, I know you have a gun in your right pocket," a voice behind me said.

Not *a* voice.

The voice.

"Don't turn around. Easy out of the pocket and out to the side. I'm armed and pointing my weapon at your back. It's a fully automatic Glock 18, so I'll put a dozen rounds in you before you inhale your last breath. And as tempting as that is, I prefer to handle the end of our relationship another way."

I pulled my hands out of my pockets. Held them straight out to the sides. Gripped the Colt by the barrel.

"Now drop the gun."

I did.

"Without turning around, kick it into the shadows."

I kicked the Colt ten feet down the balcony.

"Now, Stewart, arms still outstretched, turn and look at me."

I'd never seen the killer's face before. In each confrontation, he'd worn a ski mask. But I'd seen a picture of Dr. Marcus Moore in the Meridian staffing files.

It was him.

The Glock was pointed at my chest. A thick rope tied into a

noose and a large, neatly folded blue tarp were at his feet. He stood at the rail, his back to it. I was eight feet away from him, in front of the silverback.

His mouth fell open. "Little Engine."

"Fuck you, Moore."

He composed himself and even laughed. "I'm impressed."

"I don't give a shit. Until you're dead. Then I'll give a shit."

"Of course you will."

I gestured down at the rope and the tarp. "You had plans for Sinclair. Sorry to mess them up."

"That is unfortunate. I detest loose ends."

"I detest you."

"Grade-school attitude to the end."

"Logan knows it's you."

"Yes, he had his task force parked at my West Side penthouse. Fortunately, I don't live there, so he was Wrong-Way Corrigan again, as I anticipated and planned for. But you, Little Engine. You are, if not smarter, more resourceful than you appear."

"And you're more fucked. Sinclair is safe. He'll take the lawsuit public, and your reputation will be ruined for the rest of time. You'll be broke and shamed. Licenses revoked. Not that it will matter. By tomorrow, your face will be on every law-enforcement screen in the country. You'll spend the rest of your life in prison."

"By tomorrow, I'll be in a foreign land with a new persona. But you, Little Engine, will be dead. So who is truly more fucked in this scenario? Who is the *most* fucked as our tragic relationship comes to its inevitable end?"

"What kind of sick motherfucker abuses and extorts his grieving patients to the point of a lawsuit?"

"Not sick, Little Engine. *Particular.* I'm particular about human behavior and my reactions to it. These soft, emotionally feeble men deserved nothing less than abuse for their constitutional weakness. Extortion was simply an easily understood manifestation of such abuse."

"Grieving is not weakness. It's human nature."

"That definition does not change the fact of its weakness. And frailty, in all its many expressions, is disaffirmed by strength."

"Abuse is not strength."

"He said, she said, etcetera, ad infinitum. As usual, I grow tired of you after a few moments. Shall we get on with it?"

My heart raced. How could I have been so close and still so far away? I'd beaten him to the spot and still lost. Tears threatened again. I wanted to tell Jimmy how sorry, how profoundly wrecked and wretched I was to have failed to avenge him. But Jimmy was dead. Murdered by Moore. There was no one for me to tell. I was stuck with my own self-pity.

"What's with the rope and the tarp?" I said.

"Can you imagine a more fitting death for such a psychologically fragile man? Hung by the neck from the balcony rail in his literal inner sanctum to symbolize his internal emotional insolvency, eyes shot out of his head to signify his lack of vision?"

"I've never been so happy to rain on someone's parade."

"Same sarcastic spew as your father. Nothing more than a deflection of fear in each case."

My anger boiled up. "Not fear, douchebag. Rage."

He tossed me the tarp. "Let's put an end to that, shall we? Plans change, Little Engine. Mine, yours, Stewart's, everyone's. Adaptation is the one constant of nature. Rage is among its ugliest exemplifications. Open the tarp in front of the silverback and lie down on it. Face up, please."

"So you can shoot my eyes out and then hang me from the rail?"

"There's a weakness to you I find repulsive. Stewart's fate fits you fine."

I dropped the tarp and kicked it away. "Fuck you."

"No problem, Little Engine. We'll do it your way."

He aimed the gun at my face. I was past tears. Past fear. Past everything.

"Take this to your grave, Moore. I got here first. I beat you in the end."

"You have a curious definition of victory. And of the end. This is not the end for me, Little Engine. It's the end for—"

He looked to his right.

I looked too.

Fu charged toward us like a wild animal, a mad bull, an enraged rhino, flying down the oval.

Moore froze.

I froze too, stunned again by how fast and graceful and powerful Fu was.

Five o'clock. Four o'clock.

Moore snapped out of it and shifted the Glock onto Fu, refocused his aim and squeezed the trigger.

But as he did that, I ran forward, smashed into his chest, and we both tumbled over the balcony rail.

Like Olympic divers, we did a one eighty with a twist in midair, and the world spun out of control. Up was down. Down was up. Left was right. Right was left. I lost myself in space and time. I lost Moore.

And then, *bang*, I crashed into something hard on my left side, something that gave way, and then I hit the ground with a thud.

I was woozy but conscious. I assessed my ribs, my back, my shoulders, my neck, my hips, knees, arms, and legs. It hurt to breathe, but that I was still breathing was a good sign. No blood. No overpowering pain. I decided nothing was broken and gave myself a talking-to.

Stand up, Kate. He's getting away.

Somehow—I didn't know how—I got to my hands and knees, opened my eyes, and forced myself to find my bearings.

I was in the herd of gemsbok. I'd smashed into one of the animals, who'd broken my fall in the luckiest way and saved me from a far worse fate.

I forced myself to stand. My entire left side hurt, but I reminded myself nothing was busted or crushed or shattered.

Where is he? He'd gotten away again. I was sure of it.

But I was wrong.

Four feet away, Dr. Marcus Moore had been less lucky than me.

Moore had been impaled by two gemsbok horns that had pierced his chest like African spears. He was face up, arms and legs dangling. Blood leaked from his mouth and nose. He was sixty seconds from death. But he wasn't dead yet. And he was conscious. His face filled with incredulity, pain, and blood.

I took two steps to him, leaned close and said, "That's for my father, you scumbag piece of shit. And my name's not Little Engine. It's Kate. Kate McCall. I'm Jimmy McCall's daughter, and I got you, motherfucker. I got you for Jimmy."

I locked my eyes on his. He blinked twice, and then he died.

59

WHAT WAS IS, WHAT IS WAS

I was crying like a baby by the time Fu got to me. Aside from when I'd first found out about Jimmy's murder, I don't think I'd ever been so overwhelmed with emotion in my entire life. Everything that had happened since the end of July rolled into one wild, hysterical ball in one crazy, culminating moment. Vengeance had been sweet for all of a minute, and then the hole in my heart that was *Jimmy Gone Forever* had reappeared, to be decidedly unfilled for the rest of time, since there was nothing and no one left for me to avenge. The emptiness in my soul since my father's death was still there even *after* Moore's murder-by-gemsbok. I'd known deep down it would be, of course, but chasing Moore had been about as complete a distraction from that pain as possible. Now, there was nothing to divert my attention. Now, I would have to live with my loss.

Fu checked Moore, lifeless on the horns, then looked at me. "Killer dead."

"I'd say so."

"You not dead."

"I'm alive."

"Why cry?"

I bawled and bawled. "I'm so sad."

"Fu know what feel."

"You do?"

"Fu know first."

And then the smirk that came with the smartass remark. It was like a cold bucket of water in the face when you're fast asleep in the saddest dream you've ever had.

"You couldn't possibly know how I would feel when I finally got him before I finally got him and felt what I'm feeling. You're a lot of things, but my personal mystic philosopher psychologist is not one of them. You don't know what I feel before I feel it."

"What was is, what is was."

"What does that even mean? What kind of crazy thing is that to say to me at a time like this? Why in the world would you say something like that?"

He reached out and gently wiped the tears from my face. "No more cry."

I hadn't even realized I'd stopped crying. On top of that, I thought I might not cry again for a long time. I didn't really understand why I felt that way. Maybe Fu was telling me there were distractions unknown coming my way. Maybe he was telling me my pain was universal and the mitigation of it would be as well. Who really knew about the secrets of the emotional universe as told by an exiled Chinese-mob assassin? I realized there might be one and only one explanation: *What was is, what is was.*

"No more," I said.

"Fu say good."

And then I threw my arms around his neck and hugged him. He hugged me too. I would never be able to tell him how much he meant to me.

"I have to call Logan now," I said as our embrace ended.

"Fu know first."

This time there was no snark. This time we both smiled.

"He's going to bring the task force," I said. "You can't be here."

Fu nodded. Turned to leave, then spun back to me. "Owe Fu more parrot."

"What? Why?"

"Fu save life."

"You didn't save my life. I saved your life. If anybody owes anybody a parrot, pal, you owe me one."

He held my eyes for a long time, and I realized he'd set me up.

"Fu say yes. You take Joe."

And just like that I knew. We were coming to the end. Maybe this was goodbye, or maybe it wasn't, but goodbye was close at hand, no doubt.

I took a sad, resigned breath. "Yes, Fu. I'll take Joe."

He nodded and walked across the Great Hall toward the exit. "Fu know you say that."

"I knew first," I said.

He laughed out loud, and then he was gone.

I finally got the last word, I thought as I dialed Logan's number.

The task force arrived at the armory like, as Logan might say, the Seventh Fleet. Logan looked at Moore's body, still hanging from the horns, dead as Dillinger, and claimed a seating area in the center of the hall as his home base for the hunt-club finale.

Jesse sat me on a sofa near the guilty gemsbok, where I was checked and cleared by the paramedics and then interviewed by a long line of detectives, forensic specialists, and other investigative task-force team members who did I had no idea what. I told them all the same story, which was mostly true—except for the part about Fu. I left Fu out. Fu would remain a mystery. Sinclair would, of course, mention the large Chinese man who'd stopped him flat with a hand to the chest and then later escorted him to a cab. But my take was I'd met a random Chinese linebacker on the street and asked him to help me because, well, I'd needed help.

When the last detective had questioned me to his satisfaction, Jesse escorted me to Logan's hunt-club living room and put me in a chair across a bamboo coffee table from the head of the task force himself. Cops came and went with alacrity and focus. The no-nonsense end of the hunt had happened at the hunt club and all hands were on deck.

Good thing because there was a ton of cleaning up to do— reports to write, explanations to explain, models to manifest, notions to actualize, theories to substantiate. Logan was on a hyperdrive investigative loop—giving information and updates, answering questions, and issuing orders. Detectives continued on and commenced apace with the dusting for prints, the measuring of measurements, and other investigative practices and procedures that blended and blurred and mixed and melded into one long episode of *Law & Order*—on which I was the special guest star.

"I should be satisfied and grateful, McCall," Logan said.

"Satisfied and grateful at the least. Satisfied and grateful should be your starting line, Logan. Over the moon and indebted to me is where you should be striving."

"But instead I'm aggravated and frustrated you didn't take him alive."

"You're going to have to get over that. Just like me."

He looked at me a long time, and then nodded. "Don't press your luck, McCall. I ran out of patience with you back in July. I have no trouble throwing you under the bus with the following headline: *Renegade Amateur PI Guilty of Douchebag's Death by Deer.*"

"You're going to have to charge the gemsbok with that one, I'm afraid."

"He got the job done, I'll tell you that."

"He did indeed."

"I'll read your statements, make an assessment, and reach out if I think you're full of shit."

"You always think I'm full of shit."

"There's a reason for that."

"Which is?"

"You're always full of shit."

Jesse stepped into Logan's living room and held up the Colt. "Lew."

Logan looked at the gun, looked at me, looked at the gun, looked at me, and shook his head in disbelief and despair. "You've got to be fucking kidding me."

"It's in the report, Logan," I said. "Full disclosure."

"Full can of crap more like it," Logan said.

"What do you want me to do with it?" Jesse said.

Logan glanced my way and caught me checking my watch. "Am I keeping you from something, McCall?"

"In fact, you are," I said.

"Private-investigation related?"

"In fact, it is," I said.

"You going to tell me what further nonsense you have planned in my city?"

"In fact, I'm not," I said, and held out my hand. "May I have my gun, please?"

"Take McCall to the Thirteenth and lock her up," Logan said. "We'll deal with her and her omnipresent gun tomorrow, when this mess is settled."

"You're arresting me?"

"Since the summer, it's what I do."

"On what charge?"

"Inconceivable innocence."

"No such thing."

"Just made it up."

"I'll call Shavelson," I said, though it would be as unpleasant for me as for Logan.

"You can't call him," Logan said, "on account of it being Sunday. Because as the Good Book says in the King's English, *And then, lo and behold, God created Mel Shavelson on Saturday and said to the people, Fuck it. Everybody, including Me, especially Me, gets a break from this smokestack asshole prick on Sundays.*"

"Okay, okay," I said. "If you're going to bring God into it, someone may or may not try to murder my client tonight, and I have to be there to guard his body, which is what a bodyguard does, in case you were wondering."

"You talking about Rick Gotti?" Logan said.

"He hired me," I said.

"I remember," Logan said.

"Gottiguard," Jesse said.

"Funny," I said and stood up. "So can I have my gun now?"

Jesse looked at Logan, who exhaled a long, exasperated breath, nodded, and then turned his head to me. "Does your brain not work at all?"

60

THEY COULD SHOOT ME BEFORE I GO ON

LOGAN DID NOT ARREST ME FOR INCONCEIVABLE INNOCENCE, though I was probably guilty of it, so I left the hunt club and drove the White Whale back to the House of Emotional Tics. I parked on 82nd, walked around the block to the brownstone, stepped into my living room, looked at Rick, and checked my watch. Thirty minutes until we had to be at Victor Vreeland's Comedy Camp Cornucopia.

Early that morning, well before Fu and I had left for the hunt club, I'd told Rick the plan I'd planned before I'd passed out. He was still reworking his index cards accordingly but was otherwise ready to go.

He kissed me hello but was preoccupied. Concern on his face. Disquiet in his voice.

"It's either the last performance for the rest of my life or the first performance of the rest of my life."

"Could be both," I said, trying to cheer him up, continuing to my walk-through closet. "Last show for this chapter. First show of the next chapter."

"Could be neither," he called out. "They could shoot me before I go on."

"Or I could shoot them," I called back.

"You're a terrible shot, and you don't like guns," he said.

I chose a stylish pants suit (charcoal gray with matching lacy T-shirt under the jacket) because I didn't want to be wearing a gown if I had to move fast or punch someone in the nose but still wanted to look like a woman Rick Gotti would fall for and propose to. I sat at my vintage vanity, put on the blonde wig with the heavy bangs, slipped in the green contact lenses, slid on the five-carat, hand-cut, hand-polished cubic zirconia engagement ring to make your eyes pop, and said hello to Jennifer Lily Lane.

We got to the club an hour before the guests were scheduled to arrive. A fleet of Pinnacle trucks was parked out front near a convoy of local and national TV news vans. The NYPD was here. As were the paparazzi. They were all over Rick. He wasn't in the mood to be famous. I didn't blame him.

Inside, a small crew of Comedy Camp staffers bustled about, fine-tuning last-minute minutiae while a full platoon of Pinnacle servers, cooks, bartenders, and supervisors set the room for the Thanksgiving feast of the year. Pinnacle boss and D-Cup alumnus Melissa Kinneman was on-site and had come through in a big way. I don't mean managing the transformation of Victor's club into the coolest dining room in the city, although she'd done that in spades. I mean I noticed no fewer than fifteen Schmidt and Parker Players working the event— including Dennis and Posey employed as servers and Big Black Bald Bart arranging bottles of booze behind the bar. There was something satisfying about seeing a six-foot,-ten-inch power forward working as an undercover bartender, but there wasn't time to explore what it was. I made a mental note to circle back and put my finger on it.

I needed eyes in the room, which was why I'd called Dennis and Posey on Saturday and asked them to see if Melissa could put some Schmidt and Parker Players on her Cornucopia catering crew. But Sunday morning, after I'd told Rick the plan I'd planned to save his life *and* clear his name, I'd called Dennis and Posey and told *them* the plan I'd planned. I said they had to get it done in a day or it would be curtains for the stripper musical they were currently crafting for Rick and me to star in because Rick would either be dead or in prison for murdering Kenny Cochran. Dennis had said there were no better—or at least no faster—producers anywhere in the city, so not only could they do it, but Posey was already on the phone making it happen. I'd told Dennis I'd get Shavelson on board for legal backup. Of course, later that afternoon Logan had explained God's rule regarding Sundays and Mel Shavelson. I wish I'd known that morning when I'd dialed Shavelson's number.

I had no idea if the plan I'd planned would go as planned, but Melissa was in on it, as were the D-Cup actors, who'd been prepped by Posey prior to assuming their positions. Actors all, they knew how to play their parts. Meaning none of them, not one, gave me a second look. I was on Rick Gotti's arm wearing a ring that could sink a ship, so I must have been his new fiancée. So what? No big deal. Good for her, whoever she is.

A Comedy Camp talent coordinator escorted Rick and me backstage to the dressing room, which hadn't been updated in forty years of shows. *Hellhole* was too kind a description. *Cramped* and *dark* and *dank* were other words that came to mind, but they seemed laughable and lacking.

Rick opened his bag and pulled out Jimmy's bulletproof vest. "Maybe nothing happens."

"Maybe something does. Better safe, Rick. I think that's a lesson we've learned, don't you?"

"I'll put it on after dinner."

I shut and locked the door. "Until then, no one in or out."

An hour passed in a minute or maybe a month. I could feel it in my blood that Victor was taking Rick out tonight. Not Victor himself, of course. Maybe the bear or the pig or some new mammal yet to appear in the play. Rick would be a sitting duck on the stage in the spotlight. My mind raced with dark thoughts. I texted back and forth with Dennis and Posey to make sure all points were on point.

It'll happen when Rick's alone onstage, I group texted.

Red lights flashing, Dennis texted back.

Sirens screaming, Posey texted back.

Actors. Why be dramatic when you can be melodramatic?

Puzzle pieces in place? I texted.

Working on it, Dennis texted back.

Deal's not done until it's done, Posey texted back.

What does that mean? I texted.

Some puzzle pieces are more puzzling than others, Dennis texted back.

Some days need twenty-five hours, Posey texted back.

Is this one of those days? I texted.

Too soon to know, Dennis texted back.

There's always hope, Posey texted back.

Whatever will be will be, Dennis texted.

The future's not ours to see, Posey texted.

Que Será, Será, they both texted.

jfc, I texted.

Rick was mostly quiet, though he did call Dee to find out how the girls were doing. They were fine and dandy. I could hear them yelling and cheering in the background for Uncle Rick to break a leg. One of them, maybe Isabella, gave a shout-out to me. And then they were all shouting out to me. I was in with the nieces. If I wasn't so nervous about someone shooting Rick in the head tonight, I might have done a dance or pumped my fist.

And then the hour was over and a Comedy Camp staffer knocked on the locked dressing-room door. "Victor's ready for you. The room is full, dinner is served."

As was longstanding Cornucopia tradition, Rick, the comedian du jour, had been invited and was expected to dine with Victor at Victor's VIP front-row center table. Because I was the fiancée, that invitation had been extended to me as well.

It was a table for four—actually, it was a table for six but Victor, in tux, tails, and top hat, took up three seats. The fourth guest was Ruby Gold.

I hadn't seen Ruby since she'd been whisked away after the bear shot Rick at her Silvercup pilot. She'd been beautiful and impressive then, but tonight she was regal and majestic in all the ways a living legend queen of comedy could and should be. Her gown sparkled. Her eyes shined. She was bedecked and bejeweled from head to toe.

She remained seated as Rick and I arrived at Victor's table and apologized for the horrible set of circumstances at the pilot, saying she'd never felt worse about anything in her whole long, storied life. She reached for my hand and gave it an emotional squeeze. I apologized for accusing her of shooting Rick in the chest as her handlers handled her off the set. We shared a phony theatric smile and told each other it was water under the bridge. Showbiz bygones.

Victor was Victor times two. He lifted his huge bulk to welcome us and smiled at me. "Are you armed?"

"No," I said, returning his smile. "My fiancé says I can't be trusted with weapons around waiters."

We all had a good laugh at that one. Though Rick laughed in a way that couldn't quite hide the fact he knew weird, bad shit was coming down the pike.

Throughout dinner, Broadway bigwigs, Hollywood heroes, Wall Street heavyweights, kings of comedy, professional athletes, runway supermodels, and a steady stream of fans and friends stopped by Victor's table to give thanks, gawk and fawn over Ruby Gold, and wish Rick luck. Between genuflections, the four of us chatted about nothing. How fabulous the food was, how on point the service was, how beautiful the room was, how impressive the crowd was, how gorgeous my ring was, how delighted Victor and Ruby were by our engagement, how fortunate we all were to be in this particular place at this moment in time. The drinks flowed. The food kept coming.

And coming.

And coming.

Victor drank three full bottles of wine, downed four bowls of roasted acorn squash soup, consumed five overflowing plates of turkey and fixings, and devoured an entire apple pie, half a pecan pie, half a pumpkin pie, two pints of vanilla ice cream, four double espressos, and four double sambucas. It was the most effortless and stunning display of gluttony I'd ever witnessed—and I'd eaten dinner with him at Oxbow Tavern, which had been the record holder until tonight.

In the end, we all gave thanks and toasted our great good luck at being happy and healthy and, okay, a little bit rich and famous. Except for Rick, who was more than a little bit famous, and Ruby, who was a whole hell of a lot famous.

Of course, the lifelong friends didn't know *I* knew they were lifelong friends. And that they were a *little bit rich* wasn't nearly the truth, the whole truth, and nothing but the truth. Then again, they also didn't know I wasn't Jennifer Lily Lane, Rick Gotti's fiancée.

As dinner ended, the dishes were cleared, and coffee and drinks were replenished. Victor took the stage and presented Rick with the traditional Comedy Camp Cornucopia Silver Platter, a large, oval, heavy-as-hell, real-deal silver-plated platter engraved with Rick's name, an artist's rendering of a pilgrim's cornucopia overflowing with Thanksgiving fare, the Comedy Camp logo, and Victor's sprawling signature. Victor had given such a platter to every Cornucopia host throughout the event's history. The Presenting of the Platter was a long-standing ritual that involved Victor welcoming his guests as an ensemble to his humble holiday shindig, fast and furious flashbulb photography, and a preset standing ovation for Rick. The Presenting of the Platter was the official signal that dinner was over and the show was about to begin.

With his arm around Rick, Victor made a joke that in his club, comedians were innocent until proven guilty...or until they died onstage. It was all at once a comment on Rick's legal predicament, a well-worn show-business joke, and a precognition of the near future.

Everyone laughed but me.

61

RICK WAS A DEAD MAN IN THREE, TWO—

RUBY SAID TO BREAK A LEG, VICTOR SAID TO KNOCK 'EM DEAD, and I accompanied Rick backstage as the lights dimmed and the club buzzed with excitement. If I had to pick one word to describe the vibe between us, that word would be *intense*.

"People in place?" Rick said.

"People in place," I said.

"And the puzzle?"

"Wait for the high sign."

I knew that wasn't an answer. He knew that wasn't an answer. But it was too late to say more because a Comedy Camp staffer was onstage and the microphone was hot.

"Ladies and gentlemen, put your hands together for the one, the only, *Welcome to the Jungle* Rick Gotti!"

Three hundred fifty people, boozy with Victor's booze, feasty with Victor's feast, rose to their feet and whooped and hollered as Rick took center stage.

I was backstage right wing, leaning against a wall, silver platter at my feet. I could see Rick in the spotlight and maybe one or two tables deep into the club. Meaning I could also see Victor and Ruby. The rest of the room was dark, and the stage lights were too bright and glary to see beyond. Chloe appeared at my side. As planned, one of Melissa's Pinnacle people on the back door had let her in.

"How did you do?" I said.

"She's in the dressing room," Chloe said.

I nodded. "What about Roger?"

"On his way."

"Alone?"

"With company."

"And the others?"

"Coming to a club near you."

"All of them?"

"That's the word."

"Good to know. I'm going to work the club. Put them in the dressing room and keep them there until it's time. You're in charge of the dressing room. You and Roger."

"Like second assistant directors?"

"Why is that important?"

"I'm going to put it on my resume. You never know."

That was especially true of Chloe. "You never do."

I went into the club and cruised the shadows, eyes everywhere all at once, looking for someone to make a move, reach into a pocket, open a purse. I made eye contact with Dennis and Posey. I shared a look with Big Black Bald Bart. He was a hell of a bartender, for what it's worth. His tip jar was jammed with tens and twenties. (I guess that's what it was worth.) I gave a grateful nod to the other Schmidt and Parker Players, who went about their catering business but were on alert for suspicious behavior. If something went down, we might just catch it before it went all the way down.

Rick was killing it on the Comedy Camp stage. Smooth and nasty and cutting and funny as shit. Nothing but jokes and laughter for twenty-five solid minutes.

And then what I thought might happen happened.

I was at the end of the bar closest to the stage. From there I could see the whole floor and Rick in the spotlight. At the other end of the bar, the bear was on the move.

"That's him," I said to Bart. "That's the bear."

"I got you," Bart said.

"Wait for a big laugh," I said.

"Don't leave me hanging, Little Rick," Bart said as he moved down the bar toward the bear.

Midbar, Bart waved him over and gestured for him to lean in—to discuss some kind of bar business, I guess, though it doesn't much matter. When a six-ten bartender flags you down, you lean in no matter what kind of business he wants to discuss.

Just as the bear was moving in to Bart, Rick landed a punchline that made the room roar. At that moment, Bart grabbed the back of the bear's head like he was palming a basketball and slammed his forehead into the rounded edge of the bar. Not so hard as to kill the bear or even knock him out, but definitely hard enough to make him way wobbly in the knees.

Bart nodded my way, I moved over to them, and together we escorted the bear, like a drunken bum, backstage, where we gagged him, blindfolded him, zip-tied his hands behind his back, and deposited him in the dressing room, where Chloe was second AD in charge.

I knew everyone in the dressing room, all of whom had been coerced to attend the event—some, but not all, against their will. I would owe Shavelson big. Unfortunate peripheral damage. Anyway, I was one puzzle piece short.

"Roger?" I said to Chloe.

"Parking."

"Perfect."

That's when I saw the bulletproof vest on the dressing-room table. With everything whirling and swirling around us, Rick had forgotten to put it on before taking the stage. I'd forgotten to remind him.

Shit. Double shit.

I returned to my position backstage right, waiting for word from Chloe that Roger had arrived with his guest so I could give Rick the high sign...when the pig appeared backstage left. He took out his gun and aimed it at Rick.

I froze. After all the planning and finagling and wriggling and wrangling and threatening and pleading, after all that, I was in the wrong place at the wrong time.

Rick was a dead man in three, two—

And then there was Roger, who'd made the most fortuitous backstage wrong turn in the history of backstage wrong turns. Instead of being on my side of the stage, he'd swerved the other way and ended up in the wing with the pig.

It would have been the best luck ever except Roger froze as well. Guns will do that to you was something I'd learned along the way.

Which meant the end of the road for Rick.

All of this took half a blink. But before the other half—the tragic half—could happen, Wendy Bell took a gun out of her purse, put the barrel on the back of the pig's head, and whispered something in his ear. The pig lowered his arm without turning around, and Wendy, with her six-seven leverage (six-nine in her go-go boots) took his gun and whacked him on top of the head with it.

The pig crumpled. Roger caught him under the arms.

Blink of an eye.

Wendy smiled and waved at me, holding both guns. I waved back and gestured for them to come around to my side of backstage. Wendy put the guns in her purse, and she and Roger carried the pig together.

Statuesque isn't a big enough word for Wendy Bell. Resplendent doesn't do her justice either. She was clubbed out for action. Fire-engine-red micro-mini skirt with a skintight, burnt-orange turtleneck top. Deep-red, blunt-cut bob wig. Blinding-white go-go boots with two-inch heels. Diamonds on the souls of her shoes. Like the Paul Simon song. She showed them to me. Actual freaking diamonds.

"I love Rhymin' Simon," she said. "Forest Hills boy."

Diamonds everywhere, in fact, because, as she'd explained over massive martinis, diamonds were the new black.

I told her she knew me as Emma, but my real name was Kate, though tonight I was Jennifer, and I could never thank her enough for what she'd just done.

"I always carry a concealed weapon," she said, "because a girl like me can't be too careful. There's a name for that. Do you know what it is?"

I smiled and sent a Pinnacle person to the bar. "Tell Bart I need the biggest martini anyone has ever seen and to deliver it himself. Time to play the game for keeps."

"I will love you forever, Jennifer Emma Kate," Wendy said and went into the dressing room with the other folks.

Wendy Bell was the last piece of the puzzle. We would turn the tables on Victor Vreeland and Ruby Gold or we would die trying.

62

VICTOR VREELAND AND RUBY GOLD, THIS IS YOUR LIFE

Rick glanced my way, and I gave him the high sign. He nodded, smiled a determined smile, turned to the club crowd, and said, "Who wants to play a game?"

The Cornucopia campers were all in, cheering loud and strong. "*Yes, yes, play a game, play a game,*" they shouted.

"It's an old game, a classic game, a timeless game, an illuminating, enlightening, and entertaining game," Rick said. "A game whose very name begs the question: *Are you ready to have some freaking fun?*"

They *were* having fun, of course. The *most* fun. It was Thanksgiving, for Macy's sake, and Rick had them in the palm of his hand. And now they were ready to have even *more* fun. Some *freaking* fun.

"That's what I thought, you degenerate pilgrims," Rick said. "So without further ado, let's play...*Victor Vreeland and Ruby Gold, This is Your Life!*"

The club went bonkers. People pounding the tables, stomping their feet, howling and hooting. Crazy town.

"Victor, Ruby, stand up, face your fans, and take a bow," Rick said.

Front row. Center stage. Victor took Ruby's hand. They stood, and the crowd exploded. Ruby waved like the comedy goddess she was. Victor tipped his top hat and did a jig. Everyone was having the time of their lives.

Best. Thanksgiving. *Ever.*

Then Victor and Ruby took their seats and got ready for their happy, funny, delightful stroll down Memory Lane.

Like the late great Ralph Edwards, Rick pulled a thin stack of index cards from his pocket, and the game began.

"Let's go back," Rick said, "*way* back to when Victor and Ruby first met in Washington Heights, when they were five years old, when Ruby was Robin Goldmacher and Victor was already planning to rule the world."

The crowd *oohed* and *aahed*. So cute, so sweet. None of them had known any of this.

"They fast became best friends and soul mates and have stayed that way all their lives. Just how close were they? Just how close *are* they? Well, let's hear it from our first special guest. Ladies and gentlemen and decadent pilgrims, please welcome, all the way from Paramus, New Jersey, Victor's father…"

Chloe had escorted Augie from the dressing room to where I was standing, backstage right. Augie had a cane tonight. No wheelchair. He reeked of reefer.

"He keeps grabbing my butt," Chloe said.

"Keep your hands to yourself, Augie," I said.

"Girl's got a great ass," Augie said. "Got to grab it."

"…Augie Vreeland!" Rick said.

"That's your cue," I said.

Augie caned his way to center stage, where he bowed to the cheering crowd.

"They love you, Augie," Rick said.

"Everybody does," Augie said.

"Are you nervous?" Rick said.

"I'm ninety-six and stoned to the gills," Augie said. "No, I'm not nervous. Where do you think Victor got his gumption?"

"I'm guessing from you?" Rick said.

"Damn tootin' Isaac Newton," Augie said.

The crowd laughed. Victor smiled, but it wasn't sincere. His body language alone said he was mortified to see his father on the stage.

"So, Victor and Ruby. Just how close were they, Augie?" Rick said.

"Cut their palms with a Swiss army knife and put their bleeding hands together," Augie said. "Five years old. Connected by blood for the rest of time. That's how close."

"Would Victor do anything in the world for Ruby?" Rick said.

"Anything and everything," Augie said.

"Buy her flowers?" Rick said.

"Every rose in Rotterdam," Augie said.

"Sing her songs?" Rick said.

"A sides, B sides, all the sides," Augie said.

"Give her money?" Rick said.

"Millions and millions," Augie said.

Victor's fake smile dulled but didn't disappear. Ruby's smile froze on her face.

"Augie Vreeland, everyone," Rick said.

The crowd whooped and hollered as Augie exited stage left, where Bart waited to escort him to a Schmidt and Parker Players car that would deliver him pronto to the Belvedere Health and Rehabilitation Center, where he could smoke weed and grab ass for the rest of his days.

"Our next special guest is famous in her own right," Rick said.

Roger appeared at my side with Lillian Pearl. "She threatened to shoot me in the head. Says she should have done it when she had the chance."

"Tell her you'll kill her dog," I said, locking eyes with Lillian. "That shuts her up."

"I'm not happy about being here," Lillian said.

"Tell it to Shavelson," I said.

Here's what Jimmy had said about Mel Shavelson: *"Lawyers come in two kinds, Kate. One kind knows everyone, the other kind everyone knows. Shavelson's both. Nobody wants to know him, you understand, but they're connected to him in a way they wish they weren't and can't cancel the connection because he's such a goddamn tornado of a hurricane of a mess of a man. A dirt magnet. Knows every secret in the city, but you can't kill him because he's a human booby trap, with hidden tapes and secret files and private videos and access to every illegal, immoral thing you wish you never did. You just learn to live with him. Like bad breath or arthritis or plantar warts."*

Shavelson had told me he had dirt for days on Lillian Pearl, which was the only reason she was standing beside me.

"Ladies and gentlemen and ne'er-do-well pilgrims, please give a grand Comedy Camp welcome to the one and only Lillian Pearl," Rick said.

The crowd shouted and screamed and stamped their feet as Lillian Pearl put on a smile and walked across the stage to Rick.

Ruby's eyes opened wide. But her smile stayed in place like a pro.

"Lillian is helping Ruby write her autobiography, so she knows more about Ruby Gold than Ruby Gold knows about Ruby Gold," Rick said.

Lillian tried to smile at Ruby but couldn't quite pull it off because in the second row, two tables over, she laid eyes on Mel Shavelson. She glared at the disheveled attorney for the longest five seconds in recorded history. Shavelson returned her glare with a glorious one-finger salute.

Maybe I can learn to live with him, I thought. *No, no I definitely can't. Scratch that. No way.*

"Ruby and Victor, two peas in a pod but not romantically involved?" Rick said.

"They loved and *still* love each other heart and soul, but Victor is a man's man, so to speak, and so Ruby had, shall we say, lovers elsewhere," Lillian said.

"Lovers like Kenny Cochran?" Rick said.

"Yes," Lillian said.

"Kenny Cochran and Ruby Gold had a fling-thing?"

"Yes," Lillian said.

"You know I've been arrested for his murder?" Rick said.

"Everybody knows," Lillian said.

"I didn't do it," Rick said.

"Remains to be seen," Lillian said.

"True that," Rick said. "Tell us something about Ruby Gold that nobody knows. Tell us, for instance, how much money she has on hand."

Lillian looked at Ruby, Shavelson behind her, and folded, her voice nearly invisible. "None."

"What was that?" Rick said.

"Ruby Gold is broke," Lillian said.

The crowd gasped but then laughed and then roared, thinking it must be some kind of Comedy Camp Cornucopia joke.

"Lillian Pearl, everyone," Rick said.

Lillian exited stage left, where Bart waited. Victor stood. Ruby seemed too horrified to move.

"Ladies and gentlemen and perverted pilgrims, Victor Vreeland," Rick said.

Everyone cheered and cheered. But, as per part of the plan, there were so many people crammed in tight all around him, and with Victor being the size of Saturn, that there was simply no way to get out of the way, no path of escape. He was trapped in the front row. Not to mention Melissa had placed some of the bulkier Schmidt and Parker Players in the getaway path, and they weren't budging.

Victor waved at his crowd and took his seat. It was all he could do.

Chloe escorted Danny Boy Bailey to backstage right. He wore a brown suit, brown tie, brown shoes, and a brown bowler. All he needed was a tail and the world would think he was an extra-large rat.

"He says I could make bank dancing for Parties to Remember," Chloe said.

"Have you seen her dance?" I said to Danny Boy.

"Ruby Gold and Kenny Cochran...oh to be a fly on their boudoir wall," Rick said. "If only there were someone who knew them when, someone who knew them then. Well, it wouldn't be *This Is Your Life* if there wasn't that very someone waiting in the wings. Ladies and gentlemen and depraved pilgrims, say hello to Danny Boy Bailey."

Danny Boy took the stage. Rick let the crowd settle. "Danny Boy, how exactly did you know the loving couple?"

"Through Kenny, mostly. I was his racehorse guru. Hers too, on account of them being an item," Danny Boy said.

"Ruby Gold had a pining for the ponies?" Rick said.

"Kenny got her hooked," Danny Boy said.

"You gave them expert inside info for a wedge of their wagers?"

"It's what I do when I'm not booking strippers," Danny Boy said.

Class act, I thought. I imagined Ms. Gold was thinking the same because she turned a dark shade of, well, ruby.

"Were they big spenders?" Rick said.

"Seven figures," Danny Boy said. "Big in my book."

"They must have cleaned up," Rick said, "what with your expertise."

"Cleaned out more like it. Kenny, without my blessing, bet a bundle of Ruby's money with a Coney Island bookie and lost it all," Danny Boy said. "Which is why I warned him about Mad Mike the collector. 'Cause I got scruples."

"The scrupulous Danny Boy Bailey, everyone," Rick said, and the rodent exited stage left, where Bart had him covered.

There was applause and cheering, but it was less thunderous. As if the crowd was just a crumb concerned that maybe this game wasn't funny anymore even though it was still pretty funny because Rick was Rick.

I had no expectation of Paulie Crane playing the game and had indeed discounted him entirely. But Shavelson had contacted the old man who'd sold Crane two shoeboxes of classic Bowmans and Topps for pennies on the dollar, signed him on the spot as a client, and then threatened to sue Paulie into oblivion if Crane didn't play his part. At the same time, Shavelson knew another card seller with top-dollar shoeboxes that just might have Crane's name on them, which he'd dangled as a carrot to go along with the lawsuit stick.

"Full disclosure," Rick said as Crane arrived center stage, "I've been to Paulie's Coney Island pawn shop and had some flaming-hot baseball card conversations. Flaming being the key word for those conversations. Paulie Crane, everyone."

Applause. But with hesitation. What in the world was a Coney Island pawn-shop owner doing in a game called *Victor Vreeland and Ruby Gold, This Is Your Life*?

"See anyone you know sitting in the first row or two?" Rick said to Crane.

If he'd had a gun, Crane might have shot Rick right there on the stage for burning his cards. But Bart had patted him down when he arrived so he was gunless.

"Yes," Crane said. "I see someone I know."

Shavelson held up a baseball card and waved it at him.

"Ruby Gold," Crane said.

"How do you know her?" Rick said.

"She paid off Cochran's debt," Crane said. "Vig and all. Cash in a suitcase."

"But Ruby's broke. So where did she get a suitcase of cash?" Rick said half to Crane, half to the crowd, and half to Ruby and Victor.

"Do I look like her accountant?" Crane said.

"Ladies and gentlemen and reprobate pilgrims, if you need to hock your watch, you don't go to an accountant, you go to Coney Island. You go to…Paulie Crane, everyone," Rick said.

Confused applause. The game was strange and getting stranger.

It was about to get stranger still.

63

LET'S NOT LOITER ON
MEMORY LANE

"Is there an accountant in the house?" Rick said. "Hello. Calling all accountants. And if you happen to be Ruby's accountant, that would be aces. How about it, reprobate pilgrims? If we make enough noise, maybe Ruby Gold's accountant will crawl out of the woodwork and join me onstage."

Like every other law-enforcement enforcer in the city, Shavelson had a dump truck of dirt on Oscar K. Ricci but, again, like the rest of them, couldn't dig a shovel's worth.

"Can't touch him. Even for a client. One call from Ricci and I'll end up swimming with the fishes in Jamaica Bay," Shavelson had said Sunday morning when I was planning the plan.

"I'm not your client," I'd said.

"That's what Jimmy used to say," he'd said.

So I'd had to plan a plan within my plan to coerce Oscar K. Which I'd indeed done. I wasn't proud of snatching his ninety-five-year-old mother, Maria, off the street in front of the Ricci brownstone. And I wasn't proud of using her as a lever to move her mob-accountant son, but I'd done it before, so I did it again.

Roger and Chloe had done the snatching while I'd been

otherwise engaged at the hunt club. Posing as presenters for Publishers Clearing House Sweepstakes, they'd convinced Ricci's mother to open the brownstone door and accompany them to the "studio," where she could pose with the giant check that signified five thousand smackers a week for life. Back at the D-Cup, they'd fed her milk and cookies and treated her with kid gloves.

After an hour had passed, long enough for Oscar K. to get good and worried about his missing mother, they'd called him, told him they had Maria, and put her on the phone. She'd said she was having her best day ever, that she would see him tonight at the comedy club, and that some nice lady would call him with instructions.

I was the nice lady. After Ricci had threatened to have me murdered, he'd cried like a baby boy and said he'd do anything in the world to get her back.

And so here he was standing beside me, backstage right. The Armani suit, the crooked nose, the pock-marked skin, the meatpacker hands, the diamond pinky ring. Looking across the stage to the backstage left wing, where Big Black Bald Bart had his massive paw on Maria's tiny shoulder. Mama gave her boy a wave. Oscar K. fought back tears.

"Do your deal and Mama's all yours," I said as the Cornucopia crowd made just enough noise to bring Ruby's accountant out of the woodwork.

He murdered me with his eyes but nodded he understood.

"Then that's your cue, Mr. Ricci," I said.

Oscar K. smoothed his thinning hair, straightened his tie, and joined Rick onstage.

While Rick joked with the crowd and kept them glued to the game, I became conscious of the fact I wasn't the star of the show. It wasn't me center stage, center of attention, center of the universe. It was Rick. All eyes were on Rick. I was merely the writer-director. Above the line, yes, but behind the scenes. Strictly offstage. Not normally where I saw myself. Not where I wanted to be. Not what I'd been born to do. On the heels of this realization, I expected to feel a tinge of jealously, not enough to mean anything profound but there nonetheless. But instead, watching Rick save his own life by doing what *he* was born to do—command the room and make folks laugh—gave me a feeling of pride. I was so stinking proud of Rick right then. I loved him for his courage, for his focus, for his talent, for his refusal to give up or give in or give way. I loved him for hiring me, inviting me along for the bodyguard adventure of a lifetime, for his willingness to trust me, for his blind faith in my illogical, irrational, unreasonable plan.

Whoa, I thought. What word was that? Loved? Was that the word I said in my head? Loved? A conjugation of the verb love, as in to love someone? Jesus Christ, get a grip, Kate. Circle back later, but get a grip. Oscar K.'s about to give away the store.

"...so Ruby had no rubies, right?" Rick said. "Ruby was broke and in deep dog doo and needed how much dough to dig herself out?"

Oscar K. stared past Rick to his mother backstage left. She gave him an encouraging smile. Bart gave him a thumbs-up.

"Six mil and change," Ricci said. "More than a mil for the bookie. The rest for the sitcom, to which she was committed pay or play."

"Meaning?" Rick said.

"She had to pay for it whether she shot it or not," Ricci said.

"So where did she get the money, Oscar?" Rick said.

"Victor Vreeland gave it to her," Ricci said.

"The six-million-jack generous Victor Vreeland, everyone," Rick said.

The crowd cheered but now had no idea what they were cheering for.

Oscar K. didn't wait to be excused. He rushed off stage left, put his arm around his mother like the mama's boy he was, and left the building in a hurried hurry.

In contrast, all I had to do to get Bruce Bailey to play the game was tell him he'd be center stage with Rick Gotti.

"Welcome-to-the-jungle Rick Gotti?" Bruce had said Sunday morning.

"The very one," I'd said.

"Count me in like Flint," he'd said.

So he was standing beside me, backstage right, as happy as a clam digger digging clams.

"Let's not loiter on Memory Lane, ladies and gentlemen and dissolute pilgrims. Because for your host with the most, Memory Lane has a name," Rick said. "For Victor Vreeland, Memory Lane is Mclean Avenue."

"Bruce, Bruce, Bruce, Bruce, Bruce..." I said, ushering Bailey onto the stage.

The lunatic land broker practically jogged to meet Rick in the middle, grinning and glowing like a carnival clown.

In his front-row seat, Victor couldn't have looked more uncomfortable if he'd tried. Ruby was in a kind of shock. Victor was in a kind of rage.

"Now, Bruce, if I'm reading my cards right, you go way back with Victor," Rick said. "All the way back to Yonkers, where Victor, who has a documented jones for real estate, bought a down-and-dirty acre on the elbow of Mclean Avenue from a man named Tommy Tariccone. You had something to do with that deal, didn't you? A little story you can share with these sullied pilgrims?"

"Say it for me, Rick," Bruce said. "One time, and I'll tell you the whole tall tale."

Rick smiled at me like the pro he was. Like me, he knew we were getting to the end of the show, so why the hell not?

"Welcome to the jungle..." Rick said with all the age-old energy he could bring to it.

The crowd roared back to life. They'd needed something familiar, something they collectively knew was funny as hell, something to hold on to after the pathetic spectacle of tough-guy Oscar K. Ricci crying for his mommy.

And then Bruce Bailey told the story of the dirty dirt on the elbow and the phony environmental letter and Tariccone's even dirtier deal on the table. Turns out Bruce had been both the listing and selling agent in that disaster, and was expecting to make a bundle when the deal finally closed. But Tariccone said he'd shoot the broker in the face if he so much as whispered the word *commission*, so Bruce approached Victor to intervene on his behalf, seeing as how Bruce had hung in there for two-plus years. But Victor told Bruce to go screw—*"Your business with Tariccone is your business with Tariccone."*—so Bruce had made nothing on top of nothing. Meaning there was no love lost between the land broker and the comedy king maker.

"So the Friday the six million was due, Victor was broke?" Rick said.

"As a joke," Bruce said, and then he put his off-the-cuff retort in the perspective of having said it in Victor's very own comedy club while sharing the spotlight with Rick Gotti and thought he was hilarious. As if clicking the clicker in his pocket, he went into his routine. "Bruce, Bruce, Bruce, Bruce..."

That was enough for Victor. He stood with bad intent. Anyone in his way would now be bowled over by his bulk. Flattened like a flag on a floor.

But I'd anticipated this moment and planned it into the plan. *"When Bruce Bailey informs the crowd that Victor was dead broke on Friday and had six mil on Monday,"* I'd explained to Dennis, *"step outside and tell the police we're about to solve Kenny Cochran's murder."*

I'd told Rick the same thing, and he had it covered.

"House lights, please, so Victor can see his adoring, debauched pilgrims."

The house lights came up, and in addition to three hundred fifty friends, fellows, comrades, and companions, Victor also saw ten NYPD officers with eyes on the stage—and now on him. To run for it would somehow be an admission of involvement—possession of incriminating knowledge, perhaps, or maybe a more Machiavellian connection.

Victor bowed deeply (as deeply as a man of his great girth could bow) and sat back down. The sour look of suffering on his face said it all. He couldn't run. He couldn't hide. (Not that a man of his magnitude could ever hide.) He had to sit in his club, at his own Cornucopia feast, and take it on the chin. He and Ruby both. No choice now but to settle in for the rest of the ride.

The lighting guy killed the house lights, and Rick took us into the grand finale.

64

YOUR THIS IS YOUR LIFE LIFE

"THERE'S YOUR LIFE," RICK SAID TO THE CORNUCOPIA CROWD, "and then there's your *This is Your Life* life. And if there's one thing upon which we can all agree, it's that no one knows more about your *This Is Your Life* life than your ex-wife..."

Laughs and groans from the crowd, of course, but muted somehow. As if they collectively knew it was a jokey thought with a comical delivery and returned the laugh but were losing track of what was funny-ha-ha and what was funny-uh-oh.

Wendy Bell polished off her martini and handed me her empty glass. "How do I look?"

I took her in from go-go boots to deep-red blunt-cut bob wig. "Like the Queen of Queens."

She leaned over and kissed me on both cheeks. "Oh, Jennifer Emma Kate. That's what I was going for."

"...and Victor's ex has no time for rules or fools," Rick said, "so let's get her out here. Ladies and gentlemen and devious pilgrims, Victor's ex-wife, Wendy Bell..."

Since it was annulled in a New York minute, very few folks, if anyone, knew Victor had ever been married in the first place, so seeing his ex take the stage would have been a super-sized surprise even if his ex wasn't Wendy Bell. But that she *was* Wendy Bell blew all three hundred fifty minds the moment she stepped into the spotlight.

"Hi, Wendy," Rick said.

"Hi, Rick," Wendy said, and she waved at the front-row center table. "Hi, Victor. Hi, Ruby."

Victor and Ruby smiled weakly. Did not wave back.

"There seems to be some confusion, Wendy—" Rick said.

"Well, let's clean that up right away," Wendy said. "I'm a woman in a man's body who likes men who like men."

She laughed and laughed. There was something winning about her casual honesty. Like me, the crowd couldn't help but fall for her. Despite being a six-foot, seven-inch man in a miniskirt, she was the endearing definition of endearing.

"That's awesome sauce," Rick said, "but not the confusion about which we're all confused."

"It's just that me and Victor were steaming hot in love before we went ice cold, and I want everyone to know the annulment was as much mine as his," Wendy said. "Let the record show it was a mutual migration. Me to martinis. Victor to a life of crime."

Snickering silence in the club. Was Wendy Bell trying to be funny? No. No, she wasn't. And yet there was something engaging going on.

"That's the confusion I'm talking about," Rick said. "Can you clear the life-of-crime air?"

"Like Mrs. Meyer's Clean Day Lemon Verbena," Wendy said.

"Are we talking about the six mil Victor gave Ruby to cover her pilot and her boyfriend's beaucoup horse debt?" Rick said.

"That six mil *plus* the six mil he paid Tommy Tariccone for the dirty dirt in Yonkers," Wendy said.

"Six mil and six mil is twelve mil," Rick said.

"I have an MBA from MIT. I can add it up," Wendy said.

"Be my guest," Rick said.

"Victor and me and Ruby and Kenny double dated," Wendy said. "Horse races, supper clubs, yachts, you name it. I had the best seat in the house. Kenny couldn't keep his cash in his pants as far as betting on the horses, and he lost all of his and then all of hers, which is to say what was left of the money she hadn't already lost by her little lonesome. Ruby, you're funny, honey, but you're a moron with money. Anyway, girlfriend had a cash conundrum and asked Victor to make it all better. Now, what you have to understand about Victor is he can't and couldn't and didn't say no. And then Tommy Tariccone stopped the clock on the Yonkers deal, and Victor was expanded, extended, stretched, and strained to the point where his bank accounts were busted."

"So where did he find the money?" Rick said.

Wendy put her index finger to her lips. "Don't tell anyone, but he took it from the Cabaret account."

Gasps in the crowd. Whispers. Disbelief. No one, including me, could take their eyes off the stage. Victor shook his head with fury. Ruby hid her face in her hands. We were almost there. Almost.

"Could someone prove that?" Rick said.

"If they called the participating nonprofits and asked if Victor paid them as promised," Wendy said.

"Could someone do that?" Rick said.

"I did," Wendy said.

Shock waves ran through the room. What kind of comedy show *was* this?

"Do tell," Rick said.

"I'm as curious as the next girl, so I checked the charts and made the calls. A fraction of the funds raised at the fundraiser have found their way to the nonprofits who were meant to profit from the raised funds," Wendy said. "A forensic accountant could check the Cabaret account and see what they could see."

"Which, you suspect, is what?" Rick said.

"Drano down the drain," Wendy said. "He took in twelve million for charity, and then split it with Ruby to save both their skins. Sorry, Victor, but a girl's got to tell the truth when the truth's got to be told."

Victor's face was flushed with rage. He was as incredulous as everyone else in the club. Though they couldn't believe what they were hearing, and Victor couldn't believe they were hearing it—out loud and in glorious, Wendy Bell color.

"So that's one crime to crow about but doesn't explain Kenny Cochran's murder," Rick said.

"Oh contraire," Wendy said, and she looked over her shoulder at me in the backstage right wing. "Can I get a martini, Jennifer Emma Kate? This big girl's a pinch parched in the spotlight. Where were we, Rick?"

I sent a Pinnacle server to the bar.

"We were at the part where Victor kills Kenny Cochran," Rick said.

The crowd buzzed.

"You mean motive?" Wendy said.

"Good place to start," Rick said.

"Kenny found out from Ruby that Victor had stolen the charity money," Wendy said, "and tried a bit of blackmail on for size."

"Cut me in or I call the cops?" Rick said.

"In so many words," Wendy said.

"The beautiful, wonderful, ex–Mrs. Vreeland. Wendy Bell, everyone," Rick said.

Wendy exited stage left. The people cheered not because they'd accepted the funny-uh-oh oddness of the evening, the dreadfulness of the game, the impossibilities of the possibilities, but because she had won them over.

The martini arrived in the wing at precisely the same moment as Wendy Bell. She had, not surprisingly, perfect martini timing.

"So Victor hired hitmen to kill Kenny Cochran," Rick said to the club, "and I wandered into The Joke Joint dressing room in the middle of the murder and somehow took the fall."

Wendy took the martini, hugged me, and kissed me on both cheeks. "You're my best friend in the world, Jennifer Emma Kate."

"Which meant Victor had to kill me too, before I could prove I didn't do it and he did," Rick said. "And the only way I can prove *all that*, ladies and gentlemen and devilish pilgrims, is to bring Victor's hitmen onstage for everyone to meet..."

I was tangled up with Wendy Bell while trying to keep one eye on Rick and the other on the front-row, center-stage table.

"...so Victor and Ruby, say hello to your hired hitmen, the bear and the pig."

Bart and Roger escorted the bear and the pig onto the stage.

The crowd gasped in a kind of collective shock. This couldn't be happening. Some folks jumped to their feet because their minds were too blown to sit.

Ruby laid her forehead on the table. Victor was livid, eyes on fire. He drained the last of his sambuca and bent beneath the table.

There was only one reason he would do that.

To grab the gun strapped around his ankle.

I was out of ideas. Out of time. Out of my mind.

Victor came up holding his gun, stood, and aimed at Rick.

I reached for the Cornucopia platter and ran across the stage.

Rick was frozen in the spotlight, staring at Victor.

About five feet from Rick, I dove into the air. Platter first.

I heard a gunshot. And then another.

I heard screams and panic and chaos.

I smashed into Rick, and we crashed to the ground.

He wasn't wearing the bulletproof vest.

He's dead, I thought. *I've lost him. All this for nothing.*

I heard shrieking and screeching. I heard tables and chairs being tossed this way and that way. I heard uproar and upheaval, turmoil and commotion.

The house lights blasted up to full power. I opened my eyes. The police closed in on Victor and Ruby. I tried with all my heart not to think of Rick, who'd died on the stage like Victor had said.

I realized I was crying.

"Why so sad, McCall?"

I turned. Rick was sitting up. Definitely not dead. The opposite of dead.

Alive. Very much alive.

"Such a good show," I said. "Remarkably moving."

Then I lost my shit completely. Weeping and weeping.

He put his arms around me, pulled me to him. "I'm okay, McCall. You saved me."

"I did?"

"You did."

"How did I do that?"

He gestured at the Cornucopia platter.

There were two bullets imbedded where Rick's name was engraved.

65

BOUND BY SONG AND DANCE

THE NYPD ESCORTED VICTOR AND RUBY AND THE BEAR AND THE pig out of the club and into the rest of their incarcerated lives. Thank you, God of Karmic Criminal Justice.

Plenty of police stayed behind to question the guests, the Comedy Camp staff, the Pinnacle Events staff, Rick, and me. It took hours to ask everyone what they knew, when they knew it, and how they'd come to know it.

For the first time in a long time, I told the truth, the whole truth, and nothing but the truth. Except for the parts I left out and the parts I fudged and the parts I created out of thin air. But for the most important part—that Rick was innocent of all charges—I was as honest as Oprah.

From one side of the bar, I watched Rick on the other side sign autographs for a half dozen cops. He wasn't high-profile famous anymore, but he was famous enough. I wasn't really thinking about how famous he was though. I was thinking about how handsome he was. How attracted to him I was. How close we'd become since he'd hired me to be his bodyguard. I was wondering, now that his case was closed, whether what we'd both been feeling would melt like mist in the morning.

By two a.m., the club was empty but for me, Rick, and the Schmidt and Parker Players posing as Pinnacle caterers.

The Comedy Camp general manager, blown away by the prospect of having worked his last night on account of Victor not being available to sign checks for the next twenty to forty years, handed the keys to Melissa and told her to lock up when her Pinnacle team was ready to leave. He was headed home, he said, to polish his resume.

If he'd ask me before he left, I might have explained that leaving the keys to a stocked bar featuring a stage and a piano with the Schmidt and Parker Players—with instructions to lock up *when you're ready to leave*—was unwise at best, irresponsible at worst, and reckless everywhere between the two. With a stocked bar, a stage, and a piano, the Schmidt and Parker Players might *never* be ready to leave.

And after all the excitement of a successful sting, we weren't going anywhere soon. Not now that Rick was innocent and free and one of the family.

To celebrate, Posey sat at the piano, and she and Dennis presented a sneak peek of the next D-Cup maniac musical— written for Rick, with starring roles for me, Roger, Chloe, and Big Black Bald Bart—*Stripperville!*

Running into the sun with the original idea of me as a street-smart stripper who knows the ropes of romance; Chloe as a youthful stripper with much to learn about love; Rick as the strip-club MC who falls hard for me; Roger as the club's piano player, who loves me like summer rain; and Bart as the bouncer with a heart of gold, Dennis and Posey had "improved" the plot by making Stripperville not just the name of the bar but the name of the town. The town in which everyone was a stripper. They were foggy about the plot beyond that premise (what else was new?), but songs were taking shape, choreography was coming into focus, and *Stripperville!*, which would include, based on the commercial success of

Psychedelic Sunday, at *least* two orgies, was now listed in the D-Cup lineup as officially on deck.

We drank and sang and danced until four thirty, celebrating Rick's freedom, toasting our great good fortune to be bound by song and dance as a theatrical family, and rejoicing in the knowledge that there was no place like home when home was the D-Cup.

Cornball crazy stuff, of course—even when you've been drinking tequila since two a.m.—but true for all of us musical misfits who wanted not much more out of life than to be onstage, any stage, awash in the footlights, in front of an audience, feeling alive with artistic purpose.

"So what's our next case?" Posey said.

Not surprisingly, I was at the bar with Rick, Roger, Chloe, Dennis, and Posey. She'd surrendered the piano to Bart, who played honky tonk like Jerry Lee and had everyone dancing into the boogie-woogie wee hours.

"Murder most foul?" Dennis said.

"Persons of the missing persuasion?" Roger said.

"Cheating spouses cheating?" Chloe said.

I realized, with the help of a half dozen shots of tequila, that I loved these people. Without hesitation, after my father had been killed, they'd joined my PI journey because, yes, their adrenaline-pumping participation made them feel alive somehow, part of the world in a way madcap musical theater (and less-than-scintillating day jobs and lives) did not. But mostly because they'd known I'd needed them and so had been there for me.

That's as good a definition of family as any I've heard.

"Nothing on the books," I said.

"Keep us in the loop, Kate," Chloe said. "Pretty sure you can't do it without us."

"We're the cheese to your burger, babe," Roger said.

"The honey in your hive," Dennis said.

"The blue in your sky," Posey said.

Rick smiled and poured a shot of tequila for everyone but himself (of course).

I held it up and toasted them. "You are the oddest of the odd in this whole town. That includes you, Gotti."

"Hell yes it does," Roger said.

"Craziest of the crazy," Chloe said.

"Wildest of the wild," Posey said.

"Weirdest of the weird," Dennis said.

"To us," Rick said.

"To us," we all said.

Rick and I got back to the House of Emotional Tics at five o'clock Monday morning. Not that it ever sleeps, but the city was waking as we were falling into bed.

"I want us to make love," I said. "And I know I promised this would never happen again, but I'm too tired."

"I promised too," he said, "and I'm too tired to even talk about it."

"Will you sleep with me, though? Just hold me?"

"You think that'll be okay with your sofa?"

"My sofa will understand."

He snuggled me in his arms, and I felt safe and whole and happy and sleepy-sleepy-sleepy. Drifting off...

"Don't make any plans for tomorrow," I said.

He was almost out. "You mean tomorrow today or tomorrow tomorrow?"

"Tomorrow today. We have someplace to be."

"Where's that?"

"My son's wedding."

66

NO MORE MURDER

I'D NEVER SLEPT BETTER. SO GOOD, I WANTED TO KEEP SLEEPING and maybe ease into a little late-morning sex—I thought I'd actually done that in my dreams—but the alarm went off at ten. In a few hours, Matthew and Nina would be married. A few months after that, I would be a grandmother. My eyes shot open. How's that for a wake-up call?

"Good morning," Rick said. He held two mugs of coffee. One was for me. "I think you said something about going to a wedding today as I was passing out. Do people get married on Mondays?"

"My son does. It's a popular day to get married when you're eloping."

He sat on the bed and handed me caffeine in a cup. "Is your son eloping?"

"He and his pregnant wife, yes."

"Ah, I remember now. This is the moment you've been obsessing about for the last two weeks. As opposed to obsessing about someone trying to frame me for murder and kill me before they finished framing me."

"I was obsessing about both. Obsessing's a very kind word by the way."

"I thought worrying, agonizing, distressing, and struggling were inappropriate on the actual wedding day. I made scrambled eggs with sautéed potatoes, onions, and cheese. Cinnamon raisin toast. We should eat and get ready. Can't be late, McCall."

I pulled him in for a kiss that suggested much more than a kiss. "A little late?"

He smiled. "Not for this one. Not on my watch."

I followed him into the kitchen. Breakfast was wonderful. We inhaled it. He did the dishes while I showered and got dressed. In the crazy chaos of Marcus Moore and Victor Vreeland on Sunday, I'd forgotten how happy I was to find an outfit at Screaming Mimis on Saturday.

It was a 1950s two-piece known as a patio set, featuring a coordinating top and skirt decorated with silver rick rack, ribbon, and lace. Soft, sensual, fine black corduroy. The look and feel of luxury without the luxurious price tag. Boat-neck top with raglan sleeves and zipper at the side. Midlength circle skirt with a side zipper and hook-and-eye fastener. Vintage elegance without being too dressy. Perfect, I thought, for a Monday elopement at the courthouse.

We took a cab to 100 Centre Street, the New York Criminal Courts Building, a massive, *art moderne*–style complex housing courtrooms for the Criminal and Supreme Courts, the offices of the Manhattan DA (where Matthew was a rising star), the Legal Aid Society, and a slew of other law-enforcement agencies.

As commanding and imposing a piece of architecture as any in the boroughs, the south wing was known as The Tombs and was where I'd spent the night with other criminals after Logan arrested me for murdering a coroner I didn't kill during the Harriman Affair four long months ago. Ancient Kate McCall history.

In the cab downtown, I couldn't believe how nervous I was. In the elevator up to the chambers of Judge Robert DiSalvo, my nerves decidedly doubled down or doubled up or double troubled. I was a wreck. More or less calm on the outside. An emotional basket case on the inside. I held Rick's arm so I wouldn't keel over. My legs were rubber. What a mess I was.

We weren't late, but we were the last to arrive. As we stepped into DiSalvo's dignified, dark-wood-paneled digs, I made a decision that steadied me. Today, there would be no nasty, snotty, adjectives for Nina. Today, her only adjectives would be *my son's wife, my daughter-in-law,* and *the mother, come May, of my grandchild.* No mean-girl name-calling today. That's what I promised myself.

Matthew and Nina looked radiant. Both of them glowing. Tears were already in my eyes and nothing had freaking happened yet. I spotted Nina's parents. He was a corporate tax attorney. She was an interior designer. I'd never met them. They had never met me. We'd *heard* about each other—I still can't imagine the stories Matthew told them—but that was as close as Matthew and Nina had allowed us to get until the deal was sealed.

Knowing Nina as I did, I'd expected snooty snootballs galore from her upper-crusty folks. But they couldn't have been nicer. Nicer than me. (Not saying much, I'm aware.) Pretty much nicer than most people. I liked them. And today I liked Nina. Today, I liked everyone. Today was my son's wedding.

They were all delighted to meet Rick, whose comedy and career they knew well enough. And *liked.* Nina had once written a freaking paper on the importance of welcoming people to the perceived jungle. I couldn't believe it. Of every person I knew in the world, Nina was the last one I'd have thought would be a Rick Gotti fan.

Rick won them over. I was so proud of him. Check that. I

was so proud to be with him. I was so happy he wasn't dead. Or going to jail. Or both.

I was just so stinking happy about everything today.

Today. Matthew's wedding day.

After about ten minutes of glorious anticipation and bubbly small talk I couldn't remember, Judge Robert DiSalvo, for whom Matthew had clerked after law school before joining the DA's office, in no small part due to the judge's power-packed recommendation, entered from his office in full robes. The man took my breath away. There's something solemn and Olympus-like, royal and mighty, about a man in a flowing black robe. You know what? He was charming too. His affection for Matthew, who he knew quite well, and for Nina, who he seemed to know pretty well too, was palpable.

Everyone was as happy for Matthew and Nina as I was. Everyone was over the moon. I doubted DiSalvo's serious office carried this kind of vibe during the normal course of its criminal-court business. But the word for DiSalvo's chambers today was *joy*.

Goddamn, I thought. *This is the best day of my life since Jimmy died.*

Thinking of my father didn't make me cry today. It made me smile. Today was all good things. All good memories. All good thoughts. Today was Jimmy's grandson's wedding.

The ceremony was brief but heartfelt. Nina's mother cried. I cried. Rick held my hand the entire time. I would have collapsed into a puddle without him.

Afterward we all hugged—yes, I hugged Nina, and she hugged me—and left the judge's office to walk one block to the New York State Supreme Court Building. (Which most everybody knows, or has at least seen, at one time or another.)

I say that because the front facade, the dramatic front steps of that building, originally known as the New York County Courthouse, have been featured in *The Godfather*, *Goodfellas*,

Regarding Henry, Legal Eagles, Wall Street, 12 Angry Men, Night Court, Law & Order, Kojak, Cagney & Lacey and too many others to get into on my son's wedding day. Which was today. Did I mention that?

Nina's fashion photographer friend met us at the steps to take wedding pictures. When all the family photos had been taken in all the various groupings and poses of people, everyone wanted to get a shot with Rick because, well, Rick.

I found myself standing with my son. I couldn't hug and kiss him enough. Love and joy and joy and love poured out of me.

"Logan called me yesterday," he said. No anger in his voice. No frustration. No embarrassment. No mortification. No humiliation. No shame. Just my son who loved me telling me Detective Logan had called him yesterday.

"Yesterday was madness and mayhem. I didn't want to tell you about it today."

"I know. You got him, Mom."

"I got him."

"But he almost got you."

"But he didn't."

"I can't lose you."

"You're not going to."

"No more murder cases. I can't stop you from being a PI. I know that now. It's in your blood. You got it from Jimmy. But today, on my wedding day, in front of the New York Supreme Court, I want you to promise me no more murder."

"I promise. No more murder."

He nodded. We smiled as we watched Nina and her parents coo around Rick.

"Jimmy would have been proud of you," Matthew said.

"I always hope so."

"I'm proud of you."

"You are?"

"Yes. I love you, Mom."

And just like that, all the pain and anguish and emotional suffering of the past four months melted away. Moore was dead. Jimmy was avenged. My son was married. Life pressed on.

"I love you, Matthew."

"I heard about Victor Vreeland too."

"I didn't want to tell you about that today either. Who told you?"

"Shavelson. Wanted me to know he'd come to his client's rescue."

It was true.

"I'm not his client."

"That's what Jimmy used to say."

We both laughed.

"I'm glad about that too," Matthew said. "I like Rick. You're good together."

As if the day couldn't get any better.

67

WHEN YOU KNOW, YOU KNOW

We went for a late lunch. A downtown Civic Center deli famous for rare roast beef and killer coleslaw. We drank strong coffee and ate sandwiches and slaw and laughed and laughed until it was time to go. We hugged and kissed each other goodbye with promises and plans to have dinner later in the week, and then Rick and I caught a cab to East 83rd Street.

LaTanya, Fu, Charlie, Al, and Warren were shooting an action scene on the front steps. LaTanya was doing yeoman's duty as director, director of photography, camera operator, camera crew, wardrobe, props, and craft service. The other four were acting. I wasn't listed on the call sheet due to it being my son's wedding day. The cast and crew acknowledged us with varying degrees of interest—from zero to less than zero—because I was me and Rick was one of us now.

To my surprise, Fu was covered with fake blood.

"What scene is this?" I said, since there was no Fu-covered-with-fake-blood scene in the *Kung Fu Fu* outline, which was admittedly malleable.

"This the scene where Al and Charlie, wiggy on Warren's

martial-arts magic mix, kill Fu on the front steps," LaTanya said.

"Wait...what?" I said.

"Fu's a wrap," LaTanya said. "Heading home tomorrow. Home being China. Rewrite's already rewritten."

"Wait...what?" I said.

"Says you got the parrot," Charlie said.

"Says the next guy can fix Al's flusher," Warren said.

"Fu you, Fu," Al said.

"Fu you too," Fu said.

"Wait...what?" I said.

"You the star now," LaTanya said. "Detective Peanut saves the city."

"Wait...what?" I said, and tears came to my eyes. Talk about an emotional day.

LaTanya, Charlie, Al, and Warren commandeered Rick to review the plot changes and let me have a moment with Fu.

"No cry," Fu said.

"No cry?" I said, already crying.

"This not goodbye," Fu said.

"What is it?" I said.

"This later alligator," Fu said.

I buried my head in his shoulder.

Rick came over and Fu put a concrete-crushing finger in his chest. "You take care Kate or Fu find you."

It was the first time I'd ever heard him say my name. Tears rolled down my face. I couldn't stop them.

"I will," Rick said.

"I was hoping you'd say that," I said.

"Fu hope first," Fu said.

Which made me laugh. Crying, laughing, coming, going, who the hell knew where I was? All over the map. What a day!

I pulled myself together inside my apartment, splashed water on my face in the kitchen sink, then opened the fridge, grabbed a Sam Adams for me and a bottle of Barq's Root Beer for Rick (his favorite), and met him on the living-room sofa.

He'd flipped on the TV and turned it to *Animal Planet*, an episode about birds that mate forever. Black vultures, bald eagles, Laysan albatrosses, mute swans, scarlet macaws, whooping cranes, California condors, and Atlantic puffins. The whole lot of them were so damn romantic I could hardly stand it.

"That's us," Rick said.

"What's us?" I said.

"I realize we haven't known each other very long, but I think we've lived a lifetime in the last two weeks, and I don't want to be with anyone else. No more games. No more bullshit. Just you. Just you, McCall."

"Just me what?"

"Just you moving in with me. Just us living together. In Brooklyn. In the firehouse. I have a place in LA too. So we can live there sometimes if you want to. I have money so you don't have to worry about that, unless that's something you want to worry about. You can worry about anything you want. I don't care. After all these years, I think I'm a grownup now. And I think you are too. I don't want to sound stupid, but I can ride this road anywhere it goes, as long as you're with me and I'm with you."

I kissed him like I loved him, which I think I might have. I think he loved me too. Or he might have. Probably we were falling in love. Maybe we already had.

"You're okay if I give up the brownstone job?" I said.

"I'm okay."

"I promised Fu I'd take care of the parrot."

"I'm good with the parrot."

"And if cases come my way?"

"It's your life. I just want to be in it for the rest of mine. If cases come, and you want to take them, then take them. I figure you're your father's daughter."

"And the D-Cup?"

"Same deal."

"Two weeks is crazy fast, isn't it?"

"When you know, you know."

"Lot to think about."

He nodded and kissed me, and we watched the birds spend their lives together. Rick was right, of course. We'd lived a lifetime in two weeks. We were grownups. And it didn't matter where the road went as long as we were together.

And when you know, you know.

In the end, cases *would* come, and I would take them because, hell yes, I was my father's daughter. I was a PI.

But I was also an actor.

THANK YOU

I hope you had as much fun reading *Gottiguard* as I had writing it because I had a blast. If you did, it would be most excellent if you could help other mystery lovers find the book by leaving a review and sharing the laughs.

Honest reviews of my books help introduce them to new readers. I would be deeply grateful if you could find a few minutes to post a positive review about *Gottiguard* or any of the Kate McCall Crime Capers. It only takes a minute to leave an upbeat word or two. Thanks again.

FIND OUT HOW IT ALL GOT STARTED!

Get Workman's Complication, the first Kate McCall Crime Caper, and find out how it all got started!

Kate McCall dreams of basking in the bright lights of Broadway. But after her PI dad is found dead in a NYC elevator, she has no choice but to split time between show business and the family business. When her vampire musical fails to pay the bills, she accepts a workman's compensation case that's sure to put her acting chops to the test. On her way down the trail of clues, she can't help but get sidetracked by her father's unsolved murder. Will Kate crack her cases before playing detective becomes a role to die for?

KEEP THE LAUGHS COMING!

Get Swollen Identity, the Second Kate McCall Crime Caper, and keep the laughs coming!

Kate McCall hopes she can balance her passions and her PI practice. Struggling to keep both on stage, the way-off-Broadway performer finds herself in the deep end of a billionaire's allegedly stolen identity. But her role as a super-sleuth takes center stage when a corporate crime scene replicates her father's unsolved murder. Can Kate shine a spotlight on the killer before she loses her part for good?

HOLD ON TO YOUR HAT!

Get Emboozlement, the third Kate McCall Crime Caper, and hold on to your hat!

Kate McCall dazzles audiences on stage by night but by day she searches for her father's killer. She seems to gain ground until the man who pulled the trigger sends texts that prove he's one step ahead. While investigating the murderous messages, she takes on an embezzlement case from a handsome sports bar owner who might just be her top suspect. If she can't close both cases, Kate's next intermission could be permanent. Will Kate's latest song and dance deliver justice or a fatal review?

ALSO BY RICH LEDER

ROMANTIC SHADES OF FUNNY

Juggler, Porn Star, Monkey Wrench

DARKER SHADES OF FUNNY

Let There Be Linda

Cooking for Cannibals

Extraterrestrial Noir

KATE MCCALL CRIME CAPERS

Workman's Complication

Swollen Identity

Emboozlement

Gottiguard

ACKNOWLEDGMENTS

My heartfelt appreciation to everyone who helped me travel the Kate McCall road. There are too many of you to mention, but I want you to know I could not have finished these four books without your help, support, love, and guidance. In the end, I'm just stringing words together the best I can. All of you are the reason McCall became McCall. And for that I thank you.

For all the impossibly strong, smart, and funny women I know and admire and respect and love. Rest assured there's a piece of each of you in Kate McCall.

ABOUT THE AUTHOR

Rich Leder's screen credits include 19 television films for CBS, Lifetime, and Hallmark and feature films for Lionsgate Entertainment, Paramount Pictures, Tri-Star Pictures, and Left Bank Films. He has published eight novels through Laugh Riot Press.

He has been the lead singer in a Detroit rock band, a restaurateur, a Little League coach, an indie film director, a literacy tutor, a magazine editor, a screenwriting coach, a commercial real estate agent, a wedding guru, and a visiting artist for the University of North Carolina Film Studies Department, among other things, all of which, it turns out, was grist for the mill.

Contact Rich through his website: www.richleder.com